<u>**Books by Thomas J. Doscher**</u>

The Vixen War Bride
Holdouts
Uncivil Affairs
Repatriation
Cupcake Girls
The Dark Ones

Book Cover Design by ebooklaunch.com

Follow the author on his Facebook page at https://www.facebook.com/Thomas-J-Doscher-Author-108795198074711

The Dark Ones

The Vixen War Bride
Part 6

Thomas J. Doscher

To the veterans.

Common Acronyms

- AAFES – Army Air Force Exchange Service
- AO – Area of Operations
- BX – Base Exchange (on-base department store, Air Force)
- CID – Criminal Investigation Division
- CJTF – Combined Joint Task Force
- COC – Combined Operations Center
- DFAC – Dining Facility (Nice way of saying "chow hall.")
- DFAS – Defense Finance and Accounting Service
- DLI – Defense Language Institute
- DPAA – Defense POW/MIA Accounting Agency
- DV – Distinguished Visitor
- ECP – Entry Control Point
- EOD – Explosive Ordnance Disposal
- FARP – Forward Air Refueling Point
- FOB – Forward Operating Base
- GO – General Officer
- ID – Infantry Division
- JDOG – Joint Detention Operations Group
- LT – Lieutenant (pronounced "El-tee.")
- LTV – Light Tactical Vehicle
- LZ – Landing Zone
- MEDEVAC – Medical Evacuation
- MOS – Military Occupation Specialty
- MRE – Meal Ready to Eat
- NASA – National Aeronautics and Space Administration
- NCO – Noncommissioned officer
- PA – Public Affairs
- PX – Post Exchange (on-base department store, Army)
- QRF – Quick Reaction Force
- RIF – Reduction in Force

- RIP/TOA – Relief in Place/Transfer of Authority
- SeaBee – United States Naval Construction Battalion. (Heterograph of "CB," for "Construction Battalion.")
- SGLI – Servicemembers Group Life Insurance
- SNCO – Senior Noncommissioned Officer
- TOC – Tactical Operations Center
- TTP – Tactics, Techniques and Procedures
- UNCLASS - Unclassified

Va'Shen Pronunciation

- *Aderen – Ah-dur-en*
- Alacea – *Ah-lah-say-ah*
- Alva'Rem – *Al-vah-rem*
- Alzoria – *Al-zor-ree-ah*
- Aru'Dace – *Ah-roo-dah-say*
- Azarin – *Ah-zah-rin*
- Bao Aren – *Bou Ah-ren*
- Bao Sen – *Bou Sehn*
- Basilla – *Ba-sih-la*
- Boso – *Boh-soh*
- Boto – *Boh-toh*
- Dan Huun – *Dan Hoon*
- *Dara Tang – Dah-rah-tang*
- Donya'Ta – *Dohn-yah-tah*
- Garan'Sel – *Ga-ran-sell*
- Goto – *Go-tow*
- Hesmea – *Hez-may-ah*
- Hestean – *Hes-stay-en*
- Kasshas – *Ka-shas*
- Kastia – *Ka-stee-ah*
- Ketra – *Keh-trah*
- Mezina – *Meh-zee-nah*
- Mikorin – *Me-kor-rin*
- *Myorin – Me-yor-in*
- Nadro – *Nah-droh*
- Na'Sha – *Neh-shah*
- Nazea – *Nah-zay-ah*
- Pavastea – *Pah-vah-stay-ah*
- Pelle – *Pel*
- Posha – *Po-shah*

- Runa – *Roo-nah*
- Sho Nan – *Show Non*
- Tasshas – *Ta-shas*
- Tenzeta – *Ten-zeh-tah*
- *Tesho* – *Teh-show*
- Toka – *Toh-kah*
- Toki – *Toh-kee*
- Turean – *Too-ray-en*
- Turan – *Too-ran*
- Va'Shen – *Vah-Shen*
- Voro – *Voh-roh*
- Wenlin – *When-lin*
- Ya'Jahar – *Yah-Jah-Har*
- Yarl – *Yah-ril*
- Yasuren – *Ya-soo-ren*
- Yunhee – *Yoon-hee*
- Zaishin – *Zy-shin*

Prologue

Contact

Space...

It kinda sucks.

In the movies and vids, it was different. Space was a wondrous place explored by intelligent people who were treated like professionals. Their lives aboard spaceships, star ships, star destroyers... whatever you wanted to call them... were essentially like their lives back home. They worked, they played, they hung out after work and drank together, watched vids, played sci-fi versions of familiar sports and, above all, got to look out the window and see *space*!

The problem with space in the real world was that it was in the real world. Operating in space automatically made every action, from the most vital to most trivial, a hundred times more dangerous just because you were doing that action *in space.*

Space was inherently dangerous. One wrong move and you could go spinning out into the void, never to be seen again. Or blown out of an airlock where your insides would suddenly become your outsides.

Crushed by meteors.

Crashed into a sun.

Space madness.

Space rabies.

Is that strange green mass the lunch you accidentally left in the fridge too long or a new dangerous alien life form that somehow found its way aboard your space ship?

And then... for the brave few... it got even *worse.*

Because those brave few were members of the U.S. military.

The brave few like Technical Sergeant Michael Tatsumaki of the United States Space Force.

Tatsumaki had seen the vid commercials. He had listened to the stories told to him by the Space Force recruiter who had visited his school. He had seen members of the Space Force in movies doing amazing, heroic, downright *awesome* things, and he wanted to be a part of it.

He wanted to wake up every morning, look out the window of his spaceship and see the stars, and say, *"Oh my God! I'm IN SPACE!"*

But what the commercials, the vids and the recruiters' stories showed was actually different than the reality.

Space was actually boring. Boring and dangerous. And unlike the vids, it was nothing like life back home. Getting a drink after work? Are you nuts? You can't have *alcohol* on a spaceship! You'll kill us all!

Look out the window?! You want a *window?!* Why? So you can break it while you're goofing off with the other twenty guys in your berthing area and kill us all!?

Even for Tatsumaki, someone who worked in the Command and Control Center of a massive colonial ship, the *Neil Armstrong*, looking out the window at the stars was a dream. You could look at camera feeds showing what was around the ship, look at Va'Sh spinning lazily down below you, but you could have done that on the internet at home and probably in higher definition.

Command and Control had no windows. There would be no dignified space admiral gazing out at the stars and contemplating his role in the universe as officers in pressed uniforms worked all around him. Nope. No windows. Just a large, rectangular room lined with holographic consoles manned by men and women in dark blue flight suits. Even the ship's commander didn't have a chair in the center of the room like you would see in a vid. He had to sit at his own console in one corner of the rectangle unless he was working at the large holographic display in the center of the room.

This display was probably the closest thing to sci-fi on the ship. A huge hologram showing Va'Sh and the *Neil Armstrong* in the center along with two red spheres representing the planet's nearby moons. Points of light spread across the hologram looked like stars, but actually represented satellites, drones, other ships, asteroids or comets based on the color of the light.

Part of Tatsumaki's job, as a matter of fact, was identifying those points of light as they appeared.

Like the one that just popped up on his holographic display.

The display at his station was a miniaturized version of the large one in the middle of the Command Center, stripped of its nifty graphics so that only points of light remained. The point of light that had suddenly appeared had done so from the far side of Va'Sh's larger moon.

Tatsumaki lifted a finger and tapped the new point of light. A window popped up next to it, displaying all the information the ship, through its own scanners and the network of satellites and drones spread throughout the area, had on it.

Which wasn't much yet considering it had only just come into range.

But there was something displayed there that made it worth a much closer look.

Tatsumaki reached up and touched a holographic button on his display, one that would automatically summon the current Command Center controller to his station.

A moment later, the shift controller was standing behind him, leaning over his shoulder.

"What have you got?" the controller, Major Jeff Townsend, asked him.

"New sensor contact," Tatsumaki reported as his fingers moved around the holographic display in an attempt to coax move information from it. "Just popped in behind Hobbes."

Va'Sh's moons, Nareana and Shirazea, had deep connections to Va'Shen history and mythology, but to the Space Force they were just two more moons they had to keep track of, and, not knowing or caring what their local names were, had settled on calling them Calvin and Hobbes.

"Not an asteroid?" Townsend asked. He knew Tatsumaki wouldn't have called him over for an asteroid, although even that would be strange. For some reason no one had yet been able to explain, the Va'Sh system was completely devoid of any asteroids larger than a mid-size sedan.

"No, Sir," Tatsumaki replied. "Not a lot of info yet, but doppler is showing a change in the object's blue-shift as it approaches Hobbes." He looked up at Townsend. "Whatever it is, it's slowing down."

Townsend was silent for a moment. An object caught in the moon's gravity well would be speeding up, not slowing down. "Anything on the Space Tasking Order today?" he asked.

"Not over there," Tatsumaki told him. "No interstellar arrivals scheduled for today." He looked up as his display offered more information as the nearby satellites conducted further scans.

"Could it be *Over the Rainbow*?" Townsend asked. "Got here early and overshot?"

"If it is," Tatsumaki told him, "Then it's only a piece of her. Whatever it is, is only about half our size."

Townsend turned to another station. "Communications," he ordered. "Contact the Jamieson JOC. Ask if they're expecting anything and have them contact the Chinese JOC. Maybe it's just our two networks failing to talk again."

Townsend turned and looked up at the main holographic display where the intruder blip was now showing at the very far edge.

"I don't like that it's coming in from the other side of Hobbes," he noted. "Like they're trying to sneak in without us seeing them."

No one answered his concern.

"Sir, Jamieson reports no changes to the Space Tasking Order," the communications controller told him. "The Chinese report no expected arrivals either."

"Sergeant Tatsumaki," Townsend began, "Is the bogey performing any active scans that you can tell?"

"Negative, Sir," Tatsumaki replied. "No active EM scans. No RADAR, LIDAR or doppler that I can see."

Townsend pointed at a blue light near the intruder. "Order Skylight 27 to launch an SQ-62 to do a flyby. Passive scans only. If they think they're sneaking by us, let's let 'em think it awhile longer."

Tatsumaki opened a new holographic window and selected Skylight 27 from the list of options on the dropdown menu. The space near Va'Sh was practically littered with satellites, extending the sensor range of *Neil Armstrong* hundreds of thousands of miles. Each satellite was controlled by a limited artificial intelligence. And each was equipped with a limited number of smaller drones capable of going out and collecting information on objects further away.

Tatsumaki selected the SQ-62 drone from the satellite's inventory and selected the bogey as a target for a passive sensor investigation.

And this all brought up another way that space sucked.

Space was big.

Like... *super big.*

It would take a few minutes just for the satellite to receive the orders. It would then take hours for the drone, able to go much faster than a manned ship would, just to get near enough to the bogey for a scan.

"One more thing," Townsend told him. At Tatsumaki's questioning look, the controller continued. "Have the satellites switch to laser comms only. No broadcasting in the clear until we're sure that thing isn't listening to us."

"Yes, Sir."

By switching to laser communications, the satellites would essentially become players in a really big game of telephone. One satellite with a message for the ship would have to transmit it by laser pulse targeting the next closest satellite, which would then transmit it to another satellite until it reached one with a clear line-of-sight to the *Neil Armstrong*. It was slower than regular radio transmissions, but it had the advantage of not being able to be intercepted unless the eavesdropping ship planted itself between the two satellites.

Townsend studied the holographic projection as if staring at it hard enough would get it to yield more answers. Va'Sh was restricted space, but there *were* commercial ships moving in and out of the system, mostly passenger or cargo carriers contracted by the government for moving troops and fresh food. It was *possible* they were looking at a ship that had fallen victim to an accident with their fold drive. But if that were so, they would be on the radio screaming for help.

On rare occasions, some media company would pay a private contractor to try to sneak a reporter into the system. But that had all but stopped after the Secretary of Defense had told them, personally and in no uncertain terms, that such ships would be disabled and left to float until the company responsible paid DoD the cost for rescuing them.

The most worrying possibility for Townsend was that he was looking at a renegade Va'Shen ship full of angry commandos who'd decided a glorious death in battle was better than a life on the run.

Neil Armstrong, like every other "warship" in the U.S. inventory, wasn't designed with battle in mind. The Treaty of Minot restricted the world powers from creating sci-fi inspired space navies. In a galaxy where Earth-like, habitable worlds had been found to be in abundance, there really was no need to militarize space. If a country needed minerals or space for population growth or farmland, all it really needed to do was wait a week and one would be found by Earth's space agencies.

The end result had been that, when the Va'Shen attacked three years earlier, Earth's militaries had plenty of ways to transport troops and equipment from one world to another, but no real way to protect those ships from attack. No one knew at the time that Va'Shen ships weren't really made for space combat either, but science fiction vids had convinced the entire world that if you were going to have a space war, you were going to need space warships.

Having nothing at the time, the U.S. contracted with the three largest aerospace firms in the nation, all of which were producing and operating colony movement ships, and arranged to have those ships retrofitted for some form of combat. The U.S. was also currently constructing ships designed from the ground up for combat, but the government contracting process and the usual lawsuits that followed had prevented any of them from actually being built yet.

With all the pieces moving, the only thing Townsend could do now was wait and prep his people for anything.

The "hurry-up-and-wait" phase had begun.

* * *

Over the last 10 hours, Tatsumaki must have checked his board more than a thousand times, looking for some change in the bogey that was still moving quietly behind Hobbes. The drone they had sent had done a passive flyby at the very edge of its sensor capabilities, and the data was just now beginning to come in.

"That," Tatsumaki told Colonel Dean Farley, "Is definitely *not* the *Over the Rainbow.*"

The balding Space Force commander of *Neil Armstrong* looked over the tech's shoulder to study the screen for himself. The imagery sent back by the drone came in several different forms: Thermal, electro-magnetic, and radar just to name a few. And, of course, there was the photographic image.

At such an extreme range, not a lot of detail could be made out, but it was enough to know for certain that whatever-it-was was not a human colony ship. It was darker, almost coal-black against the already dark blackness of space. It was roughly oblong in shape with rounded protrusions that were hard to make out scattered over the hull. Its propulsion system was not immediately apparent. There were no burning thrusters pushing it forward.

"It doesn't look Va'Shen either," Farley agreed. "Forward the data to the JOC," he ordered. "How long until it clears Hobbes?"

Tatsumaki checked the clock. "Two hours, seventeen minutes if it maintains its current course and speed."

"And it's still not aware of our presence?" the ship's commander asked.

The technical sergeant blew a breath of air between his lips in thought. "It's impossible to say for certain, Sir," he admitted. "I'll say this, though. It's definitely hiding. If not from us, then from Va'Sh itself."

Farley looked at the information on Tatsumaki's board. He didn't like this. He didn't like it one bit. He knew nothing about the bogey's origin, intentions or capabilities. For all he knew it was only pretending to not see them. All he knew was that it was acting suspiciously and not at all like a ship with any kind of peaceful intentions. He needed some kind of edge. And right now, the only one he knew he had was time.

"Weps," Farley called over his shoulder. "Prepare a Stellarhawk missile for launch. Fifteen kiloton yield."

"Yes, Sir," the guardian at the weapons console replied.

"Tech Sergeant," Farley said, addressing Tatsumaki. "I want you to order the Skylight network to take control of that missile's guidance system after launch and have them guide it around Hobbes to approach the bogey from the rear. Minimal power settings. Set it to impact the bogey forty-five minutes after it comes within weapons range. That should give us time to see what's what."

"Manual trigger?" Tatsumaki asked as he took notes.

"Plus a deadman's switch," Farley told him. "I want it to go off *if* our IFF beacon stops transmitting."

Tatsumaki nodded and set to work. Farley looked at the holographic display again. Launching the missile now meant the bogey *shouldn't* be aware of it. If the bogey was peaceful, they could always transmit an abort signal to the missile. If the bogey was hostile and overwhelmed *Neil Armstrong* in a fight, it would make sure that the bogey's crew wouldn't be celebrating very long.

"Sir, weapons crews report Stellarhawk ready for launch," the crewman at the weapons console spoke up. "Awaiting target profile."

"All yours, Tech Sergeant," Farley told Tatsumaki.

* * *

Two hours later, there still had been no detectable change in the bogey. The commander had ordered loading and unloading activities suspended an hour ago, enough time for the cargo crews to safely stand down. Now that it was almost time for the alien craft to clear the moon, it was time to prepare *Neil Armstrong* for battle.

"Stand by to stop rotation," Farley ordered, sitting down in his chair and pulling the safety harness down over his shoulders and down to his waist. The other Command and Control Center techs did the same thing as a soothing female voice came over the ship's loudspeaker.

"*Attention. Attention. All personnel. The ship's rotation will cease in ten minutes. All personnel must return to their berthing areas or their battle stations immediately and prepare for Zero-G operations.*"

Neil Armstrong's cylindrical hull spun in order to simulate gravity for the passengers and crew while cargo operations were conducted in the relatively motionless center of the cylinder. Cargo cranes, antennae and sensor modules protruded from the center cavity out toward the front of the ship, making it look like an empty cup with several straws sticking out of it. Like the cargo areas, the engines in the rear, at the bottom of this cup, did not spin.

The warning was repeated over the loudspeaker. The crew and passengers had about five minutes to get to their stations and strap in. After that five minutes, the ship's rotation would begin to slow and take about another five minutes to stop completely.

Farley looked at his control board and watched the holographic clocks in the corner count down. One counted the seconds until the ship would stop spinning. The other counted toward the alien ship clearing Hobbes. The ship's captain felt a knot in his stomach. There were still so many unknowns. His eyes went to the third clock that counted down the minutes until the Stellarhawk missile they had launched would impact the rear of the bogey.

The computer's voice came over the loudspeaker again.

"Attention. Attention. All personnel. The ship's artificial gravity will reach Zero-G in five minutes."

The technicians and officers in the control center instinctively tensed as they felt their bodies slowly begin to get lighter as the ship's spin slowed. After exactly five minutes, a deep *CLUNK* echoed throughout the ship as the cylinder stopped and locked into place. Anyone not strapped into something was now floating.

Tatsumaki focused on his holodisplay. One counter had reached zero. The other would follow it soon.

Two minutes after it did...

"EM spike," Tatsumaki announced evenly. "They're scanning us."

"Are we getting any new data from them?" Townsend asked calmly from his station.

As soon as the ship cleared the moon, *Neil Armstrong*'s scanner array began blasting radiation their way, trying to see what would bounce back.

The data from the scanners was analyzed by *Neil Armstrong*'s computer AI for interpretation, which then generated a report based on what it *thought* the data meant.

"Its hull isn't metal," Tatsumaki reported. "Some kind of composite material..."

"Is it still coming at us?" Farley asked.

"Yes, Sir," the tech reported.

Farley growled. The fact that it didn't slow or change course told him that they knew they were here the entire time.

"Weps, status?" he called.

"Ten Stellarhawks, ready for launch," the Weapons tech replied. "Fifteen kilotons each. Ready for firing solution. Laser cannon ready to charge."

"Open missile doors," Townsend ordered. "And charge the laser."

The Weapons tech complied with the order even as he debated it. "Sir, we are still out of range for the cannon."

Farley knew that. The laser cannon was a strictly close-range weapon, designed to blast rocks apart during mining operations. "They don't know that," Farley told him. "Rack the shotgun. Give 'em something to think about."

Both ships had now hit the other with the full force of their information gathering instruments, and both sides were now using that information to weigh the threat of the other. Seconds dragged into minutes as the two ships sized each other up across a vast ocean of empty vacuum.

"Blue shift!" Tatsumaki called. "Bogey is accelerating toward us!" He had just finished this announcement when he followed it with another. "EM spike!"

"Weps! Fire missiles one through five," Farley ordered. "Control, increase speed to full and move us toward the bogey. Close the distance."

"Stellarhawks one through five firing!" Weps called out.

Tatsumaki looked through the data on his board as the ship's AI interpreted. "Changes in EM and thermal readings!" he announced. "Rated highly probable energy weapon charging!"

"All personnel brace for imp..."

The ship rumbled under his feet before he could finish.

"Weapons impact!" the engineer tech called out. "Section Three all the way through to the cargo area."

Farley blinked in shock at what he just heard. Whatever the bogey had hit them with had struck the cylinder and gone all the way through to the center of the ship before stopping.

"Tatsumaki, check instruments!" he ordered. "Are they closer than we thought!?"

Lasers spread as they move through space. The reason *Neil Armstrong* couldn't use its laser to attack the alien ship was that the beam would have dissipated over too large an area to do any damage. The same should be true of the alien ship's weapons.

"RADAR and LIDAR confirm bogey at one-point-four light seconds," Tatsumaki said.

Not only could their energy weapons reach further than the lasers on *Neil Armstrong*, but they were much stronger as well.

Although the Stellarhawks would continuously accelerate, it would still take time for them to reach the bogey. It was like someone trying to fight a sniper with a hunting knife.

"EM spike!" Tatsumaki called. "Incoming fire!"

"Engage maneuvering thrusters sixteen through thirty-five!" Farley ordered, futilely trying to get his massive ship out of the way.

The ship shook again violently around them. Before the commander could ask for a report, the lights in the control center along with all the holographic displays went out, leaving them all in pitch darkness.

One by one, the controllers turned on the emergency key lights that hung on the front of their uniforms, giving the control room a little light.

"Everyone okay?" someone called.

"Power's out!" someone else replied.

"Yeah, no shit," another voice agreed sarcastically.

"Everyone stay calm," Farley ordered, his voice even and projecting a calm he didn't actually feel. "As soon as Damage Control..."

Before he finished, the bulkhead in front him ripped open, and the air in the control center along with the chairs that lined that wall were blown outside into the vacuum of space.

Strapped into one of those chairs, Tatsumaki cried noiselessly in horror as he suddenly realized he could see his ship spinning in front of him, getting smaller and smaller, seeming to bleed fire and gas from two very large wounds in her side.

As his eyeballs began to freeze over, a blast of dark purple light struck the ship in the side and came out the other end.

In the half second this all happened, just as his vision went black, a final thought went through his mind.

Oh my God... I'm in space...

Chapter 1

"... Then, three minutes later, at approximately zero-six-sixteen ZULU, Skylight Two and Three detected an explosion in Va'Sh orbit in the twenty-megaton range," the crackling voice on the phone continued. The pace and meter of the man's words made it obvious that he was reading off prepared notes, a calm drone that would have put people to sleep if the information it was passing wasn't so incredible. For the briefer, he may as well have been reading off the day's chow hall menu, not recounting the deaths of several thousand people.

Ben, like everyone else around the table in their tiny conference room, took notes on everything the briefer said as he continued.

"The explosion is consistent with a fold drive overload, and Skylight Two detected activated fold particles following the explosion. We can assume that this was the moment that *Neil Armstrong* was destroyed, causing the light visible in the sky over the main continent."

"Logs show *Neil Armstrong* launched missiles shortly before its destruction," another voice broke into the briefing. Ben recognized the voice as the Director of the CJ-5, the task force's plans directorate. "Any indication that they did any damage?"

"Skylight Two's sensor data shows five missiles approaching the bogey twenty-five minutes after *Neil Armstrong* exploded," the briefer replied. "The bogey then radiated some kind of weapon or countermeasure, and the missiles went completely off course and went silent when they ran out of fuel."

"So, they never got a shot in," someone on the line commented. This remark was met with several rumbles and chatter. Ben knew that the room in which this briefing was taking place at the CJTF headquarters was likely packed wall-to-wall with people.

"Actually, Sir, that brings me to my next item," the briefer broke in and waited for the chatter to die down before continuing. "Ten minutes after the missiles scattered, Skylight Eight detected a nuclear detonation, approximately fifteen kilotons, directly *behind* the bogey. Following this detonation, the bogey's course shifted by six degrees, and Skylight Eight's sensors indicate that the bogey also began a slow lateral spin at a speed of one-point-five rotations per minute. CJ-2 assesses that this may be the result of damage sustained by the bogey in the explosion from the Stellarhawk missile *Neil Armstrong* launched hours before."

"Good for them," someone on the line commented.

The briefer continued, ignoring the comment. "The bogey has since righted itself, however its course and speed indicate that the bogey is most likely adrift and is being pulled toward Va'Sh by the planet's gravity well."

Another familiar voice came over the line, and Ben reflexively tensed at the sound of Lieutenant General Walker addressing the briefer.

"How long before they enter Va'Sh's atmosphere?"

"Assuming the bogey *is* adrift and is unable to correct its own course, it will enter the planet's atmosphere in three days. If it does so uncontrolled, it will likely burn up in the atmosphere, and the remains will touch down in the ocean, sixteen hundred miles southwest of Jamieson Airfield, approximately five-hundred and fifty miles off the coast of Kashuta Province."

"Has there been any indication of survivors from *Neil Armstrong*, either alive in the wreckage or in escape pods?" a female voice asked on the line.

"The fold drive explosion would have vaporized everything within twenty kilometers of the ship," the briefer replied. "Making the odds of survivors extremely low. We are, however, having the

Skylights scan every piece of wreckage for any indication that someone might be alive."

Left unsaid, of course, was the point that almost *no* wreckage had been left by the fold drive explosion, meaning the satellites had, up until now, scanned practically nothing.

"How long until *Over the Rainbow* arrives?" another voice spoke up.

"Thirteen days if they remain on schedule," another voice replied.

"Is there any way at all to warn them?"

Ben put his elbows on the table and rested his chin in his hands as he listened to the worrisome conversation. If the hostile ship regained control of itself, it could attack the arriving colony ship the moment it came out of fold space. It would be another slaughter.

He could almost see someone shaking their head in answer to the question.

"Until they come into normal space, they won't be able to send or receive any radio or laser transmissions," someone answered. "Best we can do is have the Skylights continually broadcast a warning so that they receive it the moment they come out of the fold. If the bogey is far enough away, they may be able to get clear of the danger long enough to recharge their fold drive and escape."

"Do it," Walker ordered. "What else?"

"Do we try to talk to them?" someone at the table asked.

"We don't even know who *they* are," someone pointed out.

"Aren't they Va'Shen?" someone else asked.

"The bogey's capabilities are inconsistent with what we've seen from Va'Shen ships," the briefer informed them.

"Then who?"

Ben heard another familiar voice clear its throat and speak up, prompting him to smile grimly.

"If we rule out the Va'Shen and any potentially hostile human force, there are at least three other possibilities," Dr. Everett Sinclair, the general's cultural advisor spoke up.

"I know the three possibilities you're referencing, Doctor," another voice, one that Ben knew was the CJ-2 Intelligence director, told him. "However, we have yet to find any real substantiating evidence for those rumors."

"With all due respect, General," Sinclair replied calmly. "I think your substantiating evidence just blew up a colony ship."

"You tell 'em, Doc," Patricia muttered from Ben's right at the conference room table. Ben looked at her and found the lieutenant scribbling notes, not even bothering to look up at the speakerphone in the middle of the conference room table.

"For those of you who have not yet read the report, Dr. Sinclair is referencing stories told to us by some Va'Shen villagers of ancient enemies and servants of their gods," General Walker supplied.

Ben frowned. The way Walker had said that seemed to give the impression that what he and Patricia had reported was simply folktales and legends told to them by simple villagers rather than historical accounts from commandos and Mikorin historians.

"I recommend we act strictly on what we know for certain," the Operations director suggested in a tone that made it obvious what he thought of Sinclair's remarks.

"Agreed," Walker concurred immediately before anyone could object, effectively silencing any possible dissent.

The meeting continued, and Ben listened while simultaneously making a list of all the things he would need to do as a result of these events. His big question was what would the Va'Shen do? The explosion lit up the sky in a way that hadn't happened since the nuke attacks at the end of the war. Alacea, herself, had witnessed it. The villagers would have questions or... worse... their own conclusions.

As if answering his thoughts, Walker asked Sinclair another question.

"What is the Va'Shen position?"

Ben heard a sigh over the phone. "The palace isn't saying anything," Sinclair informed them. "They are 'investigating.'"

He heard Patricia snort and looked up at her. She saw his look and spoke up. The phone was muted on their end, so she didn't have to worry about anyone else hearing her.

"Looks like someone learned their lesson about jumping the gun," she commented.

Ben bit his lip. He and Patricia had learned only recently that the entire war between Earth and Va'Sh stemmed from a case of mistaken identity and premature declarations that could not, due to the Emperor's status as a god, be taken back. It now looked like the Va'Shen government was going to wait a bit and see how things played out before saying anything.

Finally, it seemed that the meeting was beginning to wind down. Walker ordered proposed courses of action for three possible eventualities: The bogey remained in orbit, the bogey crashed, and the bogey landed. Finally, it was time to "go around the room," usually the final part of any meeting where anyone who wished to say something or ask a question could. A few people replied by saying they would speak to Walker "offline" while everyone else replied with a "no."

Ben's eyes narrowed as the voice of Major Elkanah Keyes came over the line.

"Next meeting at eighteen hundred local," the general's executive officer informed everyone. "Jamieson out."

The line clicked, and everyone at the small conference room table threw their pens down as if exhausted by it.

"Comments?" Ben asked the room.

"Refueling schedule is probably worthless now," Senior Chief Petty Officer Chase Warren said from Ben's left. The older man ran his hand through his curly brown hair. "On the upside, the equipment that was glassed has all been replaced, and we got resupplied last week. We should have plenty of fuel for any contingency needs that come up."

Ben nodded and made a note. FOB Leonard's primary mission was to refuel convoys and helicopters moving back and forth across Va'Sh's largest landmass. Under normal circumstances, it was a pretty routine job, but with everything that just happened, they could expect a lot of last-minute additions and subtractions from their refueling schedules.

"Medical?" Ben prompted as he continued scribbling notes.

Sitting next to Warren in her mottled green Marine Corps uniform, Navy Corpsman Second Class Mina Fletcher checked her own notes before answering. "Medicinal stocks are good, though we're starting to run a little short on Cosoridan," the blonde woman said. "Both beds are available. All personnel are up-to-date on Self-Aid and Buddy-Care."

Ben nodded. The Cosoridan shortage didn't bother him too much. It was a drug used to treat herpes that the FOB was prescribing to the young vixens in Pelle who had contracted the disease from human "patrons." The refugee vixens from Garan'Sel had been exchanging sex for peace. Now that the practice had been discontinued, the need for the drug should vanish.

"Intel?" Ben prompted.

First Lieutenant Patricia Kim took a deep breath and straightened in her chair. As the FOB's intelligence officer, interpreter and second-in-command, the Korean-American woman was probably the busiest person on the base.

"Where would you like me to start?" she asked him seriously.

"Closest to the flagpole," Ben replied immediately.

"Okay," Patricia began. "It looks like things in the village have started to die down, but you can bet a big-ass light in the sky is going to stir things up. I can't say for sure how, though."

Ben blew some air between his lips. It had barely been a week since the Pelle commando, led by his own Va'Shen brother-in-law, Azarin, had dragged every Garan'Sel refugee out of their homes and forced them to pledge not to fight the humans. It was during that operation that they had discovered that the *Dara Tang*, Va'Sh's hyper-extremist secret police, had been quietly stirring up violence in his AO since the refugees' arrival and before that in Garan'Sel. There had been several casualties, including two Mikorin, the village's religious caste.

"Continue to monitor," Ben told her absently. There wasn't much more she could do at the moment.

"Yes, Sir," she said. "As for the... thing... in orbit, I haven't gotten a readout from CJ-2 yet, but I imagine it'll be coming down soon."

Ben nodded and made a note to check with every vehicle that came through the FOB for the next few days for message traffic.

"Can I ask a question?"

The Ranger captain looked up at the man sitting next to Patricia. Staff Sergeant John Ramirez had his hand up like he was asking a question in school. At Ben's nod, he lowered his hand and continued.

"What was all that stuff about 'other possibilities' as to who these guys are?" Ramirez asked.

As most of that information had come as a result of Ben and Patricia's activities, they were probably two of the few humans on Va'Sh who could answer that question with anything other than a shrug. Ben deferred to Patricia as she was the one who had learned the most.

Patricia looked around the table and began her impromptu briefing. "It looks like there are at least two other alien races out there who have had contact with the Va'Shen in their ancient past," she said. "One extremely hostile and the other *possibly* friendly."

"'Possibly' friendly?" The question came from Ramirez's right. Staff Sergeant Jared "Burgers" Baird looked huge next to the much smaller Ramirez. At six-foot-three and made of nothing but muscle, the African American Texan was one of the best Rangers Ben had ever worked with.

"We say 'possibly' because we have reason to believe that these aliens used the Va'Shen as cannon fodder for a war with the other alien race by posing as servants of their ancient gods," Patricia told him. "So 'friendly' in an 'enemy of my enemy' kinda way."

Burgers nodded. "Track'n."

"And this other race?" Fletcher asked.

"The 'Dark Ones,'" Patricia answered. "From what we've learned, they invaded Va'Sh around four thousand years ago and drove the Va'Shen to near-extinction."

"That doesn't sound good," Ramirez noted.

"They killed about ninety-seven percent of the Va'Shen population, so..." Patricia trailed off.

"Definitely not good," Ramirez concluded with a nod.

"So, which are the guys in orbit?" Warren asked.

"That's the big question," Ben asked. "Either way, it doesn't look good for us."

* * *

Alacea, Na'Sha of the People and Animals of Pelle, was trying desperately to hold onto her composure and maintain an air of calm as the crowd around her shouted their questions and worries. Standing upon the stone platform from which the chieftain or the Na'Sha spoke to the village, she, Kasshas and Yasuren tried to get the crowd to settle down so they could speak.

The villagers, however, were too frightened and excited. They had only just recently endured one terrifying event that included the loss of two Mikorin and a few members of the village's *aderen*, its ruling council. Now there were bright lights in the sky with no explanation. Like any organism placed under stress, it could only endure so much before it began to crack under the pressure. Thanks to everything that had happened in the last week, that crack was now starting to appear in Pelle.

<Please!> Kasshas called, raising his hands up above his head. <Peace!>

<Is it the Great Ones?!> someone in the crowd called. <Have they finally come to fight the Dark Ones!?>

The crowd went silent at the question. It was the one they were all asking themselves, the one they all wanted to hear the answer to.

Alacea stepped forward, her tail swishing back and forth in concern. <We do not know what the light means,> she told them honestly. <The Overlod has said it is very likely the destruction of one of their ships high above us, but, if so, he does not know the cause of that destruction.>

<Is it not obvious?> another voice called out.

The crowd turned to look at the source of the question. A middle-aged tod with stone-grey hair and a beard looked up at the three on the platform.

Alacea recognized the man as a miner from Garan'Sel, though she did not know his name. Many of the Garan'Sel miners had been followers of the now-deceased Goto, a tod deeply hostile to her *Tesho*'s people. That said, she had no memory of this tod performing any violent acts during the recent troubles.

At everyone's gaze, the miner rallied and continued. <Is this not a sign from the Gods that the time has come?>

<The time for what?> Yasuren, Kasshas's *Myorin*, asked from her position at her husband's side. The question and the tone in

which she asked it was covered in barbs. She knew what this tod was implying, and with the death of Wenlin, Hestean and Goto still so fresh, it took either a very dumb tod or a very courageous one to suggest it.

<The time to throw off the Dark Ones,> the tod continued, confirming that he was either very dumb or very courageous. <We have waited for a sign, and now that sign from the Gods has come!>

Alacea sighed inwardly. She had futilely hoped that her brother's actions had put this issue to rest, but the hatred the Garan'Sel villagers had toward her *Tesho*'s people ran deep. He was not, strictly speaking, promoting violence. He was merely asking if a greater power was.

As she was pondering how to answer this question in a way that wouldn't result in more division, a familiar blue-haired vixen stepped forward through the crowd and walked up to the tod.

Alacea's tail moved faster as she recognized her friend, Sho Nan, as the vixen now facing the tod. Like Alacea and every other Mikorin in Pelle at the moment and for the next month, she had forsaken her normal light blue and white hanbok for one made up of deep shades of red, the Va'Shen color of mourning, in honor of the departed Hestean and Wenlin. Her ears and tail were impossible to read. But knowing the Ya'Jahar as she did, she knew this was not going to end well.

The crowd parted and looked between the two. The tod, under the full power of Sho Nan's gaze, did not back down, though he did bow to her in respect.

<What is your name?> Sho Nan asked him evenly.

<I am Ketoro, Honored Ya'Jahar,> the tod replied respectfully.

Sho Nan turned to the three village leaders on the platform and raised her voice. <Alacea Na'Sha, I propose that Ketoro be named our new Na'Sha!>

The crowd buzzed at the blatant disrespect, amazed at the vixen's brash attitude. Alacea, meanwhile, braced herself and sighed.

Sho Nan, please don't... she thought in exasperation.

Ketoro's tail had puffed out to three times its volume in shock in the meantime.

<M... Me?!> he cried.

<Of course,> Sho Nan replied, her voice deadly serious. <Look upon that platform,> she continued, pointing at Kasshas, Yasuren and Alacea. <That Mikorin has spent *years* at the temple, studying, researching, learning at the feet of Jemenista Na'Sha herself. All so that the day the Great Ones return to us, she would know and be able to interpret their meaning and share it with all of us.>

The people in the crowd listened to Sho Nan with rapt attention. Some looked sheepishly away, their tails moving back and forth nervously. These were the villagers of Pelle, who knew how their Ya'Jahar thought and already had an idea of where she was going.

<And all of that time and effort was wasted,> Sho Nan continued. <For hither Ketoro, who has shown us that all one must do is look up at a light in the sky and declare 'The Great Ones have come!'>

Ears in the crowd began to flutter, slowly at first, then faster, as Sho Nan looked at Ketoro, and the miner looked sheepishly at the ground.

<Surely, a person of such wisdom should be our Na'Sha,> Sho Nan concluded. <Do you not think so?>

Alacea sighed. Kasshas looked down with ears of stone, and Yasuren's ears twitched a smile.

Ketoro's tail and ears drooped. He cleared his throat. <Forgive me,> he said. <I meant no disrespect to the Na'Sha.>

<Then you do not wish to be our new Na'Sha?> Sho Nan asked in mock surprise.

<I... I do not,> Ketoro replied, forced to continue with Sho Nan's act.

<Well,> Sho Nan sighed. <It is an honor just to be nominated, yes?>

Ketoro said nothing.

Alacea took this opportunity to seize the conversation for herself.

<When the Great Ones come,> she called to the group loudly as Sho Nan quietly made her way back to the other Mikorin, <They will send their heralds who will stand upon the top of our temple and share their words with all of us.> The crowd, reminded by Sho Nan that they did, indeed, have someone with answers among them, had their eyes glued to Alacea. <There will be no need to guess,> she continued. <They will tell us, themselves, what we must do. As they have not yet done this, we cannot assume that the Great Ones have anything to do with the light in the sky.>

Murmurs from the crowd along with swishing tails replied to Alacea's statement.

<Then, what should we do?> someone from the crowd asked.

This time, it was Kasshas who stepped forward to answer. <We do what we have always done,> he said. <We serve our Gods and our Emperor, we take care of one another, and we honor those who must be honored. Please know that we are not ignoring this. And when we learn more, we will share it all with you.>

This rather benign statement was met with grumbling, and it took a minute for Kasshas to realize what they were all thinking.

Like you shared the information about the Mikorin selling their bodies?

Although the danger of an armed insurrection against the humans at FOB Leonard was over, there was still a lot of angry feelings over what had happened. The hearts of every villager went out to those "Mikorin Zaishin," the noble damned, and they were working to help them as best they could. But feelings toward the humans had hardened.

Although not completely. Alacea and the Mikorin had made sure to speak to the villagers and emphasize several key points: That it was one of Pelle's humans that had discovered what was happening and raised the alarm, and that it was Pelle's Overlord that had put a stop to the practice and sought justice.

Pelle's villagers, who had interacted with humans in the most positive way, were more ready to accept that the acts were aberrations. The Garan'Sel villagers, however, had no wish to budge on their opinions.

<Thank you all for hearing us,> Alacea told the crowd with a bow. <Go in peace and be blessed.>

The crowd began to break up and go their separate ways. Alacea looked around and found the mop of blue hair she was looking for. Making her way through the throngs of Va'Shen, she was soon able to reach out and touch the vixen's shoulder.

Sho Nan turned and bowed to her. <Na'Sha,> she began, <Congratulations on surviving the challenge to your position.>

Alacea's tail slapped the ground in mild annoyance. <I thank you for your help, Sho Nan, but do you think publicly embarrassing that tod was the proper thing to do?>

Sho Nan's features were normally very difficult to read if you didn't know her. She was one of those Va'Shen who seemed to be able to control her ears and tail a lot more than others. But she and Alacea had known each other for years, and so the head priestess could tell by the slight hardening of her eyes that the other Mikorin was actually quite angry.

<My friend is dead because ignorant tods thought they knew better than the representatives of their community's will,> she said calmly. Nevertheless, Alacea could hear the venom in her words. <I

would prefer to kill the baby *toka* in its den than wait for it to grow into a predator.>

Alacea's ears curled inward sadly. <It was my fault things got to that...>

<Do not!>

The head priestess took a step back at Sho Nan's angry cry.

<Do not try to take the responsibility from them!> Sho Nan told her. <They have earned my anger and my hatred just as much as every other Mikorin! I will not see my friend try to take that burden from them and place it upon herself!>

<Sho Nan,> Alacea whispered. She reached out and hugged her friend tightly. <Feel what you feel,> she said. <But don't let it consume you. Hestean would not wish that for you.>

<I understand... Alacea,> Sho Nan replied softly. The use of her friend's name let the high priestess know that they were not just words to placate her.

As Alacea pulled away from Sho Nan, the two simultaneously felt the presence of another person nearby and turned. The Huntress, Alzoria, stood to the side, looking sheepishly downward. Her tail and ears made it apparent that she felt awkward at having to intrude on such a moment.

Alacea's ears twitched and she gave a short bow. <Forgive us, Alzoria,> she said. <We did not mean to make you wait.>

<No! No, Na'Sha!> Alzoria replied, bowing low to the two Mikorin. <I did not wish to intrude upon you. But I have a message from the Overlord that he asked me to bring to you.>

<*Tesho*?> Alacea asked, her ears popping up in interest. <What is it?>

Alzoria came up to her full height, which wasn't very much. She absently scratched the back of her head, once again silently missing the gold and deep red hair that had been taken from her. She had been at the FOB, looking for Ramirez, and found Patricia waiting for her alongside him when the Huntress finally found him. It was the interpreter that passed along the message.

<The Overlord asks to meet with you, the Chieftain, Lady Yasuren and Azarin this afternoon after the midday meal,> Alzoria told her. <He wishes to talk about the light in the sky.>

<Did he say what that light was?> Alacea asked eagerly. Most of the village had been asleep when the light bloomed in the stars above them, but Alacea had been one of the few to actually see it happen. She had been lying in her den with her *Tesho*, looking up at those stars through her skylight when it happened.

<No, Na'Sha,> Alzoria told her in disappointment.

<I see. May I ask you to return to him and tell my *Tesho* I will gather the others into the temple at that time?> Alacea asked.

Alzoria bowed again. <Of course, Na'Sha!>

The Huntress turned and started jogging back to the FOB. Alacea and Sho Nan watched her go.

<I will see to it that tea and snacks are ready, Na'Sha,> Sho Nan assured her.

<Thank you, Sho Nan.>

<It is good to see her appear happy again,> Sho Nan continued.

Alacea's ears twitched. <She is surrounded by people who love her, of both peoples.>

<May she ever be so,> the Mikorin cook wished quietly.

<Come,> Alacea said, turning. <We have work to do.>

* * *

When Ben entered the Mikorin temple meeting room, everyone who had already arrived rose and bowed to him. He stopped and bowed low in return. Va'Shen culture and etiquette played a large role, even in simple meetings, and even if the meeting was urgent, it was not something that could be brushed aside.

Alacea waited on the far side of the low table. The Na'Sha's hanbok was red with a dark, blood-red trim. He thought she looked good in red and silently berated himself a moment later, remembering that her choice of outfit was for the sake of mourning her lost friends.

He and Patricia circled around the others, and the Ranger captain sat at the head of the table with Alacea on his right and Patricia on his left, ready to interpret for him. Next to Patricia sat Alzoria, whom Alacea had asked to attend to help interpret if need be. At the other end of the table sat the Chieftain, Kasshas, with his *Myorin,* Yasuren, sitting on his right. On Kasshas's left and Alacea's right sat Azarin, whose slightly discolored blood-red monpei told Ben that he had come directly from work and that he, too, was deep in mourning.

<Thank you to all you for meeting with me now,> Ben said, bowing low from his seated position. The rest of the room bowed back. <I have things to say about light in the heavens.>

<Do you know what it was?> Kasshas asked him.

<Yes,> Ben told him. He gestured to Patricia to take over the translations before continuing. "The light was one of the ships that brought us here. It was destroyed by an alien ship that came into your space."

Patricia translated, pausing only once to confer with Alzoria on word choice.

<Who are these aliens?> Azarin asked with great interest. He was one of the few villagers of Pelle who knew that the humans were not actually the Dark Ones of their legends and that those Dark Ones, as a result, were still somewhere out there.

"We don't know," Ben answered in English. "Their ship was not Va'Shen. That is all we know about them."

Kasshas and Yasuren looked at one another as if wondering if they should speak of what they thought as the most likely possibility.

<Where is this ship now?> Kasshas asked instead.

"Our ship managed to damage it before it was destroyed," Ben said. "Right now, it appears to be adrift in orbit."

Kasshas took a deep breath before taking the plunge <It could be the Great Ones,> he said, preparing himself to give a lengthy explanation.

"That is one possibility," Ben replied after hearing the translation.

Kasshas's ears popped upward slightly. However, he quickly waved away his surprise. It made sense that the Dark Ones would automatically assume this new enemy was their ancient adversary.

<It could also be the Dark Ones,> Alacea announced from her position next to Ben.

Kasshas, Yasuren and Alzoria looked at her, confused by her statement. Azarin remained silent and sipped his tea.

<Na'Sha,> Yasuren began cautiously, <Are you suggesting that the Dark Ones are attacking one another?>

Alacea took a breath. This was going to be the hard part.

<Kasshas, Yasuren, the time has come to tell you the truth,> she said. <It will be difficult to hear. But I swear to you, it is all true.> She cleared her throat and swallowed.

<The Overlord's people are not the Dark Ones,> Azarin interrupted before his sister could say anything.

Alacea looked to her brother in surprise. It was a breach of etiquette to interrupt a Na'Sha when she spoke, but...

Did he do that so that I would not have to give voice to heresy?

She knew that this news would mean that the Emperor had either been wrong or deceptive. For a Na'Sha to suggest either would be a faith-shattering moment for anyone who heard it. But for Azarin to do it...

<Heresy,> Yasuren whispered and looked away from him.

Kasshas, however, merely took a breath. <Your words could lead to great punishment, Azarin,> he told him. <I could banish you from this village.>

Azarin sipped his tea as if he didn't care one bit about what happened to him. <Do as you must,> he said simply. <One way or another, the truth will soon arrive.>

He received support from a surprising source.

<I... I think so too!>

Everyone turned to look at Alzoria, who was staring down at the table in fearful guilt. She didn't look up as she continued.

<They can't be the same people,> she said.

Kasshas stared at the young Huntress.

Alzoria seemed to gather her courage and looked up at the Chieftain. <I am already shamed,> she said. <A little more shame will not hurt me.>

<Alzoria!> Yasuren hissed in disapproval. In Va'Shen society, vixens tended to be the more pious sex, and so Alzoria's drift into heresy alarmed the faithful noblevixen much more than Azarin's.

<We... are not the... Dark Ones,> Ben interjected slowly so that there would be no chance to say the wrong thing. <You... do not need believe... but is also true.>

Kasshas took a deep breath. <Azarin has served this community with great distinction, and so I have no problem overlooking his momentary heresy.>

Once again, Azarin looked like he didn't care one way or another.

Alzoria, however, looked at him with a thrashing, fearful tail.

<And it is fortunate that *no one else* here spoke up to agree with him,> Kasshas continued.

The Huntress breathed a sigh of relief. Yasuren appeared troubled by the statement, though she did not say anything about it.

<For now,> Kasshas began again, <I believe it is fully possible that these attackers are some offshoot of your people whose ways are very similar to those who invaded our world. And that because of that, they represent a threat to both our peoples.> He looked at Ben and Alacea with hardened eyes. <But that is *as far* as I am willing to believe.>

Ben took a breath and nodded. Kasshas's position was fair given that they weren't even sure *who* was up there. For all anyone knew, it could be Santa Claus.

"When we learn more, we will share it with you," Ben promised.

Kasshas listened to the translation and bowed to Ben in thanks. <We shall share what you have told us with the *aderen*,> he said.

At that, the meeting moved to the ending ceremonies: Standing, bowing and thanking. Yasuren looked to Kasshas, and the two left the room.

Ben looked to Azarin and bowed to him. <Thanks be to you, Azarin,> he said.

Azarin gave the Ranger a short bow in return and a deeper one to Alacea. <Overlord... Na'Sha...> he said with each one. With no further words, he left as well. Alzoria followed him after two bows of her own.

"Gimme a minute?" Ben asked Patricia.

She nodded. "I'll be in the LTV."

The captain turned to Alacea as Patricia left the room. The two stood awkwardly for a moment before Ben began.

<I am apologize,> he said. <Leave quickly before.>

Alacea's ears flickered an understanding smile. <You are a leader of warriors,> she told him. <Such things will happen.> Within minutes of the explosion in orbit, Ben had thrown on his uniform and rushed from the temple to deal with this newest emergency. It was only in hindsight that he realized it hadn't been a good look. Alacea, however, was not so immature as to demand her *Tesho*, a tod of great importance, remain with her when the very world could be in danger.

She reached out and took his hands in hers, looking down at them bashfully.

<I cannot come to temple at this night,> Ben continued. <Things may occur. May need be close.>

<I understand,> the priestess told him. <Then I will come to your den instead.>

<Not need to,> he replied. <Den is not soft with comforts.>

She finally looked up at him. <You *are* my comfort,> she said. <I will come. That is my role as your *Myorin*.>

Ben smiled at her promise. He cleared his throat nervously. <Is acceptable nip in temple room?> he asked her.

The fur on Alacea's ears stood on end in the Va'Shen version of a deep blush. <*Tesho*,> she said quietly. <You *marked me* in this temple,> she reminded him.

His face and neck turned red at the reminder. <Um... yes...> he admitted. He pointed upward. <Did not want make... um... Great Ones... angry.>

<It is no sin to show the Great Ones or the Gods that we are happy,> she assured him. To prove it, she leaned up on her tip-toes and softly bit his left earlobe.

Ben swallowed as he blushed like a schoolboy.

<Lady Patricia awaits you,> Alacea told him. <You have much to do.>

He took a step back and bowed. <I will see you in the evening, *Myorin*,> he said.

She bowed back, her every move made with the elegance of a dancer. <And I you, *Tesho*.>

Chapter 2

Patricia looked up from the documents she was reading as Ben climbed into the driver side of the LTV and shut the door. She looked over at him and smirked.

"Is Alacea all right?" she asked innocently.

"She's fine," Ben said as he put the LTV into gear and started down the road.

"Just checking," she said, casually continuing to look through her notes. "Thought there might be a problem since you were at the temple until like zero-two this morning."

Ben cleared his throat guiltily but said nothing.

Patricia's smirk turned into a full-blown grin. "Good for you," she remarked.

"It's not appropriate to talk about," he warned her.

"Uh huh," she replied as they approached the gate to the FOB. "I've got a million questions..."

"And I am not answering any of them," he assured her.

"Come on!" she begged. "It is such a huge step in human-Va'Shen relations!" Ben gave her a warning look as the sentry waved them through the sallyport. "At least let me give you a questionnaire!"

"Absolutely not!" Ben cried in response.

"Please!?" she whined. "Could you at least tell me if all the... um... parts... fit?"

"No," he replied.

Patricia was silent for several moments as they pulled into the parking spot outside their office.

"'No,' you won't tell me, or 'no' they didn't fit?" she finally asked.

Ben ignored her and got out of the vehicle, Patricia following a second later.

"It's for *science!*" she tried one last time.

The Ranger didn't reply. Instead, he stepped into the office and removed his patrol cap. He found Warren, Ramirez and Burgers waiting for them there.

"How'd it go?" Warren asked immediately.

"They're pretty scared," Ben said, taking a seat at his desk. "But we promised to keep them updated, and they seemed good with that."

"So, what do *we* do in the meantime?" Ramirez asked.

"There's nothing we really *can* do," Ben told him. He pointed at the ceiling. "They've got the high ground. For the moment, let's keep the troops informed of what we know, keep everyone calm, and be ready to kill stuff that falls from the sky."

"Is there anything we can do to protect ourselves if they *do* hit us from up there?" Burgers asked, turning to Warren.

The SeaBee snorted. "If they hit us from up there, we're screwed. It doesn't even matter what they use. They can drop a bowling ball from up there and take a bunch of us out."

"It ain't gonna be a problem," Ramirez said assuredly.

"Why do you say that?" Patricia asked.

Ramirez grunted. "This is a tiny little FOB," he told her. "Of all the places they *could* hit, why bother with us? If they're gonna glass anything, it's gonna be, like, Jamieson or the capital."

"He's not wrong," Ben agreed. "So, to sum up, there's nothing we can do to stop an attack, so there's no point in trying. And we're so unimportant a target anyway that there's no point in worrying."

"Our greatest defense is insignificance," Burgers concluded dryly.

"Well, I hope you're right," Patricia told them. "Because I really hate the idea of being on *this* side of an orbital bombardment."

"Let's just hope that *Neil Armstrong* got a really good hit on them before they were taken out," Ben said. "Because until *Over the Rainbow* gets here, there's nothing standing between us and them." He tapped his fingers on the desk in thought for a moment before looking up at Warren. "If we had to completely evacuate the FOB, how long would it take?"

"Depends on where you want to evacuate *to*," the SeaBee replied. "To Jamieson? Days."

"I doubt we'd be lucky enough to get that much warning," Burgers pointed out.

"How much *would* we get?" Patricia asked.

Ramirez pointed at the ceiling. "Probably about: 'Hey! What's that!?'"

"We don't know what we don't know," Ben told them. "But I'd hate to learn we had a few days warning and didn't have a plan to act on it."

Burgers's eyes popped up as he thought of something, and his head swung to the others. "We don't need to figure out where to go," he said. "The Va'Shen did that for us. We could go to the mountain cave where we first found them."

Ben gave the idea thought and nodded. "Far enough away, and enough mountain to take a pretty good hit. I like it."

"We have the trucks to move all the FOB personnel in a couple of trips," Warren said. "Equipment would take longer, but it would take a lot less time than hauling everyone to Jamieson."

"Draw up a plan," Ben ordered. "Check out the trucks, keep 'em fueled and have the drivers ready to roll." At Warren's nod, he turned to Burgers and Ramirez. "Make sure everyone has an assault pack for a three-day mission ready to go."

"Yes, Sir," the two NCOs complied.

"What about the Va'Shen?" Patricia asked.

No one said anything, and the terp continued.

"If we're getting hit from orbit, then *they're* getting hit from orbit," she went on. "Do we take them with us?"

"I'll talk to Alacea and Kasshas," Ben told her. "And recommend they be ready to leave the village, but first priority for us has to be our people and preserving our combat power." At Patricia's concerned look, he continued. "We can't help *anyone* if we're dead."

Patricia nodded in agreement. It was a cold way of looking at things, but war was a cold place.

Ben looked up at the clock. "Next telecon is in five hours. We have work to do. Let's get to it."

* * *

By the time the next telephone conference with Jamieson came around, FOB Leonard was buzzing with preparations to bug out on a moment's notice. Ben had just enough time to get some initial updates from his folks before the voice of Major Keyes came on the line and cut them off.

The Rangers listened as the intelligence briefer gave them an update on the unidentified spacecraft.

"As of twelve-twenty-two ZULU, the bogey is still in an unpowered orbit above Va'Sh," the briefer told them. "Skylight Six made a passive scan and detected directed EM discharges targeting the planet at several points, including Jamieson. CJ-2 assesses that these are scans of the planet surface, indicating that there are... crew... still alive aboard the bogey with some limited capabilities."

"Any indication of lifeboats or landing craft?" someone from the meeting asked.

"Not at this time," the briefer replied.

Another person on the line spoke up. "Indicating that they may be optimistic of repairing their ship."

"Any attempts at communication?" a female voice asked.

"Not at this time," the briefer replied.

"What about the warning message to *Over the Rainbow*?" General Walker asked. "Are we transmitting yet?"

Another voice replied, and Ben recognized him as Colonel Winslow, the Director of the CJ-6, the communications directorate.

"The message has been uploaded to the Skylights with instructions to not transmit until they detect *Over the Rainbow*'s transponder," Winslow said. "If they start transmitting now, the bogey may detect the transmissions and target the satellites, so we've instructed the onboard AIs to conceal themselves as best as possible until then."

"Is there any change to their estimated splashdown time or location?" Walker asked.

"Negative, Sir," the briefer told him. "Estimate remains three days and five hundred and fifty miles off the coast... assuming an uncontrolled crash."

"What is the plan if it is *not* uncontrolled?" someone asked. "Intercept with F/A-202s and shoot it down?"

There was silence on the line. A lot more silence than the question warranted, Ben thought. Shooting the bogey down was a no-brainer. The Air Force had perfected the technique during the war. As long as they had a little warning, they had been able to successfully intercept and shoot down Va'Shen troop transports as they entered the atmosphere.

So why did he suddenly feel nervous?

There was some whispered chatter that Ben couldn't make out. Two people sitting next to each other seemed to be discussing something. One of them was definitely Walker.

Finally, he heard Walker clear his throat and answer.

"Fixed wing assets are not available at this time."

Again, there was silence. Only this time, it was shocked silence.

"Do... Do they have something *better* to do?" someone on the line asked. "Or did we lose some birds... Sir?"

"They're not available," Walker repeated.

There was a flurry of concerned murmurs on the line, and Patricia looked over to Ben.

"Why wouldn't they be available?" She whispered, even though the phone was on mute. "Jamieson has F/A-202s. We saw them on the flightline when we were there."

Ben rubbed his temples in thought.

"What manner of ass-hattery is this?" Ramirez asked, not bothering to whisper. "If we can blow this asshole out of the sky, why wouldn't we?"

Finally, a new voice came over the line.

"This is Brigadier General La Rouche," he announced. Ben recognized the name. He was the Air Force general in charge of air assets for the CJTF. "In anticipation of the change-over, the 84th and 27th Fighter Squadrons crated up their aircraft and shipped them to the *Neil Armstrong* three days ago."

"Oh my god," Ben muttered as he realized what had happened. The other voices on the line seemed to indicate everyone else had realized it as well. Militarily, you didn't pack up necessary equipment until replacements had arrived and were ready to take up the mission. Economically, however, it cost the government a billion dollars a day to keep a colony ship on station during loading and unloading. That meant that when *Over the Rainbow* arrived and unloaded its aircraft, *Neil Armstrong* would have had to remain on station until the old aircraft were crated up and sent up for loading, keeping two colony ships in orbit around the same planet at the same time at two billion dollars a day. Apparently, someone had decided that the situation on Va'Sh was so secure that they could risk packing up the jets and sending them up early to save time and money.

Which meant there were no operational fighter jets on Va'Sh. The Chinese on the other side of the planet had attack helicopters and a few manned reconnaissance aircraft but had never seen the need to have fighter aircraft on a world where the biggest airborne threat was the kite.

"It's done," Walker cut into the chatter. "What is important is planning to respond with the forces we have."

"Wait, what does this all mean?" Patricia asked, unable to process what she was hearing.

"It means without the F/A's, we're *F'd* in the *A*... Ma'am," Ramirez explained with a shake of his head.

"At this point, we *deserve* to get hit," Burgers muttered angrily.

"Enough," Ben interrupted tiredly and without heat. "It's their problem. I want to concentrate on *our* problems."

The NCOs went silent but continued to fume. It was a fact of life that the lives of military personnel were often screwed over by bureaucratic bean-counting, but they didn't have to like it.

There were more reports from the directorates, but nothing that had much to do with them. Afterward, Walker called to hear from the FOBs. Keyes went down the list, naming each forward operating base, after which a representative from the base would come on the line and report what they were doing. Most were reporting that they had gone to Force Protection Delta, upping the security around their posts to their maximum.

"Should we be doing that?" Patricia whispered to Ben.

He shook his head. Delta was good when a ground attack was imminent, but it also meant everything on post was locked down with no movement except on the most important matters. No post could stay at no-kidding Delta for long, and right now Ben needed his folks working on their preparations to respond or evacuate.

"FOB Leonard," Keyes called.

Ben reached out and turned off the mute button. "Captain Gibson here for FOB Leonard," he announced. "Currently, we are having everyone on the FOB prepped for an evacuation in case the bogey begins some kind of orbital bombardment. We are working with the local Va'Shen authorities and keeping them informed of what we're doing and what the bogey is up to."

"If you intend to COOP to Jamieson, we're going to have to talk about finding beddown for all your people," Walker broke in.

"Not necessary, Sir," Ben replied. "There is a place the Va'Shen dug out of a mountain a few thousand years ago that's big enough for everyone on the FOB and the village." Something suddenly occurred to Ben, and he continued. "It's likely that other Va'Shen communities have something similar. I would recommend that you reach out to your local Mikorin Aru'Dace as they would probably have that location in their records even if they haven't used it in a few thousand years."

There was some muttering on the other end of the line only some of which Ben could catch, including the question, "What's an 'arrowdossee?'"

"That's some good advice, Captain," Walker finally replied. "If any of you have questions, please talk to Captain Gibson offline. He has a pretty good relationship with the locals."

"Outpost Buckley," Keyes prompted.

They heard the familiar voice of Lieutenant Spring come back. "Yes, Sir. Similar to FOB Leonard, we're in communication with the local Va'Shen. They're a little... well... weirded out about all this. I'm not sure what else to call it. But they've been pretty cooperative, and we're keeping them informed. Their local religious leader and the captain of their militia have asked for a meeting with me tomorrow morning."

Patricia turned to Ben and whispered to him. "The Kar'El Na'Sha sounded like she doubted the official line about us," she informed him.

Ben nodded. Back when he had overseen the surrender of the Kar'El commando and brought them back to their village, he was concerned that he was causing Lieutenant Spring and his people a dangerous headache. He was glad to see that the relationship between them and the Va'Shen had become so cordial.

"That's all of them, Sir," Keyes told Walker.

"Saved rounds?" Walker called.

No one said anything.

Walker must have given Keyes a signal because his voice on next. "Next meeting at zero-six-hundred tomorrow. Jamieson out."

Ben mashed the button to hang up the phone and let out a long breath.

* * *

After the meeting, Ben went to the chow hall and made the rounds, talking to his people at different tables and trying to get a feel for how everyone was doing. His folks were nervous, of course, but not frightened. Most of them had been fighting space aliens for three-and-a-half years already. They knew the score.

In a way, it both comforted and disturbed Ben. He was glad his people weren't freaking out, but he was worried that they might be underestimating the threat. When the Va'Shen first appeared and started attacking settlements with laser rifles, there was a great deal of fear among humanity. They had been conditioned over the centuries to expect that any race they met out in the vastness of space would be technologically superior to humanity and that Earth, as a result, would be at a clear disadvantage in any war with them. But as time went by and people saw that the Va'Shen weren't as advanced as they had feared, that worry began to dissipate. Fighting aliens was hard, sure, they thought. But not overwhelmingly so.

But this could be very different, and Ben was worried that his people might approach this new threat as something routine.

After checking in with the other shops and sections on the FOB, it was almost ten at night. Va'Sh's moons sat high in the night sky beyond the glowing veil of the planet's ever-present aurora, The Blessing.

When he opened the door to his hooch and stepped inside, he found Alacea already there, sitting on her knees in the center of the room with a cup of tea. Seeing him, her ears fluttered.

<Welcome home, *Tesho*,> she said.

<Blessed evening, *Myorin*,> he replied, smiling tiredly. Somehow, without realizing it, he found that he had been looking forward to this part of his day more than any other.

She rose to her feet. <Have you eaten? Would you like some tea?>

In response, he stepped forward and wrapped his arms around her, causing her tail to swish back and forth quickly in mild surprise.

<Are you well, *Tesho*?> she asked him in concern.

<I am happy I am able to see you,> he said in slow Va'Shen.

<You are exhausted,> she told him. <Sit. Have some tea.>

He removed his uniform blouse before sitting down across from the priestess and taking the teacup she offered him. Pausing, he realized he wasn't sure what to say right now, what to talk about with her. They had been technically a married couple for months, but after the other night in the temple it was suddenly very real. Their relationship had changed, and he was now unsure what a normal conversation in that relationship consisted of. He sipped his tea to buy some time.

Alacea, he suspected, felt the same way. She remained silent as the two of them drank their tea. He didn't want to talk about work. Surely there was something the two of them could talk about.

That said, there was a cloud hanging over them in the shape of an alien spaceship with unknown intentions.

<Has there been any news?> Alacea asked him quietly.

<No,> he replied with a shake of his head. <If there is bad things, we will go to the mountain from before. Pelle people should ready for this too.>

<We will prepare,> she assured him.

Ben looked down at his teacup and decided to inject a little humor. <This time,> he said, looking up at her, <... you stay at mountain. No wed other tod.>

Her tail slapped the floor in shock, and she was prepared to scold him for thinking such a thing, but she saw his lips were curled upward and understood it was meant in jest.

<And should that ship land and a vixen appear, you must not recklessly take her,> she finally shot back.

<I will try,> he promised.

<You will do much more than try!> she scolded him.

His grin reached his ears now. <What if vixen bites me?> he asked.

<Only the worst kind of vixen would bite a hand that is already marked!> she responded. <And if she did anyway, I would berate her openly and tell her how awful a vixen she is!>

She looked at his grin, and her ears twitched a smile. <You tease me too much, *Tesho*,> she told him quietly.

<*Myorin* beautiful when anger comes,> he replied.

The fur on her ears stood on end, and she looked away as her tail slapped the floor. She peeked at him through the corner of her eye. <Tods...> she growed quietly, sounding very much like Yasuren.

<I am sorry,> he apologized. <Did not want make angry.>

<An obvious lie,> she chastised. <You say anger makes me beautiful, so you must have said those things to anger me.>

<I am sorry as so,> he said, this time wondering if he really had gone too far.

She half-turned her head to look at him. <Then you must atone for it,> she announced. <And reassure your *Myorin* of her place.>

<What must I do?> he asked.

The priestess looked down at the floor, the fur on her ears bristling as she stole quick glances at him.

<Tell me,> she began nervously. <That I am yours...>

<You are my *Myorin*,> he said obediently.

<No,> she said. <Tell me... Like that day you told Voro...> She looked away, her tail moving at warp speed in embarrassment.

At first, he didn't know what she was talking about and then it hit him. When he confronted Voro after tracking them through the wilderness, he had given the Va'Shen nobleman a warning, but his limited Va'Shen vocabulary meant he had to say it in a very basic way. He hadn't meant it as a declaration of love, but...

He moved to the vixen's side and reached out, pulling her to him. Alacea gave a quiet cry of surprise and looked up at him as he stared into her eyes.

<Alacea... is... *mine*,> he growled.

Her tail shook and then went slack as she gasped. She put her face into his chest and held onto his shoulders. <Yes, *Tesho*.>

Chapter 3

He was sleeping soundly and, thankfully, dreamlessly when he awoke to Alacea moving in his arms.

<*Tesho*,> she whispered to him. <Someone is approaching the den.>

Ben blinked the sleep out of his eyes and listened carefully. He didn't hear anything out of the ordinary, but then a gentle knock came at the door.

The Ranger captain climbed out of the tiny bed and started climbing into his uniform trousers as he called out to the person on the other side of the door.

"Who is it?"

"Lieutenant Kim, Sir," the voice of a tired woman came back through the door.

"Just a sec."

Ben put on a tan t-shirt and approached the door. He looked back to find Alacea putting on a teal robe she had brought from the temple. He waited until she was decent and then opened the door.

Patricia stood there, fully dressed in her uniform. Through sleepy eyes, Ben could see she was anxious.

"Sorry to bother you, Sir," she said quickly. He shook his head, and she quickly continued before he could say anything. "Call came into the TOC," she said.

"What is it?" he asked.

Patricia bit her lip nervously.

"The bogey is coming down. Now."

* * *

Without being asked or invited, Alacea followed her *Tesho* and Patricia to Ben's office. The lights were on, and it appeared that

Patricia had already been working late when the call came in. Papers were spread across her desk, but she had no problem instantly finding the exact notebook she needed, grabbing it off the desk as she passed it on the way to the map that hung at the back of the office.

"It's coming down powered," she reported, reading the notes she took during the call. "But the techs at the JOC think it's coming down more as a controlled crash than an actual landing."

"Probably made just enough repairs to come down safely," Ben surmised quietly. "What's the bad news?" he asked.

Patricia turned to the map and pointed at a large triangle drawn in magic marker that encompassed a good portion of the bottom half of the map. "JOC says it can come down anywhere in this triangle," she said.

"Shiiiiit," he drew out in one long, frustrated breath.

"Yeah," Patricia agreed.

"Every possible landing zone is in Sector 22," Ben commented, staring at the map.

"Just south of us," Patricia agreed.

<*Tesho?*> Alacea broke in, unable to follow the conversation. <What is it?>

<Ship is coming down,> he told her. He pointed at the triangle. <Here. These places.>

Alacea looked at the map, and her tail began to move frantically in concern.

"How long?" Ben asked Patricia, turning toward the analog clock on the wall.

"It'll be on the ground in less than an hour."

"This time of night, no infrared," Ben said with a shake of his head. "They won't even be able to do a flyby until morning."

"Which will give them a five-hour head start in whatever it is they intend to do," Patricia finished for him.

Alacea reached out and pointed at a spot on the map in the lower right area of the triangle. <They will probably land here,> she told them.

<Why you say?> Ben asked her.

<This area of Nezara Province is mostly flat plains,> Alacea replied. <The ground is soft and used as pasture. Most of the rest of Nezara is hilly, mountainous, or thickly forested.>

Ben had to turn to Patricia to get a full translation of his wife's words, and when he did, he nodded. <Thank you. That is useful words.>

"Route Blue runs through that area," Patricia noted. "Roughly sixty miles from here. There's an outpost in that area: Outpost Dineen."

"With a bunch of long-range artillery and combat helicopters that can take out that ship with no problem... Is what you're about to say next... Right?" Ben asked hopefully.

"It's about seventy guys from the Massachusetts National Guard and some LTVs," Patricia said, disappointing him.

Ben sighed. "Yeah, that sounds like our luck," he said. With occupation forces stretched thin, the military had to dig deep in order to find enough personnel to man all the necessary outposts and FOBs. In the south, which was much more peaceful than the northern sectors, most of those outposts were staffed by support troops sprinkled with some infantry. FOB Leonard was a notable exception in that so many Rangers from Persephone ended up there. Ben still had no idea what kind of accident occurred at the headquarters that kept them from being moved north, but he and his people weren't complaining. Perhaps the Army thought the Persephone survivors had suffered enough and decided to give them a break.

"JOC say anything else?" Ben asked.

"Tomorrow morning they're going to send out an MC-14 to take a look at the wreckage," Patricia told him. "As well as a ground recon force from OP Dineen for a closer look."

Ben nodded. The MC-14 was one of the few remaining manned reconnaissance aircraft in the U.S. arsenal, usually used by Special Forces groups. With the Fuzz making drones useless, they had found renewed purpose on Va'Sh.

"Any orders for us?" he asked.

"Stand by to stand by," Patricia said.

Ben nodded and took a breath. "Okay," he said. "You go get some sleep. I'll wake you for the morning meeting."

"Yes, Sir," Patricia said.

The lieutenant turned to go and that was when they realized Alacea was gone. The stealthy alien woman must have slipped out while they were talking.

"Probably went home," Ben concluded.

Patricia smiled and grabbed her patrol cap off her desk. "Good night, Sir. See you in the morning."

As she opened the door to leave, she almost ran into Alacea, who was coming from the other direction with a white cup in one hand and a handful of paper packets and creamer cups in the other.

<Blessed evening,> Patricia told her with a small bow.

<And to you, Lady Patricia,> Alacea returned with a careful bow of her own. Patricia held the door open for her, and she stepped inside.

Ben looked up and saw her coming. Smiling as she approached, he stood up and held out a hand to help her with her cargo.

<I went to your dining hall and got you some of the dirt water you like so much,> she said, handing him the cup and putting the paper packets and creamer on his desk.

<Thanks be to you,> he said, touched by the gesture. He reached for the packs and paused momentarily as he realized that, rather than

sugar packs, Alacea had brought him a bunch of salt and pepper. Not wanting to point out her mistake after such a thoughtful gesture, he decided to just use creamer instead.

<You need not stay,> he told her. <You should be sleeps.>

<I would rather stay with you,> she said. She found a chair with an open space in the back for her tail and maneuvered herself into it.

Ben sipped his coffee and sat down in his office chair. Alacea's eyes went to the map behind him, her focus on the triangle that seemed like a dagger pointed at her village.

Her thoughts went back to the night they learned her *Tesho's* people were in the skies above them, surrounding their world. She remembered the apprehension she felt as she looked up and saw what appeared to be stars moving irregularly, the roar of flying machines approaching her village and the relief she felt when the sound eventually moved away and became silent. Her tail shivered at the memory, the feeling of not knowing what would happen next but certain there was nothing she could do about it when it did.

Gods be thanked, nothing happened to Pelle. The flying machines never lingered, although they could hear the sounds of occasional fighting near them as Imperial Army units and commandos engaged Dark One reconnaissance units nearby.

She looked at her alien husband and watched him sip his coffee as he read something on a piece of bone-white paper. The people of Pelle had been very lucky last time.

Would they be that lucky again?

<*Tesho*,> she began quietly. When he looked up, her eyes fell to his desk. <What will happen if they are the Dark Ones?>

Ben didn't answer immediately. He wasn't sure what he could say to that question. <I do not know, *Myorin*,> he told her quietly. <That is truth.>

The fox-woman took a deep breath. <Will... Will your people fight them?> she asked.

He wasn't sure how they could *not* fight them at this point. The first thing they did when coming into the system was kill several thousand people. They sure as hell weren't here selling cookies.

Before he could reply, though, Alacea amended her question.

<If there is war,> she said. <Will your people help us?>

That was a very different and more complicated question. If it *was* the Dark Ones of Va'Sh's past war, then it was very likely they had come here to attack the Va'Shen, *not* the humans. If the Dark Ones issued an apology for the *Neil Armstrong* and told the U.S. they had no beef with humanity, would the U.S. intervene in a war between them and the very weakened Va'Sh?

He wanted to say that they would stand with the Va'Shen. After all, that was the message the Coalition constantly put out. The Va'Shen were U.S. allies now, friends.

But he also knew that the U.S. had a *long* history of saying the same to other people and then leaving them to horrible fates when protecting them was no longer politically convenient. The Vietnamese, the Iraqis, the Syrians, the Afghans, the Ukrainians, the Poles, the Taiwanese, the Estonians... All of them had received promises of friendship and protection, and all of them had been abandoned in their time of need when voters became impatient.

<I do not know,> he told her honestly. Reaching out, he took her hand and gave it a gentle squeeze. <I will not leave you,> he promised.

Even as he made the promise, he was kicking himself for it. It wasn't technically a deception. He meant it. If these Dark Ones started rolling in, and the U.S. decided to bug out, he had no intention of leaving Alacea to her fate.

But that didn't necessarily mean he would be able to stay and fight.

If necessary, he could have Fletcher sedate the Va'Shen woman and then bring her with them if they withdrew. He would have to.

Having seen how far Alacea had been willing to go to protect her people, he knew she would never leave willingly. And he knew she would be right out in front offering her life to protect Pelle.

It would crush her. He knew that. It wasn't that he didn't care. It was simply a matter of which horrible choice he would be willing to live with.

He could live with her hating him for the rest of her life.

But he would make absolutely goddamn *certain* that that life was a long and safe one.

Her ears twitched at his promise. <Thank you, *Tesho*.>

He smiled, hating himself for his deception. <It will be well, *Myorin*.>

* * *

Lieutenant General Alfred Walker stepped onto the Joint Operations Center floor and looked up at the wall-to-wall, floor-to-ceiling video display that showed every aspect of Coalition forces on Va'Sh in as close to real-time as he could get it. The constant sound of ringing phones as well as the murmur of a hundred voices discussing their own individual piece of the Coalition pie made for a steady background buzz as he studied the map.

The JOC director, Army Colonel Anthony Thomas, stepped down from his desk at the top level of the JOC and made his way to Walker to report.

"How does it look?" Walker asked as Thomas stepped beside him.

"Skylight Six got some high-altitude imagery of the bogey after it landed," Thomas reported. He pointed at the black-and-white image that filled a good quarter of the screen in front of them. "Looks like it landed hard, left a debris field a mile long behind it. But it's mostly intact."

"How soon until the reconnaissance aircraft makes its first pass?" Walker asked.

"It should be over the target area now," the director answered immediately. "We won't be able to get any answers from them until they return, though. Two hours, maybe."

"What about the ground team?" Walker asked.

"They should be in position near the craft already, but, again, we won't know anything until they can get to reliable comms."

"Goddamn Fuzz," Walker murmured. "Can't the Skylights get anything better than this?" he asked, disappointed in the multi-billion-dollar satellite system that couldn't seem to do better than grainy black-and-whites.

"Clouds moved over the area about an hour ago," Thomas told him. "This is the best we've got until a reconnaissance bird gets something from low-level."

Walker grunted and nodded. So far everything seemed to be going all right. If things continued like this, it might not be the crisis he was afraid it might be.

"Let me know the second the recon bird lands," Walker ordered.

"Yes, Sir."

Walker turned and started toward the JOC exit.

Yes, he told himself. *Perhaps, this will not turn out as bad as I feared.*

* * *

Specialist Bill Carson came to and blinked rapidly. He was lying in a pool of warm liquid behind a fallen tree and felt his heart beating extremely fast.

Go-Juice, he thought as the memories started coming back to him. Someone had taken his injector and stabbed him in the thigh with it. Just before that, though...

Struggling to lift his head under the weight of his helmet, he managed to look down at himself and let out a choked sob.

Two bloody stumps tied off with tourniquets just above the knee were all he could see of his legs. The stumps were resting in a pool of blood mixed with a brownish sludge. He hurriedly looked around but couldn't see where his missing legs had gone. He tried to remember what happened, but all his overclocked brain could recall was running to cover and suddenly falling down. Someone had dragged him behind this fallen tree while he screamed and quickly tended to his wound.

That's when he realized that it wasn't just his legs that were missing.

He didn't see any other members of the ground recon force near him. Nor did he hear any gunfire to suggest they were still in the fight.

Was it over already? Did they win?

Carson swallowed dryly. He didn't think so. His thoughts were still fuzzy, but he definitely remembered that things weren't going very well after they saw the reconnaissance plane get shot down. The lieutenant said they were going after them. No one had argued against it. Never leave a man behind and all that.

But as they got closer to the ship...

Carson shivered. He felt cold. *Real* cold. He was in shock.

He heard something moving on the other side of the tree and froze. Looking around again, he saw his M-31 lying on the ground above his head. He reached up for it, his fingers just barely able to touch the buttstock.

Then he saw it step over the tree and stop, looking down at him. Carson froze again, this time in mind-numbing fear.

It was taller than the average human; seven feet and change perhaps. It wore flat black armor over its entire body. Its face was concealed by a glossy, black, bowl-shaped helmet like a black pearl.

Its arms were longer than a human's and instead of hands, they ended in long, sharp claws that surrounded slick, wavy tendrils like a sea anemone's. Long spikes protruded from its shoulders, almost a foot long. The chest plate of its armor had several white knicks in it, places where bullets had impacted and, as Carson now recalled, did absolutely fuck-all to put the creature down.

The soldier looked up and made one last lunge for his weapon as the creature's clawed hand shot down at his throat, pinning him down by the neck. The tendrils of its "hand" emerged and wrapped around his throat. Carson could feel thorny barbs bite into his neck as the tentacles squeezed.

But the creature stopped there. Reaching down with the claw of its other hand, it ripped Carson's helmet off and seemed to study him, although it was impossible to know what the thing was looking at through the faceplate of its helmet.

Reaching back, it pulled something from its waist, a black, smooth piece of oblong polymer perhaps six inches long, and attached it to the wrist of the arm holding Carson down.

As if Carson hadn't seen enough crazy shit already this morning, he watched in awe as the creature's armor began changing colors, a beautiful kaleidoscope of different hues like a tie-dye t-shirt that continuously shifted its color and pattern.

A guttural voice coming from the box on its wrist startled the soldier, causing the barbs in the creature's tentacle to dig deeper into his neck.

<WHAT. ARE. YOU.>

The voice was in Va'Shen, and Carson had never bothered to learn any Va'Shen.

<WHAT. ARE. YOU.> the box repeated.

Carson gritted his teeth. He didn't know what it was saying, but he had an answer ready to go already.

"Go fuck yourself!" he hissed at it with all the venom he could muster.

The creature stared at him, motionless, perhaps trying to understand the strange human. Color emanated from the box and ran up and down the creature's armor. More colors blossomed across the creature and flowed down to the source of the voice on its arm.

<GOFUCKYOURSELF,> it repeated. <WHERE. DOES. GOFUCKYOURSELF. COME. FROM.>

Carson spat at the creature's helmet and was almost heartbroken when he saw the glob fail to make it all the way to the helmet.

It looked down at him. The creature had never been spat at before, but it understood the sentiment. It jerked its arm back, and the barbs of the tentacle around Carson's neck sawed through his windpipe and spine in a fraction of a second.

The creature reached down and picked up the soldier's head with its clawed right hand. It studied it, moving the dead soldier's hair with its tentacles as if checking for something and not finding it. Its search done, it reached up and stuck the head on the end of the spike protruding from its left shoulder like some kind of grisly accessory, Carson's dead eyes frozen open in the horror of his last moments.

Turning, the creature looked back across the downed tree over the bodies of the dead man's comrades that littered the field near its crashed ship. Other members of its caste walked among the bodies, examining them or the unfamiliar equipment they bore.

Perhaps this would not be as difficult as they feared.

Chapter 4

Space Force Sergeant Kaitie St. John bopped along to the beat as she steered the LTV up Route Blue back to Jamieson. Her friend and fellow Space Force Band member, Specialist Layla Goldsmith sat in the passenger seat, playing her oboe to pass the time.

Their return trip from R&R at Camp Wagner had, so far, been uneventful. Camp Wagner didn't have much more than Jamieson had. If anything, it had less. But it was different scenery, and it was near the beach, and it was absolutely NOWHERE close enough for their supervisor to come in at the last minute for an "emergency" tasker that wasn't in any way, shape or form an emergency.

Route Blue had been smoothed out and graded by the Army Corps of Engineers, making it far and away better than 99 percent of the other roads on Va'Sh. It let them go a good forty miles per hour with barely any bumps.

St. John continued to vibe to the oboe player's music as she drove but was a little annoyed at herself. As a vocalist in a band, it drove her nuts that she couldn't identify a song when she heard it. Goldsmith, however, was playing classical music, and she was never big on classical. She decided to give it a shot anyway.

"Perry?" she asked Goldsmith hesitantly.

The dark-haired oboe player stopped playing and looked at her friend with an expression just short of contempt.

"Swift," Goldsmith told her as if correcting a toddler who had just crapped itself.

"S'cuse me," St. John replied and went back to looking at the road.

Goldsmith brought the oboe back to her lips, but stopped as something on the road ahead of them caught her eye. "What's that up ahead?" she asked.

St. John squinted. Large, black shapes stood up against the flat, red grassland around them.

"Checkpoint?" St. John guessed.

Before Goldsmith could make her own guess, a flash of purple light shot out from one of the shapes and slapped the ground next to LTV.

"HOLY..."

Before St. John could finish, another bolt slammed into the front left end of the LTV. The front of the vehicle fell to the ground and caused the LTV to swerve into the ditch to their left.

The vehicle came to a stop, and the two musicians were thrown against their seatbelts. St. John shook the stars from her eyes and looked around for a hot second before undoing the safety belt.

Another bolt of purple shot over the LTV.

"Get out! Quick!" she cried to Goldsmith.

Rather than risk getting hit by the fire coming from her side of the vehicle, Goldsmith clambered over the console and followed St. John out the driver's side door. They made it about six meters when Goldsmith stopped and turned back.

"My oboe!" she said.

St. John grabbed her hand and dragged her away from the vehicle.

"Forget the damn oboe!" she yelled.

More blasts of purple light hit the LTV, blasting chunks of the vehicle away with each hit. The two dived into the deepest part of the ditch and moved further away.

"Is it the Va'Shen?" Goldsmith asked.

"No, it's the Boston Philharmonic!" St. John shot back.

The fire from the unknown enemy increased, moving closer to them.

"Just stay down!" St. John cried.

St. John tried to get her bearings. The shapes she had seen, which she had taken for vehicles at a checkpoint, had been perhaps a quarter mile away. Which meant it wouldn't take long for them to get to them.

She pulled her sidearm from the shoulder holster under her left arm and checked the action with shaking hands. The pistol felt unnaturally heavy in her hands, and she struggled for a moment to pull the slide all the way back and chamber a round. Energy bolts continued to zip over their heads.

"Hear that?" Goldsmith asked.

St. John listened. Over the electric buzzing of the energy weapons, the sound of an LTV engine coming closer filled their ears.

Taking the risk, St. John crept up and looked over the top of the muddy berm they were hiding behind. An LTV traveling perpendicular to the road was racing toward them, bouncing over the uneven terrain as it did its best to dodge weapons fire.

"Get ready!" St. John ordered Goldsmith, who quickly crawled up and joined her.

The LTV skidded to a stop next to them.

"GET IN!" a man's voice shouted.

Energy bolts began tracking closer to the vehicle, and the two bandsmen popped out of the ditch and threw the LTV doors open.

Before they were even fully inside, the vehicle tore off again back the way it had come.

St. John, who had gotten into the passenger seat, looked up at their savior and found a soldier, his right arm completely missing beneath the shoulder, driving, his uniform covered with grime and blood.

"One of you get on that gun!" he called to them.

St. John looked up at the M-270 machine gun in the unmanned turret.

"I don't know how to use a machine gun!" she cried. She looked back at Goldsmith sitting in the passenger side backseat next to another soldier. "Do you know how to use a machine gun?!" she asked.

Goldsmith blinked, still in shock from everything that had happened in the last two or three minutes.

"Is it anything like playing an oboe?" she asked.

"What about you?" she asked the soldier sitting in the other backseat. She froze when she saw the man's lifeless eyes looking down at the front seat, one of his legs completely missing.

"Forget the gun!" the driver called. "Are they coming after us!?"

Goldsmith peeked over the backseat and out the back window. The fire had stopped, and there was no one behind them.

"I don't think so," she called back.

St. John studied the driver. A tourniquet was tied around the stub of his right arm, stopping the bleeding, but his face was pale and covered in sweat. There was a smattering of blood on the side of his face that reached up into his dirty blond high-and-tight.

"Let me drive," St. John told him.

"How's Simmons?" he replied, ignoring her offer.

Goldsmith looked at the body of the African American soldier in the seat next to her. The nametag on the right side of his chest identified him as Simmons.

"He's... um... He's dead," Goldsmith answered.

The driver didn't say anything. The LTV seemed to bounce over every rock and hole on Va'Sh as they continued their frantic escape.

"Hey!" St. John tried again. "Let me drive! You're all screwed up!"

"Not yet," the driver replied. "We gotta get further away first. Who are you with?" he demanded.

"Space Force Band of Starlight," Goldsmith supplied helpfully.

"Fuck me running," the driver grumbled. "I'm Grafton," he said. "54th Infantry Regiment, Massachusetts National Guard. Find a pen and some paper. You got Go Juice?"

The two guardians started checking their pockets and the storage compartments of the LTV. Goldsmith passed a gold autoinjector up to St. John.

"Go Juice," she said.

"Hit me with it," Grafton ordered, his eyes not leaving the road.

"How many have you had?" St. John asked him.

"Not enough!" he irritably bit back at her. "Hit me!"

St. John jabbed the autoinjector into the meaty part of the man's right thigh. The man's eyes went wide as the drug raced into his bloodstream.

"Paper! Pen!" he called out.

"Got some!" Goldsmith called.

"Okay, listen closely," Grafton began, his voice calm but with its own sense of urgency. "If I don't make it, you need to get somewhere with comms and contact the JOC at Jamieson. Tell them everything I'm about to tell you. Got it?"

St. John nodded while Goldsmith called back. "Okay."

"Okay," he said, trying to calm himself even as the Go Juice put every nerve and muscle into hyperdrive. "Found the unknown ship at zero-six this morning. They shot down the recon plane. We went in to get the crew out and were engaged by enemy ground forces. We never even got close to the wreckage. My entire platoon was shredded."

Goldsmith scribbled as Grafton spoke.

"Okay, size..." he continued. "I don't know. *A lot.* In the hundreds, at least. They have vehicles too. Some kind of hovercraft transports with big guns on them. They're heading north. That group you ran into is some kind of vanguard, making sure no one else comes along to interfere with their assembly."

"Va'Shen don't have vehicles like that," St. John pointed out.

"They're not Va'Shen," Grafton told her. "They're... something else. Big motherfuckers. Taller than Simmons, and that dude's a fucking giant. They're wearing some kind of armored space suits or something. Six-point-eight does jack-shit to them unless you're right up on them. But I think our sniper got one..."

St. John let that sink in for a moment. So far, the best news Grafton had given them was that their sniper *might* have killed *one*.

Grafton was starting to breathe faster, and his head began to dip as he rapidly blinked his eyes.

"They're using some kind of energy weapons that liquify whatever they hit."

"You mean melt?" Goldsmith asked.

"I mean liquify."

"What's the difference?" St. John asked.

Grafton turned to her with wild eyes. "When you're looking down at a puddle that used to be *your* arm, YOU'LL KNOW THE FUCKING DIFFERENCE!" he shouted at her.

"Okay! Sorry!" she cried.

"Did you get all that?" Grafton asked Goldsmith.

"Yeah, I got it."

"Okay," the infantryman wheezed. "I think... I think I'm gonna sack out for a bit..."

St. John screamed and grabbed the wheel as Grafton's head slumped forward and hit it. Reaching over the console with her left leg, the bandsman kicked at the man's legs until she found the brake pedal and smashed down on it until the LTV skidded to a stop.

Throwing the vehicle into "park," St. John reached out and touched the man's neck. His pulse was fast but weak.

"What do we do?" Goldsmith voice broke the momentary silence.

"We get the hell out of here," St. John told her. She opened the glove box and looked for a map. Anyone driving on Va'Sh had to take a course on how to read one since navigation aids were completely useless. At the time she had found the class quaint, like learning how to churn your own butter. Now, she was hoping she remembered enough of it to save their lives.

Pulling the map out, she opened it and tried to get an idea of where they were. In the meantime, Goldsmith had gotten out of the LTV and opened the driver-side door, the small woman struggling to pull the larger, heavier man out of the vehicle without hurting him.

St. John looked at the LTV's fuel indicator and back at the map again. There was an outpost south of them, OP Dineen, but something told her that Grafton hadn't gone that way for a good reason. The next best option was north. If they went far enough west, they could head north cross-country and then east again until they picked up Route Blue, hopefully north of the whatever-they-are's. But if they hit a hole wrong, ran into forest or rocks, they would be screwed.

But it was better than going back the way they had come.

"Little help?" Goldsmith called from outside.

St. John dropped the map and got out of the vehicle, circling around to the other side. Goldsmith had Grafton by the armpits, so she grabbed his feet and lifted.

The two struggled but finally managed to lift the infantryman into the backseat next to the body of his friend. Breathing hard from the exertion, the two women looked at each other for a moment before St. John spoke.

"We need to get to a phone," she said.

"Back to Wagner?" Goldsmith asked.

St. John shook her head. "Too far. LTV's running low on fuel."

"Where to, then?" the oboe player asked.

"Map says there's a FOB north of here," St. John replied. "I think we can make it on the fuel we have if we're careful and get back on Route Blue ahead of these things."

"What if we get there and these things are already there?" Goldsmith asked.

"Then we're screwed," St. John replied with a fatalistic shrug.

Goldsmith thought hard for a minute. They weren't infantrymen. They were musicians. This was so far outside their training that it was a miracle they had managed to get *this* far.

"Okay," the oboe player said.

St. John nodded. "Okay."

The two got back into the LTV, St. John in the driver's seat.

"You're gonna have to read the map, because I'm gonna be busy," the vocalist told her.

Goldsmith picked up the map and started studying it.

"We're about here," St. John said, pointing at what she guessed was their position. She put the LTV into gear, and the vehicle lurched forward.

"What's the name of the place we're going?" Goldsmith asked, as she searched the map for their destination.

"FOB Leonard," St. John said.

* * *

"Recon bird never made it back to Jamieson," Ben told his assembled staff. "No word on the ground team either."

The officers and NCOs assembled in his office, sitting on chairs and desks, looked at one another in concern as Ben shared with them his notes from the morning meeting with the JOC.

"Command is considering whether or not to risk another bird," the captain continued. "But we've been given a WARNO that we may need to refuel a couple of choppers on the way to insert another team."

"No problem there, Sir," Warren promised him.

Ben nodded as he racked his brain for something optimistic to say. Without more information one way or another, he couldn't promise anything.

"I guess the good news is we don't have to worry about an orbital bombardment anymore," Burgers ventured.

"True," Patricia agreed. "But now we have to worry about them being right on our doorstep."

Ben turned and looked at the map on the wall behind him. "I want to put an observation post here," he said, pointing at an area of the map just a few miles south of them. "Overlooking this bridge over the river here. If trouble comes, it'll probably come from there."

Ramirez and Burgers examined the map and nodded, recognizing the area. "There's a ridge overlooking that bridge," Ramirez said. "Perfect spot for an OP and overwatch."

"Set it up," Ben ordered.

"All the way, Sir," Burgers replied.

"Anything else?" Ben asked.

"Are we still looking at a COOP?" Patricia asked.

Continuity Of OPerations was a nice way of saying "bug out." Now that the threat of orbital bombardment was gone, was there still a need to be ready to evacuate to the mountains? If the ship had touched down anywhere else, Ben might have said no.

"Yeah," he replied. "Until we know more about what we're dealing with. Anything else?"

Heads shook all over the room.

"Okay, get to work," Ben ordered. The group dispersed and headed for the door. The Ranger officer sat back in his chair and let out a breath, looking at the map as if staring at it hard enough would give him some new insight.

"It could still be nothing to worry about," Patricia said hopefully.

"It could be *anything*," he countered. He never hated the Fuzz more than he did right now. If communications still worked, the recon plane and the ground team would have been able to update the JOC every step of the way. Without that, they were blind.

As a mental exercise, he tried to place himself in the shoes of the ship's commander. If he and his Rangers had crashed on, what was to them, a hostile world, what would he do? First question he would ask would be, "Is there a way to get back *off* that world?" If their ship had been repairable, they wouldn't have landed in the first place. They were relatively safe in orbit. That indicated that a landing now was preferable to a crash later, when they could still determine for themselves where they would end up.

Okay, so they *chose* to land in Sector 22. Why? Perhaps it was simply the least worst option. Alacea had already told them that the terrain was good for a landing. That may have been all there was to it. But that didn't sit right with him. It meant that, across the entire planet of Va'Sh, there was no place better to land than within a stone's throw of its most heavily fortified area. If the Air Force commander hadn't carted up the F/A-202s, the ship might already be a smoking hole in the ground. So, why risk it? If it had been him, he would have looked for a landing zone far enough from Jamieson to make it as difficult as possible for an air intercept to happen.

Which would indicate that they *wanted* to land close to Jamieson.

But why?

Was the ship's commander that confident that his crew, without any support, could take on the entire planet by themselves? Was that confidence warranted? If so, landing so close to Jamieson made a weird type of sense. If they could take out Jamieson and the communications hub there, they could take out comms for the entire CJTF. The Coalition forces wouldn't be able to talk to each other *or* the *Over the Rainbow* when it arrived.

Who knows what kind of havoc they could cause while everyone tried to figure out what was going on?

Before he could take the exercise any further, a Ranger in full battle-rattle opened the door and ran inside.

"Sir!"

Ben turned to him as the Ranger made his report.

"LTV just came through the gate with wounded!" the sentry reported quickly.

* * *

"Get him up on the table," Fletcher calmly ordered the two SeaBees who had been nearby when the LTV skidded to a stop outside the clinic. Two Space Force guardians had jumped out and announced that they had wounded with them.

The SeaBees gingerly placed Grafton up on the examination table. Fletcher had already confirmed that the other man in the backseat was dead. If she didn't do something soon, she was pretty sure Grafton would be joining him.

St. John and Goldsmith looked on from not far away.

"What happened?" Fletcher asked them, her tone all business. She was carefully examining Grafton's amputated arm.

"He said they were attacked by something not Va'Shen," Goldsmith supplied.

Fletcher nodded. "No powder burns, no cauterization," she said out loud. "Almost looks melted."

"Liquified," Goldsmith corrected.

"What's the difference?" Fletcher asked.

"We don't know, but it's really important," St. John said.

"Go Juice?" Fletcher asked.

"A lot, I think," St. John told her.

They turned as the door to the clinic clamshell opened, and Ben and Patricia walked in.

"What have you got?" Ben asked.

"One wounded with a missing arm," Fletcher told him, not bothering to pause her examination. "Another KIA in the LTV outside. These two guardians brought them in."

Ben looked at the soldier and, seeing the Minuteman patch and the Massachusetts National Guard insignia on his uniform, knew immediately who he was.

"Will he make it?" Ben asked.

"Probably not," Fletcher replied, looking at up him. "He's got more adrenaline and Go Juice in him than blood right now."

"Do your best. We need a debrief," Ben told her.

"Aye aye, Sir," Fletcher promised.

"Sir!" St. John called to him. "Sergeant Grafton saved us. He gave us as much information as he could before he passed out and told us to pass it to the JOC."

"Who are you with?" Ben asked. He hadn't recalled any Space Force units being mentioned as part of the ground recon team.

"Space Force Band of Starlight," St. John and Goldsmith replied in unison.

"Captain Bennett's people?" Ben asked, remembering the vocalist who had come to entertain the Va'Shen during the Arbor Day festival.

"Different ensemble, but yes, Sir," St. John supplied.

Ben nodded. "Okay, let's go to my office. We can call the JOC there. Come on."

As the two guardians followed Ben and Patricia, Goldsmith nudged Patricia with her elbow to get her attention.

"I lost my oboe in the attack," Goldsmith told her. "Am I going to get in trouble?"

Patricia looked at her, puzzled by her priorities. "I think you're good," she told her.

* * *

"I don't know, Sir."

St. John looked equal parts frustrated and humiliated as people on the JOC conference call continued to pepper her with questions she didn't know the answers to. She had already stated, several times in fact, that she hadn't actually been at the battle, and was only relaying what Sergeant Grafton had told her before he passed out. Nevertheless, the colonels, majors and captains on the other end of the call seemed to think that if they just asked the same questions often enough, she'd suddenly give them the answers they wanted.

"What other weapons did you see?" someone asked.

Ben looked at the Space Force NCO with sympathy as she took another breath and tried desperately to hold onto her calm.

"I didn't see anything more than what hit our LTV," she said.

Again.

"Sergeant Grafton said they used energy weapons that liquified on contact," she explained.

Again.

Ben and Patricia hadn't asked any questions. They were busy jotting down notes on everything St. John said. Ben looked at the map behind his desk and grimaced. Everything St. John said seemed to make things worse for them.

"Sergeant St. John, we are going to need you to come to the JOC and give us a debrief in person," another voice said. "Some things we want to ask can't be said over an unclassified line."

"I understand, Sir," the vocalist said. "However, I really don't know anything more than what I just reported."

"Something else may come to you," the voice explained. "We're going to send a chopper to Leonard to pick you up. It'll be there in an hour."

"I understand, Sir."

"All right. Out here."

With that, the call ended, and St. John collapsed into one of the chairs on the opposite side of Ben's desk. The Ranger captain handed her a cup of coffee, and the bandsman slugged it down gratefully.

"I'm sorry, Sir," she said, feeling disappointed by her debriefing.

"Don't be," Ben told her. She didn't look up at him. "Sergeant," he prompted.

St. John looked up at him, exhausted by the horrific things she had seen today.

"You did good," Ben assured her. "You got Sergeant Grafton back alive. You passed on his report. You did everything right today."

St. John took a deep, cleansing breath. "Thank you, Sir."

"You got an hour," Ben said. "Why don't you and Specialist Goldsmith go get some chow, maybe a shower. You're probably going to have a long day once you get to Jamieson."

"Thank you, Sir."

With that, the two guardians stood up and started for the door. Ben turned to the map and rubbed his temples.

"It's bad, isn't it?" Patricia asked quietly.

"What's your assessment?" Ben asked her. Although she spent most of her time as an interpreter, Patricia's primary job was to be his intelligence officer.

Patricia sighed as she studied the map. "They're heading north. So, the most obvious targets are Jamieson and the Imperial capital further north after that. And we're right in their way."

"Assuming those are the targets, is there any chance they'll bypass us and attack from a different direction?" he asked, already knowing the answer.

Patricia shook her head, confirming his guess. "Northwest of us the mountainous terrain makes moving a large group and vehicles just about impossible," she said. "And the biggest bridge crossing the river is here in Pelle. They'll have to come through us, over that bridge and into the valley on Route Orange if they want to hit Jamieson anytime soon. And the longer they take, the more time Jamieson has to prepare for an attack." She shook her head again. "Their best chance of hitting Jamieson and continuing to the capital will depend on their moving quickly before we can mass forces to stop them."

"If you were the CJ-2, what would you advise Walker to do?" Ben asked.

Patricia pointed at a spot on the map north of them, about halfway between Leonard and Jamieson. "I'd tell him to mass whatever forces he can as quickly as he can right here. The terrain creates a bottleneck that the enemy would be forced to go through. If the Coalition is going to hit them, they should hit them there."

Ben considered the assessment for several moments and finally nodded.

"Is Alzoria on the FOB?" he asked. He corrected himself a moment later. "Stupid question. Of course she is. Find her and tell her to go to Kasshas. Tell him to call an *aderen*. Now."

"Yes, Sir," Patricia replied and started for the door.

* * *

"What this?" Alzoria asked, pointing at one of the many miscellaneous items arranged on Ramirez's bunk.

"Medicine," he told her while simultaneously lifting the med-kit and attaching it to the combat vest he was wearing.

"What this?" the vixen asked again, pointing at a bandolier with several black cylinders attached to it. She reached out and touched it, but Ramirez snatched her wrist.

<Much caution,> he told her in Va'Shen. "Flash-bangs. Big boom." He pointed at the ring on top of one of them. "Pull this, big boom. Run fast."

"Big boom," Alzoria repeated, her tail swishing back and forth. "What this?" she asked, pointing at something else.

"A snackerdood."

"Snacker...dood..." she repeated. "What do?" she asked.

"It doods snackers," the Ranger replied casually.

Alzoria looked at him, her eyes full of questions and unsure which to ask first.

Ramirez waited a few heartbeats before lifting the item in question and turning it on, shining a light on the vixen's face.

<I joke. It light.>

Alzoria slapped him in the shoulder three times.

"Douchebog," she said, but without heat.

Ramirez grinned. Like any good Ranger, he was going through his gear and making sure everything in his assault pack was ready for whatever misfortune was about to befall them. Other Rangers in the NCO hooch were doing the same, packing equipment and checking over their gear. The fact that Alzoria, a female, was in their all-male quarters didn't faze them.

Alzoria watched from her spot on the floor next to him as he continued to work. Her tail swished back and forth on the wood floor in concern.

"You will fight?" she asked in a low voice.

"Maybe," he told her, not pausing in his work.

<The Dark Ones... are dangerous,> she told him in Va'Shen.

He looked at her and saw her eyes and ears turned downward in worry.

The Ranger smiled. "So are we," he assured her.

A knock at the door interrupted them, and one of the other Rangers went and opened it, revealing Patricia on the other side. Seeing her target already there, the human woman smiled.

<Alzoria. Good. Glad you are here. You do thing for Overlord?> she asked.

Alzoria stood up and faced the intel officer. <Of course!> she replied, grateful for having something she could do to help.

<Please go. Tell Kasshas. Overlord wants to speak at the *aderen*. Very important. Need to speak to *aderen* now.>

<I'll run there now,> Alzoria promised.

<Thanks be to you,> Patricia said.

"Something up, El-tee?" Ramirez asked.

Patricia was suddenly aware of every eye in the hooch on her. She wondered if she should say something like, "the captain will let you know," but it sounded like a bullshit answer, even to her.

"A survivor from the recon team came in," she said carefully, not wanting to reveal anything that might cause a panic. "It's pretty bad."

"We bugging out?" a Ranger asked her.

"I don't know," Patricia said honestly. "The captain wants to talk to the Va'Shen. I think he'll decide then."

"Could you let him know that Fitzmorris and Levesque are setting up that observation post now?" Ramirez asked her.

She nodded. "I will."

<I'm going now,> Alzoria announced. She went to the door and turned to Ramirez, offering him a wave. <I'll see you later, okay?>

"See you later," he confirmed with a smile.

Alzoria's ears twitched a smile and then she was gone.

The other Rangers went back to their equipment checks, and Ramirez stood up, stepping closer to Patricia.

"How bad is it really?" he asked her.

"Not the apocalypse," she whispered back. "But in the same zip code."

"Fuck," Ramirez muttered.

"They're heading this way," Patricia shared with him. "The recon team was wiped out, and the airplane they sent was shot down."

"Double fuck," Ramirez replied quietly. He sighed. "Welp... Guess we're gonna get a chance to do some Ranger shit after all."

* * *

Sitting alone in his office, Ben dialed the Jamieson switchboard and waited as the phone rang several times before someone finally picked up.

"Jamieson switchboard control, Sergeant Murphy speaking. This is a nonsecure line. How may I help you, Sir or Ma'am?" the expressionless, scripted greeting made the woman on the other end sound even more exhausted than she probably felt.

"Captain Ben Gibson, Sector Thirteen," he announced. "I need a connection to the Tankara liaison officer in Ro'Tana."

"Hold one, Sir," Murphy replied.

Ben waited on hold for several minutes but tried to be patient. With everything going on right now, he imagined that the switchboard operators were probably drowning in work, connecting calls for meetings and check-ins.

"Connecting now, Sir," the voice suddenly announced, and before Ben could thank her, the phone started to ring on the other end.

"Major Washington," a deep baritone announced when the ringing stopped.

"Good morning, Sir," Ben said. "This is Captain Ben Gibson, Sector Thirteen."

There was a pause on the line. "Gibson?" Washington asked. "You the guy who put a gun to Count Voro's head?"

Ben cleared his throat as his heart sank, bracing himself for a lecture. When the Va'Shen noble kidnapped Alacea from the village, Ben had gone after them to rescue her. The resulting confrontation between him and Voro ended with his smoking pistol pressed firmly against the tod's forehead.

"Yes, Sir, that's me," Ben admitted.

"My admin NCO wants to send you a case of beer," Washington said. "I think he wants your autograph too."

Relief rushed over Ben, and he let out a breath he had been unconsciously holding.

"I'll see if I have any headshots lying around," he quipped.

"What can I do for you, Captain?" Washington asked. Ben couldn't see the smile on the other officer's face, but he could hear it in his tone.

"Speaking of Voro," Ben began, "I wanted to know if he was issuing any commands to the villages in Tankara as a result of the alien ship landing. I'm about to advise the villagers here to evacuate into the hills, and it would be a lot easier if he and I were saying the same thing."

"I wish I could help you, Captain, but Count Voro is not here," Washington told him. "He left for the capital this morning to 'offer his counsel' to the Emperor."

"I didn't realize he advised the Emperor," Ben noted, a sneaking suspicion coming into his mind.

"He doesn't," the liaison replied, and it was obvious that he had come to the same conclusion Ben had. "But it's a lot farther away from the bogey than here."

"Track'n," Ben sighed.

"If it helps any, I think the villagers are much more likely to trust you than him anyway," Washington said. "Voro is not well-liked in Tankara, and despite his best efforts, word of what he tried to do in Pelle has made the rounds. He's still looking for a new wife, but he's been having a hard time finding someone who'll give him the time of day. They know him a little too well."

Any other time Ben would have felt a smug sense of satisfaction at the noble tod's misfortune. Right now, however, he would have much preferred to discover that the little rat bastard actually took his job seriously.

"Are you and your folks staying in Ro'Tana?" Ben asked, changing the subject.

"For now," Washington said. "But we're preparing to bug out just in case. They're much closer to you, aren't they?"

"Yeah," Ben said. "Yeah, they are."

"Good luck, Captain," Washington said seriously. "If there's anything we can do here for you, let me know."

"Thank you, Sir. I appreciate it."

"Ro'Tana out."

The line clicked, and Ben put the phone down.

He was going to have to make this case on his own.

A knock on the doorframe drew his attention to the blonde woman standing at the door.

"What've you got, Corpsman?" Ben asked Fletcher as he went through his notes in preparation for the upcoming *aderen*.

The woman didn't look particularly happy to be there. "Sergeant Grafton is dead," she announced.

Ben paused and looked up. "I'm sorry to hear that," he said quietly.

"He just lost too much blood," Fletcher explained. "The Go Juice kept him going just long enough to get away."

"And put his buddy in the seat behind him," Ben added, leaning back in his chair with a sigh. "He died thinking he had saved his friend and completed the mission. We should all be so lucky."

"Yeah," the medic sighed.

"Were you able to learn anything from him?" Ben asked her. He refrained from saying "the body." It seemed too crude at the moment.

Fletcher took a step into the room and blew out a breath of air as if trying to relieve the tension she felt. "I think those Space Force folks were right," she finally said. "'Melt' *is* the wrong word." At Ben's questioning look, she continued. "The wounds and the uniform near them had traces of some kind of organic sludge, not blood. We know the Va'Shen have weapons that can make changes to matter on the molecular level. I think this is similar to that. I'm no organic chemist, but my best theory is that whatever hit them, broke the forces that hold molecules together as a solid mass."

"Well, that is... terrifying," Ben told her.

"If it hits you in the torso or the head, I don't think there'd be much hope," Fletcher told him. "But if it's a limb and you act fast, you might be able to save the patient."

Ben thought for a moment and nodded. "We have extra tourniquets in storage, right?"

"Yes, Sir."

"Break 'em out. Make sure everyone on the FOB keeps at least two on them at all times."

Fletcher nodded. "Aye aye, Sir. I'll also distribute rapid-clot patches as well."

"Good idea."

With that decided, Fletcher left, and Ben was alone again. He looked behind him at the map on the wall and did some rough calculations.

There wasn't a lot of time to waste.

* * *

Ben sat on his knees in the spot halfway around the oval of community leaders that made up Pelle's village council. He mentally struggled to not pick up his notes and review them again while the Va'Shen went through the arduous process of beginning the meeting, including the numerous bows and prayers.

To Kasshas's credit, the chieftain hadn't slouched. Two hours after Ben had sent Alzoria to request the *aderen*, he received word that they were ready to begin and asked him to attend.

He just wished there was a way to cut through the ceremonies.

<Na'Sha, how do the Gods view our community?> Kasshas asked.

On the far end of the oval to Ben's right, Alacea rose to her feet, her hands folded in front of her.

<The Gods know this is a fearful time for us,> she said. <But they continue to show their love, they have faith that our community will prevail in whatever struggle comes to us.>

The blessing seemed to put a cherry on top of the gloomy mood in the room, and Kasshas wasted no time getting to the point of the meeting.

<The Overlord has requested this *aderen*,> he said. <I invite him to speak.>

Ben stood up and looked around the oval, taking a measure of the people there. Some of the faces were familiar from previous meetings, while some were new. For them, this was their first *aderen* since their seniors were killed in the last one.

<I make promise to Chieftain,> Ben said, nodding in Kasshas's direction. <I learn things. I tell things. Things about unknown people who have come to Va'Sh.>

The tails of the assembled fox people began to move faster in anticipation of what the Overlord might say next.

<Unknown people land near here,> he said. <Attack more of my people. Move this way.>

There were gasps of shock, and several pairs of ears popped toward the ceiling.

<When will they arrive?> Kasshas asked him.

<I do not know,> Ben admitted. <They are close. May be here next day. May be here other time.>

<Who are they?> an unfamiliar voice asked.

Ben turned and saw a gray-haired tod in a brown monpei sitting across the oval from him.

<We do not know,> Ben told him. He turned back to Kasshas. <I ask you to take your people and take them to mountains like before time. Stay until it is safe again.>

<So, you do not know if they are our enemy,> the gray-haired Va'Shen concluded, breaking in before Kasshas could answer.

<They kill many of us,> Ben informed him.

<They have killed many of *you*,> the older tod corrected him.

The *aderen* was silent as everyone watched to see how this brash statement would be answered.

<Yes,> Ben admitted quietly. <They have killed many of my people. I do not know if they kill Va'Shen or no.>

<Then it is too soon to decide whether they are friend or foe,> the tod said.

<Ketoro,> Kasshas began calmly. <Are you suggesting we wait until these... newcomers... are casting shadows upon our doors before taking any action?>

<I am suggesting, Chieftain, that our actions will suggest to these newcomers which side we are on,> the tod, Ketoro, replied. <If they see us in cooperation with the Dark Ones, they may assume that we are their allies and treat us as they treat them.>

Alacea was not the only one to notice that Ketoro was being deliberately vague. It seemed that, after the episode with Sho Nan in the village square, the older tod was being careful not to declare these aliens as the Great Ones. That didn't mean, however, that such a thing was impossible.

There were murmurs within the *aderen* after this statement, and it was clear that the Garan'Sel miner had some supporters. That surprised Alacea until she realized that she and the villagers were working under two different sets of assumptions. She *knew* her *Tesho*'s people were not the Dark Ones whereas the others *knew* they were. That meant that whoever these new aliens were, they were the Dark One's enemy, which meant it was *possible* they were the Va'Shen's friends.

She also understood how much her people were seeking a way to think that everything would be all right. They *wanted* the newcomers to be friendly. They *had* to be. Her *Tesho's* people had conquered them so quickly. If these new aliens could beat the humans so rapidly, what chance would the weakened Va'Shen have against them?

<We can help move you now,> Ben said. <More time, we may not be able. May need people and things other places to fight.> Right now, he could spare trucks and personnel to move the Va'Shen to the mountains. If Patricia was right, and the Coalition was going to mass forces for a counterattack, he was going to need those trucks to move his Rangers and their gear. That order could come down anytime now.

<And if these newcomers see us riding in your wagons, surrounded by your commandos, then what?> Ketoro asked. <Will they attack us?> His tail slapped the ground as another thought occurred to him. <Or is it that you believe they will not attack *because* we are with you?>

A few Va'Shen in the hall gave quiet hisses at the implication, and it was impossible to know who they were actually hissing at.

Ben wasn't sure what to say to that. He knew this tod was from Garan'Sel, and he was reasonably sure that, were this conversation taking place in Garan'Sel, the question would not be without merit.

<Such words are not helpful, Ketoro,> Kasshas gently chastised the other tod.

<With respect, Chieftain,> Ketoro replied, <They are only unhelpful because the *Aridesho* is present. Were he not, others would be asking this question as well.>

Ben rubbed his temples, and he looked over to his alien wife. Worry filled Alacea's eyes. This discussion was not going the way it should be. In fact, it was going in the exact opposite direction.

The Ranger captain gave a moment's thought to simply *ordering* the village to evacuate. He was the overlord, right? If he ordered the village cleared, he was certain that Alacea would support it, and, if push came to shove, even Azarin would back him up.

"You can't take away the Va'Shen's agency."

Patricia's words came back to him, and he grit his teeth. He didn't want to see bad things happen to the villagers, but, at the same time, every minute he spent here trying to convince them was a minute he *wasn't* preparing his people for the fight ahead of them.

He rose to his feet, and the Va'Shen all turned and looked up at him.

<I do not command,> he said. <I tell you. I offer help. You decide.> And with that he turned and walked out of the room. Patricia hopped up and quickly followed him. The *aderen* erupted behind them, and Alacea sighed in frustration.

<We shall vote,> Kasshas declared.

* * *

"I feel like all that work we did improving our relationship with them was pointless," Patricia griped as the two left the temple.

"You can blame Keyes for that," Ben told her, putting on his patrol cap. "One 'ah, shit' erases ten 'attaboys,' like my dad used to say."

"So, what do we do now?" the terp asked him as they started for the LTV.

"If they ask for help, we help to the best of our ability," Ben told her as he rounded the vehicle toward the driver's seat. "Hell, they could be right. They've been waiting for the Great Ones to come out of the sky and start kicking our asses since the war began. Now, someone has come out of the sky and is kicking our asses. I'd be hopeful too."

"Do you want me to work with Kasshas and maybe…"

"No," Ben cut her off as they entered the vehicle and put on their seatbelts. "I need you doing intel stuff now. The Va'Shen are going to have to make their own decisions."

"And if they make the wrong one?" she asked.

Ben started the LTV. "Then it's on them."

* * *

When Alacea arrived at his hooch that evening, she told him the *aderen* had voted to wait until they knew more about the newcomers. Kasshas and Yasuren had fought against waiting, urging the others to at least prepare for an evacuation or to send the vixens and children on ahead, but the vote still went against them.

<I am sorry, *Tesho*,> Alacea told him with downcast ears and eyes.

<No be sorry,> he told her. <Village must do what village think must do.>

There was more he wanted to say, but the human officer was simply too exhausted after spending the day preparing for possible combat, and he wanted to get what sleep he could. He knew it was quite likely that very soon he wouldn't have an opportunity to sleep again for a long time.

But, even so, sleep eluded him. It was difficult for him to sleep when he was still uncertain that he had done everything he could. Sitting up in bed, the Ranger captain began pulling on his shirt and putting his boots on.

<*Tesho*?> Alacea asked sleepily.

<Sleep,> he whispered. <Back soon.>

His wife turned over and went back to sleep, and the human went to the door of his hooch and put his patrol cap on. He was careful not to let the door slam behind him, and soon he was walking purposefully toward the main gate. The FOB was quiet, but he could tell the sentries were on edge, waiting for an actual threat for the first time in a while.

Walking out the gate, he strolled past the village toward his target. He wasn't surprised to find light coming from the incomplete window as he walked up the hill.

<How did your people win?> his brother-in-law asked from the shadows to his right, causing the Ranger to flinch in surprise. <I heard you approaching for the last five minutes.>

<Not all Va'Shen good like Azarin,> Ben replied as the silver-haired tod emerged from the shadows in front of him. <No sleeping?> he asked.

<No,> Azarin replied simply. <You?>

<No,> Ben answered just as simply.

Azarin turned and started toward the house he had been building for his sister and human brother-in-law. Ben followed him without a word.

<The *aderen* will not yet leave the village,> Azarin informed him, not bothering to face him.

<Aware,> Ben told him. He was careful not to criticize the decision. In his mind, it was the Va'Shen's right to be stupid.

Azarin turned toward him and looked him over with his good eye. <What do you want from me?> he asked.

<Two things,> Ben replied, getting straight to the point. <Tell me about Dark Ones. True Dark Ones. Dark Ones that fight many times ago.>

Azarin took a breath and turned away, pouring himself a drink from a small barrel-shaped canteen sitting on a pile of lumber. It was true that he and his commando had been trained to fight the Dark Ones as they knew them, but even then...

<Not that easy,> he told the Ranger, offering the canteen to him. <Much of what was known melded with stories and legends. Most of those Va'Shen who survived the first war never even *saw* a Dark One. They went into the mountains, deep into the interior of our lands, and hid. Those who fought and lived... were reluctant to speak of what they had seen.>

Ben took the canteen and took a quick pull. It was a fruity alcohol, not *mura*, much to his disappointment. <Why call to them 'Dark?'> he asked. <They wear black on them?>

<No,> Azarin told him. <It is because they move in and take anywhere that the light retreats. They spare no village or town, no matter how peaceful or nonthreatening. If you do not continuously defend a place, it will be lost.> He took a drink before continuing. <But unlike true darkness, it will not easily give up what it has taken when the light returns.>

<Tell me more things,> Ben urged. He was having trouble following everything his brother was saying, but even the little he had learned had given him a hint to the way this enemy made war.

<Stories say too many different things,> Azarin told him. <Some survivors say they are twice as tall as a Va'Shen. Others say they crawl on all fours. They are both terrible to look at and also beautiful. One account said they reminded him of looking up at the Blessing. Some say they have claws, others say tentacles, and some say they eat their kill.>

Azarin took another drink and grimaced. <They bring monsters with them to hunt us. But without them, it is said they cannot easily detect us.> He looked at Ben. <Like your people.>

<You thought these Dark Ones were us?> Ben asked. <How?>

Azarin gave the question serious thought. <The first time I saw one of your people,> he said, <I wondered how the training could be so wrong. But four thousand years is a very long time. The stories, I

thought, had become exaggerated over time. It... comforted me... to think so. I thought it meant we had a chance to win.>

Ben rubbed the five o'clock shadow on his chin in thought. If he took what Azarin was saying at face value, it gave him an idea of the Dark Ones' doctrine, and although their physical appearance was still a mystery, it did tell him they would not be anything like what they had seen so far.

<What is the second thing?> Azarin asked, breaking into his thoughts.

Ben put the canteen on the windowsill. <May be made to leave soon,> he said. <Fight Dark Ones with other commandos.>

Azarin said nothing. For a commando like him, that wasn't necessarily news.

<Alacea will not leave her village,> Ben continued, looking Azarin in the eye. <Make her.>

<You want me to convince her to leave even if the rest of the village will not?> Azarin asked. He had an idea of what his brother-in-law was asking of him, but he wanted to hear him say it.

<Chain her, drug her, hit her on head,> Ben clarified. <I would do for you,> he added a moment later.

Azarin looked away for a moment. Truth be told, he was already planning to do something similar should the *aderen* continue in its stupidity.

<That will not be difficult,> he told Ben. <I am certain Yasuren and Sho Nan will come to me soon and ask the same of me.>

<Thanks be to you,> Ben said, bowing low from the waist.

Azarin gave him a shortened bow in acknowledgement.

<More?> Azarin asked.

<No,> Ben replied with a shake of his head. <This is enough.>

<Then you should sleep,> the commando advised him.

<I shall.>

Ben turned to leave when Azarin's voice suddenly stopped him.

<Don't be captured.>

The Ranger turned to him. <You say?>

<Do not let them capture you,> Azarin told him again. <There is no hope if you do.>

Ben thought on this for a moment and nodded. <I understand.>

Azarin watched as the human turned and left, taking another swig from his drink.

* * *

When Ben awoke the following morning, Bellatrix had not yet risen, but Alacea had already left to begin her day at the temple.

A part of the Ranger officer was, quite frankly, amazed. He had more than half-expected to be alerted during the night that their observation post had made contact with the enemy. The fact that they hadn't seemed so far-fetched to him, that the first thing he did when he arrived at the office was to go next door to the Tactical Operations Center and order someone to go and check on them.

Air Force Staff Sergeant Helena Bishop, the day-shift TOC controller, was running through her morning checklist when he arrived and made the demand. She put her clipboard down and picked up the phone on her desk.

"No need, Sir," she said. "Senior Chief hooked us up. His SeaBees ran a copper line all the way down to the OP." She dialed as she said this and held the phone to her ear.

"Shaman, Sword Maiden," she announced into the receiver. "Comms check."

"Sword Maiden, Shaman," Ben heard from where he stood. "Lima Charlie, over."

"Anything overnight?" Bishop asked the Ranger on the other end.

"Negative, Sword Maiden," the reply came. "Just... Hold one."

Bishop looked to Ben as the line suddenly went quiet. It took every strand of will he had to keep from snatching the phone from the NCO and demanding a report from the other end of the line.

"Sword Maiden, Shaman," the Ranger's voice finally came back. "We have movement on the other side of the river."

Ben turned and started for the door, intent on mustering as much of a force as he could to...

"Sir! Wait!" Bishop called. He turned, and she was still listening to the Ranger's report. She held the phone to him. "You should hear this, Sir."

Ben took the phone from her. "Slayer Six," he announced, using his radio callsign on the off chance they were being monitored.

"Multiple Va'Shen civilians approaching the bridge from the other side of the river," the man at the observation post reported.

"Va'Shen?" Ben asked, wanting to make sure he was clear.

"Affirmative," the Ranger said. "Looks like a couple hundred so far, mostly females and children. A few of them are armed, but there doesn't appear to be any hostile movement."

Ben paused, thrown for a loop. "Copy all, Shaman," he finally said. "Hold position. Do not engage."

"Copy all, Slayer Six. Shaman out."

The captain handed the phone back to Bishop. "Find Lieutenant Kim and back-brief her. I'm taking an LTV to Pelle, and then I'm heading out there. If anything new pops, reach me there."

"Yes, Sir," Bishop replied.

Chapter 5

As his *Myorin*, Alacea was entitled to a place of honor whenever she accompanied Ben. When walking, this was slightly behind and to his left, as this was considered an optimal position in which he could defend her.

In an LTV, however, they were rapidly establishing that this place of honor was not, in fact, in one of the passenger seats, but in the turret. While Kasshas was forced to sit in the passenger seat with his tail mashed up against the seatback, Alacea was breathing the fresh air while her tail enjoyed the luxury of plenty of space in the back seats.

Ben had stopped in Pelle to find the two of them and, after quickly explaining what was happening, brought the two village leaders with him to the southern observation post.

The Ranger had not been to this area yet, but it was easy enough to find based on the directions Staff Sergeant Bishop had given him, and as the LTV climbed the primitive road that led up the forested hill, the poorly camouflaged green tent came into view, nestled up against the side of a large fallen tree.

Ben stopped the vehicle and hopped out, opening the door for Kasshas to exit before Alacea climbed down as well. The priestess removed the goggles she had been wearing and placed them respectfully on the dashboard before moving so Ben could close the door.

As the three walked, two armed and armored Rangers approached from the tent.

"Sir," they both said in greeting, refraining from saluting out in the open as they were.

"Let me take a look," Ben said, approaching the fallen tree. One of the Rangers handed him a pair of binoculars, and they all followed the captain together.

As they came to the tree, the view opened up before them to reveal a wide, slow-moving river flowing past about a hundred yards away and downhill from them. A well-crafted and decorated bridge, just wide enough for a truck to cross, spanned the river just to their left, choked full of Va'Shen with packs on their backs and holding the hands of children.

Ben did a quick count. There were perhaps two hundred that he could see right now, with more coming from the far side of the river. He examined the far bank. There was a large clearing near the end of the bridge before dark red and purple trees obscured what lay past it.

He lowered the binoculars and handed them to Alacea, who looked down at the tods and vixens below.

<So many,> she muttered, her tail moving back and forth in concern.

<I must speak with them,> Ben told the two Va'Shen. <You come?> He didn't want to just pop out of the treeline and scare these people to death. Hopefully, having Kasshas and Alacea with him would make things easier.

<Yes, of course,> Alacea immediately agreed. Kasshas added his agreement, and Ben handed the binoculars back to the Rangers.

The three of them started walking back down the road from which they had come, going about a hundred yards before turning right and moving down the hill through the trees toward the road the refugees were on. As they exited the trees, he found the line of Va'Shen had already stopped and were waiting for them, some with nocked bows and a few hardlight rifles.

"I have *got* to work on my stealth," Ben muttered, holding his hands up in front of him in a non-threatening manner.

Fortunately, his wife immediately stepped forward and took charge. <I am Alacea, Na'Sha of the People and Animals of Pelle,> she announced loudly. <I bring with me my Chieftain, Kasshas, and

Ben Gibson, Overlord of Pelle. Who among you will speak with us?>

Weapons lowered in relief, and a short vixen in a colorful green and yellow hanbok with blue-grey hair pushed her way toward them. When she reached the front of the crowd, she bowed to them.

<I am Hazaria,> the vixen said. <Na'Sha of the People and River Life of Genne.>

<Hazaria Na'Sha,> Alacea began with a bow. <What has happened to you?>

Hazaria's tail was shivering, obviously still gripped by fear. She folded and unfolded her hands nervously as she began to explain.

<We were attacked,> she said plainly. <By... things...> Alacea reached out and took hold of the vixen's hands as if to anchor the other woman to reality. Taking a breath, the Na'Sha continued. <Creatures a godless black in color. They came into the village and began to destroy everything and everyone they saw. Our hunters fought them while the vixens and children fled.>

<When this?> Ben asked her.

Hazaria looked at him in fear, but Alacea reassured her.

<It is all right. Please answer him.>

<Yesterday,> Hazaria said. <Just past midday.> As Ben thought on this, the vixen continued. <Last night, we came upon others from the village of Bora'Zel. They said the same had happened to them. Their Na'Sha is somewhere ahead of us.>

<We shall find her,> Alacea promised. <In the meantime, come with us to Pelle. You will be safe there.>

<Na'Sha, I don't believe that will be true wherever we go,> Hazaria told her.

<The Overlord has many warriors there who will protect you,> Alacea assured her. <As well as Pelle's commando. Come. Rest. Treat your wounded.>

Hazaria thought on this and finally bowed her assent. <My thanks to you, Alacea Na'Sha.> She turned to a vixen with a hardlight rifle. <Please go ahead and find Traia Na'Sha. Tell her what you have heard here and that she must turn toward Pelle.>

<Yes, Na'Sha,> the vixen, a huntress by the look of her outfit, replied and began running toward the front of the column.

Ben turned to Alacea and Kasshas. <I leave these peoples with you?> he asked. <Will send wagons for hurt ones.>

<Thank you, *Tesho*,> Alacea replied. <We will guide these people home.>

The Ranger turned and started back up the hill, the sound of Hazaria's incredulous voice reaching him as she asked what Alacea had meant by "*tesho*." When he reached the top of the hill, he found the Rangers where he had left them, one of them talking on a phone.

Seeing him approach, the man on the phone stood up and gestured for him to come closer.

"He's here, Ma'am," the Ranger said into the receiver. "Hold one." He held the phone to Ben. "Lieutenant Kim, Sir."

"Slayer Six," Ben announced.

"Sir, it's Lieutenant Kim," the interpreter replied. "Is everything okay down there?"

"We made contact with Va'Shen refugees fleeing attacks from our new friends from out of town," Ben reported. "Alacea and Kasshas are going to bring them into Pelle. Have Fletcher come down here with a couple of trucks to start moving the wounded."

"Understood, Sir," Patricia responded.

"Anything new on your end?" he asked.

"Orders came down from the JOC," Patricia informed him. "Sergeant Bishop is decoding them now."

"Copy. Anything else?"

"Where are the refugees from, Sir?" she asked him.

"Two villages," Ben replied. "Genne and Bora'Zel."

"Bora'Zel?" Patricia asked in a surprised tone.

"Is that significant?" he asked.

"It's... Not on an open line. It can wait until you get back," she said.

"Copy," he said. "Anything else?"

"Negative," Patricia said. "I'll get Fletcher and some trucks out to the OP ASAP."

"Thanks," he said. "Out here."

He handed the phone back to the Ranger. "'When sorrows come, they come not as single spies, but in battalions,'" he muttered.

"Tupac?" one of the Rangers asked him.

"Shakespeare," Ben corrected.

"Never liked his music," the Ranger commented.

* * *

By the time he made it back to his office, Patricia was waiting there, two cups of coffee in her hands. Without a word, she passed one of them to him.

"Best deputy ever," he remarked before taking a sip. "Bishop still decoding?" he asked.

"Yeah, it all has to be done by hand," Patricia informed him. "I jumped on the conference call for you too."

"Anything new?"

"They managed to get a reconnaissance aircraft closer to them," Patricia told him, putting her coffee down on her desk with a sigh. "About thirty large vehicles, possibly their version of armor. Few hundred on foot. They say the pictures were fuzzy, so they didn't get a good look at them. Started taking fire before they could get too close, and it was damn accurate for someone aiming without a computer."

"Still headed north?"

"Yes, but that's what I wanted to ask you about," she said, walking over to the map. "You said Genne and Bora'Zel?"

"That's right."

Patricia picked up a pencil and made two X's, one to the left of the mark indicating the crash site and the other north of it, but further to the right.

"Genne... Bora'Zel," she said, pointing at the two marks in turn.

Ben looked at the map and instantly realized what was throwing his terp for a loop. "They're so out of the way," he said. Connecting the three X's would have made a wide zigzag generally moving north. "They must have lost a couple of *days* going after them."

"They scanned Jamieson," she said. "They have to know that's the biggest threat to them. The smart thing would be to blitzkrieg their way north and hit it before we have a chance to mass our forces. Why go after these little villages? There's nothing there. We didn't have outposts at either one."

"Maybe they got a real hate-on for the Va'Shen?" Ben guessed.

"There are plenty of Va'Shen between them and Jamieson to satisfy them if that's all there is to it," Patricia told him. "No, this is weird. We're missing something."

They turned as the door to the office opened, and Staff Sergeant Bishop entered. "Sir, orders from the JOC." She handed him a manila folder with a red and white cover sheet marking the contents as SECRET.

Opening the folder, he read the BLUF, the Bottom Line Up Front, that summarized the contents before the document delved into the details, and nodded his head.

"Kazen'Ta," he said, closing the folder. Patricia turned and studied the map for a moment before pointing at an area roughly halfway between Pelle and Jamieson along Route Orange.

Ben nodded. "That's where we're going to hit them," he said. He checked the map and chuckled, throwing Patricia an impressed look.

"You were only off by ten miles," he commented, remembering her guess from the day before.

"It's not a bad spot," she said. "It would have been my second choice," she added somewhat smugly.

"All forces with the ability to be there need to be there, ASAP," Ben informed her. He turned back to Bishop. "They say who was going to be the on-site commander?" he asked.

"Colonel Hopper," Bishop told him.

"*Drew* Hopper?" the captain asked. At Bishop's nod, he continued. "Best news we've had all day," he said.

"You know him?" Patricia asked.

"Worked with him a couple of times on Epsilon," Ben told her. "He's 82nd Airborne, one of the best field commanders I ever worked with. He's probably the best guy on the planet to run this battle."

"So, what now?" Patricia asked.

"As soon as the trucks get back from ferrying the wounded Va'Shen to Pelle, we start packing up," Ben told her. "Sergeant Bishop, get on the loudspeaker and make the announcement. All personnel on post need to be ready for a seven-day mission and ready to roll out the gate in four hours."

"Yes, Sir."

"And I do mean *all*," Ben told them both. "We're not leaving any of our people here to get hit."

"What about the Va'Shen?" Patricia asked.

Ben sighed. "I'll go talk to Alacea, let her know what's going on and try to get them to run for the hills. Now that they have some evidence that these guys aren't friendlies, they should be more agreeable to the idea."

"Should we leave some people behind to help th..."

"No," Ben interrupted. There was a few seconds of silence before he went on. "We have a job to do. We need to do it. And we may need every last person we can muster to make it happen."

"Understood, Sir."

"All right," he told them. "Let's get to work."

* * *

Alacea watched as Pelle's healer, Kastia, applied salve to a tall, older vixen's left arm. All around them in the meeting hall of Pelle's temple, Mikorin from three different villages along with their healers, helped treat and feed refugees from Genne and Bora'Zel.

The wounded vixen gave no indication of pain, maintaining a calm and regal pose fitting for her position as a Na'Sha. Although her long, dark red hair was matted and her sage green hanbok was filthy, she continued to represent the spirit of her community, and in her eyes, that spirit remained strong.

<You have my greatest thanks for your help, Alacea Na'Sha,> the vixen told her again.

<It is our honor to help, Traia Na'Sha,> Alacea returned diplomatically. <Can you tell me what happened at Bora'Zel?>

<I am not sure, myself,> Traia told her honestly. <I was in meditation when the screaming began. When I ran to the window to see what was happening, I saw my people running and buildings on the far end of town collapsing. Many of my people sought refuge in the temple.>

Kastia put the salve down and began to wrap a clean bandage around the woman's arm. <How did you get away?> the green-haired vixen asked.

<The Gods protected us,> Traia told her with a gentle twitch of her ears. <Even as other buildings fell around us, not a single shot came to the temple. When members of our commando appeared and

began to fight, we took those who gathered at the temple and ran into the forest.>

<Praise be to the Gods,> Kastia said.

<Praise be to the Gods,> Traia replied.

Several other villagers being treated nearby took up the call and repeated it.

Alacea saw movement at the doorway and stood up as Kasshas, Yasuren and Azarin headed toward her. The three took in the sight of so many wounded tods, vixens and kits, and their ears and tails showed the Mikorin their dismay.

<Chieftain,> Alacea began with a bow.

<Na'Sha,> he returned with a slightly lower bow. <How are things here? Is there anything you need that the community can provide?>

<A warm place for the displaced to stay,> she answered immediately. <We are caring for the wounded here, but we have quickly run out of room.>

<We are working on that now,> Yasuren assured her from Kasshas's left.

<What have they told you about the attacks?> Kasshas asked the priestess.

<The information they can provide is sparse at best,> she replied. <Only that they were attacked and managed to escape.>

<Genne and Bora'Zel,> Kasshas muttered in thought. <Too close to remain complacent, too far to inspire panic.>

<Chieftain, I strongly recommend we accept the Overlord's offer for assistance and move our people to the sanctuary in the mountains,> Alacea told him. <I think the question as to whether these... invaders... are our friends or not has been clearly answered.>

<I also suggest we muster the commando,> Azarin added. <If the invaders do come before we can leave, it will be easier to oppose them if we are already gathered and armed.>

There was little need to convince the chieftain. <Then we shall do so,> he said.

<I will call the muster so that we may hold the election,> Azarin announced and turned to leave.

<Why hold an election?> Alacea called to him before he could leave. Azarin halted and turned back to her. <The commando already has a captain.>

Azarin didn't reply right away. His eye fell on Kasshas and Yasuren, who seemed to want to know the answer to the question as well.

<After what has happened recently,> Azarin began, <... they may no longer find me suitable. It is better to resolve it now.>

Before they could object further, Azarin turned and was out the door.

Alacea was puzzled, but Yasuren watched him leave with pity.

Just as the priestess opened her mouth to voice a question, Kasshas spoke up.

<Na'Sha, may I ask you to come with me to speak to the Overlord?> he asked.

<Of course, Chieftain.>

They didn't have to take a single step, however, as Sho Nan appeared in the doorway a moment later and bowed to them.

<Na'Sha, the Overlord has come,> she said. <He asks for you.>

<How fortuitous,> Kasshas commented.

The three made for the temple entryway where Ben was waiting for them, his patrol cap in his hands. Seeing them, he bowed, and they bowed lower in return.

<*Tesho*, we were just coming to see you,> Alacea informed him.

Ben had a fairly good idea why, and Kasshas confirmed it a moment later.

<We wish to request your assistance in moving our people into the mountains,> Kasshas asked with a deep bow.

The Ranger sighed. He knew it.

<Regret,> he told them. <I cannot.> Confused, swishing tails met this announcement, and he explained. <Taken commands from my Overlord. I and my fighters must leave here to join others to fight.>

Alacea went rigid at the announcement, and Kasshas gave voice to the obvious question. <When must you leave?>

<Before day end,> Ben told them. <Preparing now. Need all wagons.> He bowed to them. <I am sorry.>

Kasshas growled low in his throat, but not at Ben. The tod was more angry at himself for not pushing harder to evacuate. Now, the most effective means of doing so was gone.

When the Gods hate you, they do not kill you. They just make you stupid, he remembered the old saying.

<You cannot leave.>

The human and other two Va'Shen turned to the source of the firm declaration. Alacea stood before Ben, her face appearing calm and collected. But any Va'Shen could see her tail swishing and her ears flattened down and backward. If she were human, she would be borderline panicked.

<You cannot leave,> she pronounced again. <You are the Overlord of Pelle. You have responsibilities here.>

Ben looked at his alien wife carefully. Normally, she was very understanding of when he had to leave for military purposes. But now there was something distinctly off about her.

<Must go,> he told her quietly.

<You may not,> she declared. <Your place is here. You shall remain here.>

It was Yasuren who broke the deadlock. Turning, she took Alacea by the shoulders and brought her lips to her ears, whispering gently but firmly.

<Na'Sha... Alacea... Your *tesho* is a leader of warriors,> she said. <You must not embarrass him by grasping at his tail like this. If his *myorin* shows no faith in his victory, who else will?>

Alacea knew all this. She had said similar things to countless vixens in Pelle who didn't want their *tesho*s to leave for war. This was not even the first time she had seen Ben leave for battle.

But this time was different. She was no longer a part of a political marriage arranged to keep the peace. She was a marked vixen whose *tesho* had just told her he was going to war in a few hours.

A few hours!

She was the Na'Sha. Chieftains bowed to her. Nobles bowed to her. An entire village bowed to her. She had never once felt the desire to abuse the power inherent of her position before, not even to help her friends or her brother.

But now she grasped at any tool at her disposal, dug into her mind and heart for any excuse, no matter how tenuous or untenable. She was the Na'Sha. If she said he could not go, then he could not go.

He *could not go.*

<Of course,> she whispered quietly. <Forgive me, *Tesho*. I lost sight of my duty for a moment.>

<No forgive need,> he said. He looked at Yasuren and Kasshas for help, and the noblevixen acted, taking the Chieftain's hand.

<*Tesho*, we must go and prepare the village to evacuate,> she said, leading him out the door.

Ben and Alacea were left alone in the entryway just inside the temple. Outside, the sun shone down on the village, filling the entryway with a light most would have seen as the hallmark of a nice day.

But Alacea knew otherwise. She stood in its light as if blocking the door so that Ben wouldn't be able to leave. She would not look up at him, not meet his eyes. The priestess had never felt this way before, so helpless and frightened. He could walk out the door and she might never see him again until the day she died and stepped into the Glade, and even then he might not be there to welcome her.

<It is well,> he told her quietly. <All book.>

<It is not book!> she cried, tossing the attempt at humor back at him. <It's... It is not *fair!*> she told him with a hiccup. <I just... I just found you.>

<I will return,> he promised. <I will go. Defeat Dark Things. Come back.>

It wasn't that he wasn't scared. Just like Alacea, he had never felt anything like this. When the war began, he had said goodbye to Jessie in a phone call while she was on a date, and although neither of them quite knew what to say, there was no feeling of cold, gripping fear like there was now. He wasn't the only one in danger. He was leaving Alacea and her entire village here, in the marching path of danger. That she seemed to be thinking more about his safety than this betrayal tore at his heart. He not only felt fear but self-loathing for what he had to do now.

But although these feelings were new for him, the situation wasn't. He had seen it play out numerous times at the Persephone Spaceport as wives, husbands, lovers and parents said goodbye to their servicemembers, perhaps for the last time.

For almost *all of them*, it *had* been the last time.

Now it was his turn.

<I come back,> he promised again, stepping forward and putting his hand behind her head to pull her close. <You go to mountains,> he told her softly. <I kill Dark Things and come back. Find you there.>

Alacea buried her face in his uniform jacket and took a deep breath as if gathering her strength.

<You will come back,> she pronounced as if from on high. <The Gods will see to it. I will pray for your victory.>

He bent down and gently nipped the tip of her ear.

<I will see you soon.>

Releasing her, he stepped out into the sun. He walked to the LTV and didn't look back, and neither did she.

* * *

Ritasia, Mikorin Ya'Jahar of Genne, tried to ignore the pain in her left arm as the... thing... used it to drag her through the burning village that had been her home. When the *things* attacked, it had been utter chaos. She had done her best to help, but no one quite knew what to do. So, she had run to the nearest houses, throwing open the doors to find villagers huddled inside, desperately hiding, and ordered them to run, directing them toward the temple.

By the time she had felt she had done all she could and returned, the temple was empty. Everyone had fled. Ritasia had gone through every room in the temple, checking each room and closet to make sure no acolytes remained. Once she had finished and was satisfied, she ran for the exit.

And something grabbed her.

It threw her roughly to the ground, knocking her head against the hard-packed dirt road, and before she could blink the spots from her eyes, whatever it was had latched onto her arm and was dragging her away.

Looking up at it, all she saw was black, a deep, soul-devouring black that allowed no light to escape from it.

As it dragged her, she saw the collapsed houses around her, the bodies of her fellow villagers, and absolutely no wounded. No one calling for help or dragging themselves away.

Everyone... Everything... was dead.

She cried out as the *thing* threw her forward, and she landed in the road, coughing dust out of her lungs. Her arm hurt, and she knew it was broken. She absently, out of habit, brushed her shoulder-length blonde hair back away from her eyes with her good hand and looked up.

A Dark One face looked back at her, its mouth open in horror and its eyes rolled back up into its head. Gasping in fear, she pushed away with her legs, but the thing that dragged her here grabbed her by the neck and pushed her down again.

Looking up again, she saw that it wasn't a Dark One at all. The head she had seen was posted on a spike protruding from another *thing's* left shoulder. The black monster itself looked down at her, its face hidden from her by an equally black dome-shaped helmet.

It stared down at her as if inspecting her, and then it began to change colors. A bloom of red and green light emanated from the center of its chest, followed by blues, purples and yellows that, at any other time, Ritasia would have found beautiful enough to stare at for hours.

She was snapped from the hypnotic sight by a growling, raspy voice, like someone was trying to speak with rocks in their throat.

<YOU. ARE. MIKORIN.>

Ritasia swallowed, her tail swinging back and forth in fear. Her blood pounded in her temples as she shivered in terror at the *thing's* voice.

<Y... Yes...> she admitted softly.

<YOU. ARE. MIKORIN.> it repeated.

The *thing* behind her kicked her, prompting her to answer.

<Yes!> she cried, looking down and holding her wounded arm.

<YOU. ARE. DURANDAL.>

She looked up at the creature, confused, but the terrible sight that met her forced her to look away again.

<No,> she confessed.

<YOU. ARE. NASHA.>

<No,> she replied.

The *thing* looked up at the one who had brought her there, three other monsters now having joined them. The *thing* lit up in another colorful pattern, but this time there was no voice to accompany it.

FEAST.

The *thing* began to walk away as the other monsters descended on Ritasia, grabbing her arms and legs with their claws. From the tips of those claws came small shocks of electricity, and the vixen watched in horror as her skin and flesh turned to sludge. She thrashed and screamed as the monsters continued doing this, the screaming only stopping when parts of her lungs had been liquified.

The thrashing and terror, however, continued for another full minute until she died.

As the members of its Caste sucked up the sludge with clawed hands, the *thing*, the Caste Leader, surveyed the destroyed village. Once again, their objective eluded them. They had to move north, toward the concentration of non-Va'Shen they had detected in orbit, but it would do no good until their first objective had been reached.

They had to warn the Great Caste of what they had seen. That was why its Caste had awoken from the hibernation first, to go forth and search for threats.

What it had seen so far confused and worried it. The Enemy, itself, was nowhere to be found. The Enemy's foot soldiers had replenished themselves, but they appeared weaker than before. And now these new creatures, like the Enemy's slaves but different. Their weapons, appearance, ships, even the way they made the air vibrate to communicate was different.

How many of them were there? Where did they come from? When his Caste awoke, one of the first things they discovered was an electromagnetic signal pointed at their homeworld from one of the Enemy's old agriculture worlds. His Caste and two others followed the signal back and dealt with it, ensuring nothing on the planet would be able to share what they knew of their hidden homeworld.

No Enemy ships opposed them, but what they did see was unfamiliar. It now wished it had spent more time studying them first, but the safety of their homeworld was paramount. Most of their population had not yet awoken from the Hibernation and would not for several cycles.

That was almost a cycle ago, and what they had discovered during their reconnaissance only brought further confusion. When the Caste approached the foot soldiers' world, no Enemy ships met them, just a large, spinning hunk of metals unfamiliar to them. He knew it had seen their approach.

So, they destroyed it.

But one of the ship's weapons had gotten through, and now they were trapped.

It was a failure and humiliation the Caste Leader could not allow to stand. The only hope for redemption was to complete their mission, to bring news of this new threat back to their world, to begin preparing the ecosystem to produce weapons to counter them. After four thousand years, the ecosystem was now able to produce weapons effective against the Enemy and their soldier slaves en masse. It would all be for nothing, however, if they were not ready to also face this new threat.

And so the Great Caste must be warned.

And nothing would stand in their way.

Chapter 6

As Ben drove the LTV back onto the FOB, he was met by the sound of rotors and the sight of an Army Pawnee helicopter moving to touch down on one of the helipads on the other side of base.

Got here just in time, guys, he thought. If they had come a few hours later they would have found an empty base waiting for them.

Pulling into the two-vehicle parking area next to the office, he powered down the vehicle and hopped out. Nearby, soldiers and sailors were carrying hard-cases for various pieces of equipment, loading them into the backs of cargo trucks. With any luck, they would be on the road before sundown.

Entering the office, he found Patricia at her desk, going through various typed communiques, most likely amendments and details to the orders they had received. Ben tossed his patrol cap on his desk and sat down.

"Any issues?" he asked.

"No," Patricia replied absently. "Just a lot of confusion and questions from other bases, asking if these orders are meant for them or not. As well as some very pointed replies stating that 'ALCON' means '*ALCON*.'"

"We've gotten complacent," Ben noted with a sigh. Things down in the south had gotten a little *too* peaceful. The sudden orders to drop everything and get ready for a battle a unit may or may not be ready for must have made a lot of otherwise rear-echelon units suddenly nervous.

Ben started going through his own pile of orders, communiques and commander's intents, seeing if any of it was pertinent, when the door to the office suddenly opened, and a tall, older man with graying hair entered followed by a much younger lieutenant.

Ben saw the eagle on the front of the man's uniform and hopped up to attention. Before Patricia could take the hint and mimic him, the man had already given them an "as you were" and stepped forward, reaching out to take Ben's hand.

"Captain Gibson?"

"Yes, Sir," Ben replied, checking the man's nametape. "Colonel Hopper," he remarked, suddenly remembering why the man looked so familiar to him. "Welcome to FOB Leonard."

"We worked together before, haven't we, Captain?" Hopper asked.

"Yes, Sir," Ben replied immediately. "On Epsilon. My platoon worked with one of your companies."

"Thought so," Hopper said.

"This is my intelligence officer, Lieutenant Kim," Ben said, gesturing to Patricia.

"Nice to meet you, Lieutenant. This is Lieutenant Bryce, one of my intel people."

"Please, have a seat, Sir," Ben asked, gesturing to a pair of empty chairs. He felt his stomach clench nervously. The man running the entire counterattack against the Dark Ones was way too busy to be coming out to a little FOB like his just for a meet-and-greet. Something big was about to drop.

"You caught us just in time," Ben said, pulling his chair from around his desk and sitting across from the colonel. "We got the orders to move this morning. A few more hours and we would have been on the road."

"Those orders are rescinded," Hopper informed him.

"They're calling off the counterattack, Sir?" Ben asked.

"To be more specific, those orders are rescinded for *you*, Captain," Hopper clarified. "You have new orders."

"You wouldn't have come all the way out here to give them to me if we were sitting this one out, Sir," Ben said.

Hopper blew out a breath and sat back, folding his hands in his lap. "Let me be straight with you, Captain," he began. "Our forces are spread to Hell and gone. We're doing everything we can to scrape up every last man and woman with a rifle and a working trigger finger, but time and distance are not on our side."

Ben gave a quick look to Patricia and found her biting her lip at this stark appraisal of the situation.

"Most of our heavy railgun artillery is up north," Hopper continued. "It took two full weeks of heavy lift and assembly just to get Firebase Voss set up, and that's not even the furthest one away. Just about all of our heavy combat power is up north, fighting the insurgents, and we don't have enough choppers to move everything down here all at once. The full truth of the matter is that the only real hope we have is that *Over the Rainbow* comes in and we can alert her to launch her birds as soon as she makes orbit." He shook his head. "But she could arrive anytime from tomorrow to two weeks from now depending on any delays she may have run into before leaving."

Ben nodded and turned all business. "What can my Rangers do for you, Sir?" he asked.

Hopper leaned forward and looked the Ranger officer in the eye. "I need you to buy us enough time to gather as much forces as we possibly can," he said. "Ideally, until *Over the Rainbow* arrives, but we can't count on her showing up in time. Every minute you buy us gives us another gun on the line. That's what I need, Captain. This is your AO. You know it better than anyone, and I can't even spare rotary assets to bring help in for you."

Ben took a breath and nodded. "We'll give you all the time we can, Colonel," he promised. Even as the words left his lips, he swallowed dryly. He knew very well that Hopper came to give him these orders personally because the colonel believed he was asking his Rangers to die.

"Do as much as you can and then fall back to the rendezvous point," Hopper told him. "How you do it is up to you. But you get your people clear in the end, understand?"

"Understood, Sir," Ben said.

Hopper sighed and stood up, offering Ben his hand again. "I'm sorry to be the bearer of bad news, Captain."

Ben shook the man's hand and nodded. "Bad news is our specialty, Sir."

"We brought you some mail on the chopper," the colonel told him. "Last mail you're likely to get for a bit."

"I appreciate the thought, Sir."

"I will see you and your people at Kazen'Ta," Hopper told him. "Good hunting, son."

Hopper put his patrol cap back on and led his intel lieutenant, who hadn't said a word the entire time, out the door and back to the helicopter.

Ben and Patricia looked at each other in silence for several moments before the captain finally spoke again.

"Tell everyone to stop what they're doing and report to the parade field," he told her quietly.

* * *

Rumors, like coffee, were found any place where there were more than two servicemembers present at the same time. After all the preparation the troops at FOB Leonard had begun, the order to cease those preparations immediately led to a series of educated guesses, assessments and stories beginning with the words, "I heard from..."

"I heard a SEAL team took them all out..."

"*Over the Rainbow* just came into the system and hit them from orbit!"

"Bullshit, dude. You'd see a strike like that from here."

"I heard their immune systems couldn't handle the local bacteria and they all died of the common cold."

"Oh, man, that one's a classic!" Ramirez commented with a smile as he overheard that last one from his spot at the front of the crowd. He elbowed Burgers who was standing to his left. "What's the stupidest one you've heard so far?"

Burgers arched an eyebrow under his reflective ballistic glasses and grunted. "Some SeaBee said the captain went nuts and decided to stay and fight."

"Hmm," Ramirez replied quietly.

"What?" the larger man asked him. "You wanna stay?"

Ramirez looked up at his friend and gave him a little shrug. "Honestly, a little, yeah. I sure as Hell didn't like that we were sneaking out on the village and leaving them to face these things alone. Felt like a dick move, ya'know?"

Burgers winced at the statement. He had felt the same way, but orders were orders. He tried to put a positive spin on the situation.

"Mrs. Gibson and Alzoria aren't stupid," he told the shorter man. "They would get out of Dodge long before those things got here."

"Yeah, I g..."

"COMPANY! TENCH-HUT!" Senior Chief Warren's voice suddenly boomed over their heads. Everyone on the parade field faced the front and came to attention as Ben hopped up onto their make-shift stage.

"As you were! No time to waste, you guardians of democracy!" Ben called out. "New orders just came from Colonel Hopper, himself. We're not bugging out!"

Some nervous murmurs began to bubble up from the crowd in response to this statement.

"Here's the deal," Ben continued after a moment. "The CJTF is gathering as many troops as they can north of here to hit the aliens hard as they advance on Jamieson. But they need time. And we're going to give it to them."

"Oh shit," came from someone in the crowd, probably not realizing that everyone would be able to hear it over the dead silence that now fell over the assembly.

"That's what I said," Ben replied with what he hoped was a confident grin. There were a few laughs from the crowd, but not many. "In order for them to hit Jamieson, they have to come north through Pelle. To be clear," Ben enunciated, "We are not tasked with destroying these things on our own. We just have to delay them. After that, we bug out north and join the rest of the CJTF forces. Then we wipe these things out for good."

Ben let it sink in for a moment. He knew he had just given them some very bad news. Now he had to pump them up.

"Up 'til now," he began. "These things have only fought an unarmed Air Force plane, a few infantry folks, two Space Force Band members and some unarmed villagers. They don't know what Rangers are yet, so they don't know how *afraid* they should be."

Some nods and upturned gazes met this statement.

"So, we're going to educate them," Ben promised. "They're going to learn a new human word. They're going to learn the word 'Ranger.' And they're going to learn what that word means." He paused for a moment. "*'The ones you don't fuck with!'*"

"HOOAH!" the crowd roared.

"RANGERS LEAD THE WAY!" Ben shouted.

"ALL THE WAY!" the crowd hollered back.

"And the Navy's here too!" someone called from the back, earning some laughs.

"NCOs report to the conference room immediately after this," Ben announced. "The rest of you get back to those trucks and start unloading everything that goes 'boom.' We're gonna need it." He gave Warren a nod.

"COMPANY! TENCH-HUT!"

The crowd came to attention as Ben hopped off the stage.

"As you were," he called to them.

* * *

"Good speech," Patricia commented as Ben met her at the conference room door, Warren trailing behind him.

"Thanks," Ben said. "Even I almost believed it."

They entered the conference room as Ramirez, Burgers, Fletcher and a few other NCOs began to arrive, filing in and taking their usual seats at the table. Ben stood behind his chair at the head of the table and leaned on the back of it.

He quickly took an assessment of everyone's expression and body language. The NCOs, the most experienced people he had, were all business. They were hopeful. He could see that. But they also knew this job was going to be rough.

"No idea is stupid," Ben announced. "I want ways to slow these things down with the equipment and armament we have on-hand. Because we're not getting any reinforcements or resupply. We're effectively on our own."

Silence.

"Hit and run ambushes," one NCO down the table immediately suggested. "Whittle them down little by little."

"We have enough demolition charges to take out the bridge by the OP," Warren told Ben. "With plenty left over for the bridge leading north."

"Have your guys start wiring them up as soon as we're done here," Ben told him. "I want to be able to blow them on a moment's notice."

Patricia raised her hand. "I know why we wouldn't want to destroy the bridge leading to Route Orange, but why not just blow the southern bridge now?"

"Two reasons," Ben told her. "First, refugees are using that bridge. We destroy it now, they'll be trapped on the far side of the river."

"Ah," Patricia said, the answer making total sense to her.

"And second," he continued, "If these things have scouts out and they see the bridge is down, they'll start looking for an alternate crossing now. If we wait until they're closer and blow the bridge, they have to waste time doubling back. That's what I want. We're not going to prevent them crossing that river. They'll find a way eventually. But we can make the process longer and a helluva lot more inconvenient for them."

Hearing Ben's answer, Burgers's head popped up as if a light bulb had suddenly lit up above him. "What about the mortar team? We can use them."

Ramirez shook his head. "No radios. We wouldn't be able to call down effective fire."

The Rangers had a mortar squad with them along with an M62, 120mm mortar, complete with self-guiding high-explosive, EM and anti-personnel rounds for it. But without radios or drones to provide firing coordinates, it was essentially useless, even dangerous.

"True, if we were using it for indirect fire support, but we *know* that these things are going to be at that bridge at *some point*," Burgers pointed out. "The mortar team can pre-register the weapon to hit them when they get to the far side of the bridge."

Ramirez nodded. "Then we blow the bridge at the same time and light them up with an ambush from this side of the river. I like, I like."

"Welcome to Pelle, D-bags," Burgers concluded. His voice turned sour a moment later. "Only problem is we only get one shot. Most of the ammo for it was redirected to the north. We got enough left for one good barrage. After that..."

"I like it, anyway," Ben said. "Make it happen. What else?" He paused for a moment as everyone thought. "The main road from that bridge is the most obvious way to go. Is there any way we could mine it?"

One of the sergeants further down the line shook his head. "No anti-tank or anti-personnel mines in the inventory. We have some claymores, and we could rig up some frags with trip wires, though."

"What about IEDs?"

Ben looked over at Warren, who had his arms crossed over his chest. Up until now he had been content to let the Army folks do what Army folks do best, but now he had an idea.

"Do we have enough explosives for that?" Ben asked.

"After rigging both bridges, there wouldn't be a lot left," Warren told him. "Maybe enough for six or seven good charges, but I got an idea. They don't know anything about us or really what kind of weapons we have. They don't know what our mines look like."

"Right," Ben prompted.

"We have a *ton* of old oil drums," Warren went on. "Let's make six bombs out of them and spread them out on the road. Then take a bunch of others and fill them with junk and spread them out with them. After the first few blasts, they'll learn that the drums are bad news. They won't be able to tell which ones are bombs and which are decoys, but unless they're willing to risk it, they'll have to stop and deal with each one they come to."

"That could force them to try going through the forest instead," Burgers said. "That'll slow them down."

"Senior Chief, run with it," Ben ordered.

"Aye aye, Sir."

"We can draw them into the village."

Their eyes turned to Sergeant Vickers, one of the Supply NCOs, at the other end of the table. Seeing everyone's attention on him, he cleared his throat and elaborated.

"I mean... evacuate it first, obviously," he clarified. "But if we can draw the enemy into the village and make them fight house-to-house, it'll bog them down."

Ben took a breath and thought on the suggestion. Vickers was right on the tactical level. House-to-house fighting was the absolute worst for an attacking force. Every room of every building had to be cleared or else you risked an attack on your force from behind after passing by. And every corner, every closed door, every closet had the potential to conceal an attacker, a booby trap or worse. It was pure Hell.

And it was a Hell he didn't want to bring to Pelle. Fighting house-to-house like that all but ensured the complete destruction of the village.

"From what I have heard," Ben said, "These things may not even bother to try to clear houses. They would probably just level them and move on. We'll consider it as a back-up plan."

The meeting continued as various details were hammered out. Ben ordered a new observation post on the far side of the river that could give them enough warning to set up for an ambush at the bridge. Assignments were handed out, and the meeting ended.

As the NCOs filed out, Ben sighed. Patricia stepped over to him and put her hand on his shoulder.

"You doing okay?" he asked her. Although the terp had been in combat situations twice now, this was the first large-scale battle she would be in. It was only natural that she would be nervous.

"I'm good," she said. "We'll just do what we have to do and then make a run for it." She took a nervous breath. "Sounds easy."

"Call the JOC," Ben told her. "I want whatever recon or intel data they can give us with updates every hour. I don't care how busy they are."

"Yes, Sir," she said. "What about the village?"

"I'll let them know about the change of plans and tell them to get a move on with that evacuation," he said. "If the fighting does end up in Pelle..." He left the rest of the thought unspoken.

The Ranger captain stood up and clapped his hands together. "Okay, break time's over!" he announced.

He and Patricia stepped out of the conference room, and the intel officer jogged off to the office. Just as Ben was going to start for the LTVs, a voice stopped him.

"Sir! Mail for you!" a young private called out as he trotted toward him. He stopped in front of Ben and gave him a quick salute while trying to simultaneously keep the green duffel bag stuffed with mail from falling off his shoulder. He offered Ben the letter and started off again, obviously in a rush.

Ben watched him go and absent-mindedly opened the envelope without even checking to see who it was from. Unfolding the crisp, bleach-white piece of paper within, he looked down and quickly read over it.

Then, he laughed.

Hard.

"Those assholes!" he laughed, shaking his head at the letter as he folded it and put it into his uniform shirt pocket. As the laughter faded, he shook his head again and breathed a deep sigh.

I'll deal with this bullshit later, he thought.

Right now, he had a war to fight.

* * *

Azarin watched and counted as three of his commandos arrived at the half-constructed house, concluding that they were the last. Seeing him, the three bowed and went to take their seats on the ground with the rest of the commandos. Azarin had chosen this place to hold their meeting because there was enough space to accommodate all of them. Most of the space in the temple the Mikorin would normally provide for a gathering like this was taken up by the continuous flow of refugees.

In addition to the Storm Rifles he had gone into battle with three years ago, the small contingent of able guardsmen that made up Garan'Sel's small commando had joined them, adding an additional twenty soldiers to their group. They sat together in one clump among the rest, their tails moving nervously. It was only just recently that this same commando had been holding guns to their heads.

Azarin stood straight and bowed to them in greeting. <I greet you, Storm Rifles.> To assuage any concerns, he turned slightly and bowed deliberately at the Garan'Sel tods. <And I greet the Third Duke's Stone Arrows. I now welcome you as brothers of the First Prince's Storm Rifles. Honor to the First Prince and honor to the Third Duke.>

<We honor them,> the commandos recited in unison.

The gesture seemed to work, and several tails began to slow to a stop.

<The commando is assembled,> Azarin intoned. <As most of you have heard, creatures have arrived from the stars and have attacked both our villages and the Dark Ones. Every moment brings them closer to Pelle. The Chieftain has ordered an evacuation of the village. We are assembled in the event the creatures arrive and we must protect the evacuation. This is the challenge we face.>

Tails waved to and fro in thought at this mission.

<Before we go further, we shall hold the election,> Azarin announced.

Ears popped up at this statement. Standing nearby, Azarin's friend and deputy, Tasshas, regarded the commando captain in puzzlement.

<Are there any nominations?> Azarin asked.

One of the commandos stood up.

<Whom do you nominate, Portas?> the captain asked him.

<I do not nominate, Captain,> the young tod nervously said. Unlike many other tods who typically had drab colored hair and fur,

Portas's hair was a bright blond. He had been sought after by several vixens before he suddenly married Beretes before leaving for the war. <I have a question,> he finished.

<What is your question?> Azarin asked, anticipating something concerning this strange new enemy.

<Why are we holding an election?> Portas asked him. <There has been no vote of removal and... er... you are not dead.>

Several other commandos murmured at this point.

<You elected me under much different circumstances,> Azarin pointed out in answer. <It is only right that another election be held. Also... I understand if many of you are uncomfortable after what happened recently.>

A few commandos glanced over at the Garan'Sel contingent, whom that last note was obviously pointed at.

<Are there nominations?> Azarin asked again.

<This is foolish,> Dan Huun growled as he stood up from his place at the head of his corporalship. He faced Azarin, his ears pointed at the one-eyed tod in irritation. <You were elected to perform a duty, and we demand you do it until a vote of removal is called or you die. The commando will tell you when it wants a new captain.>

<He is right, Captain,> Tasshas told Azarin from the tod's right. <It is not yet time for a new captain. We are wasting time. Lead us.>

Azarin took a breath, simultaneously touched by his tods' confidence in him and resenting it. <Very well,> he said.

Before he could continue the briefing, the slightest noise touched his ears, causing them to twitch. Briefly looking around, he saw that he was the only one who heard it.

<Have we become so complacent by our incarceration,> he asked, <That an entire group of Huntresses can come so close to us undetected?>

Ears popped up in confusion while others turned, now conscious of the noise they had heard but dismissed. Nearby, off to Azarin's right where the red grass had grown tall, the ears and heads of several short-haired vixens popped out of the grass to reveal themselves.

Azarin met the eyes of the vixen leading them as she walked forward. Bao Sen's once long, bright red hair had been cut short just above her shoulders, an act of solidarity with the Huntress Alzoria, whose hair had been forcibly shorn.

Bao Sen approached and bowed to Azarin with some trepidation, as if knowing she was in a place she shouldn't be.

<Greetings, Captain,> she said formally. <The Huntresses have come to offer you their assistance.>

<Vixens are prohibited from joining the Commando, Sister,> her brother, Dan Huun, pointed out.

<These are not normal times,> Bao Sen said to Azarin, answering her brother but not acknowledging any authority with him either. <While you were gone, it was Huntresses who stepped forward to defend our village. Was it wrong for us to do so?>

<No,> Azarin answered immediately. <It was not.> He paused for a moment. <But your brother is right,> he said at last. <Vixens cannot be commandos by Imperial decree.>

Bao Sen's tail whipped about angrily, and her ears folded downward into her head, but Azarin was not finished.

<Which means I have no authority to give you commands,> he said.

Bao Sen saw the opening the captain was giving her and was smart enough to seize on it.

<You could, however, offer us your advice and make *suggestions*,> she told him. <Surely, there are tasks we could take upon ourselves for the good of Pelle.>

<I would be honored to offer my advice, Bao Sen,> Azarin replied. <For instance, I would tell you how beneficial it would be to

Pelle to have scouts placed in hiding along the banks of the Odoro River who can warn us if the enemy tries to make a crossing.>

<That *would* be quite beneficial to the village,> Bao Sen agreed.

<I would also note how *convenient* it would be if I had more commandos at my disposal instead of needing to break off a corporalship to escort and protect evacuees on their way to the mountain sanctuary,> he continued. <As most of the threats they would face would be wild animals, I very much wish more of my commandos were experienced hunters.>

Bao Sen's ears twitched. She remembered killing the *yarl* that had attacked them on their return from the sanctuary. It wasn't just busy work Azarin was offering her. <Then I would suggest to you that such a thing would not be necessary as so many Huntresses with experience on that trail would be accompanying the evacuees.>

<Then I would be relieved,> Azarin concluded.

The commandos and Huntresses watched this byplay, fixated by how casually the two leaders were skirting around Imperial edicts.

<I regret that we may not join your commando,> Bao Sen said in faux disappointment. <However, I have just realized there are other tasks we must do to keep us busy.> She bowed to Azarin. <Thank you for your time and patience.>

Azarin bowed back. <And thank you for your courageous offer of assistance.>

With that, Bao Sen turned and walked back to the group of Huntresses waiting for her in the tall grass. As they began to walk away, they each disappeared one by one until there was absolutely no sign that any of them had even been there.

Tasshas cleared his throat. <My mother would have admired your diplomacy, Captain,> he complimented.

<If only every difference were so easily resolved,> Azarin replied.

* * *

Alacea knelt before the small statue that sat off in the corner of the temple's hall of prayer and raised the palms of her hands to either side of her head. She had spent the last hour praying to the various Va'Shen gods, searching for wisdom, patience, guidance, mercy and hope for her village during this time of crisis.

It had been a few hours since her *Tesho* had left the temple, and she knew he must by now be travelling with his commando north. That was why, at the end of her prayers for her community, she came to this statue for a final prayer.

The statue on the purple wooden pedestal was perhaps only a foot high and showed a vixen in ornate robes, her lips hidden behind a fan and her hair suspended in the air to her right as if the vixen had just completed a spin. An orb made of green stone was fixed behind her head, representing the moon that was her kingdom.

Alacea had chosen the goddess Nareana for this last prayer. As a dancer and the bride of the Va'Shen god of war Odorin, the priestess felt an affinity with this particular goddess.

<Nareana, please hear my prayer,> Alacea said aloud. <My *Tesho* goes to war alongside yours. Please keep him safe. And I ask that you return him to Pelle as soon as you possibly can.>

<Na'Sha,> Sho Nan's voice called quietly from the door. <The Overlord is here to see you.>

Alacea paused for a moment, her eyes remaining firmly shut.

<I fear you may have taken my words too literally,> she continued speaking to Nareana. <But I thank you all the same.> She bowed and put her hands and her forehead on the floor in front of her. <Blessed be the Gods.>

Rising to her feet, she turned and found Sho Nan silently waiting for her. The other Mikorin waited for the Na'Sha to walk by her and fell into step behind her without a word.

Alacea walked toward the main hall, her gait faster than normal, forcing Sho Nan to walk faster to keep up. She found the Ranger captain waiting for her. His lips curled up in a smile as she approached.

She bowed to him. <*Tesho*,> she said uncertainly. <I thought you were to head north.>

<Yes,> he said, hurriedly bowing back to her. <Change. Not leave.>

Alacea's ears fluttered happily at this. Nareana had heard her prayer and had granted her mercy, it seemed.

But, somehow, that didn't seem right.

<What change?> she asked, her ears slowing to a stop.

Ben took a breath and considered the alien woman carefully, trying to find a way to word the situation both tactfully and in Va'Shen.

<Grand Overlord need time to gather fighters to him,> he told her. <Grand Overlord tell us to fight here, make Dark Ones slow, to gather fighters to him more.>

Alacea's tail went slack and fell to the floor.

<You... You are going to fight the Dark Ones?> she asked him. <Here? *Alone*?>

<Yes,> Ben said with a nod. When Alacea didn't reply immediately, he pressed on. <Good thing,> he told her. <Now I have wagons. Can take village to hiding place in mountain. Please tell Kasshas. Will start move soon when as he is say ready.>

Ben had expected Alacea to be relieved, perhaps even jubilant. With the Rangers staying behind, she now had access to several vehicles and drivers to shuttle her people to safety. But the eyes that looked up at him were not filled with happiness, but fear.

<Bad thing?> he asked her.

She stared at him, her face and eyes expressionless even as her tail sped up at her back.

<No,> she finally said. <You have the gratitude of our community.> She ended this statement with a bow, and he returned it.

<Much to do,> he told her. <Dark Ones be here in day or days.>

<Yes,> she replied dully. <Yes.> She cleared her throat. <I shall speak to the Chieftain immediately. Will you also be able to move the refugees as well?>

<We will move until movement is not able anymore,> he promised her.

<Thank you, Overlord,> she said, her tone much more formal than before. <Then, please, go with our prayers.>

Ben paused for a moment before saying anything, his eyes scanning Alacea's face and ears for some hint of what she was thinking or feeling.

<I see you soon again,> he promised her.

<Yes,> she said.

He cleared his throat awkwardly and cocked his head toward the door. <I will go to now.>

He gave her a bow and started out the door. Alacea stood rooted to the spot, her eyes watching him as he left. She barely perceived Sho Nan coming to stand next to her.

<Your farewells were the kind that make poets weep,> she commented dryly.

Alacea said nothing in response to the jibe, and Sho Nan's ears pointed downward ever so slightly.

<Na'Sha?> she asked. <Are you well?>

<What if he dies, Sho Nan?> Alacea asked her, the priestess's voice almost a whisper.

The temple chef regarded her friend carefully. It had only been days since they had lost one of their closest friends. Now Alacea faced the prospect of losing her *Tesho*.

<Then the Gods will care for him until you see him again,> Sho Nan told her, trying to say something that she knew Alacea herself would say in her place. <The Overlord has proven himself a capable warrior,> she added confidently. <I doubt the Gods will call for him so quickly.>

<May it be so,> Alacea replied, looking down at the floor. <Come,> she said, turning to head back into the temple. <There is much to do.>

Chapter 7

<You! *Motherfucker!* Come here!>

The only word Ramirez picked up from the shouting was "motherfucker," and, almost out of habit, he pointed at himself with a questioning look.

The NCO had come to Pelle's square to check to see how the evacuation was going and see if the troops assisting the Va'Shen needed anything. Of course, he managed to arrive in the middle of some situation of which he knew nothing and was now being dragged into it. It was a typical situation for an NCO.

A specialist stood near the back of one of the trucks being used to ferry Va'Shen and gave Ramirez a "help me" look. The other characters involved he knew quite well. One of them, a tall older vixen with deep auburn hair stood in the back of the truck, pointing and bickering with a much younger vixen standing on the ground below, yelling back up at her.

It was the older vixen that had called him over, and it only took a quick moment to realize why.

<Alzoria,> he said to the younger Va'Shen woman before looking up and giving a quick, casual bow to the older woman. <Alzoria's mom. What paint and slippery does the woodshed require?>

<Tell her to get in this wagon right now, motherfucker!> Alzoria's mother ordered the Ranger.

Ramirez turned to Alzoria for further explanation.

<I have told my mother,> Alzoria began as calmly as she could, though her folded ears told him just how pissed she was, <...that you and the village need me here.>

"That is so sweet," Ramirez told her with a wide grin. He followed this up by grabbing the vixen by the waist and lifting her up toward her mother. "Now get in the fucking truck."

Alzoria's mother reached for her, but the Huntress screamed and squirmed out of his grasp until she was standing on the ground again. <No! I'm going to stay and help you fight! You need my help!> "Stay! Fight! Like last time!"

"Alzoria, you got captured last time!" he pointed out.

"You capture first!" she shot back.

"That's... true," Ramirez conceded. "But you're going to the mountain with your mom." He grabbed her by the waist again and lifted her into the truck. This time, her mother grabbed her before she could squirm away.

"Wait!" she yelled. "DERP! You need DERP!"

Ramirez snorted. "Lady, I am the *king* of 'derp.'"

Alzoria looked at him in confusion, sure that there was a mistranslation somewhere. Her ears popped up as she realized what it was.

"No! Terp! You need *terp!* For talking smack to the bitches!"

This last point gave the Ranger pause. The captain and the lieutenant could speak Va'Shen. Mrs. Gibson could understand some English, but he'd never heard her speak it. As someone who could speak both languages, Alzoria had been invaluable to them in the past. With more refugees flooding north, she really could be useful.

<No!> Alzoria's mother cried, sensing where the conversation was going. <No! Motherfucker! You tell her no!>

"You know," Ramirez sighed at the older vixen in English, "I really want to believe you don't know what that word means, but you just keep using it correctly..." He took a breath and bit his lip, thinking hard.

"Okay, fine!" he said, giving up. He reached up for her. "Come on," he groaned in defeat.

Alzoria's ears fluttered excitedly, and she hopped down into the human's arms.

"But you stay with *me*!" he ordered. "You understand me?"

"Betchar ass!" she replied in excitement.

<Alzoria!> the vixen's mother cried. <You come back up here! Right now!>

<Alzoria be good,> Ramirez promised. He leaned toward the specialist. "Show me taillights, Specialist," he muttered quietly. The other soldier ran to the front of the truck as Ramirez continued pacifying the angry vixen. <I keep close!> he promised. <Touch her many much all times!>

The vixen's mother was just about to leap out of the back of the truck, murder in her eyes, when the vehicle lurched forward and off down the road.

Ramirez turned to Alzoria, whose ear fur was standing firmly up in embarrassment.

<You good?> he asked.

Alzoria looked away from him, unsure if she should ask whether or not he realized he just told her mother he was going to "touch her much."

* * *

<Most of the refugees have been moved already,> Dosara reported to the *aderen*. With Hestean dead, the role of temple representative at the *aderen* fell to the next in seniority, who happened to be Pelle's Mikorin Donya'Tal. The aqua-haired vixen was still unused to speaking in front of so many people. She was much better at dealing with children.

She was finding, however, that the two could be remarkably similar.

<Why?> Ketoro asked from his position halfway down the oval from her. Most of the rest of the attendees had let the piece of information go by without concern, but now that the tod was making a fuss, there were more ears pointed at her. <Why are we prioritizing the refugees over our own people?> he elaborated.

Dosara's ears folded down. Normally, when a kit asked her such a question, she could tell them "because I said so." But having to constantly justify the Mikorin's actions as if she was the one making these decisions by herself was frustrating.

Before she could reply, a calm voice came from one end of the oval.

<Because most of our people need time to gather their things and secure their homes and livestock,> Alacea told him. <The refugees already have everything they have left on their backs and can move immediately.>

<Many villagers from Garan'Sel say they are prepared to move immediately,> Ketoro replied defensively.

<Then they may queue in the village square at their convenience,> Alacea told him.

Normally, a Na'Sha would not speak on behalf of the Mikorin, but with everything the priestesses had been asked to do for the past few days, the Mikorin were exhausted. Dosara was also new to her role, and the learning curve was unfortunately very steep. As a result, Alacea felt compelled to jump in and assist.

She was not immune to the stress, however, and there was a slight bend in her ears as she continued.

<And yet, they refuse to do so,> she pointed out.

<Because the leader of our commando refuses to provide escorts for the wagons,> Ketoro argued.

<Because there is no *need* for commando escorts as the threat is still to the south,> Alacea countered, her voice flavored with bitterness.

The rest of the *aderen* members watched the back-and-forth nervously, their tails moving awkwardly from side to side as they waited to see who would lose their temper first.

<The escorts are not needed to protect our people from these so-called invaders,> Ketoro continued. <They are needed to ensure the Dark Ones do not attempt any trickery of their own.>

<That is preposterous and insulting!> Alacea shot back. <The Overlord's troops are taking time and resources away from their preparations for battle in order to assist in our evacuation.>

<And you would have us believe they do this out of their own sense of altruism?> Ketoro asked. <That they do this even though there is no benefit to them?> He paused, and his ears folded downward and toward the priestess. <Or did you conduct some manner of transaction to purchase this "altruism?">

Alacea's ears popped toward the ceiling in surprise at the accusation. Her hands closed into fists, and her ears slowly bent down and dug into the top of her skull.

<Perhaps we should recess for now...> Yasuren began to suggest, but Alacea cut her off.

<No,> she said quietly, her voice covered with a layer of ice that told everyone there just how angry she was. She looked straight at Ketoro, who took a breath at the intensity of her gaze. <There are too many tasks of importance we must work through to waste time on a recess for such a *small* and *despicable* thing.>

The rest of the *aderen* was silent at the Na'Sha's words. They all, almost as a single entity, turned and looked at Ketoro.

The tod seemed to understand he had gone too far. <Na'Sha, I...>

<Let me, as the embodiment of our community, share something with all of you,> she interrupted him, her voice still quiet and frosty. <The community is *frustrated* by the actions of this *aderen*. This *aderen*, when faced with crisis, erupted into violence and death because it could not peacefully resolve the community's issues as is its purpose. This *aderen* insisted on letting go unpunished tods who attacked a young vixen on the flimsiest of excuses.>

The assembled tods and vixens looked downward in shame, their tails moving back and forth as their Na'Sha, their *community*, chastised them.

But Alacea wasn't finished.

<This *aderen*,> she continued, <Insisted on doing *nothing* to safeguard the community as a vicious and terrible enemy crept toward us, and all of these things were done because this *aderen* insists on *disobeying our Emperor*.>

<Na'Sha,> Kasshas tried to interject, <Such a charge...>

Alacea rose to her feet and looked the chieftain square in the eye. <We were commanded to cooperate with the Dark Ones!> she cried. <That was *His* order! The Dark Ones in Garan'Sel were evil! No one, not even the Overlord and his fighters, contest this! But it was the Emperor who ordered us to endure that evil! To endure the unendurable! Who are *you* to defy our Emperor?!> She looked at Ketoro. <Who are *you* to say you know better?!>

Several Va'Shen, mostly those lower ranked and younger aides, sitting behind the *aderen* members, crouched lower and covered their ears in shame. Only the strongest of the council's members were able to endure the priestess's tirade without doing the same.

<And yet here,> Alacea continued, <In a place where we have been *blessed* by the Gods, where Jemenista Na'Sha had convinced them to show us enough mercy and grace to send us an Overlord who is *not* evil, whose soul is closer to our own, you spit on that mercy and grace! You slap your tails to the ground and look away from it so that you can feel better about the disgrace of losing a war!>

Dead silence.

<I am the Na'Sha,> she told them quietly. <I reflect the will and spirit of our community. And I tell you right now: Perform the roles the community has assigned you. Obey your Emperor. Protect your community. Or the community will cast you aside and replace you with others who will!>

She sat back down, but her gaze remained on all of them.

<We shall recess,> Kasshas declared quietly. <A *short* recess,> he added, looking to Alacea. <And when we return, we shall perform our roles as the community requires.>

Everyone in the room rose. The members of the *aderen* filed out, but the aides remained an extra moment. Looking to Alacea, who had remained in her seat, they all, singly at first but then as a group, bowed to the priestess. Then, without a word, the lower ranked tods and vixens left the room.

Alacea took a deep breath and looked up at the ceiling.

<I shamed them,> she said to herself in self-reproach.

<They shamed themselves,> someone else corrected her. Looking to the door, Alacea saw Sho Nan standing there. <The entire temple heard you,> she told the Na'Sha.

Alacea closed her eyes in frustration. <I am sorry,> she said. <What I said...>

<Was said well,> Sho Nan told her. <You are the community, Alacea. Sometimes the community must make its voice heard lest its leaders forget that they are there, that their lives are at the center of their leaders' purpose, not the other way around.>

<How did you get so wise, Sho Nan?> Alacea asked her, her ears slowly twitching a smile.

<If wisdom could be found in the bottom of a stewpot, every Ya'Jahar would become a Na'Sha,> Sho Nan told her.

<You will be a wonderful Na'Sha someday,> Alacea told her quietly.

Sho Nan seemed surprised by the statement. <I would never aspire to such a thing. And I do not need to. I already serve one of the greatest Na'Shas in our history.>

Alacea rose to her feet and started toward the door. <That is too bad,> she said as she stopped in front of the cook. <I believe

watching Sho Nan Na'Sha arguing with the Gods would be one of the greatest spectacles in the universe.>

The tips of Sho Nan's ears twitched ever so slightly.

<They would lose,> she told Alacea.

Alacea reached out and hugged her friend before turning and walking out the door.

* * *

The light breeze that had welcomed him when he stepped out his door that morning had become a somewhat stronger wind by the time Azarin arrived at the top of the hill overlooking Pelle. The view from that vantage point was breathtaking, the entirety of the village spread before him was the perfect spot to show someone, at a glance, the beauty of his village.

It was for that reason that the Mikorin had chosen to bury their dead there. Any troubled soul could look up from their graves and see the community they had worked so hard to maintain.

Most humans would not recognize the hilltop as a graveyard. It was not fenced and there were no rows of tombstones. It was simply a field that would be left to return the bodies of the Mikorin to nature. Their souls were in the Glade now, and their bodies fed the land as one last service to the village.

Even so, Azarin had no difficulty finding the small rectangle of recently-disturbed land where the two most-recent deaths had been interred. Standing before it, he bowed deeply, his eyes closed.

<*Myorin*,> he said in greeting. He looked away for a moment, ashamed of himself for coming here to disturb Hestean's rest like this. <I need guidance,> he admitted.

There was no response, of course. No blue-tinged ghostly visage appeared to guide him. He did not expect one. He just thought that if he came here and spoke as if she were in front of him, he might be able to divine what she might have said to him.

<When I was imprisoned, I came to believe that the Gods had a hand in the events that led to our release,> he admitted. <I trusted to faith and was rewarded. But now... I do not know if I can do so again.>

Why not?

The question came to him in Hestean's melodious voice, and his ears twitched.

<Because I cannot comprehend why they would have such faith in *me*,> he admitted aloud. <I did not ask for this role. I never coveted it.>

The Gods put you in a place and time for their own ends, not yours, Hestean's voice told him. *If you do not covet a role they wish for you to play, then they must thrust it upon you.*

<But why?> he asked. <Why me? What do they want me to do?> His tail slapped the dirt behind him in frustration. <I wish... I wish I had taken you years ago,> he confessed. <Taken you and run away. If I had...>

Then you would not be here now where the Gods need you to be, Hestean's voice pointed out in his head. *There is no needless action by the Gods. All things happen for a reason. If it must be you, then it must be because there is something that* only you *could do.*

<Nonsense!> he growled. <There is nothing special about me. *Any* tod could do my job.>

If that is true, Hestean's voice replied, *Then it is not a matter of something you* could *do, but something that only you* would *do.*

Azarin looked away and down the hill at his village. Clouds were beginning to move over the area, signaling approaching rain. The wind was picking up again.

Would anyone else have trusted Bankipson in your place? Hestean's question was pointed. It was true. He had seen the Gods' work in that situation himself. No one else would have even spoken to him were it not for his connection to the Na'Sha. And being elected captain was what allowed him to act on it. As a corporal, no one would have believed his claims.

If that *was* the difference, then the Gods had put him there to act on it because no one else would.

He went to his knees and bowed, his head brushing the red grass.

<Thank you, *Myorin*,> he whispered. <I will see you again soon. And then forever.>

The wind blew at his back as we walked back down the hill. He knew what he needed to do now.

* * *

BA-WHUMP!

The office shook ever so slightly as the mortar outside lobbed another smoke shell high into the air on its way to the far side of the bridge where the aliens were expected to appear. With a little luck and coordination, Ben's mortar team would be able to pre-register their 120mm weapon with enough fidelity to put a rain of jagged heated steel right on top of the invaders when they arrived.

They had been forced to wait two days before attempting to pre-register. During that time, a flow of refugees from other villages had been using that bridge, and while the fact that the bridge was clear now was good for the mortar team, it also signaled something very disturbing.

It meant there were no more Va'Shen between the bridge and the invaders. And that meant they were coming this way.

Ben looked at the crude map one of his more artistic-minded Rangers had drawn on some butcher paper that showed a more detailed view of the area between the FOB and the bridge. X's marked areas where Senior Chief's SeaBees had placed improvised explosives and what few claymore mines they had left, turning the road that connected the southern bridge to the one that led north to the capital into a briar patch hellscape just waiting to happen.

Northwest of the southern bridge, represented by a few crudely drawn houses, was Pelle. Just north of Pelle was a square with the letters "FOB" printed within it. Northeast of the FOB with a road running between them was the northern bridge. Other roads were marked by simple lines of magic marker going northwest, west and east from Pelle. The road running east intersected the bridge road and continued east, forming a cross junction.

Between the southern bridge and Pelle lay a thick forest. In Va'Shen, the wooded area's name translated to "Black Forest," and this name was written there. Beneath it, written in italics, and most likely by Ramirez, were the words, "where we get our ham."

Ben bit his lower lip as he studied the map. What he wanted, what he hoped for, was that the invaders would cross the river and head directly north for the capital. If they did, the mines and a series of ambushes and tiger traps would slow them down. If they followed the pattern they had established thus far, however, they would turn toward Pelle. Ben had established defense lines in the Black Forest to deter them from doing so. Since the invaders had not encountered any heavy resistance so far, it was his hope that, upon doing so in the Black Forest, they would choose to bypass the village entirely and concentrate on moving north where his Rangers could shred them at their leisure.

And yet, he was still troubled by it. A human commander, even a Va'Shen commander, would likely do exactly that; forgo the strategically worthless village to avoid wasting men and materiel and head for the main goal. But these weren't humans or Va'Shen. He had no idea what motivated them, and that bothered him. As he had done with the Va'Shen several times before, he could just shrug his shoulders and assume it was impossible to know what goes on in an alien's mind. But while that was often true, it also ran the risk of being the lazy way out.

They *had* some motivation. But what?

BA-WHUMP!

The office shook again, but he didn't even notice.

<Brother.>

Ben jumped at the sound of the voice and spun around. Azarin stood in the doorway, a sheathed dagger in his left hand.

A few months ago, such a sight would have resulted in Ben dropping his hand down toward his holstered sidearm. But although his heart was beating a little faster, his hand didn't move.

Instead, he gave a slight bow, Azarin doing the same with him.

<Azarin,> Ben said in greeting. <You need things?> he asked. He didn't want to usher his alien brother-in-law out, but he also didn't have time to chat. Knowing Azarin as he did, however, he knew the commando leader wouldn't be here without a good reason.

The eyepatched captain stepped toward Ben wordlessly and stopped a few paces from him. Then, to Ben's shock, the tod knelt down on one knee and held the simple dagger out to him with both hands.

<I am Azarin,> the tod pronounced. <Captain of the Fourth Commando of the First Prince's Storm Rifles. I submit my commando to your leadership to use as you will.>

Ben stood there, unsure of what was happening although he understood his brother-in-law's words well enough. His hands did not reach for the dagger, and Azarin continued to kneel there like a statue.

<Why you do?> Ben asked him.

Azarin took a breath as the potential implications of what he was doing came to him for the hundredth time. What he was doing was essentially *giving* Bankipson the lives of his commandos as one would a Va'Shen field cornet. And like most Va'Shen oaths, it wasn't something done in half-measures or easily retracted. Once Bankipson took this dagger from him, he would have the right to lead his commando however he wished. If he ordered the Pelle commando to stand unarmed, shoulder to shoulder, and allow the invaders to shoot them, they would be obligated to do so. And should any of them refuse, it would be Azarin's responsibility to shoot them for insubordination on Bankipson's behalf.

But he knew this was the right thing to do. If his brother-in-law's forces fell to the invaders, the only thing standing between them and Pelle... and then the capital... was his commando. It made absolutely no sense to wait and hope the humans triumphed when the additional combat power his commando possessed could increase the chances of achieving that victory by working with them.

No other Va'Shen on the planet would ever consider doing such a thing.

And that's how Azarin knew it was the right thing to do.

<Take it,> Azarin told him. <Add my commandos to your forces. Let us fight with you. Lead me, Brother.>

Ben didn't know what to say. He knew from his experiences with Va'Shen commandos that what Azarin was doing was a huge deal, one that could lead to severe blowback from other Va'Shen even in his own village. His first instinct was to find a diplomatic way to refuse while letting his brother-in-law save face.

But...

A hundred Va'Shen commandos could make a big difference in what he was about to face. The intelligence he had seen said the standard 6.8mm ball ammunition in their M-31s were all but ineffective against this enemy at normal or long ranges. Some Va'Shen commandos with hardlight rifles could turn that around for them. Their ability to move stealthily at all times of the day would also be a huge advantage in ambushes.

He really wanted those commandos. He *needed* them.

Reaching out, he grasped the dagger and took it from the tod.

<I take,> Ben told him solemnly. <With much gratitude.> When Azarin stood up again, Ben continued. <You will lead them?> he asked.

<Yes,> Azarin replied.

Ben smiled and reached out, putting his hand on the tod's shoulder.

<I am glad you will with us fight,> he said.

* * *

<UNACCEPTABLE! ABSOLUTELY UNACCEPTABLE!>

Va'Shen rarely screamed. Their sensitive ears made doing so both unnecessary and painful. But given what Azarin had done, he could hardly blame Ketoro for the volume.

Sitting across the table from him in the mayor's office, Kasshas and Yasuren held their hands over their ears, their tails slapping the floor angrily. Tasshas, much more acclimated to loud noises and already partially deaf from his time in the war, did not cover his ears, but glared at the tod regardless.

<Calm yourself!> Yasuren snapped at the old miner.

<I will not 'calm' myself,> Ketoro shot back at her. He pointed at Azarin. <This tod has handed the lives of the community's commando to the Dark Ones!>

They all looked across the table at Azarin, who looked back at them with serene ears.

<Yes,> he said simply. <As captain that is my right.>

<Why did you do this, *Captain* Azarin?> Kasshas asked him.

<And why did you not tell us you intended to do this?!> Ketoro added.

<I did it because it increases the chance that the invaders will be defeated or deterred,> Azarin said calmly. He turned to Ketoro. <And I didn't tell you because you would have said 'no.'>

In the face of Azarin's unflappable response, Ketoro turned back to Kasshas and Yasuren. <An outrage,> he told them, trying hard to maintain his composure. Unlike his predecessor, Ketoro was not cut out to be a community leader. Where Goto could suppress his emotions when necessary, Ketoro more often succumbed to them. That was why, despite being older than Goto, the miner had been willing, even thankful, to allow Goto to represent the miners.

But now Goto and his politically savvy niece were gone, and the task of representing the Garan'Sel villagers had fallen mostly to him.

<Surely, you do not agree with what he has done?> Ketoro demanded of them.

Kasshas looked at Azarin, his ears bent slightly forward. <I admit,> he said, <I find the wisdom in this decision... difficult to comprehend.>

<It is not 'difficult to comprehend' that this young carpenter would prefer to abdicate his duty to his alien brother-in-law than risk his own tail performing it himself!> Ketoro spat.

<Mind your tone,> Tasshas spoke for the first time, his ears pressed against the top of his head as he growled bitterly at the older tod. <Our captain has faced greater dangers than you ever saw crawling around under the dirt!>

<It has been done,> Kasshas said, holding a hand out to calm his son. <What do you suggest be done about it now?> he asked Ketoro.

<Obviously, this tod is unsuitable to lead our commando,> Ketoro said, puffing his chest out. <I suggest a new captain be put in his place. Perhaps the chieftain's son...>

The clumsy attempt to get his way by suggesting Tasshas be given the honor was not lost on anyone, and the chieftain's son was particularly offended. Among the rank-and-file commandos, there was no greater dishonor than to receive one's rank due to their familial connections.

<I refuse!> Tasshas announced. <Azarin is our elected captain. Not even an *aderen* has the right to overturn that election.>

<Even though he gives your lives to the Dark Ones?!> Ketoro asked incredulously.

<Yes,> Tasshas bit out.

Ketoro looked like he wanted to reach out and throttle the young tod. Azarin silently rose to his feet and bowed to Kasshas.

<If that resolves the concern, there is a great deal left to do.>

Kasshas heaved a deep sigh, knowing that he was placed in an impossible situation. Under the circumstances, there was little he could do other than allow Azarin his way. <Go with our sanction,> he told the one-eyed officer.

Tasshas got up and followed his friend out the door, leaving his parents and a screaming Ketoro behind.

<Azarin,> he began quietly as they descended the stairs. <I am your friend and will support you no matter where you lead us. That said, are you sure about this?>

Unlike with Ketoro, Azarin actually respected Tasshas's opinion, and while he *could* refuse to explain himself, he knew it was important for his friend to understand.

<The Overlord's troops will fight these invaders,> he said. <If they fall, the invaders will come straight to Pelle. One hundred poorly armed commandos will not stand against such a force. But one hundred commandos fighting with another two hundred Dark Ones may. Now is the time to mass our forces, not divide them.>

Tasshas said nothing to this, and it made Azarin suddenly insecure.

<You do not agree?> Azarin asked.

<No, what you say is sensible,> Tasshas replied.

There was something in his tone, however, that the captain picked up on.

<What is it?>

Tasshas's ears folded downward ever so slightly, perturbed by the idea that he had to put this feeling into words.

<It is a sense, Captain,> he began carefully. <That we have been led to this. It is not just me. Many of the commandos have expressed this feeling. That the Gods move us this way.>

Tasshas's words surprised Azarin. Privately, he had felt the same way, the suspicion that the Gods had touched them, nudged them in a certain direction. It was how he justified his actions in the prison camp that led to their release. He never thought that others had felt like this.

<I feel it too,> Azarin confessed.

Tasshas's ears twitched, and the tod nudged his commander with his shoulder. <Then do not worry yourself with what that Garan'Sel whore's-get says. The Gods will tell you when you are wrong. And if not, they will tell your sister, and *she* will tell you that you are wrong.>

<*That* would be a much more *familiar* feeling,> Azarin quipped, his ears twitching for the first time in far too long.

Tasshas's voice turned serious, and he looked his friend in the eye. <We would be dead now if it were not for you,> he said quietly. <What time we have now is time *you* have given us. We cannot complain when you tell us how to spend it.>

<Then,> Azarin replied quietly, <Let us make certain that it is spent well.>

Chapter 8

"Latest intel from Jamieson," Patricia announced as she walked into the admin office, a notebook in her hand. Since Ben had ordered regular intel updates, Patricia spent most of her time in the TOC where the reports came directly. "They're on the move."

Ben sat back in his chair and absorbed that statement. "Something change?" he asked. "Or did they just run out of Va'Shen villages to raid?"

"The latter," Patricia told him. "Da'Sella fell two hours ago. Same pattern. Wiped out."

"Ten miles from the bridge," Ben mulled quietly. He did some quick calculations in his head. "They can be here tomorrow morning." He looked up at Patricia. "How are the preparations up north going?"

"Not good," Patricia replied pointedly. "Apparently, our friends from Garan'Sel weren't the only ones who thought these guys might be the Great Ones. Va'Shen partisans up north have been harassing our forces as they move south. They shot down a CH-92 that was lifting a rail-gun. We lost both."

"Shit," Ben swore with a shake of his head. "What the hell is Va'Sh-Gov doing?"

"They're sending heralds north to ask the partisans to help or, at least, not shoot at us, but..." She finished by shrugging helplessly.

"Well... at least *someone's* winning," he quipped.

The conversation was interrupted by the phone on Ben's desk ringing. He picked it up and put the receiver to his ear.

"Gibson," he said.

Patricia watched as the Ranger's face scrunched up in confusion, and then his eyes went wide. Her fingers clutched the notebook worriedly.

"We'll... We'll be right there," Ben said haltingly. Whatever the person on the other end had said, it had obviously thrown him for a loop. He hung up the phone.

"Bad news?" Patricia asked him.

"I don't even know anymore," the captain confessed. "That was the TOC. Gladius Three reports movement."

"They're here already?!" the intel officer gasped.

"Not at the bridge," Ben corrected her as he stood up and grabbed his patrol cap. "East of us. Route Indigo."

"Indigo?!" Patricia cried. "They crossed the river and flanked us?!"

"No," Ben said as he started for the door. "The contacts are Va'Shen."

* * *

Before investigating the contact, Ben decided to swing by the half-constructed house Azarin had been building to see if he was there and would come with them. The house and the land around it had become a de facto military camp, and when Ben and Patricia arrived, they saw Va'Shen tents arranged in circles littered throughout the dark red grass.

The hum of hardlight rifles could be heard as they shut off the LTV's engine and got out. A hastily-thrown-together firing line had been set up against a hill nearby, and a group of about ten commandos were firing at blotchy targets that looked more like camouflage than something meant to be seen and hit.

Several commandos milling around nearby saw them approach and bowed low to them as they passed, lower than Patricia would have ever expected. She also noticed that there were quite a few more hardlight rifles slung over Va'Shen shoulders than what had been reflected in her reports to headquarters.

As she mused on this, she was suddenly brought up short when Ben stopped and bowed. While she had been distracted, Azarin had silently appeared before them and bowed in greeting.

<Brother,> Azarin said in greeting. <Welcome.>

Ben got straight to the point.

<I need you,> he said.

<Then I am yours,> Azarin replied just as pointedly.

The commando captain gave a nod to Tasshas, who had stood nearby, and the young tod started for the firing line, perhaps having received a silent order from Azarin to "take over for me." The three of them turned and silently walked back to the LTV.

<How may I serve?> Azarin asked as they climbed into the vehicle. His body was turned awkwardly to the side in the seat behind Patricia, attempting to make room for his tail.

<Many Va'Shen coming,> Ben told him. <From... er... right...>

<From the east,> Patricia supplied helpfully. <We are going to see them and ask them why they have come to here.>

<I understand,> Azarin said simply.

Since they had a few minutes during the drive, Patricia decided to bring up the question she had at the Va'Shen camp. <Find more weapons?> she asked him.

<Yes,> Azarin told her. <One of our new commandos from Garan'Sel 'found' a supply of rifles in a cave near the village. It is fortunate.>

Patricia arched an eyebrow at the statement. She wasn't sure if the Va'Shen had such a thing as air quotes, but she couldn't help but hear them around the word "found." She had a pretty good idea where those weapons had come from and at whom they had originally meant to be aimed.

<It means that we can provide thirty commandos armed with rifles,> Azarin reported. <The rest have bows or knives.>

Ben pursed his lips. Thirty was a sight better than none, but he wished it was more. He couldn't even offer U.S. weapons for the rest of his commandos since they barely had enough to arm his human troops.

<Glass?> he asked Azarin.

<Four,> the commando replied. <From that vixen's supply.>

Patricia cleared her throat nervously at the venom in Azarin's statement. She knew exactly which vixen he was referring to.

Ben took a breath while simultaneously turning down another road. He, like most human soldiers who had seen them up close, hated glassers. Now he was in the ironic position of wishing he had more of them.

He looked up and narrowed his eyes as an LTV came into view, parked across the road to block it. A Ranger in full kit was walking toward them with his hand up to get their attention. Ben stopped the vehicle and rolled down the window so the Ranger could speak to him.

"Sir, Ma'am," the Specialist said in greeting.

"What have you got, Specialist?" Ben asked.

"Seventy-three Va'Shen, Sir, along with wagons and animals," the Ranger reported. "All armed. They look like Imperial regulars."

"They have a captain?" Ben asked.

"Yes, Sir," the specialist said. "I don't speak any Va'Shen, Sir, but… I think he's asking for *you*."

As they rounded the LTV blocking the road, Ben saw a large group of Va'Shen tods milling around several large furry ox-like animals pulling wagons. They all wore similar clothing, a mix of faded red and purple tunics and trousers covered by dark purple capes. One of them, speaking with two others at the front of the group, wore a red band around his bicep, the only difference in any of the uniforms that Ben could tell. Seeing them approach, this tod, sporting short, rust colored hair, turned and moved toward them.

Ben recognized the tod at once and couldn't help but smile. As he approached, they both stopped a few meters from one another and bowed.

<Captain Turan, I bid you greetings,> Ben said before coming to his full height again.

<Captain Bankipson,> Turan returned. <It is agreeable to see you again.>

Realizing introductions were in order and the situation no longer a critical one, Ben gestured to Azarin. <I introduce to you my brother. This is Captain Azarin, Captain in captaining of Fourth Commando, One Prince Storm Rifles. Captain Azarin, this is Captain Turan. Captain in captaining of Fourth Commando Third Princess Windsabers.>

The two bowed to one another.

As much as Ben would like to have the luxury of a relaxed reunion, time was short. <Why you come?> he asked Turan.

<Captain Spring took his commando to the north,> Turan explained quickly. <Before he left, he explained to us the situation and your mission. We have come to aid you.>

Ben, Patricia and Azarin were all brought up short. When he realized the Va'Shen were commandos, his first thought was that Va'Sh-Gov had recalled them to fight the invaders, but if what Turan said was true, they were acting on their own.

<Um... Why you do?> Ben asked.

Turan answered Ben but faced Azarin. <Kar'El owes a debt to Pelle that can never be fully paid,> he said. <We will help you defend it.>

Azarin's ears popped up to the sky at the statement. He had heard about what happened with the Kar'El commando and even knew that the episode had helped in a small way to get his tods released from detention. But he had never imagined that it would lead to such a thing.

He bowed low to Turan. <You have my...>

Before he could finish, a sudden and violent blast of wind rushed out of the trees and struck them, knocking several of the commandos down. A second later, a monstrous thunderclap blasted their eardrums.

Ben wasn't sure when it happened, but he suddenly found himself being helped to his feet by a Ranger. Another was nearby, scanning the tree-line with his weapon when he lowered his rifle and started to look up into the distance.

The Ranger captain followed his gaze and saw a white mushroom cloud rising into the violet sky south of them. It seemed to climb impossibly high, and Ben couldn't help but be in awe of it.

"Nuked! We got nuked!" one of the Ranger cried on the verge of panic.

"It's not a nuke!" Ben yelled at him. He turned and helped Patricia to her feet.

"How do you know?" she winced, her hand going to her head and checking for blood.

"There was no flash," he explained. "It's not a nuke."

"Holy fuck," one of the Rangers remarked.

<Gods,> Turan whispered as he looked at it. <Gods.>

Azarin turned to Ben. <One of your weapons?> he shouted.

Ben shook his head, momentarily forgetting that the gesture meant nothing to his brother. <No,> he added. <We have none here. Something different.> Azarin looked at him in confusion and Ben realized the explosion must have temporarily, he hoped, deafened him.

It only took a few seconds for him to realize what had just happened.

"That was their ship," he told Patricia.

"Oh, shit," she breathed.

<Ship,> he told Azarin and Turan. <Come!>

Together, they all ran back to the LTV.

* * *

"I still can't get through," Patricia grumbled as she hung up the phone. "Line is busy."

"Every line is busy right now," Ben told her as he leaned against his desk. They had hurried back to the FOB in the hopes of finding out what happened from the JOC, but there was no way for them to get through via the phone.

"But you're *sure* it's not a nuke, right?" Patricia asked nervously.

"When a nuke goes off there's a flash of light and heat," Ben told her. "This was big, but I'm pretty sure it's not a nuke."

It was a good thing too. At this range, a big enough nuclear detonation would, at the very least, blind anyone unlucky enough to have been facing it at the time it went off.

Ben looked over at the other side of the office where Azarin, Turan and a few other tods were huddled together. Fletcher had looked them over after the blast, checking to see if there was any permanent damage to their hearing. Fortunately, while the Va'Shen's hearing was very sensitive, their auditory organs weren't as fragile as those on a human. So, while the sound hurt the fox people immensely at the time, their hearing had returned after a few minutes.

Pelle, of course, was in a full-blown panic. The shockwave broke every window in the village and caused a few injuries. Smoke from burning trees in the south had risen and moved north, darkening the sky over Pelle. Many of the villagers had dropped to their knees and raised their hands, praying to their Gods as if the end times had come, and, in fairness, Ben couldn't blame them. It sure looked like it.

When the phone rang, it caught the two humans by surprise, and it wasn't until the third ring that Patricia snatched it up.

"Sector 13, Lieutenant Kim, this is an unsecured line," the young woman recited quickly. She looked up at Ben and held the phone out to him. "Colonel Hopper."

"Put it on the speaker," Ben ordered and pointed to the group of Va'Shen nearby. "And translate for them."

Patricia hit a button on the phone and hung the receiver on the cradle before walking over to the Va'Shen.

"This is Captain Gibson," Ben announced.

"Colonel Hopper," the gruff voice came back. "I suppose I don't have to tell you why I called."

"No, Sir," Ben told him. "The shockwave blew out every window on the FOB and in the village. Can you tell us what happened?"

"We sent a force up from Camp Wagner," Hopper explained. "Their mission was to secure the alien crash site in case they tried to double back and then push north to harass the aliens and, hopefully, crush them between us."

"Something went wrong," Ben concluded.

"We don't know what," Hopper admitted. "Last we heard from them, they were moving toward the crash site and hadn't sighted any targets. Satellite imagery shows them moving in and establishing a perimeter. Then the whole place blew. Maybe the ship was boobytrapped, maybe they touched something they shouldn't have, or maybe it was just more damaged than we thought and this was going to happen regardless. But, whatever it was, we haven't heard anything from them since. We're assuming up here that they're all KIA."

"Copy all, Sir," Ben said through gritted teeth. So far, the new Dark Ones were undefeated, and the scoreboard against the humans was just getting worse. "Any good news?"

"The detonation wasn't nuclear," Hopper assured him. "So, no radiation danger. But the blast was strong enough to throw enough debris into the air to make aerial recon in your area impossible for awhile."

"Well, that sounds... awful," Ben replied.

"What's your status?" Hopper asked him.

"We're ready to hit them at the Odoro River crossing and have mined the road north with everything we've got," Ben reported. "I don't know if we can stop them, but their trip won't be pleasant. For good news, we have two Va'Shen commando units who've volunteered to fight with us. That'll give us a little more to work with."

"You got Va'Shen signing up with you?" Hopper asked incredulously. "God*damn,* son, we should have sent you north!"

"Thank you, Sir... I think," Ben said.

"We'll call when we can get a recon plane back into your area," the colonel told him. "In the meantime, let your people know we're counting on them, and we're grateful."

"Thank you, Sir," Ben said automatically. He knew Hopper well enough to know that he meant it and that it wasn't just something they taught you to say at War College. "Out here."

He hung up the phone and turned to the group of Va'Shen. Along with Azarin and Turan were three other tods, each the de facto captain of whatever remained of their villages' commandos after the alien attacks.

<You understand of that?> he asked them.

<Yes, Brother,> Azarin replied. <It means they no longer have a way to retreat.>

<Yes,> Ben told him. <They will be ready for fight.>

The Ranger captain looked away for a moment as Patricia approached, and when he looked back, he found the five tods deep in a spirited conversation. They were talking so quickly, however, that he couldn't catch more than a few words.

"What's that about?" he asked Patricia, nodding in the Va'Shens' direction.

"They're trying to figure out who should be in overall command," she said.

"They're fighting over who gets to be in charge?" Ben asked, somewhat surprised. He realized he shouldn't have been. The way he understood it, Va'Shen elected their leaders at the company level, but when more than one company worked together, the Imperial Army would send a general officer down to lead them. That wasn't happening in this case, so the tods were now trying to fit their situation into a template they knew and understood.

"Not the way you're thinking," Patricia assured him. She nodded toward Turan. "Turan is telling Azarin that he should be in command because they are defending Pelle, and he knows the land better. Azarin thinks Turan should be in charge because he has the greater number of armed troops. The others are agreeing with Turan because Azarin also has more combat experience."

Ben bit the inside of his cheek. He had seen Azarin do things like this before. The tod didn't like being in command, and Ben could see why. He had lost people under his command too, and that responsibility weighs on you, especially if you think you're not qualified to begin with.

But Azarin *was* qualified. He was able to make hard decisions and act quickly when necessary. It was hard, sometimes, to remember that the tod was a carpenter and a draftee rather than a professional soldier. Maybe it was because of the way he carried himself, or maybe because Ben could see some of his own pain in the Va'Shen's eye.

Did he have nightmares? Ben wondered suddenly if his brother-in-law ever dreamed of fighting a human soldier while his commandos died all around him, forced to kill the same man night after night. He knew what that could do to someone, how it could sap at your confidence, make you question whether the things you've done in the past were right or not.

<I think Turan correct,> he suddenly announced.

The commando officers turned to him, surprised that he would interject like this, but not disagreeing with him either.

Azarin looked at him, not sure if he felt betrayed by his brother or gratitude for the alien man's confidence.

<Azarin should lead,> Ben said. <My vote.>

<Then it is decided,> Turan announced. The other captains made noises of agreement. <For the many reasons stated, Azarin will act as field cornet.>

Azarin took a breath and let it out, unsure of his fellow captains' decision. It was a far sight different from when he worked with the other captains in the detention facility.

<I will accept the duties,> he finally said. <But I will not accept the title of field cornet.>

Ben rolled his eyes and opened his top desk drawer. After a few moments of looking, he found what he was searching for and approached Azarin with it. The tod was surprised when the man took him by the front of his monpei and stuck a small pin of two vertical silver bars there.

<What is this?> he asked.

<This so my fighters know accept your commands,> Ben told him seriously. It was a standard practice that when foreign militaries worked with the U.S., they would wear a patch with their equivalent U.S. rank insignia on their uniform, mostly so that young enlisted soldiers would see it and know they were supposed to salute. He had been saving these bars for when Patricia eventually promoted to captain, but he would just grab another pair the next time he went to Jamieson.

Azarin and Turan looked shocked by the Ranger captain's words. They had both assumed and accepted that they and their commandos would fall under the overlord and obey his orders. Neither anticipated that he would grant them any kind of authority over his own people.

Ben hoped this demonstration of faith would help Azarin realize what the rest of them already knew: That he was the right tod to lead the Va'Shen contingent.

Azarin looked at the bars for a moment before turning to the other captains.

<Muster the commando at our base,> he told them. <We will prepare for combat.>

* * *

Alacea watched as the human vehicle belched black smoke and started down the road away from the temple. Another sat idling nearby as Kastia oversaw the loading of wounded Va'Shen into it. Aside from the truck and Kastia, the village around her was now almost completely silent. Broken glass littered the roads where the shockwave had blasted out every window in the village.

Looking to the south, her ears folded downward at the sight of the darkened sky, the white smoke rising from the fires lit by the explosion and the flaming debris that had been launched into the forests for miles in every direction. It was as if a curtain had been drawn over the sky, blocking much of the light from Bellatrix.

She had not been sure what the battle between her and her *Tesho*'s people and the Dark Ones would look like. The fighting had not even started yet, and already it looked like a punishment from the Gods.

<Na'Sha.>

She turned and found Kastia approaching her, her face lined with worry and her eyes displaying just how exhausted she was. The healer had been working nearly non-stop since the refugees had begun to arrive in their village.

<There are fourteen more in the temple that cannot be moved,> she told Alacea. <They are in a fragile condition and will not survive a trip into the mountains.>

As Alacea absorbed this, she turned and looked up at Sho Nan, who was standing at the temple's doorway. <Have the others left?> she asked.

<Yes, Na'Sha,> Sho Nan replied. <We are the last Mikorin. The other village healers and the injured that Kastia speak of remain inside. I have stocked provisions and water for them.>

<Good,> Alacea said. She turned back to Kastia. <Then it is time for you to leave, Kastia. You will take this wagon and go to the mountains.>

Kastia looked surprised. <Na'Sha, I should stay with the wounded.>

<If you remain here, there will be no healer in the sanctuary,> Alacea told her. <I will remain here with the healers and assist them as well as I can.>

Kastia looked past Alacea at Sho Nan, who took a step forward. <Then, I shall...>

<You shall go with her, Ya'Jahar,> Alacea ordered her without turning to look at her. <Our people will need you there.>

Kastia and Sho Nan shared a silent look as some kind of unspoken conversation passed between them.

Sho Nan bowed to Alacea. <It will be as you wish, Na'Sha,> she said. <I shall collect my things.> With that, the temple cook went silently back into the temple.

<Alacea, you should not remain here,> Kastia tried again. <It will be dangerous. Why must you stay?>

Alacea's ears twitched the slightest bit. <Because I am the Na'Sha. As long as there are people in need within my temple, I will not leave it.>

Kastia was about to object again when Alacea raised her hand to stop her.

<You will not convince me otherwise,> she told her. <Now get in the wagon.>

Kastia's ears folded backward sadly. <Yes, Na'Sha. We shall see you again soon.>

<Go in peace and be safe,> Alacea told her.

Kastia turned and started for the truck, looking back over her shoulder as Sho Nan came through the temple door with a straw bag in one hand and a steaming teacup in the other.

<Alacea,> Sho Nan began. <Please be careful.>

<I shall,> the priestess assured her. <You be careful as well.>

<All will be as the Gods will it,> Sho Nan told her confidently. She put her bag on the ground and offered the teacup to her friend. <I have made you one last cup of tea,> she said. <Since you will not be able to have any good tea until I return.>

Alacea bowed shortly and took the cup from her. <Thank you, Sho Nan. Go in peace.>

Her words were obviously a dismissal, and the blue-haired woman picked up her bag and joined Kastia by the truck. The two continued to look in Alacea's direction as the human driver helped them into the truck, only stopping when they saw Alacea take a drink from the cup.

The truck belched a stinking cloud of black smoke and rumbled down the road. Alacea lifted her hand and waved goodbye to them.

As the truck turned the corner, she turned and spat the mouthful of tea onto the ground and poured out the rest. Turning, she headed back into the temple.

Chapter 9

"So, I'm in the interview, and the bakery manager asks me, 'do you have any experience?'"

Ramirez was only half listening as he scanned the far side of the river with his binoculars. The sun had just begun to rise, though it was hard to tell through the black and white smoke and clouds that blanketed the sky above them. Bits of white ash fell on them from time-to-time like a grim snowfall as the forests to their south surrounding the alien crash site burned out of control. The smell of burning wood was everywhere now, even in their clothes.

Through the dim light that managed to break through the smoke, the Ranger NCO continued searching while his two squads of Rangers and another squad of commandos from Kar'El had arranged themselves behind the cover of fallen trees and shallow fox-holes.

"So, I say, 'sure,'" the Ranger nearest to him, Specialist McClellan, continued, addressing the other three soldiers in his fireteam. "'I've driven tractor-trailers, deuce-and-a-halfs, panel trucks...' and the guy says, 'no, do you have any experience with *bread?*'"

Crouched next to him on Ramirez's left, Alzoria studied her would-be boyfriend as he looked out over the river. When the word came that the aliens were coming close to the river, she had insisted that she come with him when his combined Va'Shen and human platoon was sent to the OP. She had argued, successfully, that he would need someone to interpret his orders to the Kar'El corporal, Eruto. The commando in question sat on the other side of her, he and his commandos listening to the Ranger tell his incomprehensible story in surprise. Did they know nothing of stealth?

"Well, I don't know shit about bread," McClellan said. "I applied to be a delivery driver. So, I tell him, 'well, my girlfriend had a yeast infection once.'"

"Gross," another Ranger commented.

"TMI, dude..."

Ramirez's binoculars stopped moving as he saw a group of trees on the far side of the river begin to move, spooking a group of animals that leapt from the top branches onto other trees.

"So, that's where the interview ended," McClellan said. "I step outside, and I see one of those automated Army recruiter kiosks, so I think 'why not?' After a conversation of dubious truthfulness with an Army AI, I was in the Army."

"Dude, next time someone asks you that question, just say 'free college,'" one of the other Rangers told him.

More trees were moving, getting closer to the river bank.

"Get tactical, Rangers," Ramirez ordered. "It's game time."

The soldiers who were, just a moment ago, relaxing and shooting the shit, went into action and checked their weapons before taking up firing positions. Alzoria, meanwhile, told Eruto to do the same thing.

Ramirez's orders were pretty simple. He was to wait for the enemy to arrive at the bridge and then observe as long as possible, getting as much intel as he possibly could. But once the aliens started to cross the bridge, he was to blow it up and call in the mortars, keeping up the attack as long as he thought he could before pulling back.

"Okay," he whispered to himself as the trees closest to the bank began to move. "Let's see what you assholes look like."

The far side of the bridge sported a large open area that narrowed into a road, and it was here that the first enemy was sighted. Two tall, midnight black, bipedal creatures emerged from the forest, their heads hidden by black domed helmets. Sharp, black spikes perhaps a foot long, protruded from various parts of their armor and some of them seemed to have things attached to them, maybe equipment, Ramirez thought.

His thoughts were interrupted as a group of trees nearest the far bank fell over and some kind of vehicle emerged into the exposed area. At first, Ramirez thought it was some kind of hovercraft. A black and red hull made up of several swirls, like a collection of cinnamon rolls, rested upon a sickly grey-brown bladder that glided across the ground, most of it covered by a skirt of what looked like interconnected metal plates.

"Holy shit," Ramirez muttered as the hovercraft theory flew out the window with the appearance of an armored "head" that extended from the front of the vehicle. Three antennae with knobbed ends protruded from the creature's armored helmet, moving about as if searching its surroundings before it started to move again. Parts of the bladder on which the hull rested reached out and grabbed hold of the ground, pulling it along like a snail or a slug.

More of the creatures, accompanied by more of the armored snails, emerged from the forest and took up a circular formation in front of the bridge. Ramirez counted twenty snails out in the open, but the helmeted infantry kept coming out, hundreds of them.

Ramirez broke his gaze from the enemy and looked to his left. Alzoria's ears were shivering in fear and, just past her, Eruto and his tods appeared tense. On his right, McClellan was looking at the enemy formation through the scope of his bolt-action sniper rifle.

Ramirez picked up the receiver on the field phone the OP had been using and turned the handle quickly five or six times.

"Archer, Lancer Six," he said calmly into the receiver. "Fire mission. Continuous. HE. On my command. Grid Golf Three. Repeat. Continuous. HE. On my command. Grid Golf Three."

"Lancer Six, Archer," the mortar team leader replied. "Copy all. On your command. Standing by."

Ramirez laid the receiver down and checked the other piece of 19th century tech he had with him; the detonator connected by long wires to the explosives on the bridge's pylons looked like something out of an old Looney Toons cartoon, complete with plunger. When he was sure everything looked good, he picked up the binoculars again and looked out at the enemy formation again.

More snails had appeared and a group of armored infantry was standing near the bridge, facing one another. Ramirez watched, fascinated, as the three aliens began to rapidly change colors in different patterns.

"What is that, you reckon?" he asked no one in particular.

On his right, McClellan offered an answer. "Some kind of active camouflage system?" he guessed. "I've seen SEAL guys use shit like that. Maybe the Fuzz fucks with it like it does theirs."

Ramirez was just thinking that the Ranger's answer made about as much sense as anything else when a better answer came from his left.

<They're *talking*,> Alzoria whispered in awe.

The Staff Sergeant took a closer look at the trio of aliens, and the more he watched, the more Alzoria's answer seemed to make sense.

<Right you think maybe,> he told her.

He was once again shaken from his thoughts as a cry came over the river, and he shifted his binoculars to the right. Two more black figures emerged from the trees with a Va'Shen held between them. The shorter tod's feet dragged behind them as the infantry effortlessly pulled him toward the trio.

One of the original group broke away and moved to meet the new arrivals. The spikes on his shoulders had something stuck to them that looked like antennae. It wasn't until it stopped moving and Ramirez could focus the binoculars on it that he saw what they actually were. He swallowed dryly. A pair of hands, human or Va'Shen he couldn't tell, were stuck to the ends of the spikes, palms outward. Moving his gaze back to the other two, the Ranger saw that they, too, had body parts stuck to various spikes, one of them definitely a head stuck to one alien's left shoulder.

A head *without* fox ears.

Ramirez grit his teeth and brought his gaze back to the new group and the Va'Shen prisoner. The alien with the hands on his shoulders "spoke" to the others, his body changing colors rapidly. The other two did the same. A moment later, the alien stepped forward and shoved a clawed hand into the tod's stomach, causing the Va'Shen man to scream. The alien pulled his hand out, and the tod's innards spilled out onto the ground in front of him. The alien flashed something to the guards and turned, heading back to the others.

The guards knelt over the tod, and whatever they were doing to him, it was bad, because the Va'Shen man's screams were loud enough to hear clearly across the river.

<Whore-sons!> Eruto hissed.

Ramirez said nothing in reply. One of the snails began to reposition itself at the bridge, ready to start moving, and Ramirez knew it was time.

"McClellan," he said quietly. "See the one with the hands on his shoulders?"

"Yeah, I got him," the marksman replied grimly.

"Jazz Hands first," Ramirez ordered. "When the bridge goes, fire, got it?"

"Standing by, Staff Sergeant," McClellan assured him.

Ramirez picked up the phone receiver and rested it in the crook of his shoulder before picking up the detonator in his hands.

"Archer, Lancer Six," he spoke into the receiver, lifting the plunger on the detonator. Down below them, one of the snails began to move across the bridge. "Fire for effect. Fire!"

The snail-tank was about halfway across the bridge when a distant *Whump!* came from the northwest. As soon as he heard that sound, Ramirez slammed down the handle on the detonator. At the same time, McClellan's sniper rifle boomed.

The result was that three different things all happened at the same time, and no one on the other side of the bridge knew what to do about any of them. The charges on the bridge went off spectacularly, throwing wood and stone into the air as the snail-tank traversing it let out a gargling wail and hit the water below. At the same moment, the Dark One officer Ramirez had dubbed "Jazz Hands" jerked to one side, a brownish fluid shooting from a hole in its helmet with the force of a fire hose. The creature fell to the ground as two others rushed over to it.

And as they did so, the first mortar hit, exploding dead center in the middle of the formation.

"HIT 'EM!" Ramirez yelled.

WHUMP!

Another mortar sounded as the Rangers and commandos began to fire across the river at the Dark Ones. Some of the creatures ran for cover behind snail-tanks while some fired a few shots in return, the purple energy blasts going far wide.

The mortar impacted to the left of the first shot, not quite close enough to hurt the snail-tank or the creatures taking cover behind it.

Ramirez caught sight of the target he wanted: The Dark One with the human head on its shoulder. He put the top of the carrot of his prismatic telescopic sight on the creature's chest and fired.

To his consternation, the thing didn't fall. It turned and looked up in Ramirez's direction as if it could *see* him. The Ranger continued to fire, but at that range, the only ones doing any real damage were the commandos' hardlight rifles.

As the Dark One officer continued to ignore the rounds from Ramirez's rifle, it turned and changed colors several times.

Whatever it said must have been an order. Two of the snail tanks turned and faced the ambushers, ignoring the fire raining down on them, although the occasional hardlight blast seemed to piss them off somewhat.

WHUMP!

A mortar round slammed down into the top of one of the snail-tanks, and the creature screamed, the roar of pain sounding like someone trying to cry out with melted caramel in their throat.

The two snail-tanks turning toward them stopped, and the tops of their hulls retracted. An electric hum filled the air and the swirls on the tanks' "shells" began to glow blue. A moment later there were two explosive blasts from the snails, and two pink spheres about two meters in diameter sailed over the river.

"INCOMING!" Ramirez cried, grabbing the back of Alzoria's head and pushing it down into the dirt. "TAKE COVER!"

The spheres sailed past them and struck the ground behind them, bouncing once before rolling to a stop against the trunk of a fallen tree.

Then nothing.

A few Rangers and commandos continued firing, but the rest had stopped, looking at the spheres in concern. Alzoria fought her way to a kneeling position and spat dirt out of her mouth before following everyone's gaze at the two duds.

"Holy shit, that was close," someone remarked.

Ramirez started to turn back to the fight, opening his mouth to order his men to do the same when something stopped him. One of the spheres moved, rolling to the right about a foot.

He had no idea what was about to happen, but Ramirez did know one thing for sure.

This is gonna suck!

One of the Rangers cautiously approached the spheres, his weapon up and ready, and before Ramirez could order him back, it all went to Hell.

All in the space of a second, *something* smashed its way out of the left sphere, grabbed the approaching Ranger with a pair of fleshy pink tentacles and tore him in half!

Throwing the two halves aside, the creature let out a blood-curdling shriek and pulled the rest of itself out of the shell.

It took a lot to shock Ramirez. He had seen some screwed up stuff in his life, but nothing like the thing that was looking at him now. Six tentacles covered in spiked barbs converged on a bulbous head and a toothed beak about two feet long.

Everyone was shocked frozen at the sight, and the other sphere, now for certain some kind of egg, broke open, revealing another identical creature.

"FUCKING KILL IT!" someone screamed, and everyone began to fire into the things.

The first creature shrieked again and dashed forward, grabbing another Ranger with its barbed tentacles and literally shredding the man like it was trying to make him into pulled pork.

Alzoria held her hands over her ears as the cacophony of fire deafened her. The creatures didn't seem to mind being hit with so many bullets and hardlight blasts and continued to systematically grab Rangers and commandos and shred, bite and tear them apart.

The Huntress saw a Ranger go down and ran toward him. He was obviously dead, and she needed a weapon. She pulled at the M-31 in the dead human's hands but was foiled by the Ranger's single-point sling. She started grabbing whatever she could from the man that might let her fight, but all she managed to get from him was a bandolier with several familiar black cylinders with pins protruding from each.

Sensing something, she looked up and saw one of the creatures turn to look at her. It didn't mind killing humans, but it was bred and *trained* to kill Va'Shen. Seeing Alzoria, it shrieked and ran toward her, using half its tentacles as legs while the other half grabbed stumps and trees and pulled itself toward her.

The Huntress, now decidedly the prey, turned and dashed into the trees, the creature right on her heels.

* * *

On the opposite bank, the caste leader looked toward the source of the fire they had been taking, pleased to hear it more panicked than before while no longer aimed at them. The falling explosives, however, were still a concern, and as he stood there, seemingly unaffected by it, the rest of his soldiers were taking what cover they could.

The caste leader turned back just as another explosive round landed near enough to throw rocks and dirt onto him, but he ignored it and began to issue orders. The Dark One troops saw the colors of their leader's body change and began to act, turning their armored beasts and preparing to move them per the leader's orders.

That task complete, the caste leader once again turned and regarded the sounds of panicked shouting and weapons fire in the forest across the river. If a couple of hunting pods was all it took to subdue the enemy, they should reach the next village without trouble.

And then north.

And then home.

* * *

Alzoria ran through the trees, deliberately moving toward denser vegetation in hopes that the creature pursuing her would be slowed.

But the shrieking horror had no problem squeezing its body through narrow gaps in the trees, flattening itself and pulling its way past them faster than the vixen could.

With the distance between them closing, the desperate Va'Shen did the only thing she could think of. She leapt upward and snagged the branch of a tree, climbing quickly onto it and jumping again for the next one.

The tentacled beast paused at the foot of the tree and shrieked up at her, reaching up with its toothed appendages and wrapping around the branch she had been standing on a second before.

Panting, Alzoria spared a glance downward and saw the monster climbing the tree after her. Realizing she had nowhere else to run, she decided the only thing left to do was fight. She had hung the dead Ranger's bandolier over her neck, and now she hurriedly grabbed for one of the black cylinders on it. Not thinking, she hurled one of them down at the creature, watching it bounce off its bulbous head as it reached another branch.

When nothing happened, she realized she had done something wrong. She took a deep breath and tried to steady herself. She was a Huntress. As scary as this thing was, it was still just an animal, just *meat*. And that meant a Huntress could kill it. A panicked kit couldn't. But a Huntress *could*.

Alzoria grit her teeth and pulled another cylinder from the bandolier. Seeing the ring protruding from one end, she suddenly remembered what Ramirez had told her about how they worked. She grasped the pin and pulled it from the cylinder.

Looking down, the creature was just below her. Its beak widened, giving her a close-up look at the nightmarescape that was the inside of its mouth. Tiny curved teeth were hidden behind the larger, sharp knives that lined the edges of its beak.

It screamed at her.

She screamed back and threw the cylinder down at it as hard as she could.

The creature shut its mouth and gagged as the flash-bang grenade struck the back of its throat, throwing it off for a moment. Before it could recover, a loud *BOOM* sounded, and the creature's body expanded like a balloon for a moment before returning to normal.

Alzoria watched the monster go limp and sag down toward the ground until only a single tentacle wrapped around the branch below her was keeping it off the forest floor. The rest of its tentacles hung down and brushed the ground below.

The Huntress stared down at it, breathing hard, waiting for it to suddenly turn and scream at her again, but after several moments of nothing, she began to settle down.

Grasping the branch above her head, she looked down at the dead horror with gritted teeth.

<MEAT!> she screamed at it.

* * *

Back at the ambush site, Ramirez and the half of his Rangers and commandos that were left had managed to form a semi-circle around the other creature and were continuously firing into it as it finally began to show signs of slowing down.

The creature, its body littered with burnt holes from several different weapons, crawled toward Ramirez at the center of the formation with three of its tentacles. The other three it dragged limply behind it. It shrieked at the Ranger, now barely three meters from it, still trying to complete its life's mission in the final moments before death.

Ramirez fired again and again, finally flipping the switch on his rifle to AUTO and pouring the remaining rounds in his last magazine into it. When he heard the click signifying that the bolt was locked back and his weapon was empty, he released it and let it hang from its sling, drawing his sidearm and continuing to fire into the mound of disgusting flesh.

The creature stretched out to him with its last tentacle and offered a last spiteful shriek, the clawed tip coming within three feet of the Ranger NCO before finally giving up the ghost and going slack.

Ramirez was breathing hard, the slide on his pistol was locked back, its ammunition expended. The others continued firing into the dead, unmoving beast until Ramirez finally collected himself to call a cease-fire.

His body on automatic, the Ranger sergeant dropped the empty magazine from his pistol and slapped a new one into it, hitting the slide release to chamber a fresh round. The other Rangers in the formation did the same, all of them breathing hard, from adrenaline or terror or both, it was hard to be sure.

<Tanpuki,> Eruto whispered in awe from Ramirez's right.

"God *damn*!" Ramirez cried. "My taxidermist is going to shit his pants when he sees this."

In that moment, with the terror no longer first in his mind, Ramirez realized several things. Several of his Rangers and commandos were dead. The mortars were still landing on the Dark Ones across the river. The other monster was gone. But the first thing he noticed...

"Alzoria?" he asked, looking around. Among the formation of humans and Va'Shen, there was no short pixie cut of red and gold. He looked around quickly but couldn't see her. "Alzoria!?" he called. He turned to the others. "Where's the other... thing?!" he asked. "Where did it go?!"

One of the Rangers pointed into the forest. "I think I saw it going that way, Staff Sergeant," one of the privates told him.

"McClellan, get shit squared away!" Ramirez called to the marksman as he ran into the forest. He didn't bother waiting for an acknowledgement. He wasn't even completely sure McClellan was one of the Rangers who survived, but at that moment he didn't care. His heart was racing in his chest even as a cold ball of iron began to expand in his stomach.

He was doing the exact opposite of what he should be doing, and he knew it. He should be consolidating his forces, regrouping, reloading, re-engaging, but it didn't matter.

"ALZORIA!" he shouted. "ALZORIA!"

The Ranger was so focused on the path directly in front of him that he didn't notice when a petite vixen crashed into him from the side and grabbed hold of him.

<JOHN!> Alzoria yelled.

Realizing it was her, Ramirez froze.

Alzoria's ears were fluttering in joy, her tail whipping around, collecting all manner of leaves and twigs as it swept the forest floor.

<I killed it!> she cried happily. <I killed it!> "Fucked it all up!" she told him in English.

She went quiet as the Ranger grabbed hold of her and embraced her, all but crushing her against the front of his body armor. For the first time, she heard the quiver in his breath.

"You... You're not... You're not allowed to do that anymore," he gasped out. Swallowing back his fear, he tried to collect himself but couldn't. The sight of men and tods being ripped apart by those things, the thought that she could have been one of them, her body shredded into a bloody mess, wouldn't get out of his head.

"No more," he said. "Okay?"

Alzoria closed her eyes and wrapped her arms around him, not quite able to get them all the way around his armor and equipment.

"All good in da hood," she assured him quietly. "Good to go."

"Okay," he said, his relief finally overcoming the fear. "Come on, let's get back to the others."

The two trotted back to the OP, and as soon as McClellan saw them, he waved Ramirez over to his spot at the fallen tree. The rest of the Rangers and commandos were collecting weapons and ammunition from their fallen comrades.

"You need to see this, Staff Sergeant," McClellan said as they approached. Seeing Alzoria with him, he nodded to the Huntress. "You okay, Alzoria?" he asked.

Alzoria had spent a lot of time on the FOB, so most of the Rangers knew her and liked her. So, there wasn't a single word or arched eyebrow about Ramirez going after her.

"Good to go," she said, giving him a thumbs up. "Fucked up big motherfucker," she added.

"Hell yeah," McClellan said, offering her a fist bump.

In the meantime, Ramirez had picked up the binoculars and was looking out at the far bank.

"I called off the mortars," McClellan told him.

Ramirez didn't need to ask why.

The far bank was completely empty. There were a couple of destroyed snail-tanks, but that was it. Even the bodies of the alien troops they had managed to kill were gone.

"Where'd they go?" Ramirez asked him.

McClellan shook his head. "No idea, Staff Sergeant," he said. "By the time I got up here, they were already long gone."

"Retreated back into the tree line, probably," the NCO grunted.

"Probably."

Ramirez lowered the binoculars. "How many did we lose?" he asked.

McClellan turned somber. "Six of ours, four furries," he said. "seven wounded, but not badly. We're policing up the bodies to take them back with us."

Ramirez nodded. "Okay. Good job, McClellan."

The marksman only nodded in reply.

"JOHN!"

Ramirez turned and found Alzoria pointed down toward the river bank. Lifting the binoculars to his eyes he looked across the river again, but there was still nothing.

"Alzoria?" he asked.

"Down!" she cried. "Look down!"

He turned his gaze downward at the near bank on their side of the river and found several domed heads emerging from the river. The rest of the Dark Ones' bodies appeared as they marched out of the deeper parts of the river. Soon, they were followed by the tops of snail-tanks as the creatures breached the surface. More and more of them appearing.

"The fuck?!" McClellan cried, looking down his scope at them. "They fucking *walked* through the river?!"

Ramirez swallowed as another pair of armored mollusks emerged from the river. Most of their ammo was gone along with half their manpower. And in the end, they delayed the enemy advance by less than an hour.

"Grab our guys and get back to the LTVs," Ramirez ordered. "Now!"

McClellan turned and ran back to the others. The NCO didn't have to tell him that "our guys" also meant the bodies of their fallen, and that would take a little longer.

Alzoria watched, tail shaking in fear as the Dark Ones began to take up fighting positions on the bank of the river, ready to provide cover for the others as they finished their crossing.

Ramirez grabbed the phone line and quickly turned the handle five times.

"Sword Maiden, Lancer Six. Sword Maiden, Lancer Six," he called, raising the TOC. "Enemy forces have crossed the river. Repeat, enemy forces are across the river. Lancer is falling back. Prepare for wounded. Ten KIA. Over."

"Lancer Six, Sword Maiden," the TOC operator's voice came back. "Copy all. RTB. Over."

"Lancer Six, out," Ramirez said woodenly and hung up the phone.

All of that preparation, and it had bought them less than an hour.

"Let's get the fuck out of here," he told Alzoria.

* * *

Ben listened to Ramirez's debrief concerning the less-than-successful ambush at the river and sighed, knocking his knuckles against the top of his desk. Standing nearby, Azarin listened as Patricia translated for him, his gaze cast downward and his tail twitching in disappointment.

"Intel about our weapons' effectiveness is pretty much accurate," Ramirez told them from his seat across the desk. Alzoria had managed to maneuver her tail into the seat on his right and listened as he spoke. "Six-point-eight was ineffective at long range, though 300 Winchester Mag seemed to penetrate. Mortars were effective, but it's a moot point now."

Ben bit his lip at that. The mortar team had exhausted their supply of ammunition. All that remained were a few smoke rounds.

"The... octopus things..." Ramirez continued, his voice showing fear for the first time, "... They're... They're a fucking nightmare, Sir."

"*Tanpuki*," Azarin spoke up. They all turned to him. <War beasts trained to attack relentlessly.>

"Those things we talked about when Hestean, Azarin and I spoke," Patricia explained.

"'Tanpuki,' huh?" Ramirez repeated. "Well, if that's the Va'Shen word for 'Eldritch horror,' then it's pretty accurate. Thing's a fucking bullet-sponge. By the time we were done killing them, we were so low on ammo that we couldn't have kept up the fight even if we wanted to."

Ben got up and approached the map on the wall. A large "X" was scrawled over the bridge they had blown up. As unsettling as the rest of Ramirez's news was, the fact that the Dark Ones could cross the river without using a bridge was the worst thing he had heard yet. Blowing up the crossing leading north was their last-shot contingency to slow them down. Now they couldn't even be sure it would work.

<The Cora River flows faster than the Odoro,> Azarin said as if reading Ben's mind. <They will not be able to cross it as easily.>

"But they *will* cross it," Ben finished for him. Upon hearing the translation, Azarin's tail thrashed. The Ranger captain sighed. He knew they were always going to cross both rivers at some point somehow, but that they could do it so quickly and so easily was bad news.

He studied the map, his eyes falling on the line that represented the road leading north from the observation post. The words "Damnation Alley" were scrawled above it. He turned to Patricia and Azarin.

<Captain Turan ready?> he asked.

Neither of them answered.

The sound of a distant explosion did that for them.

Chapter 10

Chase Warren had been around a lot of explosions during his time in the Navy. Sure, it had mostly been demolitions projects and not combat, but they both overlapped in certain ways.

No matter what kind of explosion it was, when it went off, you always made sure your head was covered and you were well behind cover.

And as pieces of alien gore and snail shell fell all around him, he resisted the urge to raise his head and look over the berm he was hiding behind to admire his handiwork.

It was only when he heard M-31s and hardlight rifles begin going off that he peeked over the edge to see half an armored snail blocking the road below them, the other half thrown into the air in several different directions after it had stopped and examined the painted fuel drum it found half-buried in the road.

He flinched as purple energy singed the air near his head, and he brought his M-31 up to add his fire to the rest. Down below them, the aliens had quickly found cover behind their vehicles, and some of them had run to find safety in the trees on the other side of the road.

Exactly where Warren hoped they would go.

He looked to his right and signaled to Captain Turan, who was crouched over and making his way up and down the firing line. He saw Warren waving at him and raised his crystalline saber into the air.

<DOWN!>

The firing stopped briefly as Warren hit the clacker in his hand three times. The claymore mines affixed to the trees on the far side of the road all went off at once, the Dark One's armor all but useless against them at such close range. Several trees fell over, and one unlucky mollusk, too close to the side of the road, raised its head and gargled in pain as the armor covering its slimy head was torn to pieces.

<SHOOT!> Turan commanded.

The firing continued. But although the invaders' actions were hurried, they weren't panicked, and now that they had found what cover they could, they began throwing aimed fire back at them.

One snail made high-pitched noises at them, rage or pain, none of them knew. On its back it carried a five-meter long arrowhead shaped piece of equipment that Warren knew instinctively was a gun of some kind. The tip of the arrowhead split apart, and a glowing purple orb began to hum as the weapon turned toward them.

"INCOMING!" Warren shouted at them.

A blast of purple light erupted from the mounted weapon and passed just inches above the top of the berm and then past it, cutting through a line of trees which then began to fall around them. Looking that way, Warren saw two headless Va'Shen bodies hit the ground near him. Another flash hit the berm dead on further down the line, and human screams could be heard over the sound of gunfire for a moment before falling silent.

"Someone waste that thing!" he heard a Ranger yell.

The enraged animal wailed at them as bullets and blue light struck it in several places, but it didn't stop firing. Smaller versions of the weapon, borne by the Dark One infantry, added to the cacophony of death, striking human and Va'Shen alike without discrimination, turning parts of their bodies into liquid and leaving the rest to bleed out on the ground.

Warren continued to fire down at the creatures. More armored snails were adding their fire to the fight even as a rain of fragmentation grenades fell down upon them in a desperate effort to knock them out of the battle.

More blasts of purple, more trees fell around them, more commandos and Rangers fell to the ground.

The bolt on Warren's rifle locked back, and he began to clumsily reload, but before he could, he felt a hand on his shoulder.

Turning his head, he saw Turan there, half his face covered in blood that was not his own.

"*Des'et!*" he ordered.

Withdraw. It was one of the few Va'Shen words Warren knew. Lieutenant Kim had given him a quick briefing of the commands Turan intended to give, and this had been one of them.

"FALL BACK!" he called to the human troops as Turan gave the same orders to his commandos. "Hit 'em with smoke!"

Several smoke grenades hit the ground near the Dark Ones and in the space between them and the ambushers. As the forest began to fill with white smoke, Warren moved down the line, slapping Rangers on the shoulder and ordering them to move their asses.

Only when it was just him and Turan left on the line, ducking to avoid the blind fire from the invaders, did he turn to dash into the woods.

* * *

The Caste Leader moved through the smoke as his soldiers continued to fire up into the trees at their attackers. Between the smoke from the grenades and the clouds of smoke obscuring the sun, visibility was almost impossible.

Fire began to taper off as his sub-officers began to rein in their troops. Hearing a gurgling wail nearby, the Caste Leader turned and marched toward the war animal it came from. The giant mollusk that had been near the claymore mines when they went off was screaming in pain, but aside from the damaged armor on top of its head, it didn't seem particularly hurt.

But the Caste Leader knew what it was. He had seen it four thousand years ago before the withdrawal from Va'Sh, when the biological urge to hibernate had drawn them all back to their homeworld. He had been there when the Enemy had unleashed its weapon upon the forces occupying their slave world, saw its effect up close. It had all but crippled their forces for a time when it was first unleashed.

It looked up at the creature. Its brain was being slowly fried by the electromagnetic interference that surrounded the planet. The creatures were very sensitive to such changes in the EM spectrum, it was how they sought food and avoided danger in their natural habitat. But too much of it interfered with the creature's ability to think and it was now burning away the receptors in the creature's brain.

When "The Blessing," as the Va'Shen called it, was first employed around the planet, the Enemy had hoped it would swing the war in their favor. The EM interference made the Caste weapons unreliable, drove their war beasts wild with pain and made long range communication impossible. But the Enemy's optimism did not last long. The Caste had perfected the ability to adapt to new threats. It simply altered the growth of their beasts and equipment to include safeguards against the EM field.

Within a year, it was if the The Blessing didn't even exist.

Had this happened four thousand years ago, the Caste Leader would have quickly wrapped the animal's head in a protective carapace until the armor around its head grew back, but that was not an option here.

Raising his hand, he trigged the weapon grown into his claw and blasted the creature in the head, turning the top half of it into sludge. The snail, almost gratefully, went limp. With the smoke now cleared, the Caste Leader flashed a signal to his sub-officers to deploy scouts. Several armored troops took off in three different directions. Some of them went further down the road, some of them went into the trees where their attackers had fled and more went into the woods where the claymores had killed five of their comrades.

It flashed a new order, and his sub-officers led by its second-in command, approached. Following its order, Jazz-Hands knelt down and placed a square piece of dark chitin on the sandy floor of the road. It tapped the top of the square, and it began to hum, emitting a light blue pulse that stretched out into the sand around it. The sand began to rise and reshape itself until the Dark One officers were looking at a three-dimensional topographical map of the area based on the imagery they had taken from orbit.

The road they were on led to a crossroad that would take them either to the river crossing north or the Va'Shen population center to the west. With their war animals, it would be the fastest way to either, but the Caste Leader was now wondering how many more ambushes lay in wait for them.

As if in answer to this question, the sound of another explosion further up the road caused the officers to turn toward the sound. After waiting a few moments for further sounds of battle, the Caste Leader flashed a command, and they all turned back to the map. It could already guess that more explosive traps like the one that had set off this ambush littered the road ahead of them.

If they were to fight their way to the alien base further north, it could not waste more troops and animals to such traps. Nor would it curl up and try to meekly endure more attacks.

No. It would attack. It would punish those who thought to click their claws at it with such disrespect. And, at the same time, it would find what it needed to escape this world.

Reaching down, it put the tip of its armored claw into the sand at their position and drew a line west, through the forest.

And into Pelle.

* * *

"Hey."

It was impossible for Alzoria to not have heard him, so when she failed to turn and continued walking away from the TOC, Ramirez repeated his hail and trotted up to her.

"Hey! Alzoria!"

She finally stopped and slowly turned.

The Ranger approached, perturbed by her behavior. After the battle at the river, she had seemed hyped up and excited, but since then had remained eerily silent.

"You o..."

Before he could finish the question, she reached out and hugged him, her eyes wide and her tail shivering in fear.

"Woah! You alright?"

The fox girl swallowed and remained silent. In a flash of understanding, Ramirez finally got it. The initial excitement had worn off. The adrenaline, or the Va'Shen equivalent of it, was no longer pumping through her veins, and it was beginning to dawn on her that some Eldritch horror had almost killed her, that several people she had been speaking to were now dead, ripped into bloody pieces by that same monster.

He wrapped his arms around her. <It goody,> he assured her quietly. <All done bye bye. You goody.>

A few humans and Va'Shen commandos walking by saw them as they made their way around the camp, but said nothing, giving them what privacy a small FOB could.

<Alzoria do good,> he assured her, gently rubbing her back.

<Are you okay?> she asked quietly.

"Yeah," he replied in English.

She took a deep breath.

"Um..." the human began uncertainly. "Maybe... Maybe you should go to the mountains." He switched to Va'Shen and repeated his thought. <Alzoria go hidey hide place. Away from here.>

She pushed away and looked up at him, her ears flattened against her skull.

"Blew dat out your azz!" she told him. "I stay!"

"Alzoria," Ramirez said more firmly. "That thing could have killed you."

"Thing could shoulda woulda kill you!" she shot back. "I kill it. All good in da hood!"

"*Not* 'all good in the hood,'" he said. <It is much very danger.>

She turned her head away from him and sniffed. <You cannot tell me what to do. You are not my *tesho*.>

"So, if I was your husband, you'd go into the mountains?" he asked her seriously.

One of the fox girl's ears popped upward. She opened one eye and looked at him appraisingly. "Not say yes," she said. "Not say no. Not say maybe."

Ramirez grumbled.

"But," Alzoria continued. "Would like it."

The Ranger swallowed dryly as he realized the conversation had just reached a new level of real. He understood that emotions were high right now because what they had just gone through, but at the same time...

What was going to happen to them?

The last time he had been with a woman he cared for as much as Alzoria was when he was with Mac. Back then he was just a young, stupid kid who thought there was plenty of time to think about the future. He didn't think he was ready for commitment, even the lukewarm commitment that passed for marriage in the colonies. So, the last time he saw Mac, he didn't think to worry about not seeing her again. Of course, he'd see her again. What could possibly happen?

And then, one day, she was simply not in the world anymore and wouldn't be again.

If he could do it over again, if he had a chance to say goodbye to the fighter pilot the way he wished he could, would he have? Would he have kissed her goodbye and said he loved her and made certain that she knew?

The answer was yes.

And now, with these new alien invaders breathing down their necks, the situation had come back around. They could both be dead tomorrow. Even if she went up to the mountains, he couldn't be sure she'd be safe. For all he knew, this could be their last conversation before those things launched an all out attack on them.

"Maybe I should be then," he choked out.

Alzoria's ears popped upward and her eyes widened. She hadn't thought he'd respond that way. The vixen knew the human tod was somewhat dense. She also knew that what she was saying went a-hundred-and-eighty-degrees against her overall plan. She had deliberately *not* sought out a *tesho* when the war started because it was all too likely that he might die in the war and leave her a widow.

Yet here she was, talking about the Taking with a man who could be dead by this time tomorrow. And at the same time, she didn't care. If he did die, or if she died, she wanted to see him again in the Glade. It would be okay, she thought, to spend the rest of her mortal life alone if it meant that one day she'd see him again and then for eternity.

The Na'Sha's words came back to her, and she cleared her throat. <You... You are certain?> she asked. She looked away from him, unwilling to face him when he said no.

"Yeah," he said. "Yeah, I think so," he said rapidly, trying to keep ahead of the "common sense" in his head that would be screaming at him that it was too soon, too rushed.

"Forever," she warned him. "No take-back."

He remembered what the captain had talked about during their trip to Jamieson, how there seemed to be no way to dissolve his marriage to the head priestess. Back then, it seemed to Ramirez to be a problem. But now, looking at Alzoria, that was somehow comforting. It was somehow reassuring to know that nothing would take her from him if he did this.

But what if they did this and found out later they hated each other? What if they fought? What if he screwed this up?

<What if I am bad?> he asked her in Va'Shen.

Alzoria looked down at the ground. <Then... I will thrash you,> she told him.

Ramirez's lips curled up. "You'll beat me, huh?" He looked away for a moment. "That sounds fair," he conceded.

The vixen looked up at him. <What if I am bad?> she asked him. <Will you thrash me?>

"Hmmmm," he replied with a smile, his confidence returning as the choice became clearer for him. "No," he said. <I no thrash.>

She looked down again. <So...>

They were both silent for several seconds until Ramirez put both his hands up in front of her.

"So, which hand is it?" he asked.

Before he could take it back, Alzoria snatched his right hand and brought it to her lips, biting down on the meaty part of his palm as hard as she could, until blood was running down her chin.

Ramirez said nothing this time. This was a big moment, and he didn't want to risk ruining it.

Finally, after several moments, she eased off, her teeth releasing his hand. Her eyes closed, she gently licked the bite marks as if cleaning them. The vixen pulled his hand to her cheek so that he was cupping it.

<*Tesho*,> she whispered. <You are mine, and I am yours. From now until the end of time.>

"Alzoria," he whispered, his throat constricting at the emotion in her words.

<I am *'Myorin'* now,> she told him. She looked up at him, her ears fluttering happily.

His uncertain smile became a happy grin. "Yeah," he said. "Mee-yo-rin," he tried the word on for size.

"*Myorin*."

* * *

"They've taken up a defensive position on the roadway," Ben said, leaning over the top of the speaker phone, his hands on the table on either side of it. "They haven't moved for four hours."

"Any idea why?" Hopper's voice came back through the speaker.

When the commando scouts had first told them the Dark Ones were standing fast, he had also been curious as to why. When he asked the question aloud, Patricia translated it, and Azarin was the one to provide an answer.

<They are waiting for nightfall,> he had told them.

Ben had immediately asked why. He had become so used to not knowing the motivations behind his adversary's actions that when Azarin answered, he had felt rather stupid.

<Because it will be harder to see them.>

"Our commando leader here suggests they are waiting for nightfall before trying again," Ben told Hopper. "With the smoke and the weather system moving in, it's going to be pitch black out tonight. I don't know how their night vision is, but it must be good enough that they're willing to risk it."

"Do you think you can hold them, Captain?" Hopper asked.

Ben fought the urge to sigh. "We've set up defensive lines in the Black Forest between them and the village and along the road leading north. We're trying to stay as mobile as we can because, quite frankly, we don't know which direction they'll try. But if they go for the village, I want to be able to stop them cold. If they try to circle around east, I'll be able to move forces around to intercept them."

"Can you *hold them*?" Hopper repeated.

Ben took a breath. "We'll hold them, Sir," he promised.

"I'll pass on everything you've told me to the CJ-2," Hopper told him. "We finally got word from the Imperial Palace. They're raising the commandos... what's left of them... between you and the capital. They've even requested that we release the detainees we have at Jamieson without taking the oaths you came up with. Suddenly, they're not as important as they were."

"I'd keep an eye on them, Sir," Ben warned him. "But if you can get some Mikorin from their villages to talk to them..."

"Son, I don't have enough vehicles to catch a ride to the chow hall," the colonel said. "Everything with four wheels is moving troops. Even the post shuttle busses are out there."

"Then, be careful, Sir," Ben replied. "Don't put them at your back. The *Dara Tang* have been stirring shit with them since the day they got there."

He heard Hopper sigh. "I hear you, Captain, but right now, I'd put rifles in the hands of every detainee in Alberta if I had the slightest bit of assurance they'd be pointed in the same direction as mine."

"Track'n, Sir," Ben replied in resignation. Judging by how fast the Dark Ones could move through his area of operations, desperate measures seemed called for.

"Keep us posted, Captain," Hopper told him, wrapping things up. "Out here."

"Sector Thirteen out." Ben hung up the phone and sat down with a sigh.

"So, now what?" Patricia asked from where she was standing next to Azarin nearby. "Shouldn't we attack them now while they're sitting there?"

Ben shook his head. The goal hadn't changed. If the Dark Ones wanted to sit there and twiddle their thumbs for a few hours, that was just a few more hours for the real counterattack to set up. He also didn't relish the idea of attacking a fortified position with the forces he had. The rule of thumb when it came to striking a defended position was to attack with three times the number of defending troops. He didn't have that. He would much rather make the Dark One commander try to take *his* defended positions, to fight at a place and time of Ben's choosing like they had done up until now.

As much good as it had done them...

He looked at the map and grit his teeth. They needed to slow them down, and right now the Rangers and commandos had been little more than a speed bump in the road.

<Azarin,> he said, turning to his brother-in-law, <If Dark Ones come into Pelle, can they become slowed?>

The Va'Shen commando's tail slapped the floor. He didn't like the direction the question led them, but he also understood their lack of options.

<I do not know,> he answered truthfully. <They do not seem to care about taking villages, even though they attack them.>

<What you mean say?>

Azarin thought back to what the captains of the refugee villages had told him. <When they attacked the other villages, they simply destroyed every building they came upon. Their goal was not occupation.>

Ben sighed. "Everything, huh?"

<Except for the temples,> Azarin finished.

The Ranger cocked his head. <Not temples? No destroy?>

Azarin's tail hit the floor again. <Every captain said the same thing. The Dark Ones destroyed village buildings as they came to them but seemed careful not to hit the temples.>

Ben looked to Patricia to make sure he understood what Azarin had said correctly, and when he was sure he had, he turned back to the tod.

<Why?> he asked.

The commando captain's ears turned backward in a shrug. <I do not know. From what the histories tell us, they always targeted the temples for greater brutality, knowing it would hurt us more.>

"Ask him if there's anything in the temples that the Dark Ones may want." Ben asked Patricia, not trusting his own Va'Shen for this. "Tech or intel or anything like that."

Azarin listened to the question and replied directly to his brother-in-law.

<The temples hold nothing like that,> he said. <It just doesn't make any sense.>

Ben was silent for a full minute, tapping the desktop with his fingers.

What the Hell am I missing?!

What could the Dark Ones be looking for in those temples? Could they possibly bait them with it?

<Azarin,> he said. <You go to temple. Check on hurt ones. They must be moved before Dark Ones can be to there.>

<It will be done, Overlord,> Azarin replied in a business-like tone.

<Alacea... gone to hide?> Ben asked him.

<Sho Nan and Kastia agreed to drug her before they left,> he replied. <She is likely sleeping now. When I get to the temple, I will have some Huntresses carry her to the mountains.>

Ben wanted to go to the temple himself and make sure, but he couldn't leave yet. <You make certain?> he asked his brother.

<I shall,> Azarin promised.

<Thanks be to you,> Ben said with a smile.

As long as he knew Alacea was safe, he could focus on the job at hand.

And the job at hand wasn't going very well.

* * *

Of course, Sho Nan was not there to open the temple door, bow, and say something that might have been a greeting/might have been an insult, and that automatically made the Mikorin temple feel eerie. Azarin entered without fanfare and went immediately to the main room where a makeshift hospital had been set up for the refugees.

Most of the spots where injured Va'Shen had once lay were now empty, their occupants moved carefully up into the mountains. But some of them, more than Azarin expected, were still full with healers and Mikorin from their villages moving from space to space tending to them.

He did a quick count. Twenty injured, many of them unconscious, many of them with ghastly-looking wounds. Ten healers and Mikorin. Moving them into the mountains would be difficult. For some of them, impossible.

<Brother?>

Shocked, Azarin's tail puffed out as he turned and saw Alacea standing in the doorway to the kitchen, an apron wrapped around her hanbok. She was holding a wooden tray with several bowls of steaming soup atop it.

Seeing his shocked tail and ears, the priestess's ears pointed down toward him. <Judging by your expression, you did not think to find me here,> she told him. <Or, at least, did not think to find me here *conscious*.>

<You should not be here,> he stated matter-of-factly, deliberately ignoring her round-about accusation. <You should go up to the sanctuary.>

<I am the Mikorin Na'Sha, and there are people suffering within my temple,> Alacea replied evenly. <I am *supposed* to be *here*.>

<Your *tesho* believes you are on your way to the mountains,> Azarin told her.

<And because of that, he can focus on what he needs to do,> Alacea replied. <We each have a place. I tried to take him from his, and it was wrong of me to do so. It is every bit as wrong for him or you to try to take me from mine.>

<He will not see it that way, and neither do I,> the commando informed her.

<I will leave when the last injured Va'Shen in this place is moved to safety,> Alacea said. <*Not before.*>

Azarin hissed in frustration. He knew better than to try to argue with a Na'Sha. If she was set in her decision to stay, that left him two options: Let her stay or force her to leave.

He did not want to do that. He knew what that would do to her. Although he had promised his brother he would "hit her on head" to get her to leave, the fact remained that he was a Va'Shen and a part of her community. It was one thing to do something against her will when she was not awake to voice her complaint. After all, who knows what she would have otherwise agreed to in that moment? To attack her as she ordered him to stop was no different than an attack on the community as a whole. Any Va'Shen of Pelle nearby would come to her defense, whether they agreed with Azarin or not. It was a fine distinction, and rather hypocritical when examined, but it made all the difference in the world.

<How long until they can move?> he asked her, admitting defeat.

Alacea gave a sigh of relief that her brother was seeing reason, or, at least, what she considered reason.

<The wounds are severe,> she said. <They will not be able to move for some time.>

<I will ask your *tesho* for wagons to remain here,> he growled, absolutely hating this situation. <The moment they can move, you leave with them. Do you understand, Sister?>

By referring to her as "Sister" instead of "Na'Sha," Azarin was letting her know that he would not accept another argument about a Mikorin's duty in this. He could not pull a Na'Sha from her temple, but he *could* drag a little sister from a building, kicking and screaming, if he had to.

<Once they are safe, the temple will become just wood and nails,> she assured him. <And I will leave.>

<It is decided then,> he grumbled.

<Do not tell my *Tesho*,> she cautioned him.

One of Azarin's ears popped up at the command.

<As you have said,> she went on, <It is because he believes I am safely away from here that he can fight. And he *must* be able to fight. The community *needs him* to fight. Please promise me.>

<I have already broken one promise by allowing you to remain,> he told her. <Are you certain you can trust a promise from me?>

Her ears twitched a smile. <This time you are promising your Na'Sha.>

Azarin hissed and turned away from her. <Fine!> he spat. <I will not tell him unless there is no other choice. Will you accept that?>

<I shall.>

He sighed. <Then tell me what else you need. I will see that it is brought here.>

* * *

Burgers had just finished checking over the last of his Rangers' gear and ordering them to get one last hot meal at the chow hall when he saw Ramirez and Alzoria walking through the parade grounds together. A group of Huntresses were huddled together outside the captain's office, waiting for Bao Sen to finish "receiving advice" from Azarin about what the Huntresses not up in the mountains should do next.

The group of vixens saw Alzoria, and the young Va'Shen woman responded by holding Ramirez's right hand over her head and yelling, <MEAT!>

In response, the assembled vixens squealed and rushed to her, hugging her and patting Ramirez on the back.

Burgers's eyes narrowed as he walked toward the group.

"What the hell did you do?" he demanded of his friend.

"Oh!" Ramirez said in reply, rubbing the back of his head with his hand sheepishly. "Alzoria and I... kinda... sorta... got married."

The vixens were too busy squealing and jumping up and down nearby to overhear their conversation, assuming they could understand even if they had.

"Dude, what the hell is wrong with you?" Burgers asked. "That is the primo numero uno death flag. While you're at it, you should just tell everyone how you're retiring in a couple of days and 'oh, it would be such a shame if something happened to me now!'"

Ramirez held his hands up as if to stave off an attack. "Amigo! It's cool! Absolutely nothing could possibly happen."

Burgers blinked at him in shock. "What? What is this? What are you doing right now? Are you *deliberately* trying to get us all killed?"

"C'mon! How could things go bad on such a great day? I got married, I won the lottery, I retire tomorrow..."

"Please, stop!"

Ramirez dug into his pocket. "Hey, you wanna see a picture of my baby triplets back home who I haven't met yet and can't wait to see just as soon as this is all over?"

"Dude... Just... Fuck you, all right?" Burgers grumbled in defeat. He held a hand out, and Ramirez took it, shaking it eagerly. "I'm happy for you, man."

"Thanks, Burgers," Ramirez said.

The larger man nodded and smiled. "I'm sorry to have to tell you that the honeymoon is going to be delayed. Captain wants you to take a platoon around to the east side of the road in case the motherfuckers try to flank us."

As he said this, he unrolled a crude copy of the map that hung in Ben's office and showed it to him, pointing at the spot Ramirez was to take up. "I'm gonna take the other two and some Va'Shen on the west side and make sure they don't head toward the vil."

Ramirez nodded. "I'm guessing that's where the captain thinks they're going to go?" Having fought these things once before, he knew a single platoon was going to be little more than a speedbump if they decided to hit him hard.

Burgers nodded. "If they do hit you, throw up some flares, and we'll come running. But odds are, they're coming to me."

"Keep your shit wired tight, man," Ramirez told him, punching him lightly on the front of his vest. "These things are fucked up."

"Yeah, I heard you killed an octopus," Burgers said.

"Yeah, not the best day," Ramirez said. "On that note..." He took Burgers aside and led him a few steps away from the others. "I need to keep Alzoria away from the frontlines. I'm just... worried... you know."

"I get it," Burgers said.

"She thinks she's Billy Badass after killing that squid thing..."

"I thought you killed the squid thing?" the larger man interrupted.

"There were two squid things," Ramirez said.

"So, she killed one, and you killed the other one?"

"Well... sort of..." the Ranger replied. "She killed one, and me and like... half a platoon killed the other one, so..."

"Wait," Burgers broke in again. "So, she killed one all by her lonesome while it took you and fifteen guys with automatic weapons to kill the other one?"

"Yeeeaaahhh..." Ramirez drawled out, partly in embarrassment.

"So... why is *she* the one who needs to stay off the line?" Burgers joked. "I mean, if she can do that, we should give her some stripes and a squad of her own."

"I'm being serious, dude."

The big Texan smiled. "I know, man. Don't worry, I got it."

"Thanks." The two fist-bumped. "Watch your ass out there."

"You too, Bro."

Chapter 11

Even the smallest bit of light can comfort someone in the dark. A tiny ember, a star peeking down from overhead, a little bit of light reflected from a cat's eyes. Any of it could remind a person that the world was still there, that they were still alive.

And, for obvious reasons, none of that was allowed anywhere in the myriad foxholes, dugouts, machinegun nests or other makeshift fortifications that ran from north to south in the Black Forest halfway between Pelle and the Dark One position.

That same glimmer of hope could also act like a flare, showing a waiting enemy where you were hiding and making your death the easiest thing to see.

Normally, this wouldn't be a problem for Rangers. They owned the night... with night optical devices, motion sensors, thermal imagery, direct drone surveillance uplinks and a wide array of other pieces of tech meant to drive back the darkness.

Of course, thanks to the Fuzz, none of that worked here.

Hell, even the Fuzz would have been welcome tonight. The hazy green glow of Va'Sh's ever-present aurora was hidden by a foreboding alliance of storm clouds and smoke from the forest fires burning south of them. Those same clouds blocked out Va'Sh's moons and the stars that normally poked through the aurora's light, leaving only darkness and the lingering smell of burning wood in the distance.

Pitch black.

And if Burgers could have seen the raindrops that began to land on his hand, he'd see that even they were black, the dirt and dust kicked up by the alien ship's explosion coming back down in the form of a sickly ash-like mud.

He rubbed the liquid between his fingers, feeling the grit of the dirt infused in the raindrops. Looking up from his foxhole revealed nothing. He had definitely drawn the shit duty.

The Ranger strained his ears, trying to hear anything over the pattering sound of the rain hitting the leaves of the trees overhead. But there was nothing. The Va'Shen commandos, natural-born hunters, were dead-silent, and the Rangers, no slouches themselves, did their best to compete with them.

Even the bioluminescent Va'Shen equivalent of squirrels, usually seen bouncing from tree to tree at night, were absent. Perhaps they were huddled in their dens, hiding from the rain and the smell of smoke, or maybe they could sense the approach of three sets of aliens intent on killing one another and had enough sense to get out of the way.

Thunder rumbled lazily overhead, and there was a brief flash of lightning that illuminated the forest for a half second. But it was gone before Burgers's eyes could adjust and make out anything.

The rain began to fall a little harder, but not so much that Burgers thought he had to worry about the foxholes filling up. He continued to gaze into the milky darkness, wishing for just two minutes of working night vision gear.

More thunder, another brief flash. Was that patch of darkness there during the last flash of light? The Ranger resisted the urge to see things that weren't there. Once one of them started firing, *everyone* would start firing, and then every one of their positions would be exposed.

Within the sound of raindrops striking the ground, one in particular sounded... different. Burgers's eyes turned toward the sound, but no matter how much he willed it, he didn't see anything. One good thing that came from fighting the Va'Shen, however, was that you learned to trust your senses and your instincts. The aliens were so stealthy that you might only get the barest hint of their presence before they opened up on you.

Burgers silently shifted the barrel of his rifle around and pointed it in the direction from which the noise had come. When should he shoot? At what point could he safely say that a barely perceptible noise was worth shooting at?

In the end, it wasn't a noise at all.

He felt something bump against the muzzle of his rifle and freeze as if realizing it had made a mistake.

A *big* mistake.

With one fluid motion, Burgers hit the selector switch on his M-31 to full-auto and pulled the trigger. The weapon roared in his hands and *something* lit up in bright lights like a Christmas tree before falling to the ground in front of his foxhole like sack of bricks.

Just as expected every other position opened up. Three bright red flares from three separate fighting positions fired off into the sky, bathing the forest in an eerie light.

They were moving amongst the trees, some of them stopped momentarily, distracted by the flares, something they had never seen before. But the aliens quickly got back on their game as bullets and beams of light started striking around, and in some cases, into them.

The M-270 gunner on Burgers's left began firing short bursts into the trees, trying to suppress the blasts of purple light that had begun to erupt toward them. Burgers couldn't tell how many of them there were out there, but they were going to act like it was all of them.

"CLAYMORES!" he yelled.

Explosive blasts in the forest ahead of them brought down trees, vegetation and alien bodies. The flares only had a few more seconds of life in them, and three more flew into the air along the firing line.

Burgers heard an unholy shriek and turned to his right. A... *something*... hidden in the constantly shifting shadows cast by the flares, skittered toward the foxhole on his right.

"LOOK OUT!" he shouted at them, turning to try to take a shot at it, but the surrounding noise of rifles going off was too loud and the creature too fast. The *tanpuki* leapt into the foxhole with a shriek. Burgers watched, helpless, as men and tods screamed and thrashed inside. An explosion from a frag grenade, perhaps dropped by one of the dying humans in the hole, went off, killing everyone and everything left alive in it, including the creature.

There were more screams for help as other tentacled monsters attacked, but just as many had switched to full auto and were hitting the monsters before they could enter the holes. More grenades and claymores went off, and even with the flares, muzzle flashes, lasers and energy blasts, the smoke was making it hard to see anything between them and the enemy among the trees.

Finally, the purple flashes of light tapered off. As Burgers reloaded his rifle, he searched the deadzone in front of him, but couldn't see any returning fire or hear any more hateful shrieking.

"CEASE FIRE!" he yelled. "CEASE FIRE!"

He heard the call echo down the line as others took it up. The rifle fire stopped almost immediately, and the lasers from the Va'Shen commandos began to drop off as the order was translated for them.

Soon, the forest was once again quiet with the exception of the rain falling around them. A few drops struck the barrel of his rifle and hissed as the heat turned them to steam. A few more flares popped into the air, illuminating the smoke-filled hellscape. He resisted the urge to leave the foxhole and check for wounded. For all they knew, the invaders were down behind cover, waiting for them to do exactly that. He could hear a few calls for a medic. Corpsman Fletcher was back at the FOB, preparing to accept wounded, and the Rangers and commandos would have to make do with whatever aid their fellow troops could give them.

Still nothing from the trees.

It hadn't felt like a full-scale attack, and Burgers figured what they had just seen was a probe of their defenses. Hopefully, they had given the aliens something to think about.

He heard the two-seventy gunner on his left charge his weapon after reloading, and the specialist suddenly called for his attention.

"Staff Sergeant!" he said, nervous excitement in his voice. "Check this out!"

Burgers saw that the machine gunner was pointing at the ground directly in front of their hole. Cautiously standing a little higher, he looked over the pile of dirt they had been using for cover and down at the ground.

"Holy... *shit...*" Burgers muttered.

Laying there was the body of a Dark One.

* * *

Ben rushed out of the TOC, Patricia right beside him, as several LTVs full of wounded lined up by the medical tent. They had heard the attack, saw the flares, and as planned, runners had come to report what they were up against and, later, the outcome. But the Ranger captain still felt like a shit-heel for not being out there with them. As a platoon leader, he had always been on the line with his troops. As a company commander, his place was in the TOC, overseeing the entire battlespace.

But it still bothered him that he wasn't out there, sharing the danger with his Rangers, that feeling quadrupling at the sight of the wounded being helped or carried into the med tent.

One LTV pulled up with something big strapped to the hood as if some Colorado hunter had bagged an elk. The doors opened, and Burgers emerged, a big smile on his face.

"Good morning, Sir," he said. He pulled a flashlight from his load-bearing vest and shined it at the thing on the hood. "Happy Arbor Day," he joked.

Ben and Patricia came up short as the beam of light illuminated the thing tied to the hood. "Is that what I think it is, Staff Sergeant?" Ben asked.

"Yes, Sir," Burgers replied. "Killed at point-blank range. It ain't one-shot-one-kill," he admitted. "But I reckon it still counts."

"It *is* dead, right?" Patricia asked him, as Ben got a closer look.

"Damn, I hope so, Ma'am," Burgers told her. "Otherwise, this thing is gonna be *super pissed* when it wakes up."

Ben saw the holes in the creature's armor left by the Ranger's rifle and sincerely doubted the thing was alive.

"Good work, Staff Sergeant," he said. "What about the attack?"

"They hit us with..." He pointed at the alien before continuing. "... Um... Infantry as well as those octopus things Ramirez was talking about. Maybe about a dozen infantry and half as many tentacle monsters."

"Skirmishers?" Ben asked. Without the benefit of technology, it seemed the best way to find an opposing force was to do what they did in the Civil War: Send troops out until they stumbled upon them.

"Scouts, I think," Burgers confirmed. "Ten dead, ten wounded," he finished his report.

"Any other bodies?" Ben asked.

"Nothing like this one," the NCO replied. "Either they carried their dead back with them, or we didn't actually hit any of them. A few chunks of octopus here and there."

"Take this thing to the med tent and tell Corpsman Fletcher I want to talk to her as soon as she's done treating the wounded. Anyone she can't treat here, human *or* Va'Shen, get out to Jamieson tonight."

"Yes, Sir," Burgers said.

"And as soon first light comes, reinforce the line," Ben ordered. "You can bet they'll be back."

* * *

Corpsman Second Class Mina Fletcher looked positively exhausted as she leaned forward onto the exam table. The front of her uniform was splotched with bloodstains, human and Va'Shen indistinguishable to any who saw it. She studied the Dark One body on the table and looked up at the officer standing on the other side.

"You want me to do an autopsy, Sir?" she asked. "I'm pretty sure the cause of death is 'Ranger encounter.'"

Ben gave her a tired smile. "Not an autopsy," he corrected. "I want you to dissect this thing and tell me how to kill them. Preferably, in great numbers."

The Navy medic blew a breath of air between her lips as she looked at the armored hulk in front of her. "I'm gonna need some help," she said. "I don't have the tools for this kind of thing."

"Are they specialized tools, or can you make do with a low-tech substitute?" he asked.

"Nothing too special," she said. "I'm pretty sure most of the stuff I need I can get from the SeaBees; power saws, stuff to get the armor off, things like that. I don't know what kind of gasses are building up in it, so some hazmat gear would be nice. It would be good if I can get another pair of hands in here to help as well."

"I'll find you someone," Ben promised.

She looked at the entrance to the tent. The sun was starting to come up outside. "I'll get started right away."

"It'll take a little bit to find you that help," Ben said. "Take an hour, get some rest, and start then."

"Aye aye, Sir."

Ben turned away and nearly jumped when he saw Azarin standing next to him. He briefly wondered how long the commando captain had been there. Had he followed him in from his office? He definitely needed more sleep.

Or more coffee.

<Azarin well?> he asked.

The commando was staring down at the creature on the table with almost religious awe. It suddenly occurred to Ben that, like him, this was the first time his brother-in-law had actually seen a Dark

One. For Ben, it was a scientific curiosity and a military problem he needed to think about. But for Azarin, it was like a supernatural demon from Hell was lying on that table.

<Azarin well?> he asked again.

The commando's tail slapped the ground. <I am well,> he announced, taking a deep breath. <I simply have never seen something so... evil.>

<Is dead,> Ben told him. <We killed it. We will kill more.>

<May it be so,> Azarin growled.

*　*　*

When Fletcher returned to the medical tent exactly one hour later, she found a short, skinny Asian man with a Specialist emblem on the front of his uniform waiting there for her.

"You hurt?" she asked without preamble, placing a large paper cup of coffee on her desk to steam quietly while she prepared for work.

"No, Corpsman," the Ranger replied. "The captain told me to report here. He said you needed help with a dissection."

The Navy medic studied him for a moment. "You a medic?" she asked.

"No, Corpsman," he answered promptly. "But I have a bachelor's in biology from O'le Miss."

"Close enough," the woman said, checking over the gear the SeaBees had left for her on a table in the corner. "What's your name?"

"Shinzato, Corpsman."

"Okay, Specialist Shinzato," she said, putting on a pair of clear polymer goggles and some thick surgical gloves. "Gear up. Let's get dirty."

Shinzato nodded and started donning surgical gear of his own. Once they were both done, they stood on either side of the table on which lay the alien and stared at it dumbly.

"So... Where do we start?" Shinzato asked.

The corpsman eyed the creature up and down, nowhere close to certain of the answer. As if just wanting to do *something* useful, she reached down and poked its chest with a gloved finger. Up close, she could see that tiny versions of the alien's shoulder spikes protruded from various parts of the armor, ranging from a millimeter in length up to an inch.

"I guess we should start by getting its armored suit off," she said. Her words were somewhat muffled by the surgical mask she wore. She had no idea what kind of bacteria or gasses were lurking inside this thing. "Let's look for latches or seams but be careful of anything that looks or feels sharp. We don't know if this thing is poisonous."

The two moved around the alien, carefully moving different parts of it, hoping that they might get lucky and find a big zipper somewhere that would open the suit.

Fletcher looked under its left arm and squinted through the goggles. "Over here, I think I have a seam." She brought up a scalpel and rested the blade against it. "Let's see if we can cut through here..."

Shinzato watched tensely, waiting for the thing to explode or jump up and start screaming at them. Who knew what this thing would do?

A moment later, he saw Fletcher stand up straight, surprised by something.

"What?" the Ranger NCO asked her.

"What the..." Fletcher replied, not immediately answering. She began checking other parts of the alien's body, not saying anything until she was satisfied that she was right. "Son of a bitch," she muttered in awe.

"What?" Shinzato asked again. "What is it?"

She looked up at him.

"It's not a suit."

* * *

"It's *aquatic*?!" Ben repeated in disbelief.

He, Patricia, Azarin, Ramirez, Warren and Burgers were standing around the table where the opened remains of the alien were laying, looking very different from the last time any of them saw it.

It had been ten hours since Fletcher and Shinzato had started their dissection, and what they had discovered had shocked them time after time. So enthralled they had been in their discoveries that the coffee Fletcher had brought in that morning still sat untouched and now very cold on her desk.

The corpsman, standing on the opposite side of the table from him, her uniform and apron covered in blue blood and gore, nodded excitedly.

"Yes, Sir, and hold onto your asses because that's not even the most exciting thing," she said. "I mean, people were excited when they started studying Va'Shen anatomy and physiology, but someone's gonna win a goddamn Nobel Prize working with these guys."

"Wait a sec," Ramirez asked tiredly. He had been on the line all night and then all day, engaged alien scouts twice, and was finally beginning to feel the fatigue set in. "You're saying this thing is a fucking *fish*?"

"No," Fletcher replied to the sarcasm. "I'm saying this thing is a fucking *crustacean*."

"A crab," Warren concluded.

"Who had 'crab people' on their alien invader bingo card?" Burgers asked with a grunt.

The corpsman nodded and tapped a piece of the chest armor on the table with a probe. "Like this, which we thought was body armor? It's exoskeleton, bone, shell, whatever."

"If it's aquatic, how is it functioning on land?" Patricia asked, holding her nose to keep the stench of rotting crab out of it. "Is it amphibious?"

"I don't think so," Fletcher said. She went to one side of the table where the thing's head and three pairs of large, baseball-size eyes sat. "There are parts of it that don't seem like parts of their actual bodies grafted onto them." She grabbed one side of the creature's chest and pulled it over onto its side. Two large bumps, the size and shape of the water bladders the Rangers themselves wore for hydration, protruded from the creature's back. One of them had been partially cut open.

"Under here are gills," Fletcher said. "But these protrusions here... Filled with salt water and linked to other bladders further down. I think they oxygenate the water and distribute it to the gills and a few other parts."

"Like a space suit," Ben concluded.

"Right," she replied. "And other parts seem... I don't know how to describe it. They're definitely biological but they don't seem to be... well... original stock parts. Like over here."

She went to the creature's left arm and its clawed armored hand. "We removed the... what we assumed, anyway... was the thing's energy weapon, but..." She pointed at another organ the weapon had covered. "This part here seems to have a similar function. I think the energy blast it uses like a gun is *natural* to them, and the 'weapon' either juices it up or focuses it or *something*." She took some forceps and grabbed hold of a fleshy, pink nub in the center of the thing's hand, just below where the weapon organ met the hand and another orifice that waited to be explained. She pulled the forceps and the nub was revealed to be a spiked tentacle.

"So," Fletcher went on as if teaching a college biology class. "They probably originally grabbed prey with this..." She continued to pull, and the tentacle grew to more than six feet in length. "Then pulled it in and locked onto it with its claw... Zapped it with its little taser thing, turning it into that biological slush we've seen..." She released the tentacle and pointed at the unknown orifice. "And then this sucks it up. It has no mouth like we know it. This... 'esophageal tube'... leads straight into what looks like its digestive system."

"So, its energy weapons don't liquidate people because of some tactical reason," Burgers said. "It turns people into *food*." Seeing Ramirez's tired and confused look, he nudged him with his elbow. "Like a gun that turns targets into tacos."

"I want one," Ramirez said immediately.

"Okay," Ben said with a deep breath as he absorbed this new information. "So, this is the part where you tell us that it has some easily exploited weakness that will let us kill all of them quickly and win the war. What is it?"

Fletcher cleared her throat. "You shoot it," she said. "Until it dies."

Ben clicked his tongue. "Gotta admit, Corpsman, I was kinda hoping for more."

"Wish I could give you more, Sir," she said apologetically. "But wherever these guys are from, it's a bad neighborhood, and it evolved to live in it. It has two hearts, and I can tell you exactly where they are, right in the center of the chest, one on top of the other. But those hearts are also behind three inches of that exoskeleton. Its 'head' is in the usual spot, but what is exposed behind those domes are just its eyes. Its brain is a little lower, again, protected by thick armor." She shrugged. "With what we have here, that's about as much as I can tell you. Maybe the docs at Jamieson can look at its body chemistry and find a chemical or biological solution, but that's beyond my expertise or capabilities here."

"Any idea of what *might* be a weakness?" he prompted again. "Anything at all?"

"Big ass pot of boiling water," Ramirez suggested.

"Shitload of butter from the chow hall," Burgers threw in.

"Ooh!" Ramirez cried and turned to Warren. "Senior Chief, can your SeaBees make us some giant claw crackers like in the seafood restaurants but like hella big?!"

"No," Warren answered immediately, arms crossed over his chest. A moment later, he thought to add more. "I mean... yes, we could, but we're not going to."

"Hit them with the biggest guns you have as many times as you can," Fletcher told the captain. "It's like any other creature in that sense. Do enough damage, and it'll die. It's just a matter of getting through its shell."

Ben rubbed his temples. He had dared to hope that the science fiction movies were right, that an alien species would have some weakness, but, as they had learned with the Va'Shen, the movies were mostly bullshit.

"Good work, Corpsman, Specialist," he told the two. "Pack this thing up and send it onto Jamieson with your report. Anything we can give them will help when these things reach the ambush site."

"Aye aye, Sir," Fletcher said, disappointed that she couldn't be more helpful despite their discoveries.

Ben considered what he had just learned, his disappointment mixed with his awe. An aquatic species that had managed to not only leave the oceans where they were born, but their planet's atmosphere and go into space.

He nearly jumped as another thought struck him. Was this why they had never seen any signs of intelligent life, past or present, on any of the worlds Earth had colonized? They had scoured the land masses of each world, looking for some sign that someone had been there; ruins, wrecks, bones, buried treasure, but never found anything. They were still searching, even today. Planets were big places, after all, and an indication of even a small, primitive intelligent species would have been huge.

Had they been looking in the wrong place? Were these things living right beneath their feet off the coasts of their colony cities, hidden and protected by the planets' oceans? The idea was both fascinating and terrifying.

An even more electrifying thought came to him. The Va'Shen said they attacked because humans had trespassed on Great One worlds. Were the Great Ones also aquatic? If they sent submersibles into the waters of Persephone, where Ben and the Rangers used to party on the beach, would they have found the remains of sprawling underwater cities?

Would they have found *people* down there?

"So, now what?" Patricia asked as Fletcher and Shinzato began cleaning up and packing the creature's remains in bags. The question snapped Ben out of his thoughts.

"I guess that explains the Va'Shen hardlight rifles," Ben mused quietly. "No wonder they're built to punch through tanks. Every one of these things *is* a tank."

Azarin had remained silent up until now, listening as Patricia translated Fletcher's briefing for him. <Our commandos should be out front,> he suggested. <Our weapons have the best chance to kill them.>

<Not enough commandos,> Ben replied in Va'Shen. <Also things have animal things. Need work together.>

"Well, the lines are holding for now," Ramirez interjected. "But honestly, I don't think they're trying very hard."

"They're trying to figure out where we are, where the lines are weakest," Burgers explained.

"Why wait, though?" Warren asked. "They have the numbers and the advantage. They don't have to sit there and take it. They could bowl through us if they wanted to."

"But they don't know that," Patricia argued. She turned to Ben. "You were right when you said these things didn't know how to fight Rangers. They haven't met such a large resistance before now. They probably have no idea how weak we actually are."

"Maybe we *should* attack, then," Burgers suggested. "Hit them hard and maintain the illusion that we're king of the hill."

"But if the attack fails, they get a boost out of it and take the initiative," Ramirez argued. "If they're really worried that we have fire superiority, we shouldn't prove them wrong."

"The mission hasn't changed," Ben broke in. "We have to delay them, not beat them. If that means they're reluctant to move, that's just better for us. Right now, they're surrounded, and they know it. We keep them boxed in for as long as we can."

"Can we hit them with the mortar again?" Patricia asked.

"We don't have any ammo for it left and we couldn't use it anyway without risking our guys," Ben said. "We'd have to pull them back first and then try. But the moment they start getting hit, they'll try to move out of the way..."

"And we won't be there to stop them," Patricia sighed. "How long can we keep going like this, though?"

"As long as we have to," Ben told her.

* * *

Ben walked up to the group of soldiers waiting near the trucks and LTVs staged at the sally port of the FOB gate. Twenty enlisted troops, armed and armored were huddled around the front of one of the trucks, listening as a corporal gave them a route brief.

The sun was going down, and in the distance, they could hear occasional gunfire as their fellow Rangers took shots at alien scouts probing their defenses. None of them took notice, focused on the mission ahead of them.

Driving to Jamieson Airfield had become routine for them, but the circumstances now were far from that. No one could be sure that Dark One troops hadn't broken through the lines and lay in wait on the road. The LTVs and trucks were hauling wounded men and tods as well as the alien cadaver. For them, it was a no-fail mission.

Ben watched the route-brief, listening as they went over what to do in the event of an ambush or if one of them got lost, every possible eventuality.

Finally, the group finished and broke up, heading to their respective vehicles. Ben approached the corporal, Harrison, who stood at attention but was careful not to salute.

"Sir," he said.

"You got everything you need?" Ben asked him.

"Yes, Sir, good to go," Harrison told him, the slightest hint of a Brooklyn accent coloring his words.

"Listen," Ben told him. "When you get there, they may try to 'requisition' your vehicles. Don't let them. If they try, tell them to talk to Colonel Hopper. When the time comes, we're going to need these vehicles to bug out, and I don't want us out here with our asses in the breeze because some colonel decided he wanted an extra staff vehicle."

"No problem, Sir," Harrison said.

"How are the wounded?" Ben asked.

"We got 'em all tucked in and comfy," Harrison said. "I'm a little worried about the Va'Shen wounded. If something goes wrong with one of them, we wouldn't know how to treat them, but Ms. Alacea said they're stable, so it should be okay."

Ben nodded. "Okay, good, just..." He paused and gave Harrison a hard look. "Who did you just say said they're stable?"

"Ms. Alacea, Sir. At the temple."

"You mean the translator, Alzoria," Ben corrected him, feeling a lead ball start to form in his chest and move steadily downward into his gut.

"Well, yes, Sir, she translated for Ms. Alacea," Harrison said. Seeing the look on Ben's face, the Ranger became nervous. "Is there something wrong, Sir?"

Ben grit his teeth. "No, Corporal. Get going. Be safe."

"Yes, Sir."

The captain didn't move as Harrison dashed for the lead LTV in the convoy. The sally port and gate opened, and the vehicle started to roll away.

Leaving a very pissed off Ranger officer to seethe in the dust and exhaust.

* * *

Alacea rose to her feet from where she had knelt while leading a small group of wounded commandos in prayer. While Healer Fletcher was more than willing to care for the Va'Shen wounded, she would be the first to admit that she wasn't an expert on caring for them. So, in the end, she would stabilize the wounded commandos and then send them to the temple where Va'Shen healers and volunteers could provide them with the follow-up care they needed.

Part of that follow-up was spiritual, and Alacea had, among other tasks, led that task herself. Physical and emotional wounds often walked hand-in-hand, and she wanted to be there to help her community come to grips with all of them.

<Rest peacefully,> she told them with a bow.

The commandos, all bandaged in different ways, some missing limbs, all bowed to her as best they could. <Honor be to our Na'Sha,> they said as one.

She bowed a second time and turned to head toward her next task. Before she could take a single step, she ran headlong into something hard and unyielding. Blinking, she looked up and into the eyes of her alien husband.

The priestess often had difficulty reading his emotions, but, somehow, she could tell he was angry to the point of wrath.

<Te...> she began, but he interrupted by snatching her wrist in his hand and turning, all but dragging her toward the front door of the temple. When they arrived, she saw an LTV with a pair of Rangers standing next to it.

He released her and pointed at the vehicle. <You get in. You go,> he told her sternly. <Fighters take you to mountain hills. You stay at place.>

Her ears flattened against her head in anger. <Did my brother tell you I was still here?> she asked.

<Azarin say nothing,> he replied, and by the bitterness in his tone, she knew for certain he was telling the truth. <Find out other way. You get in. You go.>

<I will not,> she told him, regally raising her nose into the air as her tail waved behind her. <My place is here.>

<Here is danger!> he snapped at her. <Mountain not danger!>

She pointed back toward the temple. <Then the people within that temple are also in danger,> she told him evenly. She knew getting angry and shouting would not win her this argument. As much as she cared for her *Tesho*, she knew that, in this aspect, she was the more skilled. <You would have me abandon them?>

It was a shot at his honor, but not one that went too far as the question was an obvious one. Against her brother, it had worked well.

<Yes,> he said simply in response, leaving her somewhat flatfooted. At her silence, he pointed at the temple himself. <You want ask them?> he demanded. <Ask commandos if Na'Sha danger good? Should Na'Sha go or stay? Let us ask. What they think say to you bad or good?>

He was so worked up that his grasp on her language was slipping, and she took a breath.

<*Tesho*,> she said softly. <You would not leave your people, even if they asked it of you. It is part of what makes you an honorable tod and leader. I cannot leave my people here to face such danger alone.> She paused for a second before throwing the killing blow. <Would you dishonor me by forcing me to?>

"Damn you!" he snapped at her in English, turning and running his hand through his short haircut. He remembered what she said while explaining Azarin and Hestean's relationship, that dishonoring someone you loved was the absolute worst thing a person could do. She was warning him this was a line for which she would not forgive him crossing. He shook his head and looked away.

Alacea looked down at the temple steps. She knew her refusal to comply with his demand, to ease his mind, hurt him. It wasn't that she believed her role more important than his. She wasn't even offended by what he was trying to do. It was simply an unfortunate truth that she couldn't, in good faith, do what he was asking.

<I did not want you to know,> she said gently. <Because I did not want your mind and heart to be split between me and what you must do.> She bowed to him. <I am sorry.>

He turned back to her and quickly looked away again, not ready yet to see her drooping ears and slack tail.

<I...> he began before trailing off. <I... cannot... lose you.> he told her carefully. <I... want... die... me-self... instead.>

<I feel the same way,> she replied, stepping toward him. Reaching out, she touched his cheek with her fingertips. <But I will not, and neither will you. I am a Na'Sha, but I am no martyr. We will both fulfill our roles as the Gods intended, and then we will be together again. So, you must live, and I must live.>

He took the hand at his cheek in his and squeezed. "I love you," he told her in English. At her questioning look, he searched for a way to say it in Va'Shen. But he knew that if he tried to translate it, it would only sound goofy. He wanted to tell her the way he felt it. Leaning down, he nibbled her left ear, prompting her to close her eyes.

She wrapped her arms around him and squeezed, a hiccup leaving her throat before she could rein it back in.

<Entrust this place and these people to me, *Tesho*,> she said. <I promise, they and I will be here to welcome you later.>

Several moments passed before his reply came. <Yes, good,> he muttered softly. Reluctantly, he pulled away from her. <Must leave now.>

<Yes,> she said, regaining her composure.

<If... things be bad,> he said. <I send people and wagons. Get all you from here.>

She bowed to him. <We shall be ready.>

Chapter 12

"What in the hell happened to you?" Patricia asked as the Ranger entered the room. "You get hit?"

Ramirez, still kitted out in his battle-rattle and weapon, stopped and looked at the terp curiously. "What do you mean?" he asked.

She pointed at the shoulders of his body armor, which were beginning to turn red from the blood dripping from the fleshy parts of his ears.

He looked down and saw the stains, then reached up and touched his ears with gloved hands, checking his fingertips and seeing blood there. "Oh!" he said. "That! Yeah... I... um... I fell?"

Patricia's narrowed her eyes at him. "What did you do?" she demanded.

"Captain around?" he asked, ignoring her question for the moment. "I need to let him know I'm gonna reconfigure our positions on the east side of..."

"What did you do?" she asked again.

"Actually... Alzoria... did this," he admitted, almost mumbling.

"Alzoria hit you?" she asked, the words not making sense.

"What?! No!" he replied. He cleared his throat. "You see... Alzoria and I... kinda... sorta... got married..."

Patricia pursed her lips. "You know that's a lot more permanent than your 'I love the Air Force' tattoo, right?" she asked irritably.

"How did you know about my tattoo?" he asked, puzzled.

"*Everyone* knows about your tattoo!" she snapped back. "Staff Sergeant..."

He held his hands up in surrender. "I know! I know! I remember what the captain said. It's forever and ever and ever... And I'm good with that."

The terp sighed. "Well... As long as you're aware of it..."

"C'mon, Ma'am!" he said good-naturedly. "You know, when you enlist in the Army, you're *supposed* to take on commitments that officers disapprove of. Like buying a new sports car with a twenty-five percent interest loan and getting engaged to an exotic dancer! Way I figure it, this is a lot better than that."

"So, then, why did she hit you?" she asked, getting back to the main topic.

"Oh, no!" he said, waving his hand to ward off any misunderstanding. "You see... Va'Shen don't kiss like humans do. I guess it really freaks them out. They nibble ears instead."

"Those aren't nibbles," Patricia pointed out. "That's a mauling."

Ramirez grinned. "*Yeah, it is!*"

She growled low in her throat at how proud he looked. "You break that girl's heart, and I'll beat your ass," she warned.

"I break that girl's heart, half the company will beat my ass," he replied. He held up the papers destined for Ben's perusal. "I'mma just leave these here on his desk."

"Fine," she relented. "Then swing by Fletcher's and have her spray those with antiseptic or something. 'My wife kissed me too hard' is a really stupid way to get sepsis."

Ramirez gave her a grin and a jaunty salute before taking off again. Patricia smiled. It was nice to see the two had finally gotten over their mutual case of the stupids and done something.

She just hoped that it would be a long marriage. Given the way things were going, it wasn't a sure bet.

* * *

The next attack was the following morning. This time, the Dark Ones hit both the east and west defense lines simultaneously, and, once again, it didn't seem to Ben that they were giving it their all.

"I'm sorry," Patricia said from the back of the TOC where she, Ben and Azarin were trying their best to follow the battles using only telephone and messengers. "I know I'm not some high-speed operator, but this is too easy."

Ben looked at the large map of the area hung on the wall at the front of the TOC. After the first couple of skirmishes, the Rangers had gotten better at anticipating the Dark Ones' movements and tactics. On the other hand, it looked to him that the Dark Ones were getting better at judging their movements as well.

Staff Sergeant Bishop put the phone down in the cradle and turned to Ben. "Lancer reports enemy forces are breaking off."

"Tell them to hold position," Ben replied woodenly. The phone rang again, and the TOC controller picked it up. A moment later, she hung up again.

"Saber reports..."

"Enemy forces are breaking off," Ben finished for her. Another battle, another all too easy victory.

<They are learning about you,> Azarin spoke up. Somehow, despite the language barrier, he had picked up on his brother-in-law's uneasiness.

<Learn them?> Ben repeated. It had taken a lot of effort to resist the urge to punch the commando captain in the face when he heard that he had concealed Alacea's presence at the temple from him. It wasn't the time to let things like that get in the way of the mission. He had resolved, however, to give him a good right hook when this was all over.

<They fight at night. They fight at midday,> Azarin explained. <Now they fight in the morning. They want to know if there is a time of day when you are languid; eating perhaps or at prayer.>

"Makes sense," Patricia mumbled.

A thought occurred to Ben, and he turned to Azarin. <Time when Dark Ones bad at fight?>

<I do not know,> Azarin replied. <It was not in the records.>

<Records?> Ben asked.

<Before we left for the Thornbush, I was allowed to read the historical accounts within the temple.> Azarin's tail moved back and forth at the memory. <It was useless then.>

The Ranger captain briefly wondered how Azarin, who was at that time not a captain but a regular trooper, managed to get access to such documents. It wasn't difficult to deduce the answer.

Hestean showed them to him.

He bet the blue-haired vixen would have had a lot to say about their adversary now.

Bishop picked up another ringing phone. "Sword Maiden," she said, calm and business-like. She listened for a moment, and her face scrunched up in confusion. "Say again, Saber," she requested. She listened again and turned to Ben and Patricia. "Sir, Saber Six is requesting you go out to the western defense line."

"Something happen?" Ben asked, throwing his armor on in preparation to go.

"The enemy forces seem to be trying to communicate."

"That's good," Patricia commented as she, like her captain, suited up for combat.

"You need to hear this for yourself, Ma'am," Bishop said ominously.

* * *

They kept their heads low as they made their way from the field where they parked the LTV to the wooded area where the humans and Va'Shen had established the western defense line that prevented the Dark Ones from approaching Pelle. They were almost to the line of firing positions when they heard it; a growling, inhuman voice calling to them from somewhere in the trees beyond their line of sight.

As they got closer, they were surprised to realize that some of the words the voice was saying were in English. They were even more surprised when they made out what those words actually were through the echoes and growling noises.

Burgers saw them coming and made his way to them, staying low. He beckoned the three of them to follow him, and he led them to a sandbagged firing position half buried in the ground and covered with fallen trees. Someone had camouflaged it with red- and white-leafed branches. A Ranger manning an M-270 machine gun was the only other occupant.

"Started just after they broke contact," Burgers explained, shouting over the sound of the alien voice. "Same message over and over again. I know the last part is in Va'Shen, and the first part... well..." He shrugged, not knowing what to make of it, himself.

Ben listened carefully as the message began to repeat again.

GOFUCKYOURSELF.   DE'SHAR. GOFUCKYOURSELF. DE'SHAR.

"What's the Va'Shen word?" Ben asked Patricia. "I don't know that one."

"It means 'submit,'" Patricia supplied.

"So... 'Go fuck yourself and surrender?'" Ben asked.

One of the commandos further down the line scrabbled up to the top of his packed-dirt firing position and shouted back at the voice.

<GO FREEZE!>

Some of the commandos nearby cheered the tod, their ears waggling in mirth.

The Dark Ones answered with a bolt of purple light that turned the top half of the tod into sludge, which splashed down with his lower half all over his two compatriots waiting in their foxhole.

"Suppressing!" the 270 gunner cried before opening fire into the trees in short bursts. The rest of the firing line opened up as well, turning the forest into a killing field crisscrossed by beams of blue light and red tracers.

Patricia knelt down and held her hands over her ears. Azarin, his own ears stuffed with cloth, covered his own anyway. Ben concentrated on observing, waiting to see what the Dark Ones would do next.

"CEASE FIRE! CEASE FIRE!" Burgers called down the line. The lasers and gunfire tapered off, leaving nothing but silence and a smoking deadland for a hundred meters in front of the line.

For a moment, there was no sound.

GOFUCKYOURSELF.   DE'SHAR. GOFUCKYOURSELF. DE'SHAR. GOFUCKYOURSELF. DE'SHAR.

"They're out there," Burgers commented quietly.

"Sure as hell are," Ben agreed. "And waiting for someone to pop their head up again."

"I don't get it," Patricia said. "They open up the channels of communication, and when someone communicates, they shoot them."

Ben looked at Azarin. The tod's cold eye looked back. The Ranger captain knew the commando had been right. The Dark Ones wanted to see how they'd react, nothing more. They weren't actually interested in entertaining a surrender. Perhaps they had been hoping that the humans would obediently stand up and throw down their weapons, allowing the aliens to gun them down.

You never know until you try, I guess...

He looked up at the sky, at the dark clouds mixed with smoke and the ash that had resumed falling around them after the rain had stopped. It was remarkable how quickly a place as beautiful as Tankara Province had become Hell.

"If we get more rain, are you guys going to be alright?" Ben asked Burgers.

"The guys in the foxholes are already standing knee-deep in water," the Ranger told him. "The alternative is getting your head shot off, so they'll deal with it." He looked at his captain and paused for a moment before asking the question on everyone's mind. "Any news from up north?"

Ben shook his head. "Orders stand. Hold as long as we can."

"We keep using ammo like this..." Burgers let the thought trail off. They were a refueling base, not meant for full-on combat, and so they weren't supplied for prolonged battles like this had turned out to be.

"How long?" the captain asked.

Burgers sighed. "They keep attacking like this at the same rate... Couple of days."

"Tell your folks to conserve their ammo," Ben said. "Only shoot at what they can hit. These things are bullet sponges. We need every round to land."

"All the way, Sir," Burgers said.

"All the way," Ben replied with a sigh. "All the way to the end."

* * *

The Caste Leader examined the three-dimensional map formed in the dirt where they had made their fortress-like camp. If its people were good at anything, it was defense, a specialty and compulsion built up within each of them over the course of tens of thousands of years of evolution. As a result, even if these Gofuckyourselfs were to attack, they would soon find themselves bogged down in traps, overlapping fields of fire, and the tentacles of war beasts. And if they managed to get through all that, they would have to overcome the hills of dirt reinforced with shell shielding grown specifically for the purpose.

So, the Caste Leader could feel at perfect ease as it prepared the next move. It had its troops attack in small numbers, both to test the Va'Shen defenses and give the impression that its forces were weaker than they were. It wanted to know where they were weakest and when. It wanted them to feel under constant attack but also overconfident in their capabilities. So that when the final blow came, the shock would be overwhelming and crippling. It had needed time to prepare for that attack, anyway, and buying that time had been worth it.

They only had the ability to gestate a few war beasts at a time, and as quick as that process had become over the millennia, it would never be instant. It was a risk. If this did not work, they would not be able to gestate any more.

And so, in the meantime, it looked for an advantage. It was forced to give the enemy commander credit. There were no obvious weak points that it could find, but its people were not the kind to only attack when the advantage was theirs. *They* were their own advantage. They had remade themselves over and over again, remade their world over and over again, until only their strongest forms were created.

So, even though there was no great weak point, it would make do with the weakest of the strong points. It pointed at an area of the map that corresponded with the defensive line's right wing. That side had been the slowest to return fire and had the lowest number of Gofuckyourselfs compared to Va'Shen. The Va'Shen weapons were stronger, yes, but these Gofuckyourselfs were much more disciplined, much more likely to hit their targets and much less likely to collapse.

It turned to its officers, and its carapace lit up in a swirl of colors. **PREPARE TO STRIKE.**

* * *

Jozoto had been one of the few Hunters in Garan'Sel. Unlike Pelle, which depended much more on agriculture, Garan'Sel did not need as many Hunters to keep the number of wild animals down to protect their crops and livestock. In a village where every tod was a miner, he had been almost an outsider.

But after arriving in Pelle, where they had no mines, but plenty of animals, Jozoto was suddenly indispensable. His talents were appreciated, although they were not as refined as those of Pelle's Hunters. Even so, he had found himself "important."

And as he was important, he volunteered to be the forward lookout for the western defense line's right wing, anchored on the right by the Odoro River and on the left by the center strong point. Most of the right wing was made up of Va'Shen, including almost all of the Garan'Sel commando, who, for obvious reasons, objected to fighting alongside the Dark Ones. The captains had conceded to this, and only a few Dark One soldiers had come with them, welcomed by the commandos of Pelle and Kar'El, but ignored by those of Garan'Sel.

Looking back, even his sharp eyes could not make out the figures crouching in their foxholes or bunkers two hundred meters away. Dawn would not come for two more hours, and the branch midway up the tree he had found to station himself had been anything but comfortable for the last six.

He wanted to sleep.

But he couldn't. Should the new invaders attack, his job was to rush back and warn the others, and if he could not do that, he was to use the orange weapon the Dark Ones had provided. The snub-nosed flare pistol was set firmly in his belt, and Jozoto once again went over the process of firing it in his mind.

Point up, pull back the switch on the back, then pull the trigger set below it.

When he did, a bright red firework would fly high into the sky and warn of the invaders' approach. He would, of course, prefer to run back and warn them, but that might not be possible. If they were too close by the time he spotted them, his plan was to fire the flare and then climb higher into the trees, leaping from branch to branch like he did as a child in the forests around Garan'Sel. Safe in their branches, he would wait for the attack to end and then return.

As if affirming this for him, the tree he was sitting in swayed in the wind. Leaves rustled in the trees around him, and he sniffed the air, hoping, perhaps, to get a scent on the wind.

It was then that he realized that there actually *wasn't* any wind. The air was still.

The tree swayed again, and he reached out to hold onto the trunk. In that moment, something wrapped around that arm that bit into the flesh all around it.

He cried out and looked at it... and then up.

A tanpuki, five of its six tentacles wrapped around the branches above him, with the sixth wrapped around Jozoto's arm, opened its jaws silently and lunged down at him.

The flare gun... along with several pieces of Jozoto... fell to the forest floor below as the trees above continued to shudder and sway like a wave heading straight toward the right wing.

* * *

"Shouldn't you be sleeping?" Patricia asked him as she rested on the desk one of the two coffee cups she was holding.

Ben looked up from the reports, maps, and intelligence assessments he had been going through for the better part of three hours and smiled wearily. "Can't sleep."

The young terp leaned against her desk and took a sip of coffee. "I thought you Rangers were supposed to sleep any chance you get."

"Believe me, I'd love to," Ben told her, leaning back in his chair. "I just can't. Too much to think about."

"We've been able to hold them back just like Hopper wanted," Patricia said supportively. "It could be going a lot worse."

"Then why isn't it?" he asked. "They could have bum rushed us and been over the river by now, so why aren't they? They want something. Something from Pelle. But what?"

"You don't think, then, that they're afraid of us," she said cautiously.

He shook his head. "The more I think about that, the more it doesn't make sense. If we were stronger than them, we would have repelled them when they first showed up at the river. But we didn't. When Turan hit them on the road, they drove us off. They *have* to know that we're not strong enough to take them head-to-head, so why pretend that they don't?" He sighed. "It would help if we knew what they actually wanted."

"To take Jamieson and then the capital, I thought," the lieutenant posited. The intel assessments she had were filled with all the bad things the Dark Ones could do if they took Jamieson. It was only a stone's throw from there to the Imperial Palace.

"You see, I don't know about that either," Ben told her, leaning forward and resting his elbows on his desk. "They get stranded here, surrounded by their enemies, so they say 'fuck it, let's go for it,' and try to win an interstellar war all on their own?"

"All right," Patricia sighed, not sure what answer she could give that would ease her commander's mind. "What would you do if you were *their* commander?"

"They're aliens, I'm not sure that will translate," he admitted.

"At some level, *all* lifeforms are the same," Patricia said. "If nothing else, all lifeforms have the desire to preserve their own lives. If you and your Rangers crash landed on Va'Sh early on in the war, what would you have wanted?"

"Easy," Ben said. "Get the hell off it again."

It was a flippant answer, as true as it was, and at Patricia's annoyed look, he gave the answer more thought.

"Well," he said, putting his company commander hat on. "First, I would want my forces to evade capture."

"Okay, that tracks," Patricia said. "They're doing that too. It's just that, instead of running and hiding, they're on offense."

He nodded. That could very well be true. Perhaps it was simply their doctrine to establish a position of strength as a way of maintaining their freedom. They certainly had the forces for it.

The sound of distant gunfire broke into their conversation, and the two looked in that direction.

"Another raid," Patricia sighed.

"We should start setting our watches by it," Ben commented dryly.

"Then what?" she asked. At his questioning look, she clarified. "You evade capture, and then what?"

Ben thought about going to the TOC, but if the raid was like all the others there was no immediate need, and if anything happened, they'd come get him.

"Okay," he said. He thought hard for a moment. "If I was under these same circumstances..." He paused and bit the inside of his cheek in thought. "Shit, I don't know. I know I wouldn't attack. What would be the point? I'd have an entire planet working against me and no way to escape. Even if we... I mean the Va'Shen... had any ships..."

He trailed off as the truth stood up in front of him, took the CJTF phone book off his desk, and smacked him in the face with it. The only ship the CJTF had capable of escaping the system had been the *Neil Armstrong*. All that was left at Jamieson they could fly were sub-orbital cargo lifters.

And one ship they *couldn't* fly.

But one the Va'Shen, theoretically, *could*.

He looked at Patricia and wondered if she saw it. The puzzled look she was giving him made it apparent she didn't.

"The Emperor's escape ship," he said. "The one at Jamieson that we took a tour of. It can still fly."

Her eyes went wide. She stood up straight and worked the possibility around in her mind. "But they *can't* fly it," she pointed out. "There aren't any Mikorin pilots left, remember? The briefer said very few Mikorin can actually fly them."

"Yeah, but there's no way for *them* to know that," Ben pointed out, rising to his feet and grabbing his cover off the desk. "All they know is what their scans of the planet can tell them, and that's that there's a ship at Jamieson. They've fought the Va'Shen before. They probably know more about how those ships function than we do!" He shook his head. "That's why they've been hitting the villages. They're looking for a pilot!"

"It wouldn't make sense to blitz all the way to Jamieson only to find out there isn't one around," Patricia noted with a breath. "It... It tracks."

"They find a Mikorin who can fly, push north, grab the ship and go," Ben said. "Then they fly home and tell their leaders all about the new squishy aliens they found on Va'Sh and how easy it is to blow their ships up."

"We need to warn Hopper," Patricia said. "Tell him to blow that ship up or..." She paused a moment later and cleared her throat. "*If* there was a Mikorin to fly it," she corrected, "Then he would need to blow the ship up."

"Right, *but*," Ben said. "That means it would be safe to use it as a lure for a trap. Draw them in, let them think they're close and then nail them with heavy artillery."

"It could work," she agreed.

He rested his hand on the phone. "Let's tell..."

Just as he was about to pick up the receiver, a Ranger practically knocked down the office door rushing in.

"Sir! They need you at the TOC!" the man gasped.

"What's happening?" Ben demanded, already starting for the door.

"The aliens hit the western defense line *hard*!" the Ranger reported. "The right wing has collapsed! They're breaking through!"

* * *

"They're in the fucking trees!" Burgers heard someone shout amid the screams and gunfire. He was already halfway down the center of the line, making his way toward the right wing when he heard it. The troops he was passing, human and Va'Shen, were holding their fire, not seeing any signs of the enemy ahead of them. Even those closest to the right wing couldn't make out any weapons fire coming from that sector.

It was only when Burgers got closer, heard the shout, and saw beams of blue light and red tracers shooting upward into the sky, that he realized it.

"We got squids in the trees!" he shouted. "Look up! Look up!"

The Rangers and commandos moved their attention upward, some firing their weapons into the branches of the trees above them anytime the wind moved them. That only made them move faster, which prompted more troops to fire upward.

Burgers ran toward the right, as red flares flew into the air, casting even more moving shadows onto the ground and into the trees, making the confusion even worse. He saw a Ranger heading toward him from the other direction and was about to call out to him when a dark, tentacled mass dropped from the tree above the trooper, snagged him, and pulled him into the branches.

Burgers, shocked, froze for a moment, his eyes upward as the Ranger began screaming. Finally, he brought his M-31 up, switched to full auto and raked the branches with automatic fire.

The screaming stopped.

As the gunfire into the trees continued, new weapons fire began coming at them from the ground to their east. Bolts of purple lightning whizzed through their lines, locking onto the sources of the hardlight blasts and tracers.

Burgers threw himself on the ground and quickly changed magazines. "CONTACT FRONT!" he shouted. He fired into the treeline, not even seeing the Dark Ones shooting in their direction, just hoping his one rifle and the few others that heard him could suppress the fire up front long enough for the rest of the line to shift fire again.

A long, gargling wail came from the tree-line, followed by several others, and the Dark One small arms fire was joined by larger blasts from the guns mounted on the giant armored snails.

The situation was, as the Army liked to say, less than ideal. On his right, Burgers could see human and Va'Shen shadows, moving backward, some of them retreating in good order and returning fire, while others flat-out ran. On his left, the return fire was vastly inferior in volume to what was being directed at them. And to his front, he could just start to make out tall, inhuman shadows moving closer.

"Fall back!" he shouted. "Fall back!" He heard the cry begin to echo up and down the line.

The Dark Ones had broken through.

* * *

"I can't raise Saber, Sir," Bishop reported. "But Watchtower reports the western defense line is breaking and trying to fall back."

"Signal them to fall back to the second defense line," Ben ordered, a cold ball of steel forming in his stomach.

Bishop picked up the receiver and spoke quickly, but calmly into it. "Watchtower, Watchtower," she said. "Blue Light. Say again. Blue Light."

A few seconds later, a series of three blue flares flew into the air from the central watchtower on the FOB, the visible signal for all forces to fall back to the second defense line near the village. The map NCO rushed forward to the map on the wall and began drawing red arrows from the western defense line to another line that butted up against Pelle.

Ben bit his lip. "Contact Lancer and Assassin," he told Bishop. "Tell them to make their way to the village."

The TOC controller looked like she wanted to say something. The logical, military thing to do right now would be to have them hold position in case this was a feint to draw attention from their real objective to the north. But after his conversation with Patricia, Ben knew he would have to gamble. If they were right, this wasn't a feint or a distraction. They were going to Pelle.

The door opened, and Azarin entered.

<Our sentries on the eastern rooftops are reporting movement,> he said. <What has happened?>

<Dark Ones go to Pelle,> Ben told him simply. <Fort breaked. Moving to next fort.>

<Gods,> Azarin whispered.

<Please tell Alacea,> Ben told him. <Sick must leave place now. Not later time. Now. Understand?>

<Yes, Overlord,> the one-eyed captain replied.

As he headed toward the door, Ben turned to Patricia. "Tell Fletcher to get her wounded on the LTVs and ready to go. Then she needs to get some vehicles to the temple and pick up whoever they can. Regroup here and then floor it north."

"Yes, Sir!"

Ben turned to the Ranger who had summoned him to the TOC. "Find Senior Chief and tell him to get everyone over the bridge to the north side of the river and prepare to blow the bridge."

"Ye... Yes, Sir!"

Patricia and the Ranger rushed out of the TOC, and Ben looked back at the map showing him the end of the world in near-real time.

The second defense line wasn't nearly as robust as the first, and it wasn't meant to be a place to regroup after an all-out retreat. The sound of gunfire from the Black Forest was becoming more sporadic. His people were either retreating or dead.

It was time to leave.

* * *

The moment the lead LTV rolled to a stop outside the temple, Fletcher hopped out and started yelling to her volunteer stretcher bearers to get a move on. The other passengers of the LTVs began opening the backs and preparing to load them with as many wounded Va'Shen as they could.

She spun around as the sound of automatic gunfire, a constant background noise in the village, suddenly seemed closer, but as much as she scanned the street in either direction, Pelle appeared to be a ghost town without a soul, human or alien, in sight.

Alzoria joined her as she lowered her M-90 submachine gun, her Huntress senses heightened as much as they had ever been. When her *Tesho* and Burgers had asked her to stay and help Fletcher translate for the Va'Shen wounded, she had assumed they were trying to keep her out of the way. Now, she saw they had entrusted her with an important mission.

Fletcher saw the stretcher bearers were almost done unloading and turned to Alzoria.

"Go tell them we need to start moving them now," she ordered. "Ask how many people are in there."

"Aye aye aye!" Alzoria replied before quickly running into the temple. She didn't have to go far. Alacea had heard the vehicles approach and was on her way to meet them.

<Na'Sha!> Alzoria greeted quickly and with just as quick a bow. <We have to go! The Dark Ones are coming!>

Alacea's tail whipped about in sudden fear and concern. She could hear the weapons fire moving closer to the village and had feared this was about to happen.

<We are already preparing them,> she assured Alzoria.

<How many are there?>

<Twelve wounded and four assistants,> Alacea answered.

By this time, Fletcher had seen the two talking and came up to join them. <How many?> she demanded.

Alzoria translated what the priestess had said, and Fletcher bit her lip. They had six LTVs. They were going to have to cram everyone into every possible space. From the sound of things, there wasn't going to be a second trip.

"All right!" she shouted to the others. "Get in there and start moving them out!" She looked up at the troops in the LTV turrets, scanning the area anxiously behind their mounted weapons. "Keep shit real out here," she told them. "We'll be as quick as we can."

"We gotcha, Corpsman," one of the gunners called back.

<Is it bad?> Alacea asked the medic, pulling her attention away from the street for a moment.

Alzoria translated the question, and Fletcher nodded. "Real bad."

<Is my *Tesho* safe?> Alacea asked. Despite the dignified composure Alacea maintained, it was obvious she was worried.

"He's fine," Fletcher said with a reassuring, but meaningless, smile. "Right now, we need to get you and your people over the river and out of here."

Hearing the translation of her words, Alacea bowed quickly and returned to the temple to oversee the evacuation. As the stretcher bearers began to emerge from the temple with wounded, Fletcher checked each patient, disappointed to see that many of them had wounds with no easy fix. Many of them, she thought, would die regardless of what they did unless they could somehow get them to a modern hospital.

The loading was slow, as the stretcher bearers were volunteers rather than trained medics, and getting the wounded and passengers situated was taking longer than Fletcher would like, especially as the gunfire seemed to be getting closer.

<They're already in the village,> Alzoria whispered just loud enough for Fletcher to hear. <They must have gotten through the commandos... or around... or...>

The medic said nothing. All she had heard from Lieutenant Kim was that the aliens had broken through the line in a massive attack, and they were trying to retreat. A retreat in good order was a difficult maneuver to pull off in the best of times, when all the units involved had worked and trained together and knew each other's tactics. Between multiple units of different species' militaries and languages, it would be all but impossible. The Rangers, she knew, would be okay, but she had no idea what condition the commandos would return in.

She saw Alacea exit the temple again. "How many more?" Fletcher demanded.

<Just three!> the priestess answered.

"Just three more," Fletcher repeated to herself. She started to turn to the gunner in the lead LTV when the vehicle blew over onto its side as if struck by a charging rhino and caught fire. It hadn't even stopped rolling when several blasts of purple light began flying over their heads and all around them.

The remaining gunners didn't waste time, turning their weapons toward the source of the incoming fire and opening up on them. Fletcher snagged Alzoria by the wrist and dragged her behind one of the remaining vehicles for cover. She looked at the burning LTV ahead of them for any signs of life, but nothing but a burning hulk of metal and brown organic sludge remained.

"CORPSMAN!" She looked up and found the gunner of the LTV she was hiding behind calling down to her. "CORPSMAN, WE GOTTA GET THE FUCK OUT OF HERE!"

"The wounded are..."

Before she could finish her reply, a bolt of purple light zipped over the LTV, taking the top half of the gunner with it. Fletcher felt something thick and gooey splash down on her and nearly wretched when she realized it was the remains of the gunner. Next to her, Alzoria, also covered head-to-toe in brown gore, was shaking, her eyes wide and her tail shivering in fear.

The corpsman choked back her fear and panic. "MOVE OUT!" she called, opening the passenger door of the LTV and shoving Alzoria into it before climbing in on top of her. The driver had his window open and was firing his pistol blindly at an enemy he couldn't actually see.

Fletcher slapped his armor to get his attention. "DRIVE!" she screamed at him.

"YES, MA'AM!" the young private cried in response. He threw the LTV into gear and stomped on the gas. Although she was lying down on the seat on top of a terrified alien girl and didn't have a good look out the window, she could still see flashes of purple light passing by them. There was a loud boom behind them, and she could make out the sounds of screaming as another LTV further down the line was hit.

"DON'T STOP!" she shouted at the driver.

The private didn't answer, even when a flash of light slammed into the windshield between them, passed through the vehicle and out the back.

They drove for several minutes, until the flashes of light, explosions and screaming had stopped, before coming to a slow stop outside the FOB fenceline.

"Alzoria?" Fletcher asked, shaking the vixen below her with her hand. "You okay?"

The vixen opened her eyes, having kept them closed tightly since being pushed into the seat.

"Mina?" she asked in a shaking voice. "You... You are good in da'hood?"

"Yeah. Alzoria good?"

"Alzoria good," the girl confirmed.

Fletcher began to rearrange the two of them into a more vertical position, packed into the vehicle like sardines.

"Private, you good?" she asked.

"Yeah... Yeah, I'm good, Corpsman," the driver's shaky voice said. He was looking over his shoulder at the back of the LTV, his face pale.

Following his gaze, she saw that three Va'Shen wounded had been loaded into that LTV, side-by-side. The one in the center had been completely liquified, and the other two were moaning in pain, their arms nearest the center patient completely gone at the shoulder.

"Fuck," the private gasped. "Fuck me..."

Fletcher looked further back and found only two LTVs parked behind them, waiting. One of the turrets was empty, the windshield below it coated with brown sludge. The driver had turned on the wipers to try to regain visibility. She wasn't sure about the LTV behind that one.

<The Na'Sha,> she heard gasped into her ear. <Where is the Na'Sha?>

Fletcher understood enough of the question to know what Alzoria was worried about. The last time she saw Alacea, the priestess was in the temple doorway. Did she run back into the temple or had she tried to get into one of the vehicles?

"Private," she muttered, wiping some of the sludge from her face with a shaking hand. "Get us back on the FOB."

The vehicle began to move. Fletcher shut her eyes tightly, trying not to break down, herself, as Alzoria's hiccups and the moans of the wounded filled the LTV.

* * *

Azarin entered the TOC and marched straight up to Ben, who was standing over Staff Sergeant Bishop's shoulder, straining to listen to the voice on the end of the phone in his hand.

"We were able to link up with what's left of Saber," Staff Sergeant Ramirez's voice came over the line, filled with static. "We managed to secure the northernmost quarter of the second defense line, but they've got us pinned down pretty good."

"What about the village?" Ben asked.

Ben could hear another voice talking to Ramirez and was relieved to realize it was Staff Sergeant Baird. A second later Ramirez was replying to his question.

"As soon as they broke through, they made a dash straight for the village," Ramirez reported. "Left just enough forces to keep us occupied and out of their way. Ammo is red." He was silent for a moment before continuing. "Sir, I don't see a way to break through them and get into Pelle."

"What about Captain Turan?" Ben asked, worry encasing him like a frozen, wet blanket.

"We split up just before the vil," Ramirez called back through the static. "I think he was going to try to circle around south of the village and try to flank them. But we haven't heard anything since then."

Ben growled and rubbed the five o'clock shadow on his chin with his hand.

"Can you pull back north to the FOB?" Ben asked. At this point, asking his people to throw themselves at the Dark Ones with little ammo and God-knows-how-many wounded would do nothing but send them to a meaningless death.

Again, he heard the two NCOs conversing amongst each other.

"Roger that, Sir," Ramirez finally answered.

"Out here."

The line went dead, and Ben put the phone down into the cradle. The captain took a breath and looked up to find every eye in the room on him.

"Bishop," he said quietly. "Contact the JOC. We're bugging out. Have Watchtower send the signal. All forces to get to the bridge and over the river. I want every remaining noncombatant on the FOB gone in the next ten minutes."

"Yes, Sir," Bishop said, picking up the phone again.

Ben turned to Azarin, not sure what to say.

<Pelle is lost,> Azarin supplied for him.

<Yes,> Ben admitted. <I am sorry.>

<The community is safe,> his brother-in-law stated matter-of-factly. <Our duty now is to reform and defend the capital.>

"Sir!"

They both looked up and found Patricia jogging through the door into the TOC. "Senior Chief said the bridge is ready to blow anytime."

"Good," he said.

"I saw the flares," she said. "We're bugging out?"

He nodded. "They're either in Pelle already or will be there soon," he said. "Ramirez and Baird have their backs against the wall. They're going to pull their guys back here. Turan may or may not be trying to circle around south of the village to try to hit them from the south." He gestured to Azarin, asking her to translate all that for him.

The terp began speaking quickly in Va'Shen, and Azarin listened wordlessly.

"What about the wounded?" Ben asked her.

"Fletcher's convoy should be back any minute," she replied.

Ben sighed in relief. That meant Alacea was safe.

"As soon as they get here, take as many full vehicles as we have and haul ass over the river."

"What about you?" she asked, worried for a moment that her captain was about to try to go down with his ship.

"We'll hold here to regroup as best as we can and get out before the Dark Ones get here," he assured her. "Right now, one of us has to be there to push the plunger on those explosives. That's you, Lieutenant."

"Yes, Sir. Have you talked to Hopper yet?" she asked.

He shook his head. "No, not yet. Gotta do that next. Let him know we're moving out and hope he's got some good news for us. As a matter of fact…"

The Ranger officer picked up the phone receiver and dialed the JOC switchboard.

What met his ear was a faint voice overwhelmed by static.

"Ja…son Air….d S…..board, this is .. no….ure line."

"This is Captain Gibson at Sector Thirteen," Ben announced. "I need a direct line to Colonel Hopper."

"I c.. ba..ly ….you. Say a…n, pl…..."

Ben hung up and redialed. The static was still there. After a few minutes of trying and failing, he hung up.

"We're going to have to be our own messengers," he said.

Patricia nodded.

<Bad tidings?> Azarin asked. He had waited patiently for a translation up until now, but one hadn't been forthcoming.

<Cannot call to grand overlord,> Ben told him. <Tell to him things of importance.>

<Our retreat?>

Ben nodded, adding a moment later. <And other thing about Dark Ones... we think it is.>

One of Azarin's ears popped up in interest. <What is that?>

Exhausted and not at his best speaking Va'Shen, Ben gestured to Patricia to explain.

<We think Dark Ones want to take Va'Shen ship waiting up north.>

Azarin's other ear popped up and he took a step forward. <A ship? We were told all of our ships were destroyed.>

<One remains,> Patricia said. <Near to where you were prisoner.> She saw his eyes widen and his tail began to thrash and held her hands up to head off his concern. <Is good. No pilot for ship. They cannot fly...>

<A Duran'Dal,> Azarin whispered.

<Um... Pilot is Duran Doll?>

Ben watched his brother-in-law's ears and tail as the commando leader did the math on his own and came to, what he thought, was the same conclusion they had. But he was surprised at what he did next.

Azarin reached out and grabbed Ben's arms.

<We must get to Alacea!> Azarin cried. <Now! Right now!>

Without waiting for an answer, the Va'Shen went to the weapons rack and snatched up his hardlight rifle.

<What?> Ben asked. <Why problem Alacea?>

Azarin turned to him at the doorway.

<Duran'Dals,> he began, his tail thumping the wall and floor in panic. <Are all *former Na'shas!*>

"Sir..."

They turned to the sound of the voice near the door, and Patricia gasped, her hand going to her mouth. Standing in the doorway, still covered in the sludge remains of some Ranger or commando, were Fletcher and Alzoria. The Huntress ran to Azarin and began to speak rapidly, blubbering something between fearful hiccups. Fletcher remained in the doorway.

"Medical convoy got hit at the temple," she said plainly. "Lost three LTVs, six of our guys, five Va'Shen patients."

Ben stared at her, his face a frozen mask.

"Alacea?" he asked her.

Fletcher opened her mouth to answer and closed it again. Ben began to breathe faster as the worst possibility seemed to get closer and closer to reality.

"I don't know," Fletcher told him honestly. "She was near the temple entrance when we got hit... I..."

Ben turned and calmly walked to the cross-like stand where he kept his armor and helmet. Throwing it over his head and fastening the clasps, he began giving orders.

"Load up the wounded," he told Fletcher and Patricia. "Get everyone else out. Get over the river and send a messenger to Hopper. Tell him to blow up the Va'Shen ship now." He donned his helmet and fastened the strap beneath his chin. "Lieutenant, once everyone is over the bridge, blow it."

"What about you, Sir?" the terp asked him nervously.

He picked up his M-31 off the weapons rack and checked the action. "Don't worry about us," he said. "Blow that bridge. Stop them here."

"Even if we did, they might still..." she began to argue.

"Then they work a little harder for it!" Ben shut the argument down. "We're counting seconds now, Patricia. Get our people out, blow the bridge. If it looks like the Dark Ones are going to cross before then, blow it then." He turned to Azarin. <You prepared?>

<Yes,> the commando replied. <Alzoria will pass my orders to Turan to escape when he arrives.>

<That is good,> Ben said woodenly. He gave his gear one last check and nodded. <We go.>

Patricia, Fletcher and Alzoria watched the two men exit the TOC and head toward the pedestrian gate at a trot.

Chapter 13

Alacea fell right on her backside onto the temple steps when the LTV flipped over and caught fire, her hands going to her ears as the Rangers in the turrets began shooting back in the direction of the incoming fire. Things seemed to have been going well, but in the space of a few seconds, had become something out of nightmare. Humans and Va'Shen screamed in pain and terror, their cries barely audible over the sound of gunfire.

It was difficult to make anything of what was happening, with the situation so chaotic, but her eyes fell onto a Va'Shen woman strapped to a stretcher laying on the ground halfway between the temple stairs and the LTVs. One stretcher bearer lay dead nearby, and the other, one of the Va'Shen healers, crouched over the injured vixen, protecting her with her body.

Climbing to her feet, Alacea rushed to the two vixens and shook the healer's shoulder to get her attention. Not bothering to try to make herself heard over the noise, she instead pointed at the end of the stretcher closest to the vixen's head and went to the other end, grabbing both handles.

The healer complied, and within a few seconds, they had lifted the wounded woman, carrying her quickly back to the temple. Looking over her shoulder so that she wouldn't run into anything while walking backward, Alacea looked back for a moment and saw the remaining LTVs rolling away, trailing fire, smoke and gore behind them.

<Inside!> she shouted at the healer. <Quickly!>

They carried the vixen into the temple toward the main hall where another injured tod with a wounded leg and a healer had been waiting for their turn to board the LTVs.

<The invaders are here!> the healer on the other side of the stretcher cried. <The Dark Ones have abandoned us!>

There was a lot Alacea wanted to say in response to such a statement, but there wasn't time. The true Dark Ones were very likely heading this way to look for survivors. There was no way they could escape carrying the injured.

They needed a place to hide.

Alacea looked from side to side in a panic, searching for inspiration. Her ears popped up to the ceiling as the answer came to her.

<Come!> she said, pulling the stretcher and the healer with it toward the dining hall. <This way!>

The other healer helped the tod with the injured leg up and the two followed them as best they could into the large dining room where the Mikorin took their meals. Two long rows of wooden tables and several chairs stood atop a spotless and polished wood floor.

Except for one spot in the corner where the faint outline of a trapdoor, made to blend into the rest of the floor, waited for them. Alacea quickly led them to it and set her end of the stretcher down.

Her fingers traced the almost invisible seams of the door until she found a part of the wood that was loose. She grasped the tiny, three-by-three-inch square of wood with her fingernails and pulled it out. Inside was a latch, which she quickly pulled. There was a loud *click*, and the end of the door popped up several inches.

<Help me,> Alacea ordered, taking the end of the trapdoor and lifting it upward. Below them was a short set of wooden stairs and some inert water lamps.

<What is this?> one of the healers asked her.

<Storage for emergency provisions,> Alacea explained quickly. <Sho Nan also uses it for pickling vegetables. Help me get her down there.>

The sound of fighting outside was getting closer but also less intense. Once the Dark Ones were done dealing with whatever resistance remained near the temple, they would most likely be coming inside.

The three able-bodied vixens struggled to maneuver the stretcher down into the food cellar. The priestess tried to tamp down her panic, knowing that this was taking far too long. Finally, the stretcher was downstairs with one of the healers, and they turned to the tod with the bad leg.

The other healer helped him down into the cellar much more easily than they had done with the stretcher. The healer looked up at Alacea and waved for her to come down.

Instead, the priestess grabbed the edge of the trapdoor and pulled it closed. There was no way to close the door from the inside, meaning the Dark Ones would instantly discover them if someone didn't close it from the outside. She replaced the latch cover, and, just like that, it was as if there had never been four Va'Shen and a food cellar.

Her ears flew upward as the sound of the temple doors being ripped open and falling to the floor echoed throughout the building. Looking around for a place to hide, Alacea quickly dashed to the kitchen and knelt down behind a counter above which hung several iron pots and pans.

She peeked around the corner as the sound of... not boots or feet... but something hard clacked against the polished floor approaching the dining room. The kitchen was open with no doors separating it from the dining room. Another entryway behind Alacea led out into the hallway and back into the temple proper but she was too scared to try to run that way with the monsters so close.

The clacking steps came closer, and Alacea put her hands over her mouth to keep from gasping out in fear. She looked out into the dining room and quickly pulled her head back at the sight of a black, armored... *thing*... standing in the dining room.

Her eyes were wide, her tail shivering and her breaths coming quickly as some primal, evolutionary fear overtook her. It was if something inside her *knew* instinctively that whatever that thing was, it existed only to kill her. Steeling herself, she managed to get herself to look around the corner again.

The thing was coal black, although there were flecks of white on its body here and there. Spikes of various lengths protruded from its armor, including on both shoulders. On one of these spikes was impaled the head of a human, its expression frozen in terror. Its long arms ended in sharp claws, three on one side and two on the other like it had two "thumbs." Its head was concealed by a smooth glossy black dome, like a helmet, making it impossible to see where it was actually looking.

It turned toward the kitchen, and Alacea pulled back in fear, trying to make herself as small and as quiet as she could.

She heard the sound of its steps again, moving away from the kitchen, and she looked again. To her great relief, the creature was beginning to move toward the exit on the far side of the dining area. It seemed like it would continue its search elsewhere, which might give Alacea an opportunity to escape.

Her hopes were dashed when her delicate ears picked up the muffled sound of a vixen gasping in pain, a sound that came from the corner of the dining room.

The creature stopped cold.

Its upper body turned to face the direction of the storage cellar. It took a step toward the wounded Va'Shen's hiding place, and Alacea covered her mouth in cold fear.

It moved closer, and it was obvious by now that it suspected something under the floor.

Alacea swallowed. She had to do something. Looking up above the counter, she saw the iron pans hanging on hooks hung from the rafters by tightly corded rope. She looked back at the creature, and her tail whipped about in terror.

Gathering her courage, the priestess slapped the pan hanging nearest to her, which caused it to hit the pans next to it with a series of loud clangs. The thing turned quickly to face the kitchen, but Alacea didn't wait around. The Dark One caught a fleeting glimpse of her tail as she ran out the other end of the kitchen and into the temple toward the stairs.

Rising to its full height, it pursued, having to be careful that it didn't trip as its clawed armored feet stabbed into the wood floor with every step, leaving jagged cuts as it moved.

It passed the swinging pans and bulled its way through a paper wall in its pursuit of the Mikorin.

* * *

As frightened as they were for Alacea, both Ben and Azarin made sure to keep a steady, careful pace as they made their way through Pelle's alleyways. Ben let Azarin lead the way, as the tod had grown up in Pelle and obviously knew its layout much better than he ever could. He kept a few steps behind and to the tod's right, his M-31 up at the ready and keeping watch on the right side. To his left, Azarin's hardlight rifle was similarly at the ready, the commando sweeping its barrel left to right as they quietly moved toward the temple.

The sounds of hardlight rifles mixed with the sound of the Dark One weapons perhaps only two hundred yards ahead of them. There were no human weapons to be heard. Ben felt a pang of guilt at the idea that he and his Rangers had abandoned Pelle, but he knew, objectively, that wasn't the case. There would be a time for his Rangers to get payback later when the rest of the CJTF forces hit the Dark Ones on their way to Jamieson. Right now, the only human who owed anyone in Pelle anything was him.

The two stopped as the alley ended and opened into a side street that crossed in front of them. Azarin held his hand up and waved it up and down.

Ben froze. The gesture had meant nothing to him. Azarin looked back at him and seemed to realize his mistake. He pointed at Ben, and then pointed at the right corner. The Ranger nodded and moved over, covering the right side of the street while his brother-in-law checked the left.

Azarin's ears popped up as he caught a sound too slight for the human to hear. He looked back at Ben.

<Tsst!>

At the sound of the quiet hiss, the human officer looked back and saw Azarin point at another alley on the other side of the street. Looking that way, Ben saw a Va'Shen commando with dark brown hair crouched in the darkness, waving at them with one hand while holding his hardlight rifle in the other.

<We... are... clear... this... end...> Ben whispered, enunciating each word carefully.

<Right side is clear of enemies,> Azarin whispered back. <You go first. I will watch over you.>

Ben nodded, looked both ways down the street, and then dashed across it to the other alley. As he ran, he spared a glance at the buildings around him. Several of them showed signs of damage, while one further down the street was on fire. Past that, the sound of weapons-fire floated toward him.

He reached the alleyway and turned, checking both sides of the street and taking up a firing position at the corner. The waiting commando took up a position on the other corner, and Ben waved to Azarin to come over.

The commando leader was across the street in half the time Ben had taken. Once he was there, the commando who had signaled them pointed further down the alley, silently instructing them to move that way.

The two complied while the commando remained to guard the entryway. They didn't have to go far before they found four other commandos in the alley, talking amongst themselves. Ben saw a familiar mop of rust-colored hair and called to its owner with a whisper.

<Turan!>

The Windsaber commander saw him and gave a quick bow. <Overlord,> he said. He bowed to Azarin a moment later. <Cornet. I have no good news for you.>

<We expect none,> Azarin assured him. <I thank you and your commandos for your courage, but now it is time for you and your people to escape. Did you not see the flares?>

<We did,> Turan admitted. <We wanted to slow their pursuit as much as possible first, but I think we may have exhausted our abilities here.>

<Go over river,> Ben ordered. <Go boom soon.>

Turan didn't need an explanation. He knew what the plan was. <You did not come out here yourselves to tell me this,> he stated. <What has happened?>

<The enemy seeks a Duran'Dal,> Azarin explained quickly. <We must keep the Na'Sha from being captured. We are going to the temple.>

Turan's ears folded downward. <They are already there,> the commando captain told him. <They surround the temple now and have sent warriors into it.>

Ben felt anger and fear well up in him. He knew Alacea was in that temple. There was no way she would abandon it if there was even one person still seeking shelter there. He tried to remind himself that, if anything, the Dark Ones wanted to take her alive, but what if they didn't bother to check first? What if she had been killed during the attack on Fletcher's convoy?

Would he fight his way to the temple only to find her battered, broken body lying on the temple steps? Or would it be even worse than that? No sign of her whatsoever, just puddles of brown liquid that *might* be her? Would he lose *another* wife with no body to mourn, no casket to weep over? Would she simply disappear and leave nothing behind but a Servicemember's Group Life Insurance payment on his next bank statement?

<We go,> he stated firmly. He looked to Turan. <Take your commandos. Leave. Now.>

Turan looked to his commandos and to Azarin, his tail slapping the ground behind him. <We will go, Overlord. And we shall attempt to draw some of them away from the temple as we do so.>

Ben felt some of the tension ease his chest as he finally remembered that he wasn't in this alone.

<I thank you,> he said quietly.

<We owe your *myorin* a debt,> Turan stated simply. <Today, we shall pay it.> He gestured to his commandos and pointed down the alley from which Ben and Azarin had come. <Gather the commando,> he ordered them. <We will hit the invaders and then fade away.>

<Yes, Captain!>

At that, the two groups split again, Turan and his commandos going the way Ben and Azarin had come, and the two captains going further down the alley in the direction of the temple. Upon reaching the end, they once again checked each side for movement. Ben's nose itched at the smell of smoke, which had hung over the entire area for days now, had become even more intense, and he realized that there was a fire nearby.

Peeking around the corner, he could see a plume of white smoke rising from somewhere within the village to their east. Then he noticed another and another. The Dark Ones were destroying buildings as they came upon them.

Azarin turned to him and whispered just loud enough for Ben to hear him over the sound of energy weapons going off nearby.

<We can cross here, go through the tavern, the temple is beyond that.>

<We go, we wait for Turan to make attack, then go more,> Ben suggested.

<I will go first,> Azarin told him. He pointed at a dark brown stained door on the other side of the street below a colorful sign adorned with Va'Shen lettering. Without waiting for Ben's signal, Azarin dashed across the street.

It almost killed him.

Purple light erupted from the window of a building further down the street. The Dark Ones sweeping the inside of the building had seen Azarin's dash and opened fire, scorching the sides of the brick Va'Shen building on either side of the door.

Azarin slammed his shoulder against the door, breaking it open, and fell down inside the doorway. Kicking his legs, he managed to get them both inside as more blasts of purple struck the ground near his feet. He heard the sound of his brother's rifle firing down the street at the source, but from where he was, he couldn't see or hit the source of the fire.

The Va'Shen captain cautiously leaned out the door with his hardlight rifle and fired a shot at where he thought the fire had come. He was answered by several more flashes of light, and he quickly ducked back inside.

He made eye contact with Ben and pointed down the other side of the street.

<Go around!> he called to Ben. <That way! I will keep them here!>

Ben grit his teeth and watched as the Dark Ones' energy blasts continued to rake the building in which Azarin was trapped. Two more hardlight blasts emerged from the door in response. He was pinned down, and there was no way for Ben to join up with him without exposing himself to heavy fire.

<I go!> he agreed to Azarin's plan.

Doubling back, he found a narrow doorway that led into the building and away from the Dark Ones' position. Ben braced himself and raised a heavy booted foot, smashing it down on the door close to the lock. The door slammed open, and Ben entered, rifle up and at the ready, sweeping the room from side to side for ambushers. But the darkened room was empty.

He could still hear the sound of Azarin's hardlight rifle firing as he made his way further into the building toward the opposite end. Another door, this one unlocked, led to the next alley with the wall of the next building waiting for him.

Ben found a window, its glass blown out, and began to repeat the process all over again, leaving the sounds of battle further and further behind him.

* * *

Alacea turned the corner into the second floor hallway and rushed down it toward the Mikorin sleeping quarters, trying desperately to keep her footsteps light and silent. The thing pursuing her didn't bother to do the same, smashing the wooden steps of the stairway with its clawed armored feet as it ascended after her. She had managed to lead it on a fruitless chase so far, but she was running out of places to go. She would duck into one room, wait for it to approach or pass, and then flee down another, drawing it further and further away from the dining hall.

But every room in which she hid was smashed open and destroyed by the monster or monsters looking for her, making them, one by one, useless as hiding spots.

She needed a place to hole up and wait for them to leave or to escape entirely.

The priestess decided to get to the staircase on the far end and go up another floor. Dashing forward, she turned the corner just as the creature behind her entered the hallway and got a fleeting glance of her tail.

She quickened her pace and all but flew up the stairs to the third floor. Rushing to one of the windows, she looked out and prepared to hop out of it onto the sloping tiled roof but stopped dead at the sight of more monsters milling around below, completely surrounding the temple.

Ducking back down, her tail thrashed in panic as she realized just how trapped she was. Why were there so many out there?

She heard the sound of her pursuer climbing the stairs nearby and ducked into the prayer room across the hall. Statues of various Va'Shen gods looked helplessly at her as she searched desperately for somewhere to go. In her panic, she had boxed herself into a room with no other exit.

Cleanliness was a virtue, and clutter was a symptom of a chaotic mind, so the Mikorin thought. This now presented a problem for the priestess as most rooms in the temple were clean, neat and limited to the bare essentials, leaving very few places to conceal herself.

Standing in the back of the room was a tall, ornate cabinet made from purple guum wood. With nothing else coming to mind, she ran to it and pulled the doors open. A broom and rags, other cleaning supplies filled the cabinet, but there was just enough room for her to squeeze in. She just managed to pull her tail in after her and close the cabinet when she heard the sound of the creature's footsteps approaching the room from the hallway.

She closed her eyes and said a silent prayer. Maybe it wouldn't know what a cabinet was and wouldn't know to open it. That was her only hope at this point.

Please, just walk by! There's no one here! Just keep going!

If it went past the prayer room, she could, hopefully, leave and double back the way she came and back down to the first floor.

The sound of wood breaking and paper tearing forced her eyes open. It was smashing through the door to the prayer room, too lazy to fumble with the latch to open it. The thumps of its footsteps entered the room and stopped.

Just go away! Please just go away!

She shut her eyes and held her breath, trying to remain perfectly silent, but the sound of her heart continued to bang in her chest, as loud to her as thunderclaps that she was certain the creature would hear. All the running and fear had left her tired, and if she breathed it would come in loud pants.

It was going to find her.

* * *

The Caste Leader entered the room filled with small, three-dimensional representations of the primitive creatures' deities and looked around. The Mikorin had escaped to this floor, it knew, but exactly where it did not.

Having seen for itself how stealthy and fast the Va'Shen were, it understood that it must be patient in its pursuit, careful to let it run without giving it an avenue of escape. Let it tire itself out in the chase until exhausted. Then, left with nowhere else to run, it would stop in despair and give itself up to death at the creature's hands.

But before that death, it would ask what it was. And if it was a Duran'Dal or a Na'Sha, it would get to live a little while longer.

There was a Va'Shen ship to their north. A ship capable of entering folded space. It represented the only avenue of escape for the remains of the caste. Even if only one of them escaped this system, it would be enough. Their duty now was clear.

They had to warn the Great Caste Leaders of this new race of slave warriors. Warn them and share with them what they had learned on how to kill them.

The Enemy had given their slaves the ability to transport their cannon fodder armies to other worlds, but the controls were limited to the mental processes of Va'Shen. The pilots of these ships, the Mikorin Duran'Dal, possessed the necessary concentration that would allow them to move the ships from one system to another simply by telling the ship what it wanted.

If it was really lucky, it would find a Duran'Dal. But even if it didn't, a Na'Sha would do. It was the Na'Shas from which the Duran'Dal were drawn, having received the blessings of their puppet Emperor that allowed the ships to recognize them.

It was fortunate that it was his caste four thousand years ago that had captured one of these ships. Had taken that ship's Duran'Dal and forced it to reveal its knowledge.

The humans who had captured Va'Sh's last Duran'Dal thought the Mikorin vixen had killed herself to hide her secrets, but it was just as likely that she had heard how the Dark Ones, the *real* Dark Ones, obtained information and so knew that tearing her own throat open would be far less painful, far quicker and easier, than the death they would have given her.

Like the death the Caste Leader had given that Duran'Dal four thousand years ago, liquifying her piece by piece, forcing her to watch as it ate her alive, feeding her to their organic machinery which consumed the vixen's body for fuel until only a series of bloody stumps attached to a head and chunks of torso remained.

Then the caste leader threatened to make her live.

She told them everything.

And then they ate her.

They would do the same to this Mikorin, Duran'Dal or Na'Sha, it made no difference. She would comply with their demands or it would begin to take pieces of her just as it had before. The Mikorin did not need hands or feet or legs or arms or eyes to fly the ship. Just her mind.

And the caste leader knew how to keep that part alive for a long, long time.

It surveyed the room and found, among the statues, a large wooden box standing upright in the back of the room. It carefully stepped forward, wary of a possible trap. Its whiskered antennae, hidden by the dome of its pressure helmet, twitched as it sensed something nearby.

The caste leader stretched forth its claws to take hold of the cabinet handle.

It stopped as the sound of weapons fire, very close by, came to it through the window. Turning, it paused, letting the vibrations of the air touch its shell. The weapons were that of its people and those of the Va'Shen, quite a few of them in fact.

Exiting the room, it approached the window Alacea had been looking out earlier and saw some of its caste lying dead in the road with more firing back at unseen enemies down the street.

It heard the sound of something crashing up the stairs and turned to see its sub-leader joining him. The sub-leader, adorned with the hands of a slave soldier it had killed on its shoulder spikes in mockery of a Va'Shen prayer, flashed a message to him.

The enemy attacks in force from the east.

Then kill them, the Caste Leader ordered.

Reports indicate other slave soldiers are escaping over the river to the north, the sub-leader added.

Then kill them too.

I shall leave four warriors here and pursue the enemy with the rest, it announced.

Do so.

The sub-leader flashed his obedience and turned to leave. The caste leader looked out the window, watching as its soldiers began to advance toward the source of the hardlight weapons fire, their own weapons belching purple disruption blasts at them in turn.

It turned back to the prayer room and marched toward the cabinet. Its patience was beginning to run out. Grabbing the handle, it ripped the cabinet door off its hinges.

A broom, some cleaning supplies, nothing more.

It seemed the hunt would continue.

* * *

Alacea heard the monster rip the cabinet doors open and thanked the Gods for giving her the courage to sneak out while it was distracted. She had not, however, been able to go far, managing only to get to the room next door. It was a Mikorin's sleeping quarters holding little more than a cushioned den for sleeping, a round wooden table and a short dresser for her clothes.

Once again searching for a place to hide and not finding any good options, the priestess began to panic. Then, an idea came to her, and she turned her eyes upward.

The rafters that criss-crossed the ceiling. If she could get up there, it was possible the creature wouldn't think to look upwards.

She looked back down at the dresser. Leaping up on top of it, she had to stop for a moment to regain her balance as one of the dresser's legs seemed to be wobbly. Breathing a sigh of relief as it stopped moving, she looked up and braced herself to jump. Crouching, she focused on the rafter above her and put all her strength into her legs.

The moment her feet left the dresser, she felt something wrap around her ankle and yank downward. The priestess slammed into the polished wood floor hard enough to knock the wind out of her and crack her ribs.

Whatever had a hold of her ankle bit into her flesh as it pulled her across the floor toward the door. Shaking the stars out of her eyes, she looked up and cried out in terror as she saw the monster standing over her, a barbed tentacle protruding from its clawed hand and around her anke.

She struggled to get away, clawing at the smooth, shiny floor, but it was a brief and useless struggle. The tentacle released her ankle as a clawed arm wrapped around her body and lifted her off the ground, the tentacle now wrapping around her neck.

The creature lifted her up until she was face-to-face with its domed head, its head and eyes hidden behind the opaque obsidian protective substance that made up its helmet.

She managed to get her hand up and around the tentacle, pulling at it futilely. The spikes only dug further into the delicate skin of her neck.

The priestess froze in shock for a moment as the monster's armor began to rapidly change color and a low, gritty voice emerged from it.

<YOU ARE DURAN'DAL.>

Alacea continued to struggle, and the creature responded by pushing her roughly against a support beam, making her see stars again.

<SPEAK IN ANSWER.>

Alacea blinked and grit her teeth as her senses came back to her. <I am Alacea,> she hissed. <Na'Sha to the people and animals of Pelle. And may the Frost take you!>

She couldn't tell if the monster was satisfied by her answer or not, but a moment later, it was turning and lumbering back through the door, its prey suspended in the air by its arm and tentacle. The priestess began kicking at the creature's chest, her attacks doing little more than annoying the beast.

<Let go of me!> she demanded, knowing that the creature wasn't just going to put her down but feeling she should make the demand anyway.

Her ears twitched as they picked up a new sound rapidly approaching, but before she could turn her eyes to it, she found herself falling to the ground with the monster, striking the floor again. The clawed arm was no longer holding her, but the tentacle tightened around her throat. She grasped at the appendage, digging into it with her nails but stopped in surprise when she looked back at the creature and found a mottled green form thrashing on top of it as it lay on its back.

<*TESHO!*> she screamed.

*　*　*

Ben had watched silently through the window of Kasshas's house across the street from the temple, counting the number of Dark One soldiers surrounding it.

Too many. Even if Azarin were here with him, there was no way they could fight or sneak through that many. As he began to run through possible alternative plans, blue bolts of hardlight began striking the Dark One troops, dropping two of them immediately and forcing the others into cover.

"Thank you, Turan," Ben whispered, moving to the closed front door. Opening it a crack, he watched as the Dark Ones returned fire. The incoming Va'Shen fire began to slack off somewhat, and some of the Dark One invaders began moving off in pursuit, leaving only a few of the crab-like monsters behind to guard the temple.

Seeing an opening, Ben quietly opened the door and sprinted across the road while the nearest Dark One was looking away, firing down the road after the retreating Windsabers. He dived over a short wall of decorative red bushes into the temple garden and lay prone there for a moment, waiting to see if anyone had taken notice of him.

All he heard, however, was the sound of fighting moving away from him.

Having gotten onto the temple grounds, he began to high crawl along the bushes toward the garden entrance into the temple, the same one he and Alacea had walked through their first night together. Reaching it, he moved himself into a crouch and began to scan the entryway, searching for any signs of movement, friendly or otherwise.

Looking back for a moment, he checked to see if there were any signs of pursuit, but it appeared as if the remaining sentries had no idea he was there. He turned back and crept quietly into the temple.

The place was a wreck. Smashed paper doors either hung open or lay on the ground. Furniture had been tossed aside and deep gouges in the wood floor made it a hazard to walk upon. He listened for sounds of movement. If there was one good thing about the Dark Ones it was that, unlike the Va'Shen, they didn't seem to care much for stealth.

Rifle up at the ready, he moved slowly down the hall, briefly checking each room he passed, wanting to rush but knowing how dangerous that could be if he missed a hidden danger.

He heard thumping above him and looked up, ducking instinctively to find cover but seeing nothing but ceiling rafters. The thumps continued, coming from the third floor.

He increased his pace, making his way to the stairwell and cautiously climbing the shattered wooden steps. The Ranger heard a familiar voice but couldn't make out the words. As he emerged on the third floor, he stealthily approached the corner and looked around it.

<Let go of me!>

Perhaps 40 feet away stood one of the monsters facing to his right, Alacea trapped in its grip. His pulse pounding in his ears, he reflexively raised the rifle for a shot, but stopped, realizing he could very easily hit the priestess if the creature moved suddenly.

With no time to think, Ben did the first thing that occurred to him. Sprinting forward, he saw the creature begin to turn toward him just as he slammed his body into it like a runaway train. The difference in size between them was significant, but the additional weight of Ben's armor, helmet, vest and weapon gave him enough mass to knock the monster over onto its back, dragging Alacea down with them.

<*TESHO!*> Alacea screamed.

The creature had been caught by surprise, but it recovered quickly, swinging its other arm up and knocking Ben in the head with it. If it hadn't been for his helmet, the Ranger was sure the blow would have killed him. He tried to bring the muzzle of his rifle down to the creature's domed head, but as it thrashed against him, the best he could do was smash the butt of the weapon against the faceplate.

Which, to be honest, did absolutely fuck-all to injure the Dark One monster.

The creature caught the weapon in its claws and flung it down the hall. It reached up with the other claw, the one trapping Alacea, dragging her with it as it tried to kill the annoying fleshy animal that had attacked it.

Ben grabbed the alien's arm, wrapping his arms around it in a strange hug to prevent it from being able to grab hold of him, but the other claw came around and struck him in the back, hitting the armor plate covering his back with the force of a bullet.

The Ranger grit his teeth in pain. He was sitting on top of a crab creature, his arms wrapped desperately around one arm while the other stabbed at him with razor sharp claws. The rotting face of Specialist Carson stared up at him, the stench making Ben want to vomit.

Another strike against his back, and Ben felt his ribs crack at the force. The Dark One was simply beating on him at this point, unused to and ill-equipped to fight something in such close proximity. It had evolved to fight in the water and, with the armored Ranger fighting on top of it, was simply too heavy to easily get up onto its feet again.

Alacea, meanwhile, continued to pull at the tentacle around her neck. The creature must have been panicked, because she could feel it tightening around her throat, forcing her to see spots in front of her eyes. With her *Tesho* holding its arm up, she had been forced into a crouch next to him. She tried to call him for help, but the words couldn't escape her strangled throat.

She looked at her alien husband, barely able to keep one of the creature's arms occupied while the other beat on him like a drum. Her eyes came to rest on the front of his armor and on the knife secured in the inverted sheath strapped to the front.

Seeing her *Tesho*'s knife spurred her to action. Reaching down to her belt with her right hand, she felt for the hilt of the mini-Kabar he had gifted to her for their wedding. The creature reared up suddenly in an attempt to throw the Ranger off, causing her fingers to slip over the hilt.

She heard her husband scream and looked over to find that the creature's claw and struck him at his left waist, below his armor. Red blood coated the monster's hand, but Ben still managed to keep the left arm immobile, knowing that if the Dark One was able to use the weapon grafted to it, it was over for both of them.

Alacea grit her teeth and wrapped her fingers around the knife's hilt. Pulling it, she gurgled a scream and swung it upward against the tentacle, slicing halfway through it.

The monster's armored shell began turning bright white and red, its version of a scream of pain, and the tentacle loosened its grip on her. She fell to the floor and gasped for breath, the knife still in her hand.

Not sparing a moment, she turned and grabbed onto the Dark One's arm, helping Ben immobilize it. Its other claw was still digging into her *Tesho*'s side, scraping his hip bone and tearing into the muscles there.

But with Alacea's help, he could finally use one of his hands for something else. Reaching down with his right hand, he pulled his sidearm from its holster. Shoving it between his body and the creature's arm, he pointed the weapon down at the domed head and just a little lower where Fletcher had told him the brain would be.

Shoot it until it dies...

He pulled the trigger over and over again. Although the armor was heavy, the domed face mask was not as tough, and at that range the pistol was just strong enough to penetrate it.

Alacea grimaced and kept hold of the arm as the sound of the weapon deafened her again and again. She shut her eyes and endured the pain as much as she could, feeling as if someone was taking a hammer to the sides of her head. She felt some sort of liquid splash against her, and she briefly wondered if it was the creature's blood, her *Tesho*'s, or her own.

Finally, she felt the creature's arm slacken in hers. Opening her eyes, she saw several holes in the obsidian dome, clear, brackish liquid dribbling out of it mixed with dark blue.

Ben, the empty, smoking pistol still grasped in his white-knuckled hand, fell against the monster's chest, breathing hard, painful breaths. Its other claw fell away from his hip, covered in scarlet blood.

<*Tesho*!> Alacea cried, resting her hands on his back but unsure as to what to do.

Ben looked at her with exhausted eyes, not even attempting to get up yet.

<You are book?> he asked her weakly.

She hiccupped. <Yes,> she sobbed. <Yes, I'm book!>

<All right,> he sighed. <Everything is book now.> Grimacing, he started pushing himself up and off the dead creature below him. He knew time was a factor, and there were several things that needed to happen immediately, but he was exhausted. He decided to start with the easiest thing first and thumbed the button on the magazine release for his pistol, dropping the empty mag on the wood floor with a *clack* and pushing a new one into the weapon.

<You are injured,> Alacea announced. <You must...>

<There is no allotted time,> he said. <We must...> He stopped as he heard heavy armored steps crashing up the steps from the first floor below them. He pulled himself into a crouch. <Be behind me!> he hissed to her and raised the pistol, pointing it at the top of the stairs.

A black dome cleared the stairwell and started to turn toward them. Ben took careful aim with shaking, exhausted hands, putting the front sight post on the helmet when a dull hum sounded and a streak of blue light followed the creature up the stairs and through its side, coming out the other as if it had gone through nothing but tissue paper.

The monster stumbled for a moment and fell face-down onto the floor. Ben and Alacea froze. They heard lighter footsteps on the stairs and then a familiar Va'Shen face with an eyepatch emerged.

<Brother!> Alacea cried in relief.

Azarin cleared the stairwell and quickly checked the hallway and closest prayer room with his rifle at the ready before finally rushing toward them.

<Are you alright?> he demanded of his sister.

<I'm just a little bruised,> she told him. <But *Tesho* is injured.>

<You did not die,> Ben remarked, sitting with his back resting against the dead Dark One.

<Neither did you,> Azarin commented. He quickly assessed the situation. <What happened here?>

<*Tesho* fought the Dark One before it could take me away,> Alacea explained quickly as she fumbled with the emergency first aid kit strapped to the front of Ben's armor. She knew from their experience in the wilderness that he could use it to stop the bleeding.

<Gods above, Brother,> Azarin said, crouching next to him and checking his wound. <Is there a monster on my world you *won't* fight bare handed?>

<This one,> Ben told Alacea as she searched the aid kit. He pointed at an Insta-Clot patch. Taking it, he looked down his left side at the mangled bloody meat the Dark One had left for him there. <And that... um... long... skinny thing,> he said, pointing at the Go Juice auto-injector.

With Azarin and Alacea's help, Ben cut open his uniform shirt on the left side, fully exposing the wound. The priestess hiccupped at the sight of it, and Ben tried not to think about it as he slapped the Insta-Clot patch against it, hearing the familiar sizzle as the chemical in the patch fused the wound closed.

<How many more await us?> Ben asked Azarin.

<None,> his brother-in-law answered. <I killed three quietly, then followed the last in here. Captain Turan has led many of them away, but I could see from the rooftop across the street before coming in here that he was moving his commandos to the bridge. There is not much time.>

Ben nodded absently and jammed the Go-Juice injector into his thigh. It was the second time in only a couple of months that he used Go-Juice, and he knew the effects would not last forever. They would, however, linger long enough to get to the bridge and over the river. After that, he could collapse all he liked.

The pain in his ribs and back faded away, and the wound in his side became little more than a throbbing sensation. His eyes cleared, and he felt his energy return.

<We must go,> he said, rising to his feet. <Now.>

<There are injured people in the basement storeroom,> Alacea told them.

<Then they are safer there than we are,> Azarin told her. <We *must* get you away from here.>

<I cannot leave...> Alacea began to argue.

Azarin grabbed her arm and looked into her eyes, his ears beginning to fold downward. <Sister, the Dark Ones want *you*, specifically. They intend to steal the a ship and flee the planet. If they cannot have a Duran'Dal, a Na'Sha is the next best thing.>

That is why it did not kill me, the priestess realized. If that was true, then her very life presented a threat to everyone around her.

She took a breath. She did not want to leave the injured behind, but if she left, she might be able to draw the Dark Ones away from them. As long as she remained, the temple would continue to be a target.

<I understand. We must go then.>

Ben, meanwhile, had found his rifle and picked it up, checking for any damage that might make it dangerous to use.

<We go,> he announced.

<I will lead,> Azarin told them, heading for the stairs. <Please watch over my sister.>

<I shall do,> Ben told him.

They followed Azarin down the stairs to the demolished first floor, and the two soldiers checked down the deserted hallways for targets, but it seemed Azarin was right. They headed for the door to the garden and were about to exit when they saw a Dark One standing on the road outside the garden.

Alacea gasped, and the three of them ducked back inside the temple, but the creature saw them and turned, raising its arm to fire.

It paused suddenly, its attention diverted by a new sound approaching. It turned just in time to see an LTV turn the corner and run right at the stunned alien.

The LTV's driver must have seen it, but instead of turning away, the vehicle leapt forward as the driver slammed on the gas. The Dark One, faced with a choice of shooting or diving out of the way, did neither for a critical second, and the vehicle rammed into the alien at full force, driving it into the low stone wall that surrounded the garden and crushing it at the waist, pinning it there like a butterfly in a case.

The driver-side door crashed open, and Ramirez hopped out, raising his rifle and firing three shots into the creature's helmet at close range without even a pause.

"Yeah, how's that bumper taste, asshole?" he asked it.

Burgers's towering figure emerged from the passenger side as the LTV began to smoke and hiss from the damage it took ramming the walking tank and the garden wall. The Texan climbed up and began removing the M-270 machine gun from the turret's mounting.

"Baird?! Ramirez?!" Ben called from the temple door. "What the hell are you two doing here?!" he demanded angrily. "You're supposed to be over that river!"

Ramirez strolled toward them as casually as if he was at a day at the market. "Hey, Sir," he greeted, ignoring his commander's angry tone. "El-tee told us what was up, so we came to give you a ride ou..." He stopped short and quickly looked at the LTV, the engine of which had just caught fire and was now burning merrily. He turned back to them. "We came to walk you out," he finished.

Burgers joined him a moment later, the light machine gun looking almost small in the man's hands. "Everyone else is over the river," he reported to Ben. "Captain Turan has some of his guys sniping at their... um... big snails... to keep the route open, but it's not gonna last long."

"I'm gonna Article 92 both of you," Ben promised without heat.

"Hell, Sir," Ramirez said with a grin. "One more of those, and I get a free crockpot!"

<We are leaving or not?> Azarin demanded.

<Leaving,> Ben answered. "All right, Ramirez take point and get us the hell out of here. No matter what happens, Alacea gets over that river. They can't get her, understand?"

"All the way, Sir," Ramirez replied, trotting in the direction of the bridge.

"Baird, watch our asses," Ben instructed.

The group set out, following behind Ramirez while Ben and Azarin stuck to either side of Alacea like an honor guard. Alacea was shocked at the sight of her village. A haze of white smoke filled the air as houses burned nearby. Some homes had collapsed, including many of the buildings built for the Garan'Sel villagers, barely a month old. In the distance, she could hear the other-worldly screams of the armored snails as commandos peppered them with harassing fire.

And there were the bodies.

Thankfully, not as many as there could have been had this attack occurred before the evacuation, but enough to break the vixen's heart. Most of them were commandos; Pelle's, Kar'El's or those from the other refugee communities. A few were human, and she looked at her *Tesho*'s face to see his reaction to them, but the Ranger captain remained focused on the mission at hand. There would be time, he knew, to mourn and whip himself for not doing more to prevent their deaths. But that time was not now.

There were quite a few Dark One corpses, most of them riddled with the neat, burnt holes from hardlight rifles. Some were blown apart by explosives and chewed apart by heavy machine guns. As with the bodies of their own people, the group passed by them in silence.

They were nearly to the bridge when Ramirez stopped and threw his fist up, ordering everyone to stop. Ben grabbed Alacea and pulled her down next to the brick wall of the building they were walking past. Ramirez was checking around the corner of that building, looking toward the bridge.

They all turned as the sound of a snail tank screaming came from behind them.

Close behind them.

Down the street, three buildings behind them, the slimy, armored head of a giant snail peered at them from around the corner. Several Dark Ones dashed across the street from it to take up cover.

"GO!" Ben ordered, raising his rifle. "BRIDGE! GO!" He and Burgers began laying down suppressing fire while Ramirez led Azarin and Alacea around the corner. The river was on their left now with the bridge perhaps 100 yards away.

The snail screamed and came around the corner, following them as the Dark Ones around it fired at the two humans.

Ben and Burgers broke cover and ran around the corner after the other three, hauling ass toward the bridge, which could now be made out through the smoke ahead of them.

Just as Ben thought they were going to make it, a massive explosion threw the five of them onto their backs. A thick cloud of dust and smoke rose from the river ahead of them where the bridge had been a moment before. Burning wood and blasted stone rained down around it, smashing into buildings and splashing into the river. To make matters even worse, the responding screams from several giant snails ahead and to their right, hidden by the nearby buildings, underlined just how screwed the group now was.

"Shit!" Ramirez cried, climbing to his feet.

"They must have been right on top of the bridge," Burgers reasoned. "El-tee wouldn't have blown it otherwise."

<Are we trapped?> Alacea asked Ben.

The scream of the snail tank approaching behind them answered that question for her.

"I think it might be Alamo time," Burgers commented.

"We're going to have to swim for it," Ben said, grabbing Alacea's hand and rushing toward the river. They changed course and made directly for the riverbank, stopping at the edge and looking down. Burgers turned and took up a firing position, waiting for the Dark Ones and the snail to clear the corner.

Unlike the Odoro River south of them with its calm and gentle current, the Cora was wide, rough and swift.

"That's a long swim, Sir," Ramirez remarked dubiously.

"Not much choice," Ben said, removing his helmet and undoing the straps on his armor. Ramirez followed suit, and as soon as he was done, he traded places with Burgers so he could prepare as well.

Ben turned to Alacea. <*Myorin* can go through water?> he asked. If she could, great, but, if not, he was going to pull her across.

<I can swim, *Tesho*,> the frightened priestess told him. She took his hands in hers and squeezed, searching for some kind of comfort. The Dark One forces were getting closer, and the sound of another armored mollusk approaching from the other direction filled her ears.

<You will be book,> he assured her. <Hold to me.>

<Yes, Te...> Her tail puffed up as she saw the snail appear around the corner behind them.

Ben turned and saw it as well. "GO!" he ordered. "GO! NOW!"

Just as they were about to jump, the snail in front of them screamed, its armored shell shattering and its greyish flesh ripping apart as if shredded. The building next to it began collapsing as well as chunks of stone flew apart and partly buried the dying creature.

BRRRRRRRRRRRRRRRRRRRRRRTTTTTT!

The familiar sound, loved by ground troops everywhere, followed a second later, causing Ramirez to whoop in joy as an Air Force F/A-202 attack aircraft flew over them, its 25mm cannon having turned the snail into chunks of broken shell and mush.

"I LOVE YOU, AIR FORCE!" Ramirez screamed as another jet made a gun run on another Dark One position.

"We're saved!" Burgers cried with a laugh. He quickly changed his tune as the buildings near them began to explode as other approaching fighters dropped bombs nearby.

"Nope!" Ramirez cried, running by him toward the water. "Still boned!"

"INTO THE RIVER!" Ben cried, pushing Alacea and Azarin toward the water again. He knew that, without the benefit of communications with the ground, those jets probably had orders to destroy anything moving on the ground in Pelle and command would sort it out later. He didn't know how much ordnance it would take to destroy the Dark Ones, but he knew how much the Air Force was going to use.

Every bit of it they had.

Ramirez and Burgers dived into the water and started swimming hard against the current. Azarin and Ben each took one of Alacea's hands and prepared to jump.

<Swim as...> Ben began to say when another explosion blew a brick building apart behind them. He felt something hard hit him in the back of the head, and he fell forward. Alacea cried out behind him, dragged into the water with him.

And then nothing but darkness.

Chapter 14

Beep.

Beep.

Ben groaned.

Beep.

"Jessie," he croaked. "Turn off that goddamn alarm..." he muttered painfully. He started to turn over in his bed but came to a stop as he felt something tug at his wrist. Opening his eyes, he was confronted by blinding white light. When his eyes finally adjusted, he saw that there were intravenous tubes attached to his right arm at several points.

His head hurt. His tongue felt swollen, and the inside of his mouth felt like a sewer.

Blinking in confusion, he looked around and found that he was lying in a modern hospital bed, wires leading from his arm, chest and head to several sophisticated machines that provided holographic displays of his vital signs and even images of his head.

"You're up."

He turned his head to his left and found Patricia sitting in a cushioned chair. The woman looked tired but smiled genuinely at seeing him wake up. A familiar-looking book sat open in her lap, and it surprised him to see it was "A Highlander's Love," the book Dr. Morant had once lent him.

The Ranger closed his eyes as the pain in his head decided to remind him it was there and that it deserved a lot more of his attention. He rested his head against the pillow and took several deep breaths. He wasn't sure what to ask first.

Patricia made the decision for him.

"You're on Jamieson," she supplied. "In the Hard COC, lowest level. They have a small ICU here for critical patients so they can use modern equipment."

Well, that was one thing explained. For a moment he had wondered if he was still on Va'Sh.

"Can you dim that light?" he muttered.

"Yeah, sure."

The bright light battering his eyeballs was turned off, leaving only the soft, orange light of a table lamp nearby.

"Alacea?" he asked.

"She's fine," Patricia said with a smile. "So are Azarin, Ramirez and Baird. They all made it across the river. We found you and Alacea almost a mile downstream."

He tried to remember what had happened at the riverbank, but his head hurt way too much. "Did I get shot?" he asked stupidly.

"No," she said, leaning back in her chair. "You got hit with some flying debris from the bombing. Between that and the wound in your side, you're lucky to be alive."

"Mmm," was the only reply he could come up with.

"Pelle... and Leonard... They're... um... gone," Patricia told him in a sad, halting voice. "Wiped off the map, gone."

"Yeah, I figured," Ben whispered.

"But so were the Dark Ones," she said with a little more optimism. "And almost everyone got over the river in time..."

She looked away guiltily, and he studied her through half-closed eyelids.

"You did right," he told her. At her look, he repeated himself. "You did right. Blowing the bridge when you did. It was the right call."

"I trapped you there," she confessed.

"It was a hard call, and you made it," he said. "Don't sweat it."

She sighed. Apparently, the decision had weighed on her.

"How long have I been out?" he asked, changing the subject.

"A week," Patricia said. "They had to put you in a medically induced coma while the nanites repaired the damage in your head. Good news is you'll be good as new in a couple of weeks."

Ben grunted and paused before bringing up the next painful question he had.

"How many did we lose?" he asked her.

Patricia looked away for a moment and bit her lip. "Forty-four humans, sixty-two commandos."

"I'm gonna need the list so I can start writing the letters..." he began.

"No, you need to rest right now," Patricia ordered. "It'll wait for a little while. The whole planet is in a tizzy right now, anyway."

"Yes, Ma'am," Ben replied, too tired and hurt to argue.

"I'm going to tell the doctors you're up," she said, rising to her feet. "Get some rest, okay?"

He was already asleep again by the time she walked out the door.

* * *

It was another three days before he felt good enough to sit up and have a real conversation. In that time, Patricia would drop by periodically to check up on him and let him know what was going on outside the CJTF's underground headquarters.

"Leonard's a tent city right now," she informed him. "But Senior Chief says he and his folks will have it back up and running again in no time."

Ben nodded. The CJTF still needed a refueling post, and Pelle was still the ideal geographic area for it. It didn't surprise him that they would rebuild the FOB there.

"Kasshas says they're going to rebuild Pelle," Patricia went on, taking a bite from a cheeseburger she had brought with her from the Jamieson DFAC. "He even submitted a request to Civil Affairs asking for help with the reconstruction."

"Must have made their day," Ben noted, pushing around a green cube of gelatin on his hospital tray.

"Pelle is going to end up looking like the Atlantis Resort," she joked. "Kasshas also said they're going to rename the village to 'Pel'Garan.'"

Ben nodded in approval. It was a symbol that the two communities were truly becoming one.

"I... uh... tried to get permission for Alacea to come visit you," she said. "But because this is such a secure area, they can't let her in."

"It's all right," he said. "I imagine she's busy anyway."

"She was asking Senior Chief for an update on your condition almost every hour for a week," the terp told him with a smile. "He finally just told her that the phone was broken, and he couldn't check."

Ben smiled. It warmed him to know his alien wife, his *Myorin*, was concerned about him. He felt bad for making her worry.

"Any word on who's taking over down there?" he asked her out of the blue.

She looked at him and blinked. "Um... No?"

He let out a breath and nodded. "Well... Now that I'm feeling a little better, you and I should start doing a hand-over so you can run things down there until they send you someone new or they give you the FOB."

Patricia gave him a confused look. "What are you talking about?" she asked. "You're only stuck here for a couple of weeks. You'll be back in Pelle in no time."

Ben cleared his throat and looked down at his lap. With everything that had happened, he had almost forgotten about it. He had told himself he'd worry about it *if* he survived the Dark One attack, and now the time had come.

"I'm not going back to Pelle," he told her.

"What are you talking about?" she demanded.

"Remember just before things kicked off, Colonel Hopper brought us that last sack of mail?" he asked her.

"Yeah?"

"I got the notification," he said. "From CJ-1. I'm being RIF'd."

Patricia looked at him, shocked by the words.

"What?" she gasped.

He nodded. "I was supposed to report to Jamieson within three days of notification for out-processing. I was actually supposed to go home on *Neil Armstrong*."

Patricia put her cheeseburger down into the cardboard to-go box and shook her head. RIF, Reduction in Force... DoD's answer to having too many people and spending too much money. She had seen the Jamieson base newspaper articles about it and knew a lot of the troops on Leonard were nervous about it, but she never would have expected the captain's name to come up.

She shook her head again. "No," she said. "No way. After what just happened, they can't really be thinking..."

"I got another note today," Ben interrupted. "Warning me that my failure to report for outprocessing means they're going to contact my commander for disciplinary action." He smiled. "The private they sent to deliver it took one look at me and said it was the stupidest thing he'd ever seen. I told him he just hadn't been in the Army long enough."

Patricia jumped to her feet, the to-go box falling to the perfectly cleaned hospital room floor. She pointed at the door in what she must have thought was the direction of the headquarters.

"I was in the CJ-2 today!" she cried angrily. "They're talking about putting you in for a *Medal of Honor!* They can't just toss you out!"

"Two different things, Patricia," he said, his voice tinged with sadness and a little bit of humor at the absurdity of it all. "They'll thank me for my service and then put me on a ship for Earth. That's all there is to it."

"Can't you fight it?!"

"Sure, I could," he said. "But they'll make me fight it from Earth while I outprocess. By the time it's all said and done, even if I somehow manage to stay in, they won't send me back to Va'Sh."

The interpreter sat back down, the expression on her face making her look like someone just took her puppy away.

"It's not fair," she muttered.

"No one ever said the Army was fair."

"What about Alacea?" she asked. "Is she going with you?"

Ben took another breath. "She won't," he said. "She might want to, but she wouldn't. She's the Na'Sha. Her people need her now, more than ever before. She won't abandon them to go to Earth."

"It's just not fair," she said again.

"Just do me a favor," he said. "If they do send you a new captain... Don't let him marry any priestesses on the first day, okay?"

She stared at him, trying hard to keep her lips from curling up in a smile. "Jeez, it was just the *one time...*"

* * *

"You still doing good, Sir?"

Ben gave the Ranger NCO an annoyed look. "You keep asking me that, Staff Sergeant, and I'm gonna beat your ass just to make you stop."

Ramirez grinned, and the two started walking down the narrow hallway of the underground hospital. The Ranger had come to visit a few days after Patricia had to return to Pelle, and Ben had suggested taking a walk.

He still hurt, and every so often he would stop and wince for a moment as some muscle in his side would tense up. The nanites did good work rebuilding muscles, but they were essentially brand new, never used before, so even if they were healthy, they took some breaking in.

Deciding to change the subject, Ben asked the younger man, "How's married life?"

He wasn't sure what to expect. Now that the danger was over, he had been concerned that Ramirez would decide he had made a mistake and would go looking for an exit. It had, after all, been the first thing *he* had done upon realizing he was married to Alacea.

"It's great," Ramirez said, and nothing in his voice made Ben think it was bullshit. "Since we're all living in tents anyway, they gave me and Alz... um... *Myorin*... one to share. Her mom was *super* pissed, but since it's a done deal, there's nothing she can say about it."

"No regrets?" Ben asked him seriously.

"No regrets," Ramirez replied.

"You register it with CJ-1 yet?"

Ramirez nodded. "Did that before coming here. Poor dude at the Personnel desk wasn't quite sure what to do, but we got it sorted."

They walked in silence for a moment before Ben asked his next question. "So, what are you going to do when your deployment is over? You taking her to the next base or..."

The NCO cleared his throat nervously as if he had been caught in something he was ashamed of. "Actually, Sir... I... um... dropped my papers."

Ben stopped and looked at the Ranger in shock. "You what?"

Ramirez nodded. "I'm taking the money," he said. "I'm doing the Persephone deal, getting out and taking Alzoria to Vega."

"No shit?" Ben asked in awe.

Ramirez smiled. "Yeah, I know, right? It's just... I figure it's time, you know? I have a wife now, and after everything that's happened, I figure I've done my part..."

"You certainly have," the captain told him.

"So, get out, introduce *Myorin* to my parents and Abuela and maybe open up a burger joint," Ramirez said. "'John's Burgers.'" He paused. "I know it's not catchy, but it was worth it just to see the look on Burgers's face when I told him."

"Congratulations, Staff Sergeant," Ben said with a pained chuckle. "I hope it works out great."

"If you and the Missus are ever on Vega, stop by."

"What about Baird?" Ben asked. "He going to open a restaurant across the street?"

"Actually," Ramirez replied, "Burgers said he decided to stay in. Says that with the new aliens in town, they're probably going to need Rangers." He gave Ben a nervous look. "I heard about..."

"Yeah, can you believe that shit?" Ben asked, knowing exactly what the NCO was talking about.

"Yeah, I can," the Ranger NCO said with bit of contempt. "But, you know, it's their loss. We all think so, Sir."

Ben smiled. "Thanks, Staff Sergeant."

* * *

It was difficult to quiet one's thoughts with the sound of hammering and sawing going on so close, but Alacea made do for the sake of the two vixens standing in front of her. The large red and blue tent that had been set up for the Mikorin to use was situated close to the ruins of the temple and was filling the role as best it could. Alacea told herself that the sounds of construction around them was something to take joy in as it was the sound of life returning to Pelle.

But after a few hours, it did grate on one's ears.

The two sisters each held one of Alacea's hands as they prayed for the soul of their commando brother who had died in the Dark One attack. Searching through the rubble for survivors had been the first priority upon their return. Thankfully, the village had been cleared out first, and only a few people other than commandos and Rangers had remained. Alacea had been relieved to find the healers she had left in the vegetable cellar had been brought up alive, if a little thirsty.

Once that task was complete, it had been time to gather their dead. Most of those had been commandos, and the funerals had taken up most of the Mikorins' time, with some exceptions. Sho Nan and the other Ya'Jahar devoted themselves to checking for food and water sources to sustain the village during its reconstruction.

Through it all, no one had given voice to the question... no, the fact... that they all knew shouldn't be true. That it had been the Dark Ones who had destroyed their village... and that it had been their occupiers who had fought for it.

Alacea finished the prayer, and the three lifted their hands up and bowed their heads.

<Our thanks to you, Na'Sha,> the older of the two sisters said.

<Your brother will be missed by all of us,> Alacea told them. <We honor him.>

They all bowed to one another, and the sisters turned to go. They, like everyone else in Pelle, were extremely busy.

Alacea took a breath and decided to rest for a moment. She had been so loaded with work that she barely had time to eat what little food they could offer her. Fortunately, Lady Patricia had been able to help with that issue, and they were expecting food aid to arrive any day now. This time, Kasshas had felt no reluctance in asking for assistance.

There was another reason she had kept busy. Every time she stopped, even for a moment, her thoughts went to her *Tesho*. She had been in constant worry since she had come to on the riverbank next to him and found she could not wake him up no matter what she tried. The commandos that found them hours later had found her a hiccupping, wailing mess.

After one of the flying machines had taken him and other wounded away, she had spent her time worrying and waiting, asking for updates at every opportunity. She even tried pulling her rank again to make someone take her to him, but although her *Tesho*'s people were sympathetic, they refused.

When Expert Engineer Warren came and told her Lady Patricia had called and told him *Tesho* was awake, Alacea had fallen to her knees and thanked the Gods. He was still hurt, but he would recover.

But when she next saw Lady Patricia face to face, the human woman looked grim. Fearing her *Tesho* had taken a turn for the worse, she grabbed the woman's arms and demanded to know. She was relieved that her *Tesho* was still well, but the news that he would not be returning to Pelle... ever... struck the priestess like a hammer blow to the head.

To hear *why* he would not be returning enraged her. If they had told her his wounds were too severe and he had to be taken away as a result, she would have accepted that with grace. But to hear that his Grand Overlords were dismissing him because they had no further use for him, after everything he had just done, was a dishonor she could not easily accept.

She wasn't sure what his people thought of what he had done. Perhaps they just considered it the expected accomplishments of an expendable asset. But she knew what her people thought.

The priestess looked up as the tent flap opened, and Alzoria entered. Her purple and red camouflage shorts and vest were stained with blood, and the quiver on her back was down to two arrows. The Hunters and Huntresses had been busy lately. Although the forest fires to their south had burned themselves out, their loss coupled with the destruction of the village meant the loss of several hunting grounds while the animals that had fled the fire were now settling into the woods closer to Pelle.

Including the dangerous ones.

Alacea's ears twitched at the Huntress's arrival. <Blessed day, Alzoria,> she said.

<Blessed day, Na'Sha,> Alzoria greeted with a bow. <*Tesho* has returned. He said he saw the Overlord and he is doing much better now.>

<Wonderful!> Alacea breathed in relief.

<He also told me... that... the Overlord will not return,> Alzoria said reluctantly. <Is... Is that true?>

The priestess's ears drooped at the question. <It is true,> she admitted sadly. <He is no longer *needed*,> she added with a growl.

<It is strange,> Alzoria said. <When he first arrived, Bao Sen and the rest of the Huntresses were planning to kill him for you. Now... I am sad he is leaving.>

Alacea's ears unconsciously twitched a smile at the memory of those early days. How stupid she *and* he had been. How close had both of them come to doing something irrevocably awful to one another without realizing it was totally unnecessary?

<Is there nothing we can do, Na'Sha?> Alzoria asked her quietly.

<I am afraid not,> Alacea told her.

<Then you are giving up?>

They both turned to the new voice that had suddenly entered their conversation. Sho Nan, wearing a worn hanbok that had seen better days, held open the tent flap and stood in the entryway.

<Sho Nan,> Alacea greeted while Alzoria bowed to her. <You look tired.>

<I am quite tired, Na'Sha,> the blue-haired vixen confessed as she fully entered the tent. She stopped and lifted a brown jug of water from the floor, drinking deeply from it before continuing. <But I am

now content that the community will not starve or die of thirst in the near future.>

<That is good news,> Alacea told her.

<Indeed. But what is this news of the Overlord never returning?> she asked.

<It is true,> Alacea once again confessed. <His Grand Overlord has declared his usefulness complete. And, so, they will send him away.>

She had to force the hiccups threatening to leave her throat back down so as not to lose her composure in front of the other two vixens.

<And you will not go with him?> Sho Nan asked.

<I cannot,> Alacea told her, putting on a brave set of ears and tail. <Our community needs a Na'Sha here and now.>

<And the Na'Sha needs the Overlord,> Sho Nan declared. <And if the Grand Overlord has no need of him, then he should be made to stay with the community.>

<I have no power to command such a thing,> Alacea told her. <If I did...> She turned away and took a breath to strengthen her resolve.

<Tch...> Sho Nan replied in such blatant disapproval that Alzoria, standing nearby, flinched at the apparent disrespect. <This is like the nipping all over again.>

<Sho Nan,> Alacea began, feeling anger rise in her.

<Stop giving so much,> Sho Nan told her firmly. <And start taking. If not for yourself, then for your community. Do you think our community wants a Na'Sha torn apart from grief during this time? The community does not have the strength to rebuild itself *and* its Na'Sha at the same time. The community needs a strong Na'Sha, and if the Na'Sha needs her *Tesho* to bolster that strength, then for the good of the community, he must be made to return.>

<I told you!> Alacea shot back. <I do not have the power to command such a thing!>

Sho Nan folded her arms over her chest, and her ears twitched just the tiniest bit, perhaps happy to finally see her friend letting her emotions come to the fore.

<Then,> she told her friend. <Borrow it.>

* * *

A week had passed since Ben had been allowed to leave the hospital and move into a six-person B-hut in the sprawling, flat and dusty expanse of Jamieson where Transient Housing was located. The transient area was where newcomers and those soon to be leaving Jamieson were housed until either permanent billeting was found for them or their ship departed Va'Sh. Dusty and dirty, it was a far cry from the amenities afforded the rest of the base inhabitants.

It did have a DFAC, gym, BX and recreation room, but you still had to walk a bit to get to the toilets and showers. A bus ran from the transient area to the base proper regularly.

As he walked from the bus stop to his B-hut, Ben heard a scream from his right and turned, his hand reflexively dropping to his side to draw a sidearm that was no longer there. His blood pumped in his ears, and his heart threatened to explode from his chest as any of a hundred scenarios came to mind as to the cause for the scream.

Another attack?!

Dark Ones who survived?

Green on Blue?!

He watched as an Air Force enlisted man ran from one of the polymer porta-johns with his pants around his ankles. The cause for the humiliating retreat appeared at the doorway of the toilet a moment later when an obviously frightened Va'Shen *kashu* furred lizard skittered from inside the porta-dumper and ran for its life in the opposite direction.

Troops hanging out at some picnic tables nearby and in the vape-pit began to applaud the Airman for the impromptu show.

"Welcome to Va'Sh, Air Force!" a Marine at the vape-pit called to him with a laugh.

Ben let out the breath he had been holding and rubbed his eyes. *Get a hold of yourself, man,* he thought to himself.

Ben was in a rear area now, as safe as a human being could be on Va'Sh, and yet, after everything he had seen and been through, it was difficult for him to relax.

Perhaps it *was* time to leave.

Not like he had a choice. For the last few days, he had been forced to attend several debriefings as each directorate tried to learn as much as they could about the Dark Ones as possible while also having to attend the multitude of appointments and briefings required for his outprocessing of Jamieson and his unit. It meant full days, every day, with no down time.

Not that outprocessing was necessarily hard. It was simply tedious. Travelling forty-five minutes by bus to an office on one side of Jamieson to spend five minutes getting a signature from an office he had never before had contact with, and then another forty-five on the bus to be just in time for a briefing on why you shouldn't try to take Va'Shen animals back with you to Earth.

Then there were the medical appointments.

Those were fun.

"What the hell happened to you?!" a medic would cry as they looked him over.

"I fell," he would answer.

"Out of a plane!?" the medic would then ask.

Ben sighed.

He supposed the only good news was that he had no personal baggage to account for. Everything he'd brought to Va'Sh with him had been in his hooch when the Air Force bombed Pelle. It was all gone.

Including his last picture of Jessie.

The photo he had just managed to print out on *Neil Armstrong* before coming down to Va'Sh, the only remaining image of his late wife and best friend, burned to nothing with the rest of his belongings.

It was as if she were only now truly gone.

He wanted to see Alacea. He had requested permission to go back to Pelle for a quick visit, but as soon as he emerged from the hospital they had put him on pre-departure quarantine status. He wasn't permitted off-post, and he wasn't to have any interaction with Va'Shen.

Which, he had thought, was a little weird and rather stupid and unfair. You usually didn't enter quarantine status until you were three days out from your departure. But base administration had insisted that he remain in quarantine status from the jump, citing some nonsense about his injuries.

It was *really* weird.

But, in the end, the Army was stupid. He had argued, they had denied him permission anyway.

The closest he had been able to get was a phone call from Master Sergeant Marcus's office. The public affairs NCO had hooked him up one last time, letting him use his phone to call the tent city outside Pelle. Patricia had run to Pelle and found Alacea, bringing her back so they could talk.

For the first few moments, neither of them said anything. It was hard for the Va'Shen to use a regular phone, their ears being in the wrong position for it, but they still made it work.

The most important thing he wanted to know was that she was okay. The most important thing she wanted to know was that he was as well. After that, he wasn't sure what to say.

<I must go,> he told her. <I am sorry.>

<Do not be sorry,> she said in reply. <The Gods will have their way in the end, and you will return.>

The fact that she seemed so certain he would come back made him both happy and guilty at the same time. Even if he could return, it would take a long time. He would have to somehow secure a civilian position in the U.S. government or as a contractor and then get on a very short list of civilians who were permitted to work on Va'Sh. That list, he knew, would get longer as time went by, but how much time would pass before it happened was unknown.

He looked up at the two moons overhead, past the green and blue aurora that silently protected Va'Sh. In a few days he would board an orbital spacecraft that would take him to a passenger transport, the "Freedom Bird," that ran between Va'Sh and Earth. *Over the Rainbow*, for obvious reasons, couldn't leave Va'Sh, so smaller transports were being sent instead. It would be a much less comfortable trip, but it would get him to Earth.

Then he would start the long, arduous process of returning to Va'Sh.

But, he swore, he *would* get back.

Chapter 15

"Is this some kind of joke?" Ben asked the Space Force guardian on the other side of counter.

The Jamieson Space Force Passenger Terminal looked more like an airport desk from a mid-twentieth century rural airport than the hi-tech spaceports he was used to. The Fuzz, of course, reduced the normally technologically savvy space service to low-tech methods of getting passengers off Va'Sh and into orbit.

For instance, paper tickets, orders and passenger manifests.

None of which, it seemed, Ben had, despite several promises that today, guaranteed, he would be leaving.

It was the same guarantee he had received for four straight days.

"I'm sorry, Captain," the blonde Space Force NCO told him sympathetically. It was the same tech he had seen each of the last four days. "But you're not on today's manifest, and there's not even any orders here, so I can't even put you on a space-available ticket."

Ben sighed and rested his elbows on the counter. What in the actual fuck was going on? They wanted him to leave Va'Sh, and he was leaving. Why was this so hard?

"Let me give Personnel a call," the NCO told him. "It *is* weird that this keeps happening."

Ben thanked her, and he checked behind him. There was no line behind him, so at least he wasn't inconveniencing anyone else. The seats in the waiting area were crowded with uniformed personnel who *had* been ticketed for the flight up to the orbiting Freedom Bird, apparently not running into the kinds of problems he had.

"This guy has been coming here every day for a week," he heard the pax terminal technician say into the phone. "He says you keep telling him to come, but there's some kind of disconnect."

He listened, trying to pick up what the person on the other end of the phone was saying, looking for some hint at what the problem was.

"How is that even possible?" the tech asked, this time whispering into the receiver. She looked back at him, this time with a surprised expression. "Oh... um... Yeah, okay. Thank you."

She hung up the phone and turned to him, clearing her throat. "They say there's been some hold-up with your orders, but it should get straightened out by tomorrow."

Ben gave her a look, knowing for *certain* that that was *not* what the person on the other end of the line told her.

"What is it really?" he asked.

"I'm afraid if you want details, you're going to have to talk to CJ-1," she said sympathetically.

CJ-1 Outbound Personnel, he knew, wasn't going to tell him dick. He had been there three times now, trying to find out what the hold-up was. No one would tell him.

"Okay," he said with a sigh. "Back to the B-hut, I guess."

"I'm sorry, Sir," she said. "Try again tomorrow."

He had already turned his back, but he gave her a wave as he walked to the door with his small, black overnight bag.

This is bullshit.

What he needed was a little more rank to force the issue.

And he knew where he might get it.

* * *

Colonel Hopper rose from behind his desk and reached out his hand to shake Ben's with a smile. The last time he had seen Hopper was after he woke up in the hospital. The Airborne commander had come to congratulate him for a job well done keeping the Dark Ones at bay until *Over the Rainbow* arrived. It was he who had filled him in on what had happened in the final hour before he had been knocked unconscious.

Apparently, while the Dark Ones were moving on the river, *Over the Rainbow* had dropped out of fold space close enough to Va'Sh to enable instant communication with the JOC, which had immediately begun screaming for help the second the colony ship had shown up on their screens.

After a few conversations between the ship's commander and General Walker, *Over the Rainbow* had her contingent of F/A-202's armed up for the first orbital combat drop since the end of the war. The fighters, made to enter a planet's atmosphere from orbit, conduct operations and then land planet-side, didn't need to stop at Jamieson first. They dropped from their mothership, entered the Va'Shen atmosphere, and made for Pelle at a comfortable Mach 6.

And then proceeded to destroy everything they saw on that side of the river using every piece of ordnance available to them short of nuclear weapons.

The smoke from the forest fires meant they had to come in low beneath the smoke and clouds, otherwise Ben and his group would never have even seen the aircraft overhead. They would have dropped their ordnance from twenty miles away and called it good.

"Good to see you up and around, son," Hopper told him. "Take a seat. What can I do for you?"

"Sir," Ben said as he sat down on the other side of the desk. "I need help. You know they RIF'd me, right?"

"Buncha bullshit if you ask me," Hopper told him sympathetically. "But there's nothing I can really do about that, son."

"I know, Sir," Ben replied. "The problem is I was supposed to leave Va'Sh a week ago, and I keep getting stopped at the door, and no one will tell me why. They keep saying it's some kind of glitch, but I'm getting the sense that it's something else. But try as I might, I can't get *anyone* to tell me what's going on. Can you help me?"

Hopper held up a hand as if to stop the captain and gave a nod. "Let me make some calls," he said. "They got some of my Airborne guys working in CJ-1. I'll get you an answer."

"Thank you, Sir," Ben said with relief.

"It's the absolute least I can do, son, after what you pulled off," Hopper told him. "I'll be honest... I was certain that we were looking at another Task Force Smith. Giving you those orders was the hardest thing I'd ever had to do. I'm pushing to get you and your people the highest awards I can swing. You deserve them all."

"Thank you, Sir," Ben said again. He shivered slightly as if someone just walked over his grave, the thought of what Hopper had told him making him realize just how hopeless he had thought the situation was. Task Force Smith, the U.S.'s first, catastrophic attempt to slow the North Korean invasion of South Korea in the mid-twentieth century had pitted under-trained, under-equipped and under-armed U.S. troops rushed from occupation duty in Japan to face off against the advanced, Chinese-supplied North Korean armored columns racing south. It had been a complete disaster, with outdated U.S. anti-tank rockets bouncing off heavily armored T-34 tanks. The U.S. force had essentially bought a few hours with their lives with no real hope of stopping the North Korean forces from the start.

It could have been that way for his people too. If not for the support from Turan's Windsabers and the Pelle commando, that fight would have looked *very* different.

"You go to lunch," Hopper told him, already picking up the phone. "Come back in an hour. I'll have an answer for you, or I'll take you up to General Walker's office myself to get one."

Ben rose from his seat and shook Hopper's hand again. "Thank you, Sir."

"We'll get it sorted, Captain. Don't worry."

With those words, Ben left the colonel's office, walking aimlessly to the exit and toward the Jamieson base exchange. He thought about getting a bite to eat but had no appetite. Instead, he browsed the military department store.

He stopped as something caught his eye. It was a copy of the coffee table book he had given to Alacea, *Earth and Her Colonies*. Picking it up, he thumbed through it for a moment before bringing it to the counter to buy it. He knew Alacea's copy was very likely destroyed in the bombing, but he could get her a new one and ask Master Sergeant Marcus to make sure it got to Alacea via Patricia or Warren.

Buying the book made him feel better. It was only one little thing that he could do, but even that small accomplishment helped his mood, and he celebrated with a sub sandwich from the BX food court. By the time he was done, the hour was almost up, and he returned to Hopper's office.

The colonel was waiting for him there, his face much more grim than when Ben had left.

"Everything all right, Sir?" Ben asked from the doorway.

"Take a seat, Captain," Hopper told him.

Uh oh...

The Ranger took the same seat he had before and waited for Hopper to give him what would obviously be bad news.

"Here's the deal, son," Hopper told him. "They haven't been able to complete your orders because they can't get diplomatic clearance for them. State Department put a hold on you at Va'Shen request."

Ben worked that around in his mind for a moment. "Wait," he said. "Are you saying it's the *Va'Shen* who won't let me leave?"

"Apparently, Va'Sh-Gov is raising a stink and demanding we allow their officials to meet with you."

"Why?" Ben asked.

Hopper took a breath. "They won't come out and say it, but the issue has gone up to General Walker and even the U.S. ambassador to Va'Sh. The only time they ever do this is when they want one of our guys to answer for breaking some Va'Shen law."

Ben's jaw dropped. "They want to *arrest me*?!"

Hopper nodded.

Ben's first thought was that the idea was ludicrous. Then, he thought back to his time at Pelle and how some of what happened there had been construed by others, including some Va'Shen.

Forcing a Na'Sha to marry him.

Threatening to murder a Va'Shen count.

Undermining Va'Sh-Gov's authority in the release of Va'Shen detainees.

Unknowingly allowing forced prostitution in his AO.

Allowing a pogrom to happen under his watch.

The complete destruction of a Va'Shen village.

The deaths of nearly a hundred Va'Shen commandos quite likely placed under his command illegally.

He felt himself go cold. He knew Va'Sh's secret police, the *Dara Tang*, had no love for him. Was this their attempt at revenge before he had the opportunity to escape?

So, that explained it. Va'Sh-Gov wanted him to account for the things that happened under his watch, and the CJTF was trying to shield him without causing a diplomatic incident. That was why they wouldn't let him off base or meet with any Va'Shen.

The irony of it all made him sadly laugh, shaking his head. After trying to bring Major Keyes to justice for what he had done, the Va'Shen were now going to come after *him* instead. Keyes had made the effort to cover his tracks, but Ben hadn't. He never felt the need to. He had always done what he thought was right.

Then again, so had Keyes.

No good deed goes unpunished.

Hopper watched the young captain in concern. "You all right, Captain?"

Ben sat back in the chair and laughed again.

"Don't worry about it, son," Hopper told him. "There's no way in Hell we would ever let this happen. They just want to look for a way to do it without pissing off the Va'Shen any more than they have to. If need be, they'll say 'fuck the clearance' and put you on the first transport out."

Ben frowned as Alacea's face flashed before his eyes. If it came to that, if he snuck off the planet in the middle of the night, he'd never be able to come back. DoD could never risk it. He'd never see Alacea again.

And worse than that...

How would it affect *her*?

To know that her *tesho* had fled from the planet to save his own skin, leaving her behind to face the consequences alone?

The worst thing a tod can do to a vixen he loved, he remembered her saying, was doing something that would dishonor her.

A few months ago, he probably wouldn't have cared and left the planet with a clean conscience, knowing that he had done everything legally and ethically. And if the Va'Shen didn't like it, they could go and fuck themselves.

But it wasn't a few months ago.

"I need to speak with General Walker," he said quietly.

* * *

"You're taking a big risk, Captain."

Standing in the brightly lit CJTF conference room, sipping bland coffee from a paper cup, Ben fought back the urge to snap at the man. He knew he was taking a risk. This same man had reminded him of it every few hours. But that man was a general, and snapping at him was only going to make things monumentally worse, not better.

Lieutenant General Walker was seated at the head of the table, looking at the young captain critically. When Colonel Hopper had called his office requesting a meeting about "the Gibson thing," he knew something was about to go wrong. Sure, Captain Gibson had caused him a few headaches here and there, but the man had gotten results when no one else could. They had also, essentially, asked him and his Rangers to give up their lives in exchange for a few precious hours to give them time to assemble a defense of Jamieson, and quite a few of Gibson's people *had*, in fact, died doing exactly that.

So, despite the headache, despite the fact that the man was a self-righteous pain in his ass, he felt he owed him. Which was why he was doing everything he could to shield him from the Va'Shen authorities until he could get off-world.

Technically, he didn't have to listen to Va'Sh-Gov. He could have sent Gibson away without diplomatic clearance, but doing so would have caused problems in the relationship, which had been thrown into further turmoil with the arrival of these new alien invaders.

To be perfectly frank, if Va'Sh-Gov wanted to make trouble in the north, right now was the perfect time to agitate the Va'Shen insurgents. Most of the troops stationed there had been rushed down to Jamieson for the defense against the invaders, and not all of them had been able to return yet. If the Va'Shen really wanted Gibson, they had leverage they could use until those troops were back up north again. After that, Walker would have a stronger hand.

But Gibson wanted to hear the Va'Shen out. Walker told him in no uncertain terms that if the conversation went south and the Va'Shen demanded he be placed under arrest, things would get messy. The U.S. Ambassador wanted this to go away. Being able to say, "Sorry, he already left," was a much different answer than, "Fuck off, you can't have him." One might be diplomatically acceptable to the Va'Shen. The other definitely wouldn't be.

And if it meant avoiding further attacks on his people, he'd give them Gibson. The Ranger had asked for this. The consequences would be on him. Walker didn't like it, but it was the way things would have to be.

The CJTF Judge Advocate had been apoplectic. They didn't know enough about Va'Shen law to mount a defense.

This is going to be a fucking disaster, Walker thought.

"Sir, they're here."

Walker heard the Army master sergeant's announcement and rose to his feet. He turned and saw Dr. Sinclair enter the conference room followed by an elderly bearded tod with long graying hair tied in the back. The Va'Shen man wore ornate, dark green robes trimmed with silver and a tall forest green hat on his head very similar to a Korean gat but with a smaller brim.

Ben and Walker bowed to the tod, who bowed back regally. The Ranger gave a look to Sinclair and found that the man looked nervous. He hadn't known who Va'Sh-Gov was sending for this meeting, but something in his expression told Ben that he hadn't been expecting *this.*

Sinclair cleared his throat and gestured to Walker. <I present Lieutenant General Alfred Walker, Grand Overlord of Combined Joint Task Force Unified Resolve.> The tod bowed again as Sinclair then gestured to Ben. <And Captain Ben Gibson, Overlord of Pelle.>

The tod bowed to Ben, and Ben bowed back. Then the older Va'Shen expert turned to the two men.

"Gentlemen," he said, "This is Baron Boravin, Keeper of the Imperial Pen."

They bowed again, and Walker aimed a question at Sinclair. "What does that mean? Keeper of the Pen?"

Again, Sinclair appeared nervous. He cleared his throat again. "The Keeper of the Imperial Pen is the member of the Imperial Court responsible for transcribing all of the Emperor's edicts. He is the only one permitted to transfer the Emperor's spoken word into writing." After a momentary pause, he added a further explanation. "They sent someone as close to the Emperor as they could possibly get without sending an actual imperial family member."

Shit, Ben thought. He thought they'd send some bureaucrat, maybe even a member of the *Dara Tang*, but to send someone from the Emperor's Court?

This was going to get serious. Fast.

"Please ask him to have a seat," Walker told Sinclair, gesturing to the chair to the general's right. The chair had been specially designed to allow Va'Shen to sit comfortably despite their tails. The noble sat down, his every move smooth and courtly. Ben figured by the tod's age, he had probably spent years, maybe decades, working in the palace.

The humans sat down, Walker at the head of the table with Ben at his left and Sinclair next to him. Walker folded his hands on the polished wood table in front of him and took a breath.

"First, I welcome the Keeper of the Pen to our headquarters," he said. "We are greatly honored by your visit."

Sinclair translated these words, and the old tod bowed in thanks.

"I very much wish that we were meeting under better circumstances," Walker continued.

<Recent events have been troubling to His Imperial Majesty, and He shares your wish that a happier occasion would warrant such a visit,> Boravin told him in reply, his voice, tail and ears completely neutral. Looking at him, Ben couldn't tell if the man was happy or boiling-over pissed. <I am happy to know, however, that you have cooperated with His Imperial Majesty's wishes to not send Captain Gibson away without His consent. His Imperial Majesty considers

this matter to be of great importance and very much wishes to stress his desire for Captain Gibson to remain until His Imperial Majesty is satisfied.>

"Before we begin, I must first stress to you that this is only a preliminary meeting," Walker said. "No matter what happens today, Captain Gibson will not be leaving this base with you."

Boravin cocked his head to the right, one ear moving only the slightest bit downward as Sinclair translated. <Am I to understand you are willing to give Captain Gibson to us willingly at a later date?>

Ben swallowed nervously at the tod's words.

"Before we consider anything like that, we would want to conduct our own investigation into these matters," Walker told him. "If Captain Gibson is to be disciplined, *we* will be the ones to do so in accordance with U.S. law and our Uniform Code of Military Justice. If your government has any input to provide, you may do so."

Boravin's ears began to lower, if not in anger, then definitely irritation. <Grand Overlord, I do not think you understand the impact of Captain Gibson's actions. While we are moving closer to becoming allies, I can assure you that removing Captain Gibson from Va'Sh without His Imperial Majesty's consent would be considered a great insult and in violation of the terms of our treaty with you.>

While Ben could keep up with most of what the old tod was saying on his own, he listened intently to Sinclair's translation. At the end of translating this point, Sinclair gave Walker a look and added a comment of his own.

"General, the Keeper of the Pen says this with a great deal of emotion," he said. "However, I am pretty certain that the Instrument of Surrender says nothing about the Va'Shen having jurisdiction over U.S. servicemembers who violate Va'Shen law."

"That's because it doesn't," Walker replied to him. "I had JAG go over that document with a fine-tooth comb. He's bluffing."

"I recommend you tread carefully, General," Sinclair told him. "If we cause him to lose face, it will be no different than insulting the Emperor himself."

"Noted," Walker remarked. He took a deep breath as he considered his next words carefully. "Tell him I understand his anger. But Captain Gibson is an officer in the U.S. Army. We will not simply turn him over to you. If the Emperor is concerned that Captain Gibson will not face justice, please assure him that, should the investigation find he acted illegally, he will be tried and punished to the fullest extent of the law."

Ben didn't like the fact that the situation had gone from him getting permission to leave to him facing an investigation, but he understood the tactics here. If the Va'Shen wanted him to face justice for what he had done, they would have to make that demand of the U.S. Ambassador's office, who would likely toss it to the Army to conduct an investigation anyway. Walker just wanted to make sure that investigation, and the decision whether or not to even proceed with one, remained with him and the Army and not the Va'Shen.

Sinclair translated the general's words, and Boravin's ears pointed at the general in irritation.

<Then you must conduct your investigation here on Va'Sh,> he told Walker. <And regardless of the outcome of your investigation, His Imperial Majesty will demand that all charges be dropped, and no punishment will be permitted.>

A heavy silence fell over the conference room as Sinclair translated Boravin's words.

"I'm sorry," Walker said. "Are you *certain* that's what he said?"

"That's what I heard as well, Sir," Ben told him.

"Let me ask again," Sinclair said, also somewhat puzzled. He turned and asked Boravin to explain in greater detail.

<It is exactly as I said it,> the older tod said in response. <His Imperial Majesty will not stand for you punishing Captain Gibson. I do not know which of your laws he has broken, but per our treaty with you, His Imperial Majesty will not allow you to remove a Va'Shen citizen from our world without His consent.>

<Waiting please!> Ben broke in finally. <Do not understand. You come take me away? Hurt to me for doing wrong to you?>

Boravin looked at him, and his ears popped up to the ceiling. He looked at Walker and Sinclair in turn. <I am afraid I do not understand,> he said. <Captain Gibson, are you in trouble with your government?>

<No,> Ben told him. <Am I in trouble with *your* government?> he asked, feeling stupid and at the same time, felt the situation was oddly familiar.

<Absolutely not,> Boravin replied, appalled at the question. <Captain Gibson, when His Imperial Majesty discovered that you were being sent away and why, he ordered your departure stopped. We have been requesting a meeting to officially inform you that His Imperial Majesty has granted you Va'Shen citizenship as well as the title of Zora'Shar.>

Silence.

Ben stared wide-eyed at the old tod. He shook his head, wondering if he was still asleep in the hospital and dreaming all of this.

<I... what?> he asked stupidly.

"What is a 'Zora'Shar?'" Walker asked Sinclair evenly.

The professor, himself shocked by what he was hearing, took a moment to collect his thoughts before answering the general.

"It is an unlanded noble title," he explained. "Its literal translation is 'Sword Bearer.' It is the title granted to higher ranked officers in the Imperial Army who do not already have a noble title of their own."

"How high is 'higher ranked?'" Walker asked.

Sinclair thought for a moment. "Their rank structure is not the same as ours," he said, "But all of the officers I had heard of bearing that title had been somewhere between what we would classify as lieutenant colonel and lieutenant general."

Boravin, not understanding the byplay, continued his explanation. <It is against the terms of our treaty for a Va'Shen citizen to be removed from Va'Sh without the Emperor's consent,> he assured Ben. <And before granting that consent, His Imperial Majesty wanted to be assured that you were leaving of your own will.> At this point, Boravin's tail twitched in nervousness.

<Why Emperor give such this to me?> Ben asked.

Boravin's tail twitched again.

<After the most recent unpleasantness, His Imperial Majesty sent investigators to Tankara Province to gather the specifics of what had happened,> Boravin told him. <In the course of their investigation, many of those interviewed talked about the Dark One who united his forces with those of Va'Shen commandos and fought to protect the village of Pelle and prevent the invaders from marching on the capital. The stories were... impressive.>

It took Ben a minute and a more detailed translation from Sinclair to understand what the courtier had said, but afterward, he frowned.

<Pelle is destroy,> he pointed out.

<The *buildings* are destroyed,> Boravin corrected him. <The community remains. Thanks, in no small measure, to your assistance in evacuating them.>

<I do what I should,> Ben argued.

<Do you know what the Va'Shen south of the capital are calling you?> Boravin broke in, perhaps annoyed by Ben's seeming inability to simply accept credit where credit was due. <They call you "The Wall of Tankara." In our culture, a Hero Name is significant and

granted only to those who have changed the course of Va'Shen history.> Boravin took a breath, and his tail moved about behind the chair, almost in annoyance. <If His Imperial Majesty *fails* to acknowledge your achievements, he will lose face. Such a thing cannot be permitted. He also recognizes that a person such as yourself could bring a wealth of knowledge and experience in war that we, after the unfortunate conflict with your people, now sadly lack and will soon need.>

Ben listened to Sinclair translate the tod's words, and a much clearer picture began to take form. Part of it was politics. Part of it was diplomacy. Part of it was military necessity. If the Emperor didn't reward someone for protecting Va'Shen territory in a situation where he could not, he would look weak and ungrateful to his people. Recognition of his acts would allow the Emperor to, in a small measure, take some credit for them. It would also, hopefully, temper some of the anger of the Va'Shen in the northern sectors to learn that it was a human who had fought to protect their Emperor, and that the Emperor acknowledged it.

By directing that recognition to Ben, the Emperor would score diplomatic points with the Coalition, who had, after the loss of *Neil Armstrong*, suffered the greater loss of life in the brief invasion. It would be a particularly poignant act, especially given that the arrival of the actual Dark Ones would prompt some very uncomfortable questions from the Coalition governments toward Va'Sh-Gov as to exactly who these invaders were and why they had attacked Va'Sh in the first place.

And then there was the not-so-subtle recruitment pitch. The overwhelming majority of Va'Shen military high- and mid-level leadership had committed ritual suicide after their defeat at the hands of the Coalition. Most of these, Ben could assume, were these "Zora'Shar," on whom the Empire depended for military continuity. With their loss, the Empire was almost completely devoid of military experts, leadership, staff officers and experience. It would take an incredible amount of time to rebuild that from scratch, time that the Dark Ones might not give the Va'Shen before attacking again. But by granting that title to a human like Ben, someone with experience leading humans *and* Va'Shen in combat against the *real* Dark Ones, they could bring on someone who could help train their new officer corps in the human way of war. It was much like the way Asian nations on Earth had imported European experts to train their forces at the end of the 19th and beginning of the 20th centuries.

In the end, it was all self-interest, but that kind of made Ben a little more comfortable with the situation. He didn't feel like he deserved such credit for what had happened. Knowing that the Emperor was giving it to him as much for his own sake as Ben's was a much more familiar feeling.

As he was thinking this, Walker chimed in.

"We are honored that the Emperor feels this way," he said. "But it is against our laws for Captain Gibson to accept such honors as a member of our military."

Boravin listened to the translation before replying.

<It is His Imperial Majesty's understanding that Captain Gibson's time with your military has come to an end and that he is now available to choose his own destiny.>

"While that is true," Walker said, "Captain Gibson must return to our world to complete his time with us, and whether he will be allowed to return is not something I can guarantee."

Sinclair translated for Walker, and Boravin's tail struck the floor behind him.

<Then His Imperial Majesty cannot approve Captain Gibson's departure,> he said. <Not unless Captain Gibson, himself, requests it.>

Upon hearing the translation, Walker turned to Ben with a sigh of relief. "I have to say, this turned out much better than expected, and it even has an easy answer. I'm sorry we didn't speak with them earlier."

"Indeed," said Sinclair. "It can be difficult when communication between our peoples is made difficult by the necessities of political maneuvering."

"All right," Walker said, gesturing to Ben. "Tell him you want to leave, and we can wrap this up."

Ben sat back in his chair, silent for several moments.

"Captain?" Walker prompted again.

"What if I *want* to stay?" Ben asked him.

The general's eyes narrowed. "Captain, you may be on your way out the door, but you're not a civilian yet. Regulations require you to return and outprocess from home-station."

"You mean Fort Accetta, Persephone, Sir?" Ben asked, perhaps a little too cheekily. Ben's home station was, at this moment, a giant hole in the ground of a dead world.

"In this case, it would be Joint Base Lewis-McChord on Earth," Walker corrected icily.

"If I want to accept his offer," Ben began, "I would just end up going to Earth and having to fight to come back anyway, right?" he asked. "It's not like I have a home on Earth or any belongings to worry about. Everything I currently own is in a duffel bag over in Transient Housing. Wouldn't it make more sense to outprocess here?"

"What makes sense and what the Army wants are two completely different things," Walker told him.

Ain't that the truth? Ben thought.

Sinclair, unexpectedly, came to Ben's aid. "General, it *does* cost a great deal of money to transport even a single person from one end of the galaxy to the other. Given that Captain Gibson's final desired destination is Va'Sh anyway, wouldn't it be more beneficial to the

Army to simply let him stay? After all, it wouldn't be the first time regulations have been bent for budgetary benefit."

Walker looked at Sinclair in angered betrayal. Sinclair was obviously referencing the carting up of the CJTF's F/A-202s before their replacements arrived, a move that could have doomed the Coalition on Va'Sh had *Over the Rainbow* not arrived when it did. As a rule, reminding general officers of their fuck-ups was not a very safe course of action.

Boravin watched the byplay, unsure as to what was happening, but not wanting to interject and possibly make things worse.

"There are other benefits, Sir," Ben said before Walker could start chewing into Sinclair's ass. "After all, if I'm here on Va'Sh, I won't have any way to communicate with anyone back on Earth." He paused for a moment to let the words sink in before adding the kicker. "Like, for instance... the Senate Armed Services Committee..."

Walker's face began to turn bright red at the implication. The events that had occurred under Major Keyes's command at Garan'Sel and Walker's decision to sweep them under the rug, still cast an ugly smell over the CJTF headquarters.

"You extorting me, *Captain?*"

"No, Sir," Ben assured him calmly. "I'm merely pointing out the benefits to every possible course of action." He smiled, and Walker looked ready to hop up and punch that grin right off the young Ranger's face.

Ben was beyond caring. He had given everything to the Army, and its thanks for his service had been to unceremoniously shit-can him. He'd done what his country had asked him to do. Now, it could do something for him. All he wanted, really, was to fill out paperwork here on Va'Sh instead of back on Earth. In the end, that was what it really came down to.

And if Walker didn't like it, well, it was an imperfect world.

The general sat back in his chair and studied Ben's face for several moments. He had known that the Ranger could make a lot of waves after he returned to Earth, but he knew if he didn't give Ben what he wanted now, not only *could* he make waves, the captain would make it his *mission* to do so.

"All right, Captain," Walker said evenly. "We'll do a waiver, and you can outprocess here." He leaned forward. "But if that's the game you're going to play, then I suggest that once you walk off this base in civilian clothes, you pretend you have a furry tail and ears and you *never* set foot on one of my installations again. Tracking?"

Ben smiled. "Thank you, Sir. I understand."

Walker grimaced and looked to Sinclair, cocking his head toward Boravin.

Sinclair smiled and turned to the Va'Shen courtier. <General Walker is happy to allow Captain Gibson the opportunity to remain on Va'Sh and bring our two peoples closer together for the benefit of both our worlds' futures," he said poetically.

Boravin bowed. <I thank the Grand Overlord for his generosity.>

Walker heard the translation with a dark expression and rose to his feet. "Please apologize to the Keeper of the Pen," he said. "But I must end things here."

"Yes, General," Sinclair said.

He and Ben both rose to their feet as Walker bowed to Boravin and walked toward the door. The Va'Shen courtier's ears twitched, savvy enough to understand that he had gotten his way despite the Grand Overlord not particularly liking it. He turned and bowed to Ben.

<Captain Gibson, I would like to add my personal thanks for your actions,> he said. <It is obvious from the way the people of Pelle speak of you that you are an honorable tod, and I will happily report to His Imperial Majesty your decision to remain.>

Ben bowed in return. <Thank you, Lord,> he said. <May I ask a final question?>

<Please do,> Boravin said.

<How did Emperor know I must leave Va'Sh?> he asked. As far as he knew, only a few people had heard he had been RIF'd. There was no reason for the Emperor to have heard of the situation promptly enough to intervene.

Boravin cleared his throat, and his tail slapped the chair nervously at the question. Everything he had said about why the Emperor was honoring Captain Gibson was true, but *how* it had come to his attention and *why* he had acted so quickly was somewhat more... complex.

How am I supposed to tell them? He had struggled with this question since the Emperor had commanded him to come and speak to the humans on his behalf, telling him to be as forthcoming as possible. But as Keeper of the Imperial Pen, he was also obligated to maintain the Emperor's dignity.

How do I tell them that His Imperial Majesty was spurred to action by a letter from his teenage crush? he thought. *Or that Her Majesty the Empress, upon learning the contents of the letter,* demanded *that the vixen's tesho be made to remain by her side to "keep an eye on her."*

He had worked in the palace since the current Emperor was a boy and remembered the incident with this vixen several years ago quite well. The Emperor had only recently entered an arranged marriage, and asking another vixen to become a concubine so soon afterward had been... upsetting... to the new Empress.

In the four thousand years since the Great Ones united the Va'Shen people under a single Emperor, there had never been an instance of an Empress doing something so remarkable as slapping her Emperor on the head with her fan...

Several times...

In front of the entire court...

So, when a letter arrived addressed to the Emperor from Pelle, every eye in the court had turned to the Empress, who demanded that Boravin read it aloud to the entire throne room filled with Imperial courtiers. The letter itself, of course, was in no way improper. It was an emotional plea for the Emperor's help and an outline of what this Captain Ben Gibson had done to protect the Empire. Learning that the sender was married to a human was shocking enough. Learning she was married to the same human his advisors had been recently telling him about was an incredible twist.

The Emperor wished to help the vixen immediately and ordered the palace to begin working on it. The Empress, at first, was against the idea... until the Emperor wondered aloud if the vixen would be permitted an Exception if her *tesho* left Va'Sh.

Fan in outstretched hand, the Empress then loudly commanded that every effort be made to reunite this couple and announced that such a person, alien or no, should be rewarded for his achievements.

Perhaps, she mused, with lands on the far side of the continent, far from the capital.

Only tods and vixens who worked in the Imperial Palace every day knew that things like this occurred within its walls. Outsiders were presented with a view of an Imperial court overwhelming with dignity and poise, but Boravin knew it could be anything but that.

Boravin cleared his throat and answered Ben.

<His Imperial Majesty's wisdom transcends that of normal Va'Shen such as myself,> he said. <He could see the many threads being woven together and could see the image they formed. From what he saw, he determined you would soon be forced to choose whether or not to leave and desired to note his wish for you to remain. If, however, it is your wish to leave, He would not have objected.>

The Empress, on the other hand, is likely to march down here herself, he added silently. *So, please agree to stay on.*

Sinclair translated the rather flowery answer, and although it didn't make much sense to Ben, he decided it was probably the best he was going to get. He bowed to Boravin.

<I thank you.>

Boravin bowed back. <I shall inform His Imperial Majesty of the good news.>

<Will I must remain in capital?> Ben asked. It suddenly occurred to him that he might be leaving one military just to join another with complete control over where he lived.

<No!> Boravin replied quickly... very quickly... His tail thrashed a bit in concern. <It suits the Imperial Family for you to return to Pelle. It is from there that you may best serve the Empire.>

Ben nodded, a little nervous at what he was committing himself to. On its face, it looked like a pretty good deal. But then again, so had the Army recruiting poster...

<Please be at peace, Zora'Shar,> the elder tod told him, perhaps sensing some discomfort. <Any task the Emperor gives you will be well within your abilities and will not test your honor. Simply being available to provide your counsel will likely be all that is necessary.>

With that, Boravin bowed again and took his leave, seeming eager to avoid any further conversation. Ben and Sinclair watched him go and were soon alone in the conference room.

"Thank you," Ben told him. "For helping me back there."

"It was the least I could do," Sinclair replied with a smile. "You've made inroads I never could. You have no idea how much more I know now thanks to the things you've done."

"Are you going to be in trouble with General Walker?" Ben asked.

Sinclair grunted. "What can he do? Fire me?" the older man said with a grin. "The only person on the entire planet even remotely qualified to replace me is *you*. That's the best part of being a civilian employee in the military. A god of old would have to descend from

Heaven and fire me himself, and even then he'd have to go through the appeals process."

Ben laughed.

"Are you really going to be okay, though?" Sinclair asked him. "If General Walker really cuts you off from access to the base, you're going to have a hard time getting medical care or even just a chance to see other human beings."

"I'll make do," the Ranger said. "That's really all anyone can do. There's nothing for me back in the Colonies now. But here... Here I have something special. I'll take the risks."

Sinclair held his hand out, and Ben took it.

"I wish you luck, Captain," Sinclair said as they shook hands. "And I'll be picking your brain from time to time if you don't mind."

"Any time, Doc," Ben promised. "Thank you."

Sinclair smiled and turned, leaving the conference room and Ben alone.

The Ranger grinned to himself.

* * *

Ben slapped the back of the deuce-and-a-half truck to let the driver know he was out and gave a wave to him through the passenger-side mirror. The truck blew its horn twice and started down the road, making a left onto a dirt packed road and passing a plywood sign with red lettering.

Forward Operating Base Leonard

Admin Operations Sector 13

Combined Joint Task Force

Operation UNIFIED RESOLVE

1LT Patricia Kim, U.S. Army, Commanding

He watched for a moment as the truck pulled up to the sally-port, and the guards at the gate began their usual inspection. Ben could have gone with the truck onto the FOB regardless of

General Walker's orders, but for some reason he didn't want or feel the need to just yet. He was starting a new life, and he didn't want the first steps of that new life to be onto another Army post.

Someone else might accuse Ben of "going native," but he wasn't quite sure that was how he felt. It wasn't like the old vids where someone completely rejects their old culture and believes the other to be superior. There was a lot about the Va'Shen he still didn't like. It was just that there was so much more that he did.

Shouldering the black duffel bag in which he kept everything he owned, he moved his hand up to adjust his cap and stopped halfway upon remembering he wasn't wearing one. It had been more than a year since he had any reason to wear civilian clothes, and the lighter, more comfortable fabric of the light blue polo shirt and khakis felt alien to him. It didn't help that the clothing options at the Jamieson BX had been so limited. In the end, he found a few pairs of khaki pants, some tan sand-tees, a couple of work polos, and a pair of black and yellow running shoes, the only ones at the BX that fit him.

Giving the FOB fenceline one more look, he set off down the road toward the distant sounds of hammering and sawing. The closer he got to Pelle... now Pel'Garan... the more amazed he was. There were already several rebuilt houses, and it appeared that the first floor of the temple was already complete with the second floor under construction.

As he entered the village proper, he noted how the rubble had been carted away in the two months since the Dark One attack and the Air Force bombardment. Although the burned skeletons of buildings remained here and there, mixed with new construction, the Va'Shen villagers had managed to make their town cleaner and neater than most human towns he'd seen that *hadn't* been utterly destroyed.

A couple of villagers saw him, and he gave them a wave. They both bowed to him.

<Blessed morning, honored Zora'Shar,> they greeted in unison.

As he walked toward the center of town, he passed more and more villagers, all of whom bowed to him and addressed him respectfully by his new Va'Shen title. It made Ben a little uncomfortable, like there was another wall between him and the community no different than the uniform he recently discarded.

The sound of hammering grew louder, and Ben found himself drifting toward it, coming to the entryway of a skeletonized building that used to be the chieftain's home. Hammering at a support beam just inside was a familiar mop of grayish silver hair tied back behind him.

Ben was about to announce himself when the tod spoke up.

<Your shoes are different.>

The former Ranger smiled as Azarin turned and faced him.

<They should be more than quiet,> he told his brother-in-law.

<They are not,> Azarin assured him. His ears twitched slightly. He looked Ben up and down for a moment before commenting. <Is that some kind of ceremonial dress?>

Ben smiled as he worked out the translation in his head. <What we wear when not a fighter,> he said.

<I will loan you something until you can find something more respectable to wear,> Azarin told him. His tone suggested disapproval, but the slight twitch in his ears told Ben his brother-in-law was just jerking him around. <You will stay?> Azarin finally asked the real question on his mind.

<I will stay,> Ben confirmed.

Azarin's tail waved back and forth once. <Come find me tomorrow. You can be my apprentice. I will teach you to nail properly.>

Ben smiled. Although he was now technically a noble and receiving a monthly stipend from the Emperor, he liked the idea of having a regular job and helping rebuild the village. He bowed to Azarin.

<You honor me,> he said.

As he returned to his full height, three Va'Shen workers passed by the house and saw him, all of them bowing to him.

<Blessed morning, Zora'Shar.>

<Honored Zora'Shar.>

Ben gave them a quick bow and watched them walk away. Turning back to Azarin he asked the question on his mind.

<They must do that every time?> he asked.

<They need not do it *at all*,> Azarin told him.

Ben felt a knot in his throat at the implication and he let out a breath.

<Have you seen the Na'Sha yet?> Azarin asked him.

<No. Go to there. Saw you.>

Azarin put his hammer down and wiped his face with a white cloth that had been hanging from a crossbeam nearby. <Come,> he said. <You will have to face the chieftain and the Na'Sha to become part of the community regardless.>

<I do?> Ben asked.

<You do,> his brother replied without looking back. Ben followed him down the road, bowing seemingly every few seconds as villagers passed him on the road to the temple.

As they mounted the unfinished steps to the entrance of the temple, Ben took a good look at the structure. The Va'Shen seemed intent on putting it back together exactly the way it was before, and even unfinished as it was, its familiarity made Ben smile.

They stopped at the top of the steps as a blue-haired vixen in a simple white hanbok with blue trim stood in the entryway. Ben bowed to her and smiled.

Sho Nan looked down her nose at the human and carpenter.

<You are here to call on Alacea?> she asked with a hint of disapproval.

<Yes, Honored Ya'Jahar,> Ben replied with another bow.

<The *aderen* is in session,> Sho Nan told him. <Follow me. I will announce you.>

<An *aderen*?> Ben asked as the fox woman turned and proceeded inside. He felt nervousness begin to well up in him.

<There is no better time to judge whether you are worthy of joining the community,> Sho Nan explained as she glided across the newly-constructed floor toward the meeting room where the *aderen* had always been held.

<I thought only chieftain and Na'Sha...> Ben began.

<The Zora'Shar must be shown the proper respect,> Sho Nan answered evenly, stopping at the sliding door to the meeting room. The imagery of the Va'Shen gods that had adorned the door in the previous temple was not there, and Ben quickly wondered if it would be remade or if some other imagery would be put there instead.

<Remain here,> the Mikorin ordered him.

Ben stood nervously as Sho Nan entered the meeting room and slid the door shut behind her.

Although Ben didn't have the keen hearing of a Va'Shen, he could still make out the voices on the other side of the door as Sho Nan spoke.

<Honored *Aderen*, forgive the intrusion.>

<We were just about to finish, Sho Nan,> Ben heard the reply, and his heart skipped a beat. It had been so long since he'd last heard that voice, and hearing it now moved him in a way he never thought possible before. Just the thought of her being on the other side of a single door made him smile giddily.

<Before you adjourn, a homeless refugee has arrived requesting to join our community,> Sho Nan announced. <More of a vagabond, really. He can't even speak properly.>

Standing next to Ben, Azarin's ears twitched at the statement.

"Fucking Sho Nan," Ben muttered in English, smiling at the vixen's act.

<That is not a very charitable thing to say, Sho Nan,> Alacea's voice came again. <There are many who need help.>

<Then shall I bring him in?> the blue-haired woman asked. <Or shall I chase him away with a stick?>

<Sho Nan!>

Ben heard Kasshas sigh. <Bring him in, Honored Ya'Jahar. We will speak with him and decide whether to welcome him.>

<Yes, Chieftain. But I would like the *Aderen* to remember that I warned them.>

<We shall make note of the Ya'Jahar's warning,> Kasshas promised.

<Very well.>

A moment later the door slid open, and Sho Nan stood before them again.

<I have told them that an honored guest has arrived,> she brazenly stated, knowing full well that they must have overheard her.

<Thanks be to you, Sho Nan,> Ben replied with a smile.

<You may enter,> she declared, gesturing grandly to the door.

Ben walked past her and into the meeting room where the village leaders sat in their usual oval on the recessed floor. On the far side of the oval, facing the door was Kasshas, who, upon seeing Ben, rose to his feet.

Sitting closest to him but facing away from the door was Alacea, her long violet hair hanging down almost to her tail. As the rest of the *aderen's* ears popped up in shock, the Na'Sha turned to see what had surprised them so.

Alacea, Ben's vixen war bride, saw him, and her ears shot up to the roof.

<*Tesho*,> she whispered, rooted to the spot in surprise.

Ben smiled and bowed to them. <Honored *Aderen*,> he said in halting Va'Shen <I like join your community. May I?>

Alacea was across the room in half a second, her arms around Ben and squeezing tightly while her tail went completely nuts behind her.

<*Tesho*!> she cried.

He wrapped his arms around his wife and hugged her as she hiccupped into his shoulder. Holding her gently, he shut his eyes and stroked her hair.

<I believe this means the Zora'Shar is welcome in Pel'Garan,> Kasshas announced with a bow. The others in the *aderen* silently concurred, standing up and bowing to Ben.

The human man took a breath and buried his face in his wife's neck. All the stress and nervousness he had felt began to drain from him to be replaced by relief and happiness.

<I am home, *Myorin*,> he told her, his voice beginning to break.

<Welcome home,> she greeted gently, holding him in her arms. <Now and forever.>

The End